THE GATES OF THE MOUNTAINS

**Center Point
Large Print**

**This Large Print Book carries the
Seal of Approval of N.A.V.H.**

ॐ श्री गणेशाय नमः

THE GATES
OF THE
MOUNTAINS

WILL HENRY

CENTER POINT PUBLISHING
THORNDIKE, MAINE

This Center Point Large Print edition
is published in the year 2001 by arrangement with
Golden West Literary Agency.

Copyright ● 1963 by Henry Wilson Allen.
Copyright ● renewed 1991 by Henry Wilson Allen.

All rights reserved.

The text of this Large Print edition is unabridged.
In other aspects, this book may vary from the original
edition. Printed in Thailand. Set in 16-point
Times New Roman type by Bill Coskrey.

ISBN 1-58547-082-1

Library of Congress Cataloging-in-Publication Data

Henry, Will, 1912-
    The gates of the mountains / Will Henry.
        p. cm.
    ISBN 1-58547-082-1 (lib. bdg. : alk. paper)
    1. Lewis and Clark Expedition (1804-1806)--Fiction. 2. West (U.S.)--Discovery and
exploration--Fiction. 3. Explorers--Fiction. 4. Large type books. I. Title.

PS3551.L393 G38 2001
813'.54--dc21
                                                                        00-050913

BOOK I
THE LOUISIANA GAMBLE
1

The day was gray and cold. A squally rain blew up the river. Between gusts, and bent to the burden of the fat deer across my shoulder, I forced along the north bank, upstream, toward La Charrette. The date as I clearly remember, was the twenty-fourth of May, 1804. The place was the part of the Missouri called the Devil's Raceground, a singular piece of water with an evil reputation among us rivermen of French métis blood. I approached it, as I always did, with a mixture of Indian fear and Gallic superstition. Mounting the low bluff, I laid the deer down and peered anxiously out over the channel.

I shuddered to a chill not of the rain. The Grand Missouri in full flood was a wicked thing to see. She was a power of nature equal to the lightning, or the wind, yet deadly to a sudden traitorous degree unknown to them or to their sister elements, which man endures and charts while somehow managing to employ with profit.

No man outwitted that sinuous mother of all yellow-brown waters. And doubly never did he think to contest her in the full fury of her spring temper. Still, he would try. He would seek to subdue her when she was rampaging; when, in her turgid rage, she sprang upon and ate away her own banks, her own skin of sandy loam, her own arteries of grass and timber, her own bones of rock and soil and root. This he would do because he was man; even as the lost poor devils my horrified glance now discovered laboring in midstream were men.

"In God's name," I cried aloud, "do they wish to die?"

"Not at all," answered a quiet voice behind me. "They wish to go up the river, and they will."

I wheeled to see two men in sorry condition from rain and mud. The taller of them nodded amicably.

"I'm George Drewyer," he said. "Who are you?"

I stared, speechless.

Drewyer, or Drouillard in the French, was a legend on the river. He had been, some said, farther north and west than any white man, saving possibly the great Alexander Mackenzie. He was the companion of such legendary figures as Toussaint Charbonneau, Hugh Heney, Simon Fraser, David Thompson, Manuel Lisa and La Charrette's own Régis Loisel. His mere name, let alone his living presence, could fire the imagination of any young fellow such as I whose entire life's dream was to ascend the Grand Missouri and see for himself those storied mysteries of the Northwest Passage.

"Frank," I stammered belatedly. "My name is Frank Rivet, of La Charrette."

"La Charrette? You hear that, Captain? We're nigh there, I reckon."

His companion, not so tall nor pleasant, shook off the information. "Damn the town," he scowled. "It's that river out there I'm worried about. I don't like the set of that current. I think Clark's wrong this time. He ought to have stayed with the bank, caving or not."

At this, it was my turn to nod swiftly.

"You are correct, Captain," I said. "If those men continue

to try to pass by the middle channel, they must fail. They will lose the keelboat and perhaps both pirogues, as well. Do you see that bad sandboil at the head of the island?"

He peered intently where I pointed. "Yes," he said, "but I fear that Clark, out there on the river, cannot."

"Again correct, Captain. Coming upstream, you are suddenly into it. The currents take you and pound you against those rocks and that is the end of your trade goods and, like as not, of your life upon the river."

He wheeled upon his companion. "Drewyer," he demanded, "do you suppose he's right? You know these people. What do you say?"

Drewyer turned to me.

"You said your name was Rivet, boy?" he asked. "Would you be related to *the* Rivet? I mean François Rivet of La Charrette?"

"Yes," I replied. "I am Rivet's nephew, named for him."

Drewyer swung back to the shorter man.

"There's your answer, Captain. This boy will know the river. Damn! I wish there was some way we could signal Captain Clark."

"We can't," said his companion doggedly. "Not in this damnable rain and roar of the river."

I cannot say why I was so bold, then. Events draw courage from us all, I suppose, and I was being drawn by the violent, ugly death awaiting those brave men on the river.

"God's name!" I shouted in sudden youthful anger. "Will you both stand there like two headless snags in the muck and permit them to drown?"

Drewyer wagged his head at me. "Don't yell at the captain, sonny," he warned. "It's no fault of his and there's

7

naught he can do about it."

"Ha!" I said, still shouting. "Stand aside and I shall show you something *I* can do about it, then!"

Drewyer's hand shot out, pinning me with the force of a bear trap. "Hold on, you damned young fool," he growled. "Just what do you think you're up to?"

"Let go of me and find out!" I challenged. "I would stand far better chance with a horse to ride, but to try on foot is better than waiting with you and your captain!"

"A horse?" said the latter, hearing me and coming up to join us. "It happens we have two of them. Yonder they come up the bluff with our hunter, John Shields."

I glanced where he pointed and saw, through the increasingly heavy drive of the rain, a man and two mounts ascending the rise. One of the animals was a bony pack brute, but the other was a clean-limbed saddler. Before either Drewyer or his sturdy captain could act further to detain me, I leaped toward the approaching hunter. I slid to a stop in front of him, holding out my rifle.

"Here," I yelled, "hold onto this!"

Surprised, he dropped the reins of the led, saddled mount, to accept the weapon. Leaping past him, I sprang on the startled animal's back. I was already slipping off my buckskin shirt and Indian moccasins as I galloped back past George Drewyer and his gruff captain. By the time the horse had pounded around the upriver bend toward the point above the Devil's Raceground, I was riding stark naked and was absolutely certain that the three men behind me must be convinced they had just met, and been had the better of, by the village idiot of La Charrette.

8

2

The chance of death was present but not probable. I was, after all, born to that river. With decent luck the wild current would bear me down and across to the island in time to warn off the men in midstream. Buoyed by this conviction, I scrambled of my mount and ran to the shelving bank of the upstream point to which he had carried me. Here, with a quick prayer, I dived into the muddy tide. At once I was aware of extreme peril.

It was like plunging into the funneled floodgate of some great pumping disgorgement of liquid earth. It was not water but a bombardment of sand, rock, gravel and suffocating fluid gumbo. Terror seized me. Then the current jammed my tumbling form against a submerged sawyer, a snag with its rooted feet sunk into the jellied bed of the river, and the blow restored my Frenchman's spirit. Rocks continued to hurtle against me, and sand and gravel to abrade my hide, but honor was involved now and I struck back with such aroused purpose that I won to the surface again and was, within a racing five minutes, dashed up onto the island's head, not completely sound, perhaps, but safe. Fortune was favoring the foolhardy. The instant I landed upon the rocks, the doomed men were just planting the setting poles into the island's far flank to force their keelboat out into the full fury of the Devil's Raceground.

At the sight of me their captain, a tough-looking man whose flaming red hair was evident even through the billowing rain, shouted for his men to stand on their poles. This they did, holding the boat in the current, while I ran out into the shallows and made effort to call out the nature of their peril to them. But the wind outcried me and the red-haired captain waved and bellowed back with a ready smile, "Never fear, lad, we'll send out help to you from the village!" I knew he had misheard me and would, next moment, order his polesmen forward into the waiting maelstrom. Again, I was left with no choice but to swim or see these poor men damned.

This time, however, I was tired. As well, I misjudged the fierceness of the current there on the lee side of the island. The prow of the fifty-foot keelboat flashed by spinningly. I recall dumbly counting the oarlocks and trailing sweeps on her starboard side—eleven, making her a twenty-two-oared craft—then I thought the river had me for her own, as my mind whirled and vision was blotted out. But the craggy-faced captain with the bright red hair failed to agree. In the instant of my sliding past his vessel's flank his gaunt body was already in the air, arching into the thunder of the channel.

In that moment he reacted only to the sight of a boy being swept to his sure death in the flood. It was not in his purview of the situation that, in the ultimate last inch of time, one of his following pirogues should nose around the turn of the island's lee and be swung to broadside of the raging current where we two—myself now supported in the captain's muscular arms—might be smashed against the smaller craft's port side and be helped, half drowned, over her gunwales.

She nearly swamped, at that, taking us all down, but the red-haired captain was a riverman. With himself plying a setting pole to virtually lift the seven-oared vessel out of

10

the water, he got her nose-to in the current once more and shortly beached her safely on the island.

Here I made it plain to him what awaited his little flotilla beyond the rocky head. He understood the degree of my service instantly. Embracing me with a bony arm, he bellowed for his other boatmen to bring the big keelboat onto the beach and set her there for bailing. By this time the second pirogue, the six-oared one, rounded into view and he likewise bawled her into coming-to for an unshipping of her cargo of Missouri mud-water.

Now ensued some swift discussion of our options by Captain Clark and myself. I held strongly for continuing by the caving, seemingly dangerous north bank Clark as stoutly repudiating the suggestion.

"Damn it, lad," he protested, "I've just tried it that way and was nigh swamped half a dozen times."

"You ran it wrong," I insisted brazenly. "Give me the tiller of the keelboat and I will take you through without shipping a teacupful."

Clark eyed my quizzically. "You crow pretty loud for a cockerel," he said. "You must be French."

"I am French," I said, straightening. "Also, I know this river. As for the crowing, you should hear me when my craw is not so full of mud and water!"

At that, he winced and grinned good-naturedly.

"Well, could be so," he admitted. "You surely did save us from poling into that bad boil yonder." He gestured toward the invisible inferno of the Raceground. "Still, you're just a colt, even if full of prance. I figure I have to make my own decisions, then set on them. Right now I mean to set on this bit of land till the wind lets up."

"That won't be until daylight, Captain. Do you have any idea how much the Missouri will rise in one night?"

"No, I'm an Ohio man, myself. That and the Mississippi. However, I don't reckon the Missouri is too vastly different from them. She'll rise maybe two feet."

"She will rise four."

"Overnight?"

"Perhaps sooner. These headland rocks are six feet out. When I went down the river this morning, they were ten feet out. How many men do you have here?"

He looked at me a little queerly. One could not say that he had turned uneasy, for this was a man of such hardness as one does not see in each spring, not even along the Missouri. This is not to say a brutal hardness, but rather an inner annealing of the spirit to go with the outer gifts of bone and sinew and iron muscle.

"Well, now," he answered carefully, "we are six oars on the white pirogue and seven on the red. With twenty-two on the barge, American arithmetic makes it come out thirty-five. How about your French figuring?"

I did not return his light spirit, my mathematics being considerably heavier than his.

"It's little matter," I replied. "What counts is that by first light of morning your men will be five, not thirty-five. Five, or perhaps as many as seven; however many can cling to what small point of the rocks will be above water by that hour."

Captain Clark dismissed his grin. Again his raw-boned arm found my shoulder.

"Lad," he said, "French or not, I like the way you stand up and say your piece." He turned to the waiting, huddled boatmen, warm grin again at work.

"Back to your oars, boys!" he order them cheerfully. "We've just hired on a new pilot . . ."

3

Sacré-bleu! Sacré coeur! Sacré Dieu!"

There could be small doubt that Uncle François was disturbed. Like our mother Missouri, the Rivet temper was on the rise. In consequence, I stood well back from the bed in the warm corner of my aunt's kitchen where *the* Rivet lay anchored with a badly injured ankle. He did not deceive me, with the hand held beneath the rough cover. I had seen him snatch the length of split hickory from the woodbox with his reach when he imagined I was occupied with embracing Aunt Célie. And that was when he merely thought I was too late home from the hunt. It was when I had told Aunt Célie the fat doe lay in the tool shed ready for skinning and she had gone out to dress the game, that I told him the full extent of my adventure with the American captains. It was also then that he burst forth with the heartfelt profanities. Yet, poor fellow, who could blame him?

To be so victimized by fate as to turn an ankle that badly he could not set foot to ground and the very moment when he was due to join these same captains in their ascent of the river was realistically tragic for any Frenchman, but for *the* Rivet it was past all tolerance.

At the least it meant that his "failure" would leave a gaping hole in the already reduced ranks of the brave Americans. Skilled boatmen who knew the Missouri like François Rivet were not to be replaced in La Charrette.

13

The settlement consisted of seven mud huts and seven poor families, all French, or French métis mixtures. And here, in this miserable atmosphere, with no adult French boatmen of the pure blood to volunteer in his place, it was I, François Rivet the Younger, his own namesake and the half-breed son of his dead brother and a heathen Pawnee squaw, who had made so bold as to offer the American captains my services as a boatman in place of *the* Rivet!

It was, naturally, an insult beyond suffrance. My uncle, however, was a man of monumental charity. "Come, Frank," he gestured forgivingly, and with what strength he had left from blaspheming my dark blood. "I would like it that you would move a little closer. The light is poor in here; I can't see you well."

I advanced cautiously, stopping out of reach of the piece of stovewood beneath the blanket.

"I'd rather not come too close, Uncle. I have a cold and would not wish you to take it from me."

"Oh? Hah! You have a cold? Caught since this morning, no doubt. You were healthy as a dog when you left for Femme Osage. Come. just one step nearer, boy."

"It is unthinkable, Uncle."

"Eh? Why is it unthinkable?"

"Because I don't care to be struck with that piece of hickory you are hiding under the covers."

He looked at me a moment, then grinned and brought out the knotty stick, dropping it on the floor, where I quickly kicked it out of his reach before seating myself at the foot of his rude bed.

"Uncle," I said, "I am truly sorry that I have embarrassed you with your *patrons*. I forgot in my excitement

14

about my Indian mother. It was only in my heart that if *the* Rivet could not go, then some Rivet must go, métis or no."

My uncle shifted uncomfortably. "Here now, boy!' he grumbled, "say no more against your mother. She was a fine woman. And leave my *patron*s to me. I will think of someone for them."

"Uncle, there is no one else, save myself."

"It's impossible. Neither of the captains would hire you, a half-breed. Let us say no more about it."

"But I have already said more about it. I talked with the captains and neither of them mentioned half-breed. I think they might accept me."

"Bah! They were being kind to you because of me. They respect me."

"Well, of course, Uncle; you are *the* Rivet."

"*Oui!* Let yourself remember it, too," he admonished me. "Now go and help your aunt with that venison. I am hungry and will need my full strength for the captains tonight. What a fate! Only one good leg and a half-breed nephew to stand on it for me. Well, damn it, there's this to be said and to be thankful for—the boy has the heart of a Frenchman, yes, and the fine mind as well. That's quite a remarkable achievement when you consider the heathen impurities of that Pawnee blood."

I left him muttering proudly to himself and went out into the early darkness thankful indeed to be even the half-breed nephew of *the* Rivet.

4

It was full dark when the captains came. I recognized them when they drew near my hiding place in the tool shed, the one of slight build, the other rawboned and powerful. A third with them, a huge fellow, towering over his companions as the genie of the lamp loomed above Aladdin and, like the genie, seeming blacker than that night. I shivered with apprehension.

In an extension of that peculiar good luck which had been attending me that day, Captain Lewis now chose to halt to regain his breath from the steep river-path climb. Clark waited with him. The third man, the shadowy giant, stood out of my line of vision, beyond the captains.

"Will," said Lewis, "what do you say to a pipe before we see Rivet? It's so pleasant here above the river."

"Well, Captain," replied Clark, "you know my weakness for the weed."

"Yes," nodded Lewis, "and you mine for climbing river bluffs. If I had your legs and lungs, Will, I could be halfway up the Missouri by this time."

"Aye," responded the other softly, "and if I had your education, Captain, I would be waiting there for you."

The men fell silent, intent on lighting their pipes. In the pause, I puzzled over the by-play between the two, wherein the one lamented the other's physical strength while the other lauded his comrade's superior training. This factor intrigued me because I was myself a young man who could both read and write and who had, moreover, attended school with the Jesuits in St. Louis since

16

early boyhood. I was hardly polished nor yet ready for an academic degree but I was, in the proper sense, educated. As well, being of French and Pawnee blood, a wild enough blending. I was hot with the lust of animal vitality. The balance—two parts of lifejoy to one of learning—thus allowed me to catch and comprehend the briefly spoken envies of the captains.

But the pipes were going well now, and the talk resuming where it had broken off.

"It's a fact, Will," Lewis said, "that you and I are different men. Indeed, the difference in us is what prompted me to suggest you to the President."

"I suppose," sighed Clark, "but a lack of schooling is a serious handicap in life."

"Not the most serious, however. Where we're going, Will, lack of another kind of knowledge would be a far more critical shortage. I refer to practical experience, the education for survival. That's your schooling."

"I hope so, Captain"

"Will."

"Yes, Captain?"

"Must you eternally call me captain?"

"It seems right."

"Shall I then call you captain, too? You know that you were promised equal rank by Mr. Jefferson."

"Aye. I'm still a lieutenant, however, Captain."

"The promotion will come through. Can't you accept that? It's not like you to be bitter, Will."

"It's not like Mr. Jefferson to forget a promise either, Captain. Yet he has done so."

"The President aside, Will, you insist on deferring to me

anyway. You invariably 'yes sir' and 'no sir' me in front of the men. Why is that?"

"I don't know, Captain. It's in some men to look to other men, I suppose."

"Rank or no rank, eh?"

"Yes, sir, I would say so."

Again they fell silent, smoking to cover the awkwardness of old friends having come too close in confidence.

Lewis, as already seemed his wont to me, led the way out of the blind place.

"What are we going to do about Rivet, Will?" he asked.

Clark shrugged. "We'll examine his leg first. But if, as his nephew told us, he can't bear his weight upon it, we must replace him, and quickly."

"Perhaps Rivet already has a replacement for us."

"I doubt that, Captain. But if he has not, I have."

"What? You do? Here in La Charrette?"

"Yes, sir, young Rivet."

"The boy! You mean that demented half-breed youth who swam to the island for us? You can't be serious, Will!"

"I'm serious."

"Well, so am I. We need a man, not a boy."

"Boys make men."

"True, but this one is part Pawnee. That's wild blood. We can't afford to risk such a replacement for Rivet."

"The boy's likewise half Rivet, Captain. That's good blood, steady and strong. I say let him come along."

Lewis took a long time with his reply. My ears hurt with the ache of hard listening, and my heart as well.

Finally, he shook his head in that quiet way of his.

"I'm afraid not, Will," he said. "Let's go in and see what Rivet has for us of information and advice."

Clark said no more. The two captains, followed by the huge dark fellow who had spoken no word the entire time, turned quickly for the door of my uncle's house.

5

My Aunt Célie's fine large woodbox was constructed to be filled from the outside, emptied from within the house. If I timed the effort correctly, I could sneak into it from the outside while the guests were being admitted at the front of the house. I could eavesdrop and spy upon all that passed between Uncle François and the American captains. Leaping from the tool shed, I sped to the rear of the cabin and was successful in stowing myself in the box precisely as I had hoped. Breath held, I crouched to peer between the wide cracks of roughsawn board which sheltered me.

Only the two captains entered. The huge third fellow stood guard outside the front door. Lewis got at once to the business which had brought him

"Well, Rivet," he began "I am sorry to see this state. I understand you cannot put weight on the limb. Do you realize what this means?"

"*Oui, Capitaine.*"

"Do you have someone who might take your place? A good riverman with something of your own skills and reliability?"

My uncle shook his head. "I have no such man, *Capitaine*," he said, "but I do have such a boy."

My heart jumped in the same moment as Captain Lewis's outraged eyebrows.

"Damn it, Rivet," complained the mercurial commander, "I'm tired of hearing about this métis boy of yours!"

"Not my boy, *Capitaine*," corrected my uncle, "but my brother's boy. You have heard of Achille Rivet, of course? This nephew of mine is Achille's true son by the Pawnee woman, Antelope, a daughter of the chief, Lame Horse. A very fine woman, now dead, may God rest her soul."

Lewis nodded stiffly. "I'm sure she was a fine woman, Rivet," he said "but you will still need to get us another man to pull your oar."

Uncle François turned impulsively to Clark.

"Please, *Patron*," he said, "take the boy, he will make a man, once up the river."

Clark's homely face showed agreement, but his reply did not. "It's not mine to say, Rivet," he answered. "Captain Lewis has made the decision and has his reasons."

Uncle François came up on one elbow, face reddening.

"Pah!" he virtually shouted. "I know his reasons and they are worthless! You will excuse it, *Capitaine*," he waved to Lewis, "but I speak the truth in my own house!"

"Go ahead, Rivet," said Lewis firmly, "speak it then."

"*Voilá!* I shall! You distrust my nephew because of one thing, alone, his Indian blood. Well, *Capitaine*, permit me to ask you just a single thing in this regard, how long have the Americans been in this land of the Louisiana? That is to say, against we French? Ha! I thought so. No time whatever. And this boy is a Rivet above his mother's blood, do you hear? There was a Rivet with La Salle. There was a

Rivet with the Vérendryes, father and son, the first white man to see this Upper Missouri where you are bound. That Rivet came all the way from Lake Winnipeg to the Mandan villages below the Big Bend. And do you recall what that date was, *Capitaine?* Aha! allow me to refresh you. It was 1738! Sixty-six years ago! Yet you will question the devotion to his land of a Rivet of this same blood, native mother or no?"

Captain Lewis accepted the charge in his blunt way, no whit persuaded by its eloquence.

"Love of land does not constitute loyalty to President Jefferson and the United States. May I remind you, Rivet, that this expedition is substantially a secret mission?"

"Hah! What of that?" demanded my uncle. "This boy's fondest dearm is to be an American. He was reared in the Louisiana and French, yes, but now that the United States has purchased this Louisiana from France, many of us regard ourselves as part of the transaction, and my nephew Frank particularly so. He tells me that your President has said he hopes that the people of Louisiana will want to join as equal citizens, that he invites them to do so. Well, I can tell you, *Capitaine,* that Frank Rivet accepts this proposal with all of a young boy's excited desires. Heart of Jesus! how can you challenge him? He was born on the prairies of Teton River, where that stream enters the Missouri above the Grand Detour. It was the winter of 1786, and that fact is recorded in the register of such things which the Jesuits keep in St. Louis. Achille, my brother, brought the baby down the river and had him baptized. The boy is legal. He is an American if he wants to be—born to this land, and of it, as much even as you. He

21

is no bastard and no half-breed and no wild Pawnee horse Indian. He is—pah!—I give up, forget the entire matter. He is a Rivet. No man can say more!"

To my vast relief both captains were smiling when Uncle François finished. It was not that they were amused by his fervor, but rather, completely warmed by it.

"Well now, Rivet," said Lewis, moving closer to his bedside, "it was never my intention to call the Rivet honor into question. Nor, indeed, to demean the lad's mother. It's his youth I object to, hence the quality of his judgment. A boy is still a boy, even a Rivet boy. As a man grown yourself, will you argue that?"

My heart plummeted. This was logic, and my Uncle François was a logical man. Moreover, I could see that Captain Lewis was a clever one. His seemingly straightforward manner cloaked a mind as sharp and cutting as a Hudson's Bay axe blade But Uncle François was not precisely a simple man, either.

"There is still the matter of the Indian blood, *Capitaine,*" he said. "A quick answer is not necessarily a true one. Would you take the boy in my place were his mother not a Pawnee squaw?"

Lewis had an oval face. Small of mouth and long and slender of nose, it was neither handsome nor attractive. It looked even less promising now as the frost settled over it in response to my uncle's confrontation.

"Captain Clark," he said, "will you be so good as to examine Rivet's leg? Our time runs short."

Clark, who was apparently the company doctor, bent over the patient, plying the ankle carefully. I could hear the bones grate. Clark straightened.

22

"It's broke sure, Captain. I'll need to get my satchel and splint it for him. You coming?"

"No, I'll stay here and question Rivet. The President wanted me to inquire after old Mr. Boone, and I would like to know for myself what news there is of Régis Loisel, Cedar Island and things in general up the river. Hurry, though. We must repack those midships lockers on the big barge so to be away with first light."

Clark departed and Lewis and my uncle resumed. In the stale-aired woodbox, I suffered the passage of the talk as best I might, helpless to move for fear of discovery.

"Coming to old Mr. Boone," my uncle began, "he is living presently down on Femme Osage Creek. Now seventy years, he is showing his age to be certain, but seems likely to last a few more winters. What a tragedy, though, eh? That such a great man in his country's recent history should be so soon forgotten. Would not one think that the famous Daniel Boone deserved better than a log hut on Femme Osage Creek a few miles from La Charrette?"

"I admit the shoddiness of the treatment," said Lewis. "Be sure and tell the old fellow that Mr. Jefferson asked after his health. Now, how about Loisel and Cedar Island?"

"Well," answered my uncle, "I have learned only this same afternoon that Loisel is coming down the river and will be in La Charrette some time tonight. He nooned at the Gasconade yesterday, and is thus considerably overdue here. I expect," added my uncle, cocking an ear, "that he may be making his landing as we talk. Don't I hear some commotion down there below the bluff, right now?"

He did, indeed, hear this commotion, for I heard it myself and knew, as he did, that it was Loisel's party.

Lewis, after a moment, nodded his agreement.

"I'll go down with Captain Clark after he fixes your leg, Rivet. Meanwhile, what do you hear of flood conditions immediately above? Also, how about farther up?"

He and Uncle François fell to discussing channel shiftings, current changes, new bars and the like, while I cursed my confinement and my despair. Down at the landing, where the Régis Loisel party was returning from upriver Indian trading, there would be high talk of wild lands and great adventure. And here was I, trapped like an animal between my uncle's bed and my aunt's cookstove until Captain Clark should return and depart again.

The following ten minutes were agony multiplied, the next fifteen worse. Yet at last the term did conclude and it was but the instant before it did that my uncle said the thing which determined the totally new course of my life. He and Lewis had progressed in their discussion as far up the river as the confluence of the Cannonball, just below the Mandan villages. My uncle had unfurled his charts of the Missouri, put his finger upon the juncture of the two streams and now, after a dramatic, deliberate pause, said softly:

"It was just here, *Patron,* that my brother Achille was swept overboard and never seen again. We searched the bank for many days but no body was ever recovered. It is why the legend persists, you see, even today."

"Oh?" said Lewis, faintly interested. "What legend is that?"

"Of my brother, Achille Rivet. The Indians say that he is still alive somewhere west of the buffalo, that he was found and taken prisoner by the Teton Sioux and traded by them beyond the Big Rock Mountains to the evil Sho-

24

shone, the Snake Indians."

"And you believe this old squaw's tale, Rivet?"

My uncle raised his eyes and crossed himself. "We never found the body," he said.

6

My father, Achille Rivet, the legend of the river, was not dead but still very much alive and a captive of the Shoshone Indians? The possibility stunned me.

I was five years old when my father brought me down the river to the Jesuit blackrobes in St. Louis and said to them, "Here is my son of a red mother; keep him and make him a white man." I was still five years old when, that same spring, my father went back up the river with my Uncle François, to be carried away by the great current at the mouth of the Cannonball. I was seven before the fathers told me that Achille Rivet had drowned in that high water of the 1791 springtime. They never hinted, nor did Uncle François or Aunt Célie, that a legend persisted after him.

Why this deception I could not now imagine. Yet, crouching there in the woodbox waiting for Captain Clark to come and be gone, I thought, in my swiftly rising resentment, that I might guess quite closely. The Jesuits, as representatives of God on earth, could afford no partnership in heathen Indian fables. Six Christian boatmen of the True Faith, in addition to my Uncle François, had witnessed the closing of the floodwater sarcophagus. They had reported my father dead. The Mass had been said for him and Uncle François had paid four prime fox pelts for it and a rosary. Mother church did not waste her labors, nor François Rivet

25

his fox pelts. *In pace requiescat Achille Rivet.*

Yet surely I must be more generous. The good fathers and my aunt and uncle had no doubt denied me the tenuous hope of the legend in the belief that it was a cruel lie and that in its useless harboring I might sicken my mind or spirit. I could not supply a better answer, nor was one needed. The news itself excused everything. What I owed the Jesuits was a better education than most in that far land. My foster parents had given me a decent home and upbringing. What my French father and wild Indian mother had bequeathed me was a tough, hard body and a totally independent mind. For myself I had added a sharp eye for subterfuge together with an optimistic determination to see the lighter side of life when fortune should fail to favor Frank Rivet.

Accordingly, what I did there in my foul-aired prison was to begin mixing a sincere prayer of thanks with an equally sincere assortment of curses at the slowness of the red-haired captain's return. This litany was at once interrupted by Clark's booming hail at the front of the house and, under cover of his cheerful entrance, I raised the outer lid of the woodbox and made good my escape into the rear yard.

My way, of course, now lay clear before me. The expedition of the American captains was bound for those very Big Rock Mountains wherein my father was rumored to lie a captive of the fierce Shoshone. I must, therefore, join that expedition this same night. As to ways and means of accomplishing this venturesome resolve, what better course than to trail the captains back down the bluff and, under the commotion of their meeting with the newly arrived Régis Loisel, stow away aboard the big twenty-two-oared keelboat?

When eventually, and far up the river, I was discovered, the courage of a lowly métis boy in undertaking such a perilous deception—and for such heart-felt reason—could not fail to captivate the friendly Americans.

I knew these men. They were not like the French and the Indians, ever ready to bend and delay or to argue meaningless legalities and traditions.

The Americans were the same as I was. They felt a thing and they did it. They didn't sit around all winter talking it over, and they never backed out once they had started. They were creatures, not of the mind, but of the heart, and I thanked God that the Jesuits and my Uncle François had let me know that I was born to this same fine heritage; that I, too, was an American, and crazy.

As the irrational pride in this idea spread tingling along my cramped limbs, I heard the captains coming out of the cabin. They were brief with their farewells at the doors and made off down the bluff trail with purposeful strides. In my hurry to keep pace them while still not risking discovery, I forgot about the third man who had been with them guarding the front of the house as they talked within. No more than two minutes along the trail I felt the prickling of the neckhairs which men reared in the wilderness understand to be a warning that something is behind them. I wheeled to flee but was too late. The great black form loomed over me, the giant hand closing on the nape of my neck as I uttered a terrified cry. Next instant my feet were dangling in mid-air, and York, Captain Clark's huge Negro servant, was presenting me like a miserable house-wetting puppy to his master.

27

"Cap'n," he announced to Clark in his liquidly soft Mississippi tones, "look here what I cotch sneaking along ahint you."

He set me down on the ground before the accusing gazes of the two captains, and Lewis said quite severely, "See here, were you actually following us, boy?"

I admitted it, saying I had meant only to go see the meeting with Loisel and to listen to the exciting talk of Cedar Island and the Teton Sioux.

"Natural enough," put in Captain Clark understandingly. "Come on along and welcome, lad. Were I your age, I'd be of the selfsame mind."

Lewis was not so naïve.

"Wait," he commanded. "Why this sneaking then?"

"Uncle François forbade me to go," I lied, but York at once waved a hand the size of a haunch of venison.

"He was hiding in the woodbox, Cap'n Lewis. I seen him. He crope out of it when you all was fixing Mister Rivet's laig."

"You were eavesdropping on us, too, boy?" Lewis charged.

"Oh, why not, Captain?" asked Clark. "He's only a kid; this is big adventure to him."

"It is to us, also," nodded Lewis. "I don't trust this boy, Will. He has something more than youthful curiosity in view. What is it, Rivet? What are you up to? Working for the British?"

"Here! here!" laughed Clark. "You can't be serious, Captain. This is the nephew of François Rivet, *the* Rivet. What would he be doing with the English?"

"Spying, perhaps."

28

"Never!" I broke in indignantly. "I, the son of Achille Rivet, a British spy? You are quite mad, Captain!"

"Well, at least quite careful," said Lewis. "Run along home, boy. Mind your uncle."

"Oh, let him tag along, Captain." Clark grinned. "He's no more than normally nosey. I like the lad."

"Go home, boy," repeated Lewis, "and stay there."

There was no compromise in his tone and Captain Clark put his calloused fingers gently to my shoulder.

"I know how you feel, Frank," he said. "I ran away from home when I was younger than you. But don't you do it, you hear? You're a smart boy. I can tell from your talk. You stay to home and keep in school."

"Yes, sir, thank you, Captain," I muttered. "You're a kind man and understand boys better than some."

"Don't be too hard on Captain Lewis now," he chided. "He's the head of this expedition and has much on his mind besides itchy-footed boys."

"I thought you were both the heads of the expedition," I said with some disappointment.

Clark only chuckled and grinned his crow's-footed, big friendly grin. "Well, now, that's so, boy, we are. But Captain Lewis he's the main head of it, you might say."

"You coming, Will?" put in Lewis abruptly.

"Yes, sir," Clark nodded, "right off. Good-bye, boy," he added, "and remember next time you want to run away, don't try it with old York around. He can hear a mouse high in a wall. Or a milkweed land in deep dust. And eyesight? Why, lad, the cat's not been littered that can move around in the night like my York!"

"Yes, Rivet," put in Lewis severely, "and don't get it in

29

your mind to follow us up the river, either. You have been told you can't go, and why you can't go. Now don't let us see you again before we sail."

I turned my back to him deliberately.

"*Bon voyage,* Captain Clark," I said.

"Thank you, lad, for whatever you said," smiled the red-headed captain, and wheeled about to follow Lewis down the bluff. Behind them trotted the giant African, York. Left alone on the steep trail, I felt the threat of misting tears and cursed manfully.

"God's name!" I cried aloud. "Do I intend to stand here and tell myself that I am this easily defeated?"

Evidently, and for the honor of my uncle's name, I did not. Within less than a full minute of the captains' departure, I was again moving for the riverfront landing.

7

I went by a secret path which I alone knew, and so encountered no more delays. As I came up to the site of Loisel's debarkment, the rain of the past afternoon was setting in again. There was great gain in this for me, since the blustery showers hid my approach to the leaping bonfire about which the men of Lewis and Clark were mingled with those of Régis Loisel. Loisel himself, that bearded raffish adventurer of the upper river, held the center of discussion. Lewis was his principal interrogator. Clark, as was his watchful way, stood back and listened. I was able to come up very close and lie behind a large cottonwood driftlog.

The interchange at once became fiercely exciting. It was all about the wild lands 200 or 300 or 400 leagues up the

Missouri. Famous and infamous Indian chiefs weaved in and out of the conversation. Tribes were named which might be counted friendly, unfriendly, trustworthy, thieving, kind, murderous. Outlandish and wondrous place names fell from Loisel's lips. Cheyenne River. Bad River. Grand Detour. Knife River. Land of the Mandan. White Earth. Big Muddy. Bear Paws. Medicine River. Musselshell. Little Manitou. Yellowstone. Prairie of Arrows. Sand Island. Vermilion River. Spirit Mound. I could scarce restrain myself from bounding up and shouting, "Come on, why do you stand here talking? Let us be aboard and poling!"

But then came the Indian tribal names. Omahas. Poncas. Loups. Pawnees. Sauks. Kaws. Arikaras. Sioux. Mandans. Minnetarees. Gros Ventres. Blackfeet. Bloods. Snakes and Flatheads and Crows. What magnificent words!

And next, the almost equally stirring names of the fabled frontiersmen of the white brother who traded or traveled through the red man's domain. Pierre Dorion. Jean Valle. John Evans. James Mackay. Pierre-Antoine Tabeau. Hugh McCracken. And, of course, the aging, great Toussaint Charbonneau. I even heard, to my startled pride, the name of my father, Primaut Achille Rivet. How can one convey the true feeling that passes over him as he hears the name of his natural parent set down in historic council between such as those of Tabeau and of Toussaint "the Squawman" Charbonneau? It was an immense thing, almost frightening.

But Loisel was speaking more swiftly now, words rattling and popping like sparks from the fire. The river *and* the Indians, once past La Charrette, were to be watched all the way up to the Mandan Nation. The Missouri was rising and falling like a crazy woman. She would be one night

31

four feet into the bank willows. Next dawn would find her dropped to the mid-channel sandbars, or her course shifted fifty feet from where the pirogues had been beached with the past darkness. As for the red men, some seditious word of the altered ownership of the Louisiana had been spread among them by the damnable British. All the warlike tribes were being deliberately alarmed with wild tales that the Americans were coming to take their hunting lands away from them, to cheat them and steal from them and do wrong things with their women. As a result, the savages were especially not to be trusted this spring. Below Teton River only hard vigilance might be required, but when it came to the homicidal and the treacherous "Tetongues," the verminous, villainous "Souex," they were the ultimate true terrorists of the upper river, and they must be treated and tread among as rattlesnakes and water moccasins of the most deadly venom.

Their territory began in the vicinity of the river named for their tribe and continued to the confluence of *Le Fleuve Couteau,* the Knife River, where began the legendary villages of the Mandan. Never forget that land nor the Sioux fiends who roamed it, advised Régis Loisel. Remember, too, their ill-famed chief, called the Partisan. He was a wolf, and his people were wolves with him.

There were the names of a few good chiefs which could be given. Black Buffalo was a wise and steady man. Second Bear, Considerable Man, Medicine Buffalo, these had some record for reliability. Yet the general council held: the Teton Sioux would kill the white man if he could. Loisel himself had barely come down the river with his own life just now, because of an ambush by these same

32

unnatural sons of hell. Now the American captains must be alert to these monsters, and . . .

The trader's grim warning carried on, but one senses the climax of a Frenchman's eloquence and I had perhaps already delayed too long in my listening. The friendly rain was thinning momentarily, weakening the cover under which I must now belatedly make my way aboard the keelboat. I slid away from behind the log and, crouching over, circled around the beach toward the big barge. I had come up to within thirty feet of her plank when a rift in the rain let me see, standing guard at this station so vital to my plan, the giant Negro, York. *Hélas!* What a cruel trick of fate!

However, there was no delay possible here. Behind me I could hear Régis Loisel rising to his final period. I must act, must risk all, or turn and flee like a whipped dog. Frantically I surveyed the winning chance.

At the helm of the fifty-five-foot vessel squatted the figure of a boatman. I knew his duty. It was to keep the debris of the flooding river from fouling the helm while the craft lay at mooring. If this sleepy steersman might be "helped" overboard into the swift water, he would be swept downstream 200 yards where he would land safely athwart a sandbar. But he would not know of this haven, nor would York; hence his seeming peril of drowning might draw the great Negro from his guardpost long enough for me to slip aboard and bestow myself among the cargo.

My problem now became how to get at the helmsman without prematurely alerting the black picket at the gangplank. The answer, if any, lay by water. I had demonstrated earlier that I was no match for York on dry land. But *how* by water? As suddenly as I asked myself, I knew. The answer lay upstream. There a certain bank current would take me neatly by the outriver flank of the moored barge. It was indeed the same current upon which I counted to waft away the sentry at the helm. *Voilà tout!* The whole thing was extremely simple, after all.

Up the bank I scuttled like some inland crab, and into the passing muddy tide, as unceremoniously, clothes and shoes included, as any French-Indian crustacean. In an instant the sluggish shore eddy swirled me out into the grip of the main shore-set, and I took the longest breath I might and bit into the current with my teeth. Down the river I went, six feet below the surface and shooting along like a slim log. Not daring to be swept past the boat, I surfaced when I thought to be abreast of her. Hell's flames! I was forty feet outside my goal, and bobbing past her with millrace speed. Wildly I clawed toward her, cross current, still struggling to stay below water and undiscovered. When breath could no longer be contained, I came up again. *Aïe Dieu!* The glistening sturgeon-gray flank of the keelboat was just sliding past. I had missed! And yet, had I? In the final second I struck out desperately atop the water, no thought or chance remaining of avoiding detection. My finger grazed, then sunk into the slimy wood of the tiller's post.

Above me the derelict steersman grunted a mildly disinterested "Huh?" then inquired mumbling of himself, "What the hell was that?" and leaned over the stern to satisfy the matter.

Automatically my arm shot upward, my hand fastening in his jacket collar. It was only after I had then jerked him clear of the deck and over my head, sprawling into the water, that I realized he wore the uniform of a private in

34

the Army of the United States.

"God's name!" I cried out unthinkingly, seeing him dashed away down the boiling current, "I have thrown overboard an American soldier! Heart of Jesus, they will hang me!"

But I was allowed no time to suffer this fear. The thud of naked feet running on deck planking raced toward the stern and the great batlike form of York soared over me to slash into the Missouri in rescue pursuit of the disappearing soldier. Still moving as if by mechanics—it certainly was not by intelligence—I hauled myself up over the low gunwale and ran forward along the river side of the keelboat's high-piled cargo. Up near the prow I dived under a loosened deck tarpaulin into the welcome warm embrace of a bale of trade blankets. Here I wormed in completely out of sight, pulling the loosened canvas tight behind me. Then, and only then, did I begin to think. What I thought, having the Gallic weakness for applying proverbs, was *tout est bien qui finit bien,* all's well that ends well. And I liked that thought so well that, as I now smiled broadly and settled back into my snug harbor, I repeated it distinctly aloud, just to relish the superior French sound of it on the tongue.

Here was another weakness, and a worse one. No sooner did the words come out of my mouth than a very familiar voice replied to them from directly outside my canvas shelter.

"Well now, Frank, that may be," said the voice, "but were I you, I wouldn't crow about it quite so soon."

"*Le bon Dieu!*" I gasped. "*Capitaine* Clark!" I groped for something to add which might help me, and came up

35

with a purely useless, "But I didn't know that you understood French, *Patron!*"

I thought I heard his warm chuckle. "It's not French I understand, lad," he said. "It's boys. I knew you'd circle around and come back. Spotted you behind the log yonder, right off. Sent York down to watch the plank. Figured you'd try to sneak on the boat that way and be caught for sure. But then you were too smart for that, all along."

I said nothing to disabuse him. *"Patron"*—my voice quavered—"what will they do to me?"

"Depends on whether they catch you."

"But you will give me over to Captain Lewis, of course?"

"Dunno, boy. Have to think about it. Sometimes takes me a spell to get my mind in order."

My heart leaped. "Captain," I whispered, "does that mean that you might—"

"Never you mind what it means," he replied sternly. "Hush up. Here comes the search party. They've fished Frazer out of the river and will want to know for certain who spilled him into it."

"They will discover me! I am undone!"

"Could be, boy. It all hangs on whether you keep on yelling, and on how long it takes me to think. As to that, I always do better setting down with a good fresh pipe."

I heard the scrape of the match and saw the glimmer of its flare through the canvas. He put it to the bowl of his cob, sucking noisily. "Over this way, men," he called out. "I thought I saw the rascal make for the forward cargo here." My heart sank at this seeming treachery, but next moment his bony buttocks were crunching down on top of me as he took his seat on my bale of blankets. "No, no," he ordered sharply to the men pounding up, "not *right* here; over there more toward the port bow. Likely under those flour bags." The feet thumped obediently off. I thought to start a sigh of small relief when another familiar American voice froze my gratitude.

"Did you actually *see* someone, Will?" he demanded suspiciously—indeed, accusingly.

I shivered. I could envision Lewis standing there, jaw thrust, neck turtled forward and eyes intent, in that focusing of utter attention which characterized his attitude toward information of any kind. But Clark was also cut of wary stuff, and watchful.

"Well no, Captain," he replied, "not precisely. There was only this general impression of somebody running forward from the stern."

"That's absolutely all?"

"I reckon. I've sat here ever since and not seen a bilge rat stir. If he's aboard, the men will find him.

"Yes, but he well may have slipped back to the stern. I will check down there. Look sharp now."

"Oh sure, Captain, you know me. I'll set right here till the last bale's lifted and looked under!"

Lewis strode off down the deck. The noise of the continuing search of the forward cargo went on menacingly, but Captain Clark had meant what he said. He was indeed a slow thinker. It was only after the last stack of trade goods had been shifted and replaced that he stood up and knocked out the embers of his pipe.

"All right, men." he said. "Let's go help Captain Lewis. There's naught up here but the night wind."

8

I did not awake until strong daylight. At first I did not recall where I was, but soon the cheery calls of the boatmen and the gruff orders of Captain Clark reminded me. *Bien!* I had done it. I was off up the great Missouri in search of my father, and more, I was with the American captains, Lewis and Clark, on their expedition to find a path by water across the vast Louisiana. The Northwest Passage! What wilder stuff might an eighteen-year-old boy feed his imagination in May of 1804?

Ah well, such provender might be fine for the mind. For the body it was inadequate.

Water! Sweet Mary, how I wanted water! Each swish of an oarsman's blade, each set and sucking retrieve of polesman's ironshod staff drove me to the brink. I believed certainly that Captain Clark had forsaken me and that by nightfall I should be dead beneath the smothering canvas of the deck tarpaulin.

From under the lower edge of this prisoning shroud I could see down the entire length of barge, bow to stern. The men were shipping their oars and stowing their poles of a sudden. A spanking breeze had sprung up and the sail had been unfurled. Beneath me the keelboat came alive, breasting the swift current with a delicious shudder. Downstream, in the angle of my view, I could also see the white and red dots of the two pirogues following the mother ship. The flash of the morning sun off their paddles, the whiteness of the sailing cloud above them, the deep blue of the clearing skies and, overall, the smells of spring on the Missouri momentarily assuaged my inner hurts.

But if I had forgotten my pangs, they soon enough remembered me. All I could see or think of was the mossy water barrel lashed to its moorings not a dozen feet from my hiding place. When, presently, Captain Clark came forward with a pewter plate heaped with boiled meat and biscuit for his noon dinner, I nearly fainted. One might think he had come to bring this food for me, save that his companion, also bearing a full plate, was Captain Lewis. Since the latter had just come aboard by canoe from a settler's cabin above us on the stream it was obvious that a serious council was upcoming. But I was puzzled by Captain Clark's deliberate manner of sitting upon a large box of glass trade beads precisely next to my bale of blankets.

"Take the powder can, Captain," he said to Lewis in his straight-ahead manner, "and let's get to it!"

I saw Lewis's feet move to a squat canister of gunpowder. Sighingly, he sat down upon it.

"All right, Will," he answered. "But first let us have this bite. I've not eaten since noon yesterday."

I could sense Clark's sympathetic nod.

"Yes it gets a bit busy now and again," he said, putting his own plate on the deck at his feet. "I believe that I shall build a pipe while you begin. For some reason I don't have much appetite. Might be I et too much of the fatback this morning."

I stared at the plate of meat and biscuit abandoned outside my lair. It was sour brisket and the gray hardtack was gritty and not altogether innocent of animal life, but to me the menu took on the aroma of roast wild turkey and spoonbread. I nearly strangled in my own saliva. Clark, compounding my misery, lit his pipe and blew me the scent of rich burley. Moreover, he deliberately got up and went to the water barrel and dipped his tin tankard full from it. He then returned and sat down, pulled a lip-smacking draft from it, and placed it upon the deck with the plate of food. In the bright sunlight I could see the beads of condensation form and trickle down the clean metal sides of the cup. I almost whimpered.

Lewis ate in silence. Clark smoked his infernal pipe. Down the deck the men continued to lounge at noon mess. Only the helmsman stood to his post. The midday breeze curled steadily and strong up the river. It was a scene of both excitement and despair.

I cursed my helplessness. Yet, even as I did, Captain Lewis put down his emptied plate and brought out his own pipe. While he was busied in loading it, an incredible thing occurred: the large, bony-ankled foot of Captain Clark adroitly shoved its owner's untouched plate in under the edge of my canvas. Next moment the same foot maneuvered the sweating tankard to follow the food dish. Covering this charity, the red-haired captain cleared his throat and spat noisily to leeward.

"Well now, Captain," he said, "what is it we must decide? The wind holds fair, the weather clear."

"Nothing to decide, Will," answered the other. "Only the matter of reviewing our instructions from the President. Mr. Oglethorpe, the settler at the creek mouth yonder, tells me the British continue to arouse the Indians upcountry. Three trading parties have come down past his place this week, all complaining of trouble."

I fell to eating, spellbound despite my ravenous hunger.

"Well," Clark said, unconvinced, "you know I don't take the dubious look at the Indian that most do, Captain. I've had my experiences with him and come off inclined to admire more than detest him."

"I realize that," granted Lewis a trifle sharply.

"But then it's not given to each of us to be the younger brother of George Rogers Clark."

My ears tingled at this. I had not realized my red-headed riverboatman was the brother of the famous American Indian fighter.

"I'll not gainsay your claim, Captain," replied Clark easily. "Being George's brother has helped a lot."

"I'm convinced of that, Will. Your brother's reputation permits you to move among the Indians with an assurance denied the rest of us. The Indians are impressed."

"So am I, Captain, to hear it the way you tell it," grinned Clark. "It's good I've a steady head for flattery."

"Yes, Will, and a stout oak heart for faithfulness, too. But we've real worries all the same. If we are to encounter major delays from the redmen, we may not get to the Pacific in time. You will recall our parting warning on that from Mr. Jefferson."

"You mean about the British also pushing to occupy the Columbia? Leastways the north part?"

"Precisely. Mackenzie, in 1799, withdrew from the British North West Company in the dispute over how best to open up Canada's western territories. We both know that by 'western territories' Mackenzie meant a goodly portion of the northern part of what the President contends we have obtained through the Louisiana Purchase."

"That's right, Captain," said Clark thoughtfully.

41

Lewis nodded, frowning.

"Will," he said, "the hard fact of this history we are involved with is that the Louisiana can mean to the United States just what we are able to make it mean. If we do not explore and map and plant the flag on what Mr. Jefferson insists is ours, then we have failed and the expedition has failed with us. The Purchase will be a diminished piece of paper meaning but a part of what you and I, with God's help and their President's foresight, have been given the chance to make it mean."

He clenched his slender jaw, frown darkening.

"This is a shadow empire we gamble to declare upon, Will," he said. "No man knows its true meets and bounds. It is as though our government had given France fifteen-million dollars and France had, for this amount, waved her hand to the west of the Mississippi and said, 'Dear friends, there is the land. We have no chart of it for you. The Spanish have measured it one way, the British another. It is for the United States to apply her own geography, to draw up and submit her own tracts of sovereignty. As for us French, *au revoir et bonheur!*' "

Lewis paused. One could sense his excitement, yet when he spoke again it was with pure frustration.

"It's a frightening prospect, Will," he declared. "It is time that we battl—time and the damnable tenacity of the British. We know they intend taking the northern reaches of this land from us, given the opportunity. This current arousal of the upriver tribes proves it and returns us to the warning Mr. Jefferson read us from Mackenzie's book. That book, Will, holds the British blueprint. You know it, I know it, the President knows it. Yet at times I wonder if we have not, all of us, been led astray by our imagination and uncertainties."

He paused once more, shaking his head.

"Still, we know that Mackenzie believed implicitly that British sovereignty did and should extend to the forty-fifth parallel. What he called his rectified boundary between the United States and Canada would have to run on a line through the southern Dakotahs and the mid-Oregon country; hence that part of the Louisiana in possible contention is vast indeed, and scarcely exaggerated by either Mr. Jefferson's or our own beliefs."

Here he hesitated a very long time. Clark did not reply. I held my breath, heart pounding.

These two plain captains and this tiny, raffish crew of French boatmen and American soldiers composed the fragile lance of empire. That lance was now in danger of being shattered by the provoked hostility of the upriver tribes. It took a powerful gift of imagination to grasp the extent of the expedition's mission, as well as its vulnerability to a few hundred naked savages with no concept of the stakes at play.

But I could see the far-glittering American star. I could see it with the passionate eye of a Frenchman and with the smoldering eye of a wild-horse Indian. And the prospect was sufficient to hold me mute and breathless.

In the stillness Lewis went on. "Will," he said, "would you think me daft if I asked you to read me that passage in Mackenzie which the President marked for us? I would like to study it again in the context of this clear air and bright sunshine. I sometimes wonder if the pipesmoke and cigar fumes at the Capitol don't defy the ear as badly as they do the nose!"

I could hear Clark's low chuckle, and evidently he reached to take the copy of Mackenzie's journal from Lewis.

"Voyages from Montreal," he began reading. "By Sir Alexander Mackenzie. Being an account of his journey by the overland route from Fort Chippewyan to the Pacific Coast. The first white man to chance this—"

"Yes," yes," Lewis interrupted impatiently. "We know all that."

"Just so," agreed Clark, unruffled.

By opening this intercourse between the Atlantic and Pacific Oceans, and forming regular establishments through the interior and at both extremes, as well as along the coasts and islands, the entire command of the fur trade of North America might be obtained from 48° North to the pole, except that portion of it which the Russians have in the Pacific. To this may be added the fishing in both seas and the markets of the four quarters of the globe. Such would be the field for commercial enterprise and incalculable would be the produce of it, when supported by the operations of that credit and capital which Great Britain so pre-eminently possesses. Then would this country begin to be remunerated for the expenses it has sustained in discovering and surveying the coast of the Pacific Ocean, which is at present left to American adventurers. . . .

When Clark closed the journal and returned it, the silence resettled itself between the captains.

"My God," said Lewis after a long while. "The entire command of the fur trade of North America? The fishing in both seas and the markets of the four quarters of the globe? Will, if that doesn't sound like a manifesto for Her Majesty's Government to move into our American Northwest, what does it sound like?"

Clark stood up, sturdy legs braced.

"Sounds more like an invitation to a boat race, Captain," he answered, low-voiced. "Let's lay to with the oars and help this Louisiana wind to win it for us."

BOOK II
CEDAR ISLAND
AND THE TETON SIOUX

9

I had no more food or water that day, the twenty-fifth of May. All the following day, which was again squalling a little rain, and cold, Captain Clark did not appear and with nightfall I had grown surpassingly despondent. He came at last, though. But then, curse him, he brought only counsel rather than comestibles.

"I warned you about running away from home, boy," he said in guarded tones. "I told you it wasn't easy."

"Food!" I whimpered. "Water, water!"

"As for the first," he replied, "you won't die for another day—or three—or five. As for the second, the river is full of it."

"Please, Captain!" I pleaded. "I'm desperate!"

"We all are," he answered. "If you listened well yesterday to that reading of mine from Mackenzie's manifesto, you will understand the state of our morale. If you come out now Captain Lewis will put you ashore without a rifle or supplies of any sort. He is in no mood to be surprised by stowaways. You set tight, lad. You've another day or so to suffer at very best."

That was the last of him for twenty-four hours. Later that night I dipped some water from the river to drink. As well, I stretched my arms and legs on the deck. Clark fed me a little next night, and the next. It was the following, fifth, evening which threatened everything. I was at my limit by then. The matters of voiding bladder and bowel, the increasing jangle of nerves five days controlled, the forays for drinking water, all conspired to bring me to the end. Or so I thought.

"Lad," Clark told me, "we've been doing badly enough. Seven miles today. You will recall that two nights ago we had only passed the mouth of the Gasconade. This evening we are scarce thirty-five miles farther."

"*Sacre coeur!*" I whispered. "We're still too near La Charrette. I am undone!"

"Not if you're the boy I risked my neck for, Frank."

This touched me. I realized his action in hiding me could earn him severe censure from Lewis. Perhaps it might even go against his name in the permanent records of the expedition. I straightened with pride.

"I am that boy," I told him. "I am cold and wet and aching with ague and shrunken-belly gripes, but I am that

46

boy. Give me the food, please."

Clark cleared his throat.

"That's another test, lad," he said uncomfortably. "Food's scarce aboard. No game ashore. Drink a lot of water tonight. It'll fill you up and ease the griping."

This time he had to leave me abruptly. Lewis was aboard the keelboat that evening and now came striding up from the stern to ask something of his co-captain. Clark went quickly to meet him and I was left alone with my misery.

Suddenly, absolutely without a sound, two of the most immense, pink-soled, bare and blue-black feet in the New World came to a rest before my bale of blankets. Next moment York had squatted down on his hams outside my nest and said in his wondrously deep voice, "don't make a sound, white boy. You let out one peep, Cap'n Lewis will throw you over the side for certain. Here," he added, raising the canvas, "the deck's clear, come on out and eat; I brang you some cold vittles."

I did not question him. The food might be gelid and greasy and of dubious origin, but it was meat and I was starving. Emerging from my hated cage, I began wolfing it down. When the last of it was lodged solidly in my wind-pipe, I leaned over the side of the boat and sucked up a pint of the Missouri's thin mud.

"York," I sighed "may the Almighty bless you until you are more handsomely rewarded. You must also thank your good master for sending you to me. Ah, what bliss!"

The huge Negro shook his head.

"Master didn't send me, boy," he said.

"What? He didn't?"

47

"Nope, he don't even know that I know you're on the boat. He'd skin me alive, happen he caught me here."

A quite large suspicion loomed belatedly.

"York," I said accusingly, "you've known all along I was on the boat. You knew it when they were searching for me at La Charrette. When Captain Clark was hiding me."

"Sure, sure I did, white boy."

"But you kept quiet because you saw that your master was protecting me, is that it?"

"Nope, that ain't it."

"No? Well then, in God's name, what was your reason for honoring my secret?"

This time he took longer with his answer, but he was very sure with it when it came.

"Because," he said, "when I was outside the door to your uncle's house, I heard what they all say in there. I heard them call you métis, and I know what that means. You ain't all white. You're part dark blood. You're part like me. I feel that inside me, white boy. I understand it. It makes something special betwixt us, me and you."

"But, York, if you protected me because we both have dark blood, how is it that you still call me white boy?"

"Because I also heard outside that door how your uncle he answered the captains. He said to them that you loved most of all to be like them, to be American, and that means a white man. So that's what you are, far as I'm concerned. And that's why I call you thataway. You understand that sort of feeling, white boy?"

"Yes," I said at last "I think I do, York."

He only nodded and gave me an awkward "good dog" pat on the head.

It was all we required between us, York and me. When presently, and without one more word, he arose and trotted soundlessly away down the deck, I understood not only the feeling the giant slave talked of, but also what that feeling meant to him beyond his simple ability to acknowledge or describe.

If in Captain William Clark I had found a friend, then in me lonely black York had surely done the same.

10

All next day it rained. York brought me a marrow bone and heel of biscuit late in the afternoon. Captain Clark came at dusk. He had no food to offer but the nature of his counsel stirred my numbed spirit to the task of enduring one more night under the deck canvas.

"I would suggest, Frank," he said, "that you be 'discovered' tomorrow. We're far enough from La Charrette for you to risk it and, moreover, the problem of getting you food has gotten to be a real chore."

"I've not complained!" I said, with some rancor.

"I've not expected you to," he replied. "All the same you'll have to come out and take your luck with the rest of the crew. Matters have tightened up for all of us with this poor hunting ashore. I can't give you any more time."

"*Patron,*" I said, "don't judge me by my bad temper. My eternal gratitude is yours. I would die for you."

"Never mind that, lad. I think we can use you alive. You write a legible hand in English, don't you?"

"Why yes, sir," I said, surprised.

"Good." He smiled. "I had you pegged right. Now, set

tight till I 'discover' you tomorrow. Be warned, though, I may need to cuff you about a bit to make it look real."

"*Patron,*" I said feelingly, "I await your blows with keenest pleasure."

He stood up, rearranging the tarpaulin to hide the signs of his visit.

"You're an odd one, Frank," he said, "and so am I. Happen the wind holds right, well make it there and back together, you and me."

I nodded thankfully, answering, "As my people say, *Patron,* 'God tempers the wind to the shorn lamb.' "

I heard his honest quick laugh.

"You're a fair tough lamb, Frank," he said, "I'm thinking you won't need too much sheltering from the elements."

"Find me early, Captain; this covert stifles me."

This time he did not reply. He had already gone away down the deck as Indianlike and silent in his elkskin moccasins as any Minnetaree or Teton Sioux.

The discovery took place about mid-morning of the next day, May 31st, a Thursday. It had continued to rain steadily the previous night and a cold wind blew with it. I was ready to be found. Even so, things went chancefully for the red-haired captain and me.

Clark contrived to work up onto the foredeck, with Captain Lewis and several of the crew in attendance. The pretext was an inspection of that part of the men's quarters contained below the decked-over prow of the big keelboat. While offering some niggling remarks to the crew about maintaining better order and cleanliness in quarters, Clark

50

suddenly raised his voice. "This bedding is crawling with vermin!" he declared accusingly. "I believe that all of you are going to have to get clean covers. Here, break open this bale of trade blankets." He banged my bale forcefully. "After you've washed and aired your own bedclothes, you can return the trade blankets as they were. The savages will never know the difference. Step lively, now!"

Again he smacked the tarpaulin, over my head, this time with a rousing clout which left my ears ringing. I was still shaking my head, when the crew tore away the canvas and spilled me out upon the deck squarely, at the planted feet of Captain Meriwether Lewis.

"Good Lord, sir!" exclaimed Captain William Clark. "It's the boy from La Charrette! Blast you, you young whelp! I told you not to run away from home!"

Before Lewis could rejoin, Clark then seized me in his bearlike grip and boxed me smartly about the head. It required no shamming on my part to howl in good effect. Indeed, my French temper was on the point of warning him that he had gone too far when he desisted and stepped back. Lewis simply waited without a word. He looked at me and he looked at Clark. He looked around also at the gathered crewmen. Finally he was ready.

"I do believe Will, that you are right," he said. "It *is* the boy from La Charette."

Baptiste Deschamps, the burly *patron* of the French boatmen, interjected grinningly. "It is indeed the nephew of François Rivet."

"Six days," put in Captain Clark, wonderingly, "Goodness me, think of him hiding in there all that time!"

"I *am* thinking of it," replied Captain Lewis, long face

51

severely set. "How did he eat? How did he exercise? Where did he relieve himself? How did he escape the search of the boat at La Charrette? Oh, I am thinking a great many things about his hiding in there all that time, Captain Clark. You may well believe that I am!"

He stared at the red-headed captain, probing him with his ready-to-pounce attitude. But Clark held fast.

"Well now, sir," he admitted ruefully, "I realize it is all my fault that he is here. I tried to advise him to do the right thing but clearly he misunderstood me."

"Yes," said Lewis. "Either that, or you didn't 'set' on it long enough."

"How's that, sir? Set on what?"

"On the idea of dissuading the boy," replied Lewis evenly. "But then, had you set on it longer, you might have smothered it altogether. The idea, naturally, not the boy."

The two captains stood looking at one another for what seemed to me like five minutes. Then Clark's sunny grin warmed the situation. "Naturally, Captain," he said.

Lewis ignored him.

"Boy," he barked at me "we are coming up on those north-bank rapids. We'll let you take the lead grip on the tow-rope. Over the side the minute we hit wading water. I believe we'll make you think twice about stowing away."

"Yes sir, Captain," I said, saluting him smartly. "Thank you very much, sir!"

"Get to the rope and stand ready!" he snapped. "I'll have none of your French trickery, you understand?"

"Yes, sir," I repeated, and went at once to my station.

Behind me, the discussion went forward, the switching of the wind bringing it to me.

"Well now," Clark was saying, "what will we do with the boy, Captain? I mean as to final disposition."

"What do you suggest?" Lewis demanded quietly.

"Well, I've one idea: since the boy is named for his Uncle François, we could simply leave the company roll as it is, with Rivet's name in place, using young Frank in his stead."

"Discipline," said Lewis sternly, "does not adjust all that easily. The very first downriver party we pass, I shall have him transferred to its care."

"But he's a fine lad, Captain, and will make a good riverman, too. It would be a pity to send him back. I mean, now that he's come so far and—well, you know what I mean, Captain."

Lewis nodded quickly, the quiet voice edged with iron.

"Yes, Will," he said, "I know exactly what you mean. And my decision holds regardless. The boy goes back."

"*Damn!*" I heard Captain Clark answer softly, and that was all.

The wind drove against us down the river beginning at noon and continuing until 5 P.M. The entire time we hugged the north bank, using the tow. Those of us on the rope were dead with fatigue when Captain Lewis ordered camp at dusk. In such a wind we were helpless to go on until it might die away. This it did by the time supper was done. But no sooner had the wind quit than other trouble blew down the river. It was a party rafting a load of peltries to St. Louis.

The *patron* was French, an agent of Chouteau's fur company. He had been trapping the past winter on the Grand

53

Osage. His companions on the raft were an Indian man and a squaw. Our American captains bid them all welcome, sharing with them the slender remains of the one deer our hunters had been able to kill. Lewis pounced at once upon the French trapper, plying him with queries about Indian tempers upstream, as well as introducing the matter of carrying me back to La Charrette.

Michaud—that was his name—convinced Lewis soon enough that all reports of poor times with the Indians upriver were well founded. The savages had just burned him out up on the Osage, permitting him to escape with his life only. The Indians did not believe, Michaud said, that the Americans now owned the Louisiana. They sneered at the idea. He added the chilling suggestion that, even should the American expedition get past the Teton Sioux—which it would not—it would still have waiting for it an even worse chief than the Partisan. This would be Le Borgne, the One-Eyed, headman of the dread Minnetarees, or Big Bellies. Le Borgne was a half- or quarter-bred white who passionately hated the Americans and was unquestionably in British pay to guarantee that he continued to hate them. Captains Lewis and Clark had better pray hard to get past the Partisan and then make a deal with the Devil to beat Le Borgne. As for Michaud, he was thankful to have come this far down the river and had no plans whatever for going back up it again next spring.

Depressed, Lewis returned to the proposition of freighting the runaway Frank Rivet back as far as La Charrette.

Michaud listened, then fastened his dark eyes on me.

"Rivet, eh?" he said "The nephew of François? The son

of Achille? I have news for you, *enfant*."

"What news?" I said bitterly. "That you will gladly agree to transport me back to La Charrette?"

"You're a Rivet, all right." Michaud answered. "Just as miserable as your damned uncle. Now, do you wish to hear my news or not?"

"Excuse me." I bowed. "Is it possible that you speak of good news?"

"It might be, cockerel. That is, were you to silence your Rivet's tongue long enough for me to divulge it."

I bowed again, and Michaud straightway told his story.

The Indians with him were not Osages but Pawnees. The squaw, She Bear, had been a girlhood friend of my mother. A particular rumor having to do with Achille Rivet, the French husband of my mother, had come down the river on the spring flood. It said that a party of northern Pawnees had traveled to the foot of the Rock Mountains, beyond which dwelled the Shoshone, the Snake Indians. The traveling band had fallen in with some Crows, a tribe known to have intercourse with the Flatheads who, in turn, traded with the Snakes. The Crows said that the Frenchman of the Big River—my father—was yet alive and being held in the camp of the Shoshone grand chief, Kooskiah. He led a strange life there, it was said. He took no squaw, lived with no warrior, and neither worked for the women of the tribe nor hunted with the men. The Flatheads had wondered at such an odd life in telling the Crows about it. The Crows then added to the mystery in passing the tale along to the Pawnees. And, Michaud now concluded, with a shrug of uplifted palms, one might be absolutely certain that the Pawnees had taken nothing from the story in passing along their version of it.

"You must be aware, *enfant,*" he added warningly to me, "that the flavor of such a rumor cannot be tasted full strength. However, the bones remaining in the pot may be sucked with some reliance. I will not say that Achille resides with this particular band of the Shoshone, nor that he is held by them in any manner peculiar or mysterious. But this I will say, if the Indians say that your father is still alive, then you may stake your sacred honor or the virtue of your favorite sister on the fact that he is alive. That is the marrow bone of the story, that you can suck on."

For a long moment no one about the fire said anything. Captain Lewis stared down at the dirt of the fireside. Captain Clark, who had come up with the two Pawnees, was watching me. The Indians were also studying my face. Michaud, like a true Frenchman, was keeping his attention where it belonged—on the man who gave the orders and paid the wages of the day—he was watching Captain Meriwether Lewis. I also watched the captain, who did not like me. The stillness became undeniably hostile.

Finally Lewis raised his head. His words went to Clark.

"This doesn't change anything, Will," he said. "We can all understand how young Rivet feels, but we're many a hundred league from the land of the Shoshone. We can't become involved with Indian fables on the way. However," he amended, eyeing me, "we share some responsibility for his having come this far." His intent eyes shifted to meet Clark's mild ones. "I'm sure you'll agree to that, Captain," he said.

"Oh yes, sir," answered Clark. "It does seem we could have been more careful in our search of the boat at La

Charrette. I blame myself for that, Captain."

"So do I," said Lewis.

Both captains exchanged nods, then Lewis continued.

"Now the complicity admitted," he said, "it becomes our charge to be completely fair in judging his case. I am going to give you the chance, Captain, to speak first. What have you got by way of a useful reason for keeping this boy among our ranks?"

Clark scowled and shuffled his feet. I could only suffer through his hesitance and Lewis's waiting intentness. Finally, Clark bobbed his head awkwardly.

"Lacking your own advantages, Captain," he said, "I thought to have young Frank help me with my entries in the journal. Also, I figure he can keep a journal of his own. You'll grant that won't hurt. After all, we are encouraging the men to keep journals, sir, and to have a truly educated young fellow along to add his to the record—mind you, Captain, educated by the Jesuits, and they're great scholars—why that, to me, just makes plain good old-fashioned horse sense."

Lewis nodded dryly. "It might also make just plain good old-fashioned horse feathers, too," he said. "Go on, Will."

"Well, the boy can also man an oar, push a pole, lay to a tow rope, hold dead center with a rifle, navigate a bar or a bad bank current and likewise, little doubt, make a steersman soon enough. Further, he's half horse Indian and we can use that 'friendly influence,' farther up the stream. His lost father is a legend up where we're going and the Indians knowing we have along the only son of Achille Rivet will be a factor most favorable to the expedition. Now, what do you say?"

Lewis pursed his thin lips. He never let his narrowed eyes wander from his companion's ruddy face.

"What I say," he nodded finally, "is why don't you come out with it honestly, Will? What is your real reason for outright lying on behalf of this, well, this extremely dirty, very skinny and, I might say, admirably tough boy?"

Clark shrugged soberly, spreading his bony hands, lowering his rough voice.

"Why, Captain," he said gently, "it's simple as sugar syrup."

He moved around the fire and came to stand at my side, putting his arm about my shoulders. Then, straightening, he met the other captain's gaze.

"You see, Captain," he told Lewis, "it's just that us Americans has got to stick together."

11

We stayed in that camp another day waiting for the company hunters. Their absence now ran to five days. The captains were concerned about this, as well as the lack of meat so occasioned. Still we all worked. There was cargo to be shifted, trade goods to be aired from the constant rains, poles, paddles, boat hulls to be repaired. Captain Lewis during this time tended to his journal of the expedition. Clark was concerned with the state of the crew and the equipment. In result his own journal was neglected, presenting me with my first opportunity to study his notes.

He brought them to me late the second afternoon, saying he thought I might care to examine them with an eye to seeing how it was done, since he still wanted me to keep my own journal of the adventure.

"A young fellow," he said, "will take a varying view of all these things to that held by older men. A boy's eyes are less spoiled, Frank."

He paused, looking off up the river, then went on.

"When the sergeants and the privates and the captains have set down the field information, folks win still want to know how lovely this great river looked in a billowing spring rain, what the sound of the meadowlark was at sunrise on the far prairie, how sharp fell the bark of the fox or thinly the distant cry of the buffalo wolf, what was the length of Captain Lewis's nose, how homely was made the face of the other captain, what vast ignorances were his and what small skills, how the grass roared on fire for forty miles around; folks will want to see the haughty stalk of a Sioux war chief, the grace of a young Minnetaree or Arikara woman, in the fashion of the savage dress, they will want to feel the moccasined foot set on earth never trod by white man before—ah, lad, there's no end to things you can tell in a way we can't!'

He seemed strangely sad for a moment there, and I took his slim journal from him.

"Thank you, *Patron,*" I murmured. "I shall do my best."

"Your best is what I expect of you, Frank" he said.

He marched off at once in his abrupt, awkward way, and I undid the oiled-silk wrappings of the journal and began to read. At first I was appalled by the crudity of his entries. Then the simple, stark manner in which he expressed himself began to invade my imagination. The man had the freshness of a child, the keen mind of a scholar. He captured a feeling in between these extremes which no edu-

59

cated writer might hope to approach. Consider this sample in which, with half a page, he describes the company's near-disastrous passage of the Devil's Raceground:

May 24th Thurs. 1804
. . . Passed a verry bad part of the River Called the Deavel's Raceground, this is where the Current Sets against some projecting rocks for half a Mile on the Labd. Side, passed a Isld. in a verry bad part of the river. We attempted to pass up under the LBd. Bank which was falling in so fast that the evident danger obliged us to cross between the Starbd. Side and a Sand bar in the middle of river, We hove up near the head of the Sand bar, the Same moving & backing caused us to run on the sand. The Swiftness of the Current Wheeled the boat, Broke our toe rope, and was nearly over setting the boat, all hands jumped out on the upper Side and bore on that Side untill the Sand washed from under the boat and Wheeled on the next bank by the time She wheeled a 3rd time got a rope fast to her Stern and by the means of swimmers was Carried to Shore and when her stern was down whilst in the act of Swinging a third time into Deep Water near the Shore, we returned to the Island where we Set out and assended under the Bank which I have just mentioned as falling in. . . .

Well, there it was. All of the meat with no fat. Captain Clark put down only those things which had honest meaning to him. He was the riverman of the two captains, Lewis for the main part traveling ashore to help with the hunting, selection of campsites, and the like. As well, it was Lewis's province to make and set down the bulk of the scientific information gathered. Clark's journal, by contrast, was as bare of concern for flora or fauna as any ocean-going master's log. Shifting channels, snags, sandbars, sets-of-current, feet-of-draft, there was the matter of front rank with the red-haired captain. Yet he had this art wherein what he did say of other things carried a peculiar impact. And his rough, old-soldier kindness in granting me his trust was the proudest hour of my life.

Nor was I ever deceived by the real nature of his work. I was a headstrong half-breed, hot-blooded, rebellious, vain, callow. As such, I was scarcely given to deeper consideration of philosophy and the orderly progression of the universe. Yet, even though I was the tool of these varied lacks, I still knew which way to spit on a windy day. Crude, unfinished, barely literate they may have been; I realized the true character of those notes beneath my hand. I was holding history in my lap.

12

The journal of Captain Clark was swiftly replaced by an oar on the keelboat. This proved work to break the back of a giant. The two days required to go on up to the mouth of the Osage pushing the fifty-five-foot barge loaded with thousands of pounds of trade goods against a twenty-mile downriver wind had me at exhaustion's edge. The second night Captain Clark tended my blistered hands, assuring me that I, and they, too, would toughen to the chore. But his medicines were small solace. It was meat that I needed, and that we all needed. One may imagine the joy, then, with which the hungry crew greeted the distant hail across the river from George Drewyer and John Shields whose two packhorses were loaded with game.

It turned out they had seven deer. As we prepared and ate these, Captain Clark went among the men urging them to wait until the meat was cooked through, this to avoid the "venison blues," a treacherous disorder of the bowel brought on by underdone deermeat. But the others were the same as I. They would not delay and so gorged and were sore and sorry the following week. But such was the esprit of these hardy rascals. They simply did not care. They were consumed by the fever of the Louisiana adventure and were, to the last veteran army private and hard-bitten French boatman, carefree as boys.

Looking at them, I was stirred in soul to be of their number. Actually, I knew very little of them. Nine of the total were young Americans from Kentucky. Fourteen were soldiers in the United States Army, volunteers every one, sworn to serve to death. There were two French rivermen, "water masters" by rating, who supposedly knew each whim and whirlpool of the Missouri, these being Peter Cruzatte and Francis Labiche. Among the soldiers were three sergeants, Ordway, Pryor and Floyd, the last-named a very fine fellow to whose mess Captain Clark had assigned me. Additionally, there was Corporal Richard Warfington and his squad of six men doing guard duty to get the expedition past the Teton Sioux. Lastly, there was the black York and the ten French boatmen, myself among the latter, hired to go only so far as the Mandan country. This was the whole of the Lewis and Clark Party.

It was not much of a host with which to strike against an

untracked enemy wilderness. Yet, glancing about the firelit sandy beach of the great river, seeing those fearless laughing faces, hearing the coarse sallies and quick gibes with which they wolfed their half-cooked meat and scalding coffee, a boy of eighteen, even with raw hands and an aching spine, must thrill to his romantic core with the knowledge that he was accepted by such men as one of them. That boy must know, too, that mere numbers presented no handicap where such character and boldness existed. If any men alive could win through to the headwaters of the mighty Columbia River—could beat the British in Captain Clark's boat race to the Pacific sea—then it was these men who were my comrades on that lonely beach.

Full of good red meat in mind and body, I reclined gratefully against a driftlog. All was right within my world. Somewhere far up the Missouri beyond the Big Rock Mountains waited Achille Rivet. With the help and sympathy of these brave comrades, and the sufferance of their two captains, I would find my father and bring him home. Together we would live in this new land, bringing greater luster to the family name with each season. In the end, people would remember us and would honor our place in this great new Louisiana. We would be Americans of the first order.

That history which I had held in my hands two nights before returned now with intensified power. I could sense it all around me. It was in the dance of the flames, the shine of the men's eyes, the flush of their faces, the hush of the low words of the captains querying the returned hunters, in the smell of the strong black coffee, the wondrous odors of the shagleaf tobacco, the lap and soft singing of the river upon the sandy beach. It was in every fiber of that early summer night there at the mouth of the Osage River. God was good. This was living. Stand aside, History, make room for François Achille Rivet! Sweet Mary, what excitement! What fearful happiness! What blind luck!

Well, perhaps. But the truth was that Cedar Island lay still 380 leagues up the Grand Missouri. The deadly Teton Sioux were waiting yet a thousand miles away. The wicked Partisan and cruel Le Borgne dwelled still a hundred days and more to the north.

The truth was, we were but eighty-seven miles by water from my uncle's house in La Charrette.

I made hasty truce with this depressing reality. In less than a full minute I dismissed the business of the small distance from home. Pah! Why be modest? I had made a superb start. Be of grateful heart and clear mind, I told myself. With these gallant companions of fellow French and American blood you are about to embark upon the great hour of your life. Bless the good God, Frank Rivet, and go to sleep.

What a poor fool I was. That night on the sandy shore where we ate the burned-raw venison and joked of beating the British to the Columbia, I envisioned a dashing attack up the river. In this gallant run, we would virtually fly to the villages of the Mandan, gliding along like racing sculls. Nothing mundane would deter us, no natural obstacle prove our superior. After all, had not the red-haired captain himself named it a boat race?

Well, it was the devil of a race. To make of it anything romantic would be quixotic. Oh, Floyd was good to me, and York, when he might leave off his employment as Clark's shadow, was similarly kind. But Baptiste Deschamps treated me poorly, being jealous of my family's reputation on the river. Neither did he permit me to forget that my mother had been a Pawnee. And Lewis, as a matter of course, was Lewis. He never gave me a friendly look or word after the brief clash with Clark in which it was decided I might stay with the company. The greatest disillusionment of all, however, was my red-headed benefactor. Clark, while he always had a smile for me when our paths crossed, seemed otherwise to have disowned me. He even assigned me to the white pirogue of Corporal Warfington, thus separating me from the keel-boat and himself. His excuse was that Warfington, being no riverman, needed a decent steersman in his craft, and that was myself.

"You are to see, lad," he told me simply, "that the white pirogue gets up the river every bit as handily as the red."

By "the red" he meant the French pirogue of Baptiste Deschamps. He was thus pitting me directly against the *patron* of the boatmen, which of course did little to enrich my relationship with that fiery, vain riverman.

But, as the French say, "Speak of the devil and his horns will appear." So I did what I might to stay with Deschamps and the red pirogue while still not exaggerating the unfairness of the match from my viewpoint. One must bear this frustration in mind. The story of interminable travail which composed the next sixteen weeks of our race against time was a hell of exhaustion. My labors to keep the white pirogue abreast of the red one continued from dawn to dusk. My every instant upon the river, my each moment in camp ashore, were alike girded by the stress of one fact: Captain Lewis was watching me. One faux pas, one error in judgment, one mistake with a snag or sandbar, and I was finished. If the white pirogue went down, I went down with it, for there remained no human doubt that Captain Lewis would send me rafting homeward on the next passing logfloat of French furs should I blunder in the trust Captain Clark had given me.

Here, then, is Frank Rivet, half-breed steersman for the white pirogue of Corporal Richard Warfington, reporting on the remaining 380 leagues to Teton River and the land of the Sioux. The company is a scanty crew of hardy paladins dispatched across the wide and wild Missouri by the American President Thomas Jefferson. The official name of the company is the Corps of Volunteers for Northwestern Discovery. The view is over the shoulder, as it were, of this great patriot leader and his two incomparable captains. They, and the forty-three other soldier and civilian minions of destiny serving under them. And especially of that wonderfully rough red-haired ex-officer of the United States Army who could neither spell nor punctuate nor pose a pretty phrase, but whose sense of life was faultless and whose faith in half-breed French and Pawnee boys was total.

12

We left the sand beach camp at six o'clock the morning of Tuesday, June 5, 1804, having first jerked the venison we had not consumed. About mid-morning, at a creek showing on our charts as Little Manitou, Captain Clark spied some fine beds of what he called "wild creases or tung grass," but which were ordinary water cress. Nothing would do for him, however, but that York and I, the prize swimmers, should breast out to the bar and fetch back a sufficient quantity of the greens for all three company messes. We did it and nearly drowned for our heroics. The proposition of swimming across an eight-mile current pushing a soggy raft of wet vegetables hardly represents sober judgment. Nevertheless, the feat served to gain me a new name, "Muskrat," and to raise me a little in the camp's social scale.

Later that afternoon, when I was two hours behind with the white pirogue, Clark sent York to see what my trouble might be. It was only some broken paddles, so York then said his master had told him that if the cause was not too serious he, York, should take me and scout the country by land. Our captain, it seemed, was curious to see to what extent my Pawnee blood might demonstrate itself effective; by which he meant effective in finding signs of other Indians.

York was a known scenthound at this work but, to my considerable pride, it was I who first found the track of the redmen going along the right-hand bank. My huge companion at once grunted, "How many of them?" and I studied the trail and replied, "Ten" which was exactly equal to his own count. York, however, confounded me by reading further that the Indians were all males and dressed for war. I immediately scowled that there was small chance to prove him wrong, to which he grinned and said, "Come along, white boy." We set out directly inland and in half an hour came up behind a rise and saw, beyond it, our band of Indians. There were ten of them and they were all warriors and all painted for war.

To cover my chagrin I made some show of identifying them as Sauks, adding that undoubtedly they were bound on a raid against the Osages, their historic enemies, with a view to stealing some of the traditionally fine Osage horses. This impressed York who, as I have remarked, was of simple mind. The larger art remained his, however, since he had impressed me and I had rather a keen intellect—well, at least keen enough to keep my tongue in my head upon our return to camp, permitting York to report our adventure. In this way I gained additional repute with my fellows through bridling my métis tendency to gild the pill, as the French say.

Early on Saturday, June 9th, we had trouble, the keelboat getting fast on a minor snag to begin with. This was at that place which Monsieur Loisel had called Prairie of Arrows. Getting the big boat off in an hour, we forged ahead, but shortly the main channel narrowed to funnel the entire tide of the Missouri into a constricted bore only 300 yards wide. The roar of the trapped flood was paralyzing. Before Captain Clark could cry out to his steersman, the keelboat struck a major snag—a great submerged deadhead—and swung herself broadside to the hammer of the raging current. Moreover, as she swung to, her lower side hit yet a third snag and her planking was stove in. She began at once to take water. Coming up just then with the white pirogue, I guided her into the lee of the keelboat and my crew leaped out to aid the other crew in heaving the heavier craft free of the menace, myself going aboard the barge to take her abandoned helm.

With luck, and Captain Clark yelling me on, I got the big

boat across the current and to a firm grounding on the right bank, so preventing her from foundering in deep water. Repairs proved not difficult and we made several more miles easily. That night Captain Clark came to Floyd's mess and announced loudly enough for all hands to hear, "That was quick work on the snag today, Frank; you're a real Rivet."

I slept that night the soundest I had since La Charrette.

With a favoring breeze, the sails set, and some timely poling, too, we did well until noon on June 12th. At dinner that day two rafts came down the river. One was loaded with peltries, one with antelope tallow and bear lard. We purchased 300 pounds of the combined greases, a most welcome addition to our diet, but the real surprise was to find that the Frenchmen had with them old Mr. Dorion. This was of course that same fabled Pierre Dorion of whom I had heard since earliest childhood.

The old gentleman was a St. Louis trader. He had more genuine years up the river than any white man alive. He was experienced with the Sioux in particular, having married a woman of the Yankton tribe and had by her a half-breed son, also called Pierre. The elder Dorion was reputed to be a violently dishonest rascal, a charge common in a trade where the richest fur merchant was most often he who got first to the most traps, his own or those of his competitors. His detractors insisted, also, that his success with the feared Sioux was due to his own implacable hatred and bad treatment of his fellow whites. But I still found old Mr. Dorion completely enchanting.

Captain Clark agreed. He said the old man's reputation was attributable to his courage. He would not be bullied nor buffaloed by the savages, and that was the deciding secret, said Clark, of dealing with them. Only stand hard and stand fast, advised our captain, and the Indians would never harm you. Take one step backward and it was all over; they would overwhelm you.

I naturally wondered about young Dorion, my fellow half-breed, and in this regard what a thrill it was when old Dorion told me he had known Achille Rivet and that he and my father had been *frères de lait,* foster brothers, for many years. What an added thrill subsequently when the doughty old trader said that he would accede to Captain Lewis's invitation to accompany the expedition back up the river. This was, as well, a crowning stroke for Lewis. Old Dorion had spent twenty winters in the Teton Nation and might succeed where Clark and Lewis never could, in getting some of the hostile chiefs to travel to Washington to visit their great father, President Jefferson. *En tout,* what a day this one was.

From that camp we worked the river like draft animals the next four days. The fifth day, June 17th being Sunday, we were finally allowed some rest. I had the chance once more of studying Clark's journal and should like to enter here the inimitable text of his notes for that Sabbath Day:

. . .We set out early and proceeded on only one mile & came too to make ores, repair our cable & toe rope &c. &c. Which was necessary for the Boat and Perogues, Sent out Sjt. Pryor and Some men to get ash timbers for the ores, and Set some men to make a Toe Rope out of the cords of a Cable which had been provided by Capt.

Lewis at Pittsburg for the Cable of the Boat. George Drewyer our hunter and one man came in with 2 Deer & a Bear, also a young Hourse, they had found in the Prarie, this horse has been left by Some war party against the Osage. This is the Crossing place for the war parties against the nation from the Saukees [Sauks] Aiaouez [Iowas] & Souix. The party is much afflicted with Boils, and several have the Deassentary, which I contribute to the water. The Countrey about this place is butifull on the river rich & well timbered on the S.S. about two miles back a Prarie coms which is rich and interspursed with groves of timber, the country rises at about 7 or 8 miles Still further back and is rolling, on the L.S., the high lands and Prarie coms. in the bank of the river continus back, well watered and abounds in Deer Elk & Bear. The Ticks & Musquiters are verry troublesom . . .

His final line puts the finger squarely upon the sore point of the entire circumstance. All of us might forget a variety of things about that camp, but none of us would forget the "Ticks & Musquiters" found there. Neither before nor after did we encounter such magnificent insects. The crawlers were as large and ill-tempered as wharf rats, the flying species of a size and disposition to shame harpy eagles.

Wednesday, July 4, 1804, was the Independence Day of the Americans. Captain Lewis celebrated it with the issue of an extra gill of whiskey per man; also, by loading and firing our four small swivel cannon which, along with Captain Lewis's unique "air gun," comprised the major dosage

71

of our "big medicine" for impressing the red men of the upper river. For myself, I was far more impressed by the bonus whiskey, becoming sick as a dog from it. I had veteran company here, Private Hall getting fifty lashes for stealing whiskey, Private Collins one hundred lashes for being drunk on post and abetting the theft. Private Joseph Fields himself bitten by a very large rattlesnake, as well, but was so thoroughly saturated with the spirits that he not only survived easily but felt much better than I next morning.

In three more days we reached the mouth of the Nodaway River. One man was taken down with sunstroke. Captain Clark bled him and treated him with compound of niter. The heat by this time was monstrous. It was the very belly of summer and all suffered unspeakably. Yet no man complained. The country, meanwhile, became lovely. Timber, grassland, winding waters, gentle. hills, dipping vales, noble expanses of handsome prairie met the eye continually. But there were other moments. On Saturday, July 14th, as we toiled up a bad channel, a vicious dark cloud blew in upon us from the north. The wind came screaming out of it and Hell itself struck us. For forty minutes we fought to keep the canvas drawn over the cargo lockers to prevent blowing water from filling the boats and sending them to the bottom. Yet, when the storm passed, it did so all in an instant. The whole of the river and all of the air above and about it lay like a plate of flat glass, soundless as some outer planet.

In another week we came to the mouth of the great River Platte. Old Mr. Dorion told us that the Sioux call this the river which is "ten miles wide and two inches deep." At its confluence, Captain Clark announced a layover of several days, since the French pirogue had shipped a good deal of water in getting past the Platte's shallow bar and her cargo must be unpacked and aired.

In making the initial announcement, Clark looked squarely at me. "Tomorrow," he then added, "will be another day. I would suggest to you all the wisdom of remembering that firmly. Frank," he added acridly, "don't 'we French' have a saying for such admonishments?"

I thought, or tried to think, swiftly. He knew I had deliberately fouled Baptiste Deschamps and the red pirogue. He was letting me know that my youth and natural exuberance to outshine the noted "Big Bat" in the management of my craft would serve once, and once only, to protect me from summary discipline. Yet, so kind was this gruff, soft-hearted bear of a man that he could not bring himself to humble even a lowly métis riverboy in front of his grown-up French peers. He was warning me over their heads while at the same time letting us all know that horseplay at work had that day enjoyed its last exercise among the Corps of Volunteers.

I straightened, facing him.

"Yes, sir, Captain," I answered. "I think that we do have such a saying—'A word to the wise is ample.' "

He still eyed me but the frost was gone from the homely, hard-weathered face.

"Good," he said, "very good," and strode away.

That night when I went to my blankets they did not want me. Something, my French conscience, my Pawnee pride, the constant eerie howling of the wolves which infested the Platte, would not permit sleep. First light was coming gray in the east when finally I did drift off.

73

Two days later Cruzatte and Drewyer, sent forward to find the local Oto Indians for the first important meeting of the American captains with upriver redmen, returned nonplused. They had located the big Oto town but no people were in it. Seemingly they had fled in our advance. Clark and Lewis began worried talks to decide the next course. For another day we waited. One man fell ill with an infected tumor on his breast. These fetid boils had been our most trying health problem the entire way. Captain Clark treated them with a hot compress of elm bark and Indian meal ordinarily, but this one defied the medication. When eventually pierced by the captain's lancet, it spewed over a pint of vile fluid, but the man mended rapidly. I do not know if the Pawnee blood was responsible, but I had had none of these tumors, not any heat sickness, nor any of the other camp disorders of the whites, including the mysterious sudden rheumatism which strangely crippled our strongest comrades. Captain Clark told me that the Americans had a saying for such immunity—"Where there's no sense, there's no feeling." He grinned but I knew he intended only to be kind and cheerful.

Another three days passed in the rest camp with no news of the Otos. The fourth morning Captain Lewis dispatched La Liberte, one of the French boatmen familiar with this stretch of the Missouri, to locate the Indians and bring them in for council. I disliked this La Liberte. He had a bad eye, was sullen, and a known "squaw-chaser."

The following dawn marked the new week of Monday, July 30, 1804. It marked, as well, the resumption of our slowed journey upstream. We did not go far. The early camp permitted another chance to consult Clark's journal,

74

now become a combined document of both captains and hence of doubled interest. The entry for this day was Clark's and unquestionably Clark's:

. . . Set out this morning early . . . Came too and formed a Camp, intending to waite the return of the frenchman & Indians . . . posted out our guard and . . . Captn. Lewis & I went up the Bank and walked a Short Distance in the high Prarie . . . the most butifull prospect of the River up & Down and the Countrey Opsd. prosented it Self which I ever beheld . . . Joseph Fields Killed and brought in an Anamle Called by the French Brarow [blaireau, badger] and by the Panies [Pawnee] Cho car tooch this Anamale Burrows in the Ground and feeds on Flesh Bugs & Vigatables his Shape & Size is like that of a Beaver, his head mouth &c. is like a Dogs with Short Ears, his Tail and Hair like that of a Ground Hog, and longer; and lighter. his Interals like the interals of a Hog . . . Jo. & R. Fields did not return this evening, Several men with verry bad boils. Catfish is caught in any part of the river. Turkeys & Geese & a Beaver Killed & Cought everything in prime order men in high Spirits, a fair Still evening Great numbers Musquiters . . .

Thus, Captain Clark proved once more peculiarly able to capture the heart of our predicament, describing perfectly the interminable minutiae which impeded our race for the upper river.

But as dark came at last and the fires died away that quiet Monday, there was some apprehension mounting in the camp.

La Liberte was still missing and there had been no sign of the Indians he had been sent to find. Had they, instead, found him?

14

La Liberte was still missing. Was he a deserter? Another man disappeared. Moses Reed, sent back to the last camp to find his lost knife, did not return. Were these the first defections?

Three days later, at the morning roll call, August 7th, Captain Meriwether Lewis read solemn notice that the men La Liberte and Moses B. Reed be thereby declared deserters. He dispatched Drewyer, Fields, Bratten and Labiche to find the stragglers. The orders were to put Reed to death if he resisted, he being a soldier of the American Army. La Liberte, being merely a French *engagé,* was to be put in arrest and returned for questioning. The first uneasiness developed among us.

The summary order to execute one of our comrades came as harsh reminder to us all that we had come a far journey to this camp at Council Bluff. When I later wondered aloud to York if Captain Lewis really would have Reed shot, the big slave told me soberly, "Yes sir, Mister Frank, he will do it, absolutely sure."

The ensuing eight days we continued slowly up the river, our scouts out in advance to locate the settlement of the Omahas higher up. An early camp was made August 15th, no word having come from the scouts. While we waited Mr. Dorion regaled us with tales of the notorious Chief Blackbird, former Grand Chief of all the Omahas, and a river pirate even greater than Le Borgne or the Partisan. In fact, said Mr. Dorion, the Omahas under Blackbird were a tribe which had invented a game of stopping upriver parties and demanding tribute of them. The old Frenchman suggested the chief's name ought to have been Blackmail, rather than Blackbird, but that in either event the smallpox had taken care of him, along with his entire nation.

It was a fearsome thing, Dorion told us, when the dread "spotted sickness" was among the Omahas. The Indians developed such a frenzy from the fatal nature of the illness that they not only burned their villages and all their belongings, including their ponies and dogs, but also put to death in the most violent and terrible ways their children and wives, this to the end that all might be together again in the "better country beyond." Mr. Dorion insisted they lost 400 people, enough to ruin them and allow the Teton Sioux to take over their power and become the dominant tribe below the Mandans.

Late that afternoon an immense wall of fire sprang up in the grass west of the river. Dorion advised Captain Lewis that the blaze was likely set by some parties of Sioux which he had been expecting on this part of the river. It was their way of signaling their presence. Since Clark was absent scouting for the Omahas, Lewis decided to send the old squawman toward the prairie fire to determine if he might find his friends, the Yanktons.

All this talk of the Sioux affected the men. I myself was still awake in my blankets at midnight. So were the others. I could hear them talking softly in the night.

Yet two long days of further waiting produced no Indians. Neither the Sioux nor the Omahas nor the Otos came in to talk. Mr. Dorion returned to report no trace of the Yankton people. Captain Clark came back to admit the same thin luck with the Omahas. Lewis was visibly upset, knowing that the meetings with these tribes were a vital part of our instructions, yet realizing full well that we could not wait forever to bring them about.

Some last-minute excitement stirred as we were cleaning up the supper things. Francis Labiche, of the party sent in search of the deserters, arrived in camp. He said the arrest party was close behind him with M. B. Reed, but that La Liberte had deceived them and gotten away.

As Captain Lewis queried Labiche, the entire company roused up and gathered quietly around. They were waiting for the party to come in with Reed. A certain nervousness spread. When the party came at last, Reed was white as a sheet. The men of my mess, like the other two messes, stood watching him intently. There was no accusation in their glances, nor any morbid curiosity, nor censure of any kind. These men were soldiers mostly. They knew the penalty for desertion in the field.

The trial of Reed began Saturday, August 18, 1804. The prisoner requested steadily enough that the captains be as favorable to him as they might, consistent with their oaths as officers. This they were, considering that death might easily have been the reward of the fugitive. He was compelled, instead, to run the gauntlet four times, the company being armed with nine-switches for striking him on each course. He was then dishonorably discharged and ordered treated in all ways as no longer a member of the party.

Since it was Captain Lewis's birthday, and had been a trying experience for the entire crew, the day was closed with the issue of an extra gill of whiskey for all hands and a rousing company dance resulted which went on until 11 P.M.

The long-sought Oto Indian party surprised us next day by appearing out of nowhere ready to talk. The Grand Chief was given a state breakfast with our captains while his scabrous subjects waited gloweringly. They were an abject, unpleasant people, naked but for breehclouts, blankets, or verminous buffalo robes. Captain Clark spoke for our side, as generally, when the business was with redmen. They referred to him at once as the Red Head Chief, a name which stuck to him in all our travels. When the two parties had orated back and forth, each of the Indians was presented with a President Jefferson medal of the second grade—Lewis had three grades of this award—and a peace paper which stated the red bearer was of meek and pacifistic intentions and recognized the President of the United States as his new father. The Grand Chief was last to receive his paper. He looked at it, sneered haughtily, handed it back to Clark. This was the testing of our nerve, the hard bluff which our captain had warned of earlier. In response to it now, Clark took the certificate and tore it into small pieces under the Indian's nose.

This mightily disconcerted the fellow. At once he wanted another certificate, but Clark had grown cold. Through our interpreter for these pre-Teton tribes, George Drewyer, he informed the chief in very rough terms that he was a liar, a cheat, a woman in his heart and had for his goal in the talks, goods, and not good intentions. At this, the rest of the Indians commenced to inflate their chests and stiffen their spines.

Our soldier guard quietly, but ostensibly, put their rifles on the cock. This action produced a sharp clicking noise, most distinctive in character. The redmen did not seem to care for it. They moved back quite suddenly away from Clark, who now made a show of generosity by bestowing another certificate upon the Grand Chief. He then had the air gun fired, presented a bottle of whiskey to the subchiefs and bid the whole shabby conclave an abrupt good afternoon. The Indians left on the double and before the Red Head Chief might again change his mind and start tearing up their peace papers.

Later that evening, with dramatic, great pain, Sergeant Floyd collapsed. Captain Clark came at once but could do little. In his journal he wrote, "Sgt. Floyd is taken verry bad all at once with a Biliose Chorlick . . . we attempt to relieve him without success as yet . . . he gets worse and we are much allarmed at his Situation . . . all attention to him." The attention failed. Floyd alternately flushed and chilled. The pain in his right side became terrible. About 4 A.M. he said that something inside of him had "give way." Clark thought he slept, but it was coma. By a little after daybreak he was dead. The captain was much shaken. He said there was no understanding it. When we buried brave Floyd and left him there, we saw something we would not see again—Captain Clark weeping.

Bitter days of progress followed. The work of poling the heavy-laden craft up the constantly shallowing channel, taken with the unbelievable August heat, crippled our strongest boatmen. Blind loops, dead-end sloughs and shoaly rapids battered our courage. The buffalo gnats, mosquitoes and sandflies undermined our will, sapped our reason. We came, in the sixth of these hellish days, to a brooding lone mountain in the plain, Spirit Mound, a sacred place greatly feared by the Indians. We were here, Captain Clark said, on the southern edges of the Dakotahs, in the Vermilion River country, an awesomely empty realm. For eleven days more forged doggedly on. Each league now brought us closer to that dreaded part of the river we all knew of but did not talk about. On August 27th we went by the mouth of the James River. Here it appeared that Shannon had become lost, having been for many days absent. The Irishman and I had become fast friends. He was the best educated of the army enlistees and we had enjoyed many a debate on Aristotle, the decline of the Romans, Hannibal and the Alps and all those elephants, and other privileged topics of the learned. I would surely miss old Shannon had he in truth gone under. But we pressed on, and ever on.

Now, with the death of Floyd and the disappearance of Shannon, Captain Clark once more took me under his personal direction. Tutelage, he called it, but it was more akin to bondage. He put me with his own mess, while leaving me to work the white pirogue. "I warned you," he reminded me when I complained, "that it would not be so easy; that you would take that white craft to the villages of the Mandan in a pace with Deschamps and the Frenchmen in the red. You will do it, too, but meanwhile you can eat with me and soak up a little something about these pesky Tetongues we shall soon be passing through."

I knew full well who he meant—the Teton Sioux—but I

81

made no answer beyond a careful nod.

"They're bad Indians, Frank," he continued. "Captain Lewis and me were given to understand by Mr. Jefferson that they have as good as shut off the Upper Missouri to our St. Louis traders. The reason appears to be the damnable British."

I indicated this was previously clear to me, and inquired uneasily what instructions the President had given them about easing the British-Sioux stranglehold.

Clark shrugged.

"Bust it wide open, that's all. Oh, Mr. Jefferson likewise expects us to rig up a lasting peace amongst the Sioux and the other tribes, but that's for certain—how do you say it, Frank—'*dorez luh pullex*'?"

"*Dorer la pilule*—gilding the pill," I replied.

"Yes, that's it. "Well, no matter, we'll manage the main part, and that's to let the Tetongues know who's the new boss up here, peaceable or powderburnt. You got any doubts you want to get shut of, boy? On that subject, I mean. I've noted you looking a lot behind you of late."

I began gratefully to unburden my several fears and weariness, but was granted no real chance to get started. Interrupting our talk, Captain Lewis stalked over to our fire and informed Clark that he was that same night sending Mr. Dorion in secret to find a band of Teton Sioux rumored to be encamped on the James River "not too far." Clark responded that he was not satisfied how far "not too far" was, and so he believed that he would double the night guard until he could make up his mind. Captain Lewis did not appear to think that at all a bad idea, and neither did Frank Rivet.

There was something about the sound of those words *Teton Sioux* and *not too far*.

15

Two nights later old Dorion came back. He had with him seventy warriors and five chiefs of the Yankton, not Teton, band of the Sioux tribe. This was his wife's band and to my delighted surprise, he brought with him his half-breed son. I could scarcely contain my desire to speak with the young fellow but, when finally I did capture him apart, he stared a hole through me, wheeled about, and stalked off dark and alien as any Teton Sioux or Minnetaree Big Belly.

Captain Clark, standing near by, moved to my side.

"Don't make more of it than it amounts to, Frank," he advised sympathetically.

"But that's just it!" I protested. "I'm not! He's a half-breed just like me!"

"No," said Clark, "that's where you make your mistake. He's a half-breed, all right, but not just like you. He's been raised by his mother's people."

"Well, where's your great difference in that, *Patron?*"

"Just this; young Dorion's a Sioux, you're a settlement boy."

I shook my head, bewildered. Clark put his hand to my shoulder.

"Frank," he said, "you suckle a wolf cub on settlement milk, he'll grow up to wag his tail. You raise him on his wild mother's milk, he'll rip your throat out. You've been raised white and you made the mistake of wagging your

83

tail just now. Don't fret it, though; you're with the right tribe, boy."

When he said that, gave my shoulder a final rough squeeze and walked on to join Lewis and the Yanktons, I nearly wept. I knew that it wasn't the entire truth he spoke. Yet, even so, Captain William Clark had just said that I was a white man, among fellow white men, and for that gentle twisting of the facts I loved him.

In the council which followed, the Yanktons complained about the cheapness of the St. Louis traders in contrast with the British factors of Assiniboine River, Turtle Mountain and the other Hudson's Bay and North West Company posts. But they agreed instantly upon gifts of tobacco, glass beads, Jefferson medals, American flags and peace papers—but mainly good old tin cups full of whiskey—to trade with the St. Louis merchants and to make and keep peace "forever" with all their Indian neighbors. This making them the first of the warlike Sioux to "come in," as the saying went, Captain Lewis had grand hopes for their example serving us with their even fiercer Teton cousins. He was especially heartened when old Mr. Dorion proved agreeable to conducting three of the Yankton chiefs back down the river to talk peace with the main Otos and Omahas and then go on with them to Washington to "see their great new father."

But Captain Clark grinned his wise grin and said to me that night at mess, "Don't you put a penny on those rascals, Frank; they took no salt with their meat. They won't be bound by anything agreed to in this council, and that peace treaty, therefore, simply ain't worth its salt."

We went on from that camp of August 29th and the

84

dubious Yankton council with an increased sense of urgency. On September 4th we passed the mouth of the Niobrara River. On the seventh we saw the first large towns of prairie dogs or "barking squirrels," as our men called them. Here also we encountered the first of the "wild goats" or antelopes, and the first of the really vast herds of the hump shouldered "curly cows," the buffalo. Indeed, the land now swarmed with game of every kind.

Human news, and very good news, too, intruded briefly the morning of September 11; George Shannon walked into camp hale and fit. He and I at once got off on a rousing debate over high and low Latin, my spirits soaring no little.

Four days thence we reached the White River, the next main stream, save one, below the Teton. All of the afternoon we poled the boats past the cliffs of a long and lofty escarpment following the Missouri in stunning grandeur for many miles. This formation was the great Pine Ridge, Captain Clark informed me, and said that it was the geographical division between the Upper and Lower Missouri countries.

"Yes," I nodded uneasily, "it even feels different up here than down below. It's like another land."

Clark smiled soberly.

"It *is* another land," he said. "This is the first of the real horse Indian country, Frank, your mother's land."

"It's wild-looking," I muttered, shivering for no good cause. "God's name, but it is lonesome and wild-looking."

Clark studied me carefully, then said in his quiet-voiced way, "It's nothing, Frank, to where we're going . . ."

The singular warning with which he heralded the

85

approaches to my mother's land proved again the peculiar presciences which were Captain William Clark's. From the white River camp, the whole air of the adventure seemed to alter itself. A loneliness which approached in its immensity replaced the rich beauty of the lower river. The scapes of plain and prairie in this higher, drier land ran off to infinity. The game remained abundant but far more restive. Like the landscape the animals appeared to recede into the distances, incalculable as to number but vague and formless, as in an uneasy dream. The grass thinned beneath a prickly rash of opuntia cactus. Limestone gave way to slate, and slate to clay. The color of the prairie faded from bight green to gray-blue at the sudden, dominant appearance of the true short grama, or buffalo grass. The river ran through this silent void between banks so pillared and perfectly sculptured that Captain Lewis actually considered them the possible masterworks of some vanished race of pre-Indian humanity. The total effect, always, remained that of the strangely hushed stillness. It was as though our keelboat and two pirogues with their cargoes of human souls did not move or breathe but were painted there forever motionless and moribund among the raw and glaring pigments of some enormous canvas.

At the same time we suffered upon the river every example of accident native to such travel. Whatever could happen to ship or sail, helm, oar, pole, keel, towrope or other trapping, did happen. We were five whole days coming from White River to the fabled Grand Detour, that weird corkscrew gorge wherein the great river within a scant thirty miles twice reverses the direction of its flow. It was, indeed, the twentieth of September and almost dark when we made our camp on a willow bar midstream of the main channel. Here we lay just below the Detour. We lay, as well, and by virtue of Captain Clark's never-ending vigilance, safely out of Indian reach of either shore. Being this past week's march by water nearer the boundaries of the Teton Sioux and not having seen a living soul, white or Indian, the entire time, our nerves were understandably on set-triggers. The night guard was posted double strength. Sleep came late and of a sketchy, restless kind.

An hour and a half after midnight, the Sergeant of the Guard came running from the head of the island. At the same time the keelboat, upon which I was sleeping with Captain Clark and six crew members, began to rock in a most alarming manner. Following the captain, I went over the side into the shallows and ran up onto the shore.

"The bank is undermining," the guard shouted. "The current has raised and reversed its set and is cutting the island out from under us!"

"Frank," ordered Clark, wheeling upon me calm as the sunrise, "you must get your white pirogue off her beaching, or she will go under when the island caves. Warn Deschamps and the Frenchmen, also. Both pirogues must be off in five minutes."

"Yes, sir," I answered, and dashed to apprise Big Bat of the situation.

There was every certainty, as confirmed in Captain Clark's journal, that all three boats would have been lost to the huge suction of the dissolving sand had we been a minute less swift in getting them away. As it was, we were forced to make camp on the opposite bank for the remainder of the night. It was a nervous remainder, but nothing disturbed the morning peacefulness save the wailing of the wolves.

Daylight revealed we had stopped in an oasis of loveliness in that gray-brown landscape. The cliffs of the gorge, towering 200 and more feet above the water, framed the river upstream. On either side of the channel, sloping to infinity east and west, the earth was a soft green inclined plain upon which incredible numbers of antelope, elk and buffalo were feeding in mixed herds. The air, inland, was full of the song and flight movement of the grouse, lark, pigeon and prairie hen, while on the river countless thousands of waterfowl rafted, filling the ear with their eerie honking cries. Everywhere the ubiquitous gray, red, black, brown and white small wolves of the prairie trotted, sat on their haunches, or lolled about panting hungrily. Amid all this tapestry of ardent life, the overwhelming sense of all-engulfing loneliness remained.

We traveled hard that day and in the after part of it came up to a high-banked island. It was some mile and a half in length, crowned with a shaggy flat-leafed conifer with which I was not familiar. Captain Clark, Lewis being ahead of us on land with the hunters, determined to camp on this island for some reason not apparent to me. He had himself, York and I landed from the white pirogue on the lower side, where he bade Warfington and the boat crew to await our return. We three then climbed the ridge of the island to a lookout point on the upstream side. There, below us, in a sort of half-moon bay lay an abandoned trading post surrounded by a stark phalanx of long vacant Sioux lodges. The post itself was of logs built behind a barricade of more logs set on end in the earth. It was the first stockaded fort I had seen, and I began to tremble with excitement.

"I wanted you to see it, Frank," said Clark, low-voiced, "before the others did." He turned to point at the dark conifers all about us. "Do you know what sort of trees these are?" he asked. And then, when I had dumbly shaken my head, he replied softly, "They're cedars, boy."

The meaning of this sank into me slowly, but it sank deeply, compounding my unnamed excitement.

"*Nom de Dieu!*" I whispered. "Cedar Island—we've come to it at last!"

"We have," said Clark. "That is the house of Régis Loisel down there, and those are the bones of the Teton Sioux camp which surrounded him last winter. It hits you a little cold in the belly, don't it, boy?"

"Yes, sir," I gulped. "One gets the distinct feeling that Monsieur Loisel was fortunate to get out alive."

"Agreed," said the rawboned captain, fixing me with his eyes. "A man can smell the death smell down there." Again he paused, watching me closely. "You still think you want to go on, lad? To keep looking for your father deeper and deeper into a land like this? Think hard on it, Frank. It's why I brought you up here. I wanted to let you smell the fear of this horse Indian country before our men camped in it and chased that fear out of it. And, remember, these Sioux are only the start of it, boy. After them comes the Arikaras, Minnetarees, Blackfeet, Crow, Snake. Take a deep breath of that quiet down there. That's 'Indian quiet,' Frank. It gets louder and louder the more you move into it."

I shivered a little and looked at him.

"Thank you, *Patron*," I said, "but there is no way for this

Rivet to go, save on with you. I can catch that dark scent down there. It stiffens the small bristles on the back of my neck. It pulls the muscles of my stomach together like the fingers of a closed fist. But my father is somewhere up ahead in that stillness. He waits for me or he waits for no one. I can't turn back, Captain."

Clark returned my look, nodding his proud acceptance of my reply.

"Well spoke Frank," was all he said. "Your father's a mighty lucky man."

The succeeding day, the twenty-third of September, we made an early camp to insure daylight for all purposes of making ourselves secure against attack. We had come a good distance and were feeling somewhat less strained, but at half after four, with the sun still bathing the prairie and with the surrounding plain seemingly visible for miles in any direction, we had visitors.

Captain Lewis and Captain Clark were seated under a shoreside cedar tree examining the idea of permanently combining their notes into one journal. Clark was paying only scant heed to this proposal of company bookkeeping. Suddenly, his eyes narrowed. He pointed over the river to the east. Lewis fell still. York crouched forward as though about to spring. I squinted hard through the westering reflection of sun on water.

"Three of them," announced Clark. "They just slipped out of that point of scrub willow into the water."

Lewis reached for his brass-bound telescope.

"Why," he exclaimed testily, focusing the instrument, "they're only children!"

"All little boys," amplified Clark, needing no glass.

"One about eight, two more like twelve, thirteen. Little one's cradleboard bare. His friends wear clouts."

Lewis holstered the telescope. I could not tell if he was amused or annoyed. This was a quality of his which no amount of familiarity could penetrate.

"Is there anything more you can tell me of them, with the naked eye?" he inquired.

Clark grinned. "Sure," he said. "They're damned fine swimmers, they're headed this way, they're most likely from the nearest camp of our Tetongue Sioux friends."

Lewis seemed to think this over, meanwhile watching the river. Presently he inclined his head.

"You'd better check the guard Will," he said. Then sharply to me, "Boy, go fetch me Mr. Dorion. We shall need him to deal with these rascals."

Clark, who had started off, stopped and came back.

"Captain, old Dorion's gone," he said. "Left first thing this morning to get those Yankton chiefs started downstream for Washington."

"The devil!" snapped Lewis. "Now what? Who can we use to interpret? Drewyer's no good to us here. It takes a horse Indian to talk with these upper river tribes." He bit off an oath, lean head turtled angrily forward. "Damn it all, I supposed young Dorion's gone, too!"

"Yes, sir," said Clark calmly, "I guess we'll have to try with Drewyer. He's all we've got."

I stepped forward, saluting awkwardly. Both captains looked at me, surprised. Lewis, of course, scowled instantly. Clark just cocked his head and waited.

"*Patrons*," I said, "excuse me. But here is a half-breed who can talk horse Indian for you."

"What?" cried Clark. "You, Frank? You talk Sioux?"

I shook my head.

"No, sir," I answered, "I don't talk Sioux, but I do talk the handsign language of this upper country. Uncle François taught me much of it. Drewyer says I do better at it than most Indians. I guess it's something that stays with you, Captain. I was only five years old when Achille Rivet sent me down the river to the Jesuits, but Uncle François said I was already at that time more of a hand-talker than the average Pawnee. Anyway, Captain, I can do it; I can talk for you."

Lewis moved in, examining me as though he had never in this world cast an eye on me before.

Finally he nodded, retracting his outthrust head.

"All right, Rivet," he said, "go ahead—*talk*."

Within the next ten minutes Clark and I had met and spoken with the three youths and Captain Lewis had come down from the shade of his cedar tree to present each of them with some blue beads and a scarlet hair ribbon. A quarter of an hour after they had waded out of the shallows on our side of the Missouri, they were reentering the water, this time the rain-swollen mouth of the creek upon which we were camped. There was no evident deceit on their parts, and very little nervousness. They told us straightforwardly that their own band of eighty lodges was camped on the next creek above. There was another band of sixty lodges of the same people on the next stream above their own. Both bands, they said, were within one easy day by the river. Captain Clark then gave the older two each a carrot of tobacco to bear back to the chiefs of the two bands, with a message to meet and talk with the white captains in the next camp upward on the Mini Sosi, the Big Muddy Waters, as the Indian youths called the Missouri. There was a bad moment for our gift tobacco when the boys plunged unexpectedly with it into the flooded prairie tributary. But in a manner miraculous to behold by any expert swimmer such as myself, the rascals held it out of the water in their strong white teeth, heads held far back, and so brought it completely across the 150-foot creekmouth without wetting a leaf of it. And that, briefly enough, was the extent of our "Goat Beach Council" with the redskins.

Oh yes, there was one more small matter which our talk with the three Indian boys cleared to the satisfaction of all parties. Captain Clark had been customarily correct in his original guess at the identity of our visitors. They were the Teton Sioux.

16

We set out very early. It was a fair day, only a bit of a soft breeze working from the east. All hands poling with a will, we made many miles by midday. In the afternoon the wind switched southeast still blowing steadily, and we hoisted sail, making better time yet. By 2 P.M. both our captains were studying the charts looking for a landmark, expected just below the boundary of "Tetongue Territory" marked for them by Monsieur Loisel. Presently they saw it; an island long and narrow and near the right shore. On the charts Loisel had crustily named it Good Humored Island, since it was here the Sioux had trapped a camp of his men and stolen their entire cache of trade goods. The island was now deserted, a fact established by the presence upon it of several head of peacefully grazing elk.

We ran on by it and came about at its head, where the confluence of a seventy-yard river appeared some one and a half miles above the island proper. Here it was that Clark wrote:

. . . the french perogue Come up early in the day, the other did not Get up until the evening Soon after we had come to . . .

The discrepancy in time here, from my 2 P.M.. to my captain's "evening Soon after," was accounted for by an accident of the river in which I had my full ignominious share; or, rather, in which Big Bat Deschamps had graciously provided me with that share. When Clark's journal remarks that the white pirogue did not get up until evening, the simple words cover a multitude of boatman's woes. But I shall not whimper. Let me only state that Big Bat had never forgiven the wetting I gave his red pirogue, in getting past the bar at Platte River. He managed on this present September 24th to catch me and the white pirogue out of sight of Captain Clark and the keelboat. It was below a great half-moon sandbar where the current ran swift as a cannon shot and where, in quartering up across it, our two pirogues rowed furiously within an oar's length of one another. Deschanps fouled me exactly as I had fouled him at the Platte. My craft broadsided and was saved from foundering only by the shallow bar beneath it. Naturally Big Bat had understood the bar would prevent a total "go under," but I still had to unload, dry and reload my cargo before going on. The wonder was that it was not far later than "evening" when we got up to that night's camp. Ashore, and still smarting, I sought out the burly *patron* of the red pirogue. He saw me coming.

"*Sapristi!*" he roared. "Look what we have here; a small wet rooster with his tail feathers draggled and his tiny heart on fire to dry them out! Ho! What is it that I can do for you, scrawny Pawnee chicken?"

"*Fort bien, mal embouché,*" I answered. "It is that you can take notice that I have orders from my captain to take the white pirogue to the Mandan country bow-and-bow with your red one. Do you understand that?"

"Careful who you call 'foul-mouthed.' " He grimaced. "However, yes, cockerel, I hear your thin crowing. Was there anything else you wished to cockadoodle from the top of your métis dungheap?"

"Yes," I replied, clenching my teeth at the mention of my mongrel blood. "I am adding a warning of my own to my captain's order: the white pirogue is not going to get up the river *with* the red one; it will be far ahead of it. Do you also comprehend that, big river pig?"

Deschamps' swarthy face contorted itself.

"Mind your tongue, water rat," he rumbled. "You would not babble so bravely with it slit down the middle like a pet magpie's."

"From a big cavern blows a big wind, " I said recklessly. "Go to hell and watch out for me on the way."

I thought then that Deschamps would experience a fatal apoplexy. Fatal for me, that was.

"Heart of Mary!" he bellowed. "I would start you on that hot journey in my place, and this instant, too, but you are born under the right planet. Here arrives *Capitaine*

Clark and his black man, as you no doubt planned all the while." His gross features melted into the grin of a full-fed bullfrog all in the moment of the sweeping bow with which he greeted Clark's approach. "Ah, good evening, Captain. Young Rivet and I were only now saying what a splendid run you made today with the big boat. It was superb. Come, now, *Patron,* there must be a Frenchman hidden in your family's chart closet. No American could court the Grand Missouri in your manner."

It was a bald-faced lie, of course, and I had not arranged for Clark and my friend York to come up just in the critical moment. However, the circumstances weighted impartially, I did not disown the intrusion. Big Bat had a deserved reputation from St. Louis to Cedar Island from being a true riverhorse, and for me to challenge him as I had was not poor judgment but insanity. It was not without genuine feeling then, that I joined the French *patron* in his feigned delight at Clark's appearance. Indeed, I nearly wept with Gallic gratitude.

When, directly, the red-haired captain ordered me to come along with him at the double, since he had some notes in need of final copying, I could easily have embraced him. I did not, of course, because Americans put different interpretations upon such familiarities than did we French. I merely went along as commanded.

For the remainder of that night our camp was quiet. The reason was not far to seek and, as usual, it was most eloquently drawn in the blunt language of William Clark's closing entry for the day.

. . . Came to about 1½ Miles above off the Mouth of a

Small river about 70 yards wide Called . . . the Little Mississou [Missouri] River, The Tribes of the Seauex Called the Teton, is Campted about 2 miles up on the N.W. Side, and we Shall Call the River after that Nation, *Teton* . . . we prepare to Speek with the Indians tomorrow at which time we are informed the Indians will be here . . . 2/3rds of our party Camped on board the remainder with the Guard on Shore . . .

BOOK III
TO THE VILLAGES OF THE MANDAN

17

The Indians are early risers but slow starters. A white man will have half the business of the day out of the way before a red one will finish his breakfast pipe. We had, then, the fore-morning to prepare the council ground. Captain Lewis supervised, as customarily, protocol being his province. In the present case he had us set a flagpole at the head of our sandbar campsite. Directly beyond the pole, he raised our largest, most gaudy canvas awning in the manner of a fly tent. Before this, he drew Warfington's squad of six soldiers as an "honor guard." He then had Clark anchor the keelboat off the bar, its bow swivel charged with a langrage of scrap iron, and a soldier standing by with lighted cord. Both pirogues were brought in from their midstream anchorages and hove to, flanking the bar. All was in readiness by 10 A.M. By eleven, with no Sioux in sight, a few nerves might be heard tuning up.

Lewis and Clark resplendent in their full-dress army officer's coats, complete with sword and pistol belts, sat beneath the awning discussing with Peter Cruzatte the procedures of the day. Cruzatte, having some Indian blood, had been named over Drewyer as interpreter for the talk. Clark, bless him, had tried to get me the work. Lewis, however, had said quite strongly that it was all well and good to send a boy to do a boy's work, meaning my talk with the three Sioux youths, but that for men he wanted a man. To confront the adult flower of the "Tetongue" Nation beneath a candy-striped canvas overflown by Old Glory required a fully grown, qualified male. The fact that Cruzatte could not read nor reply to handsigns as accurately as myself was not Lewis's point. He was out to impress the Indians and knew that to ask three main Teton chiefs to talk through a half-white settler was not the way to inaugurate the effort. Clark was compelled to agree.

This relegated me to my regular duty post aboard the white pirogue. Under the circumstances I did not resent the banishment: it was now 11:45 A.M. and still no Indians in view. Ashore, things grew tauter still.

It was perhaps five minutes later that our inland-posted scouts, Colter and Shields, came racing back to the river. The Teton Sioux were coming. There were three score chiefs and warriors, all fully armed and war-painted. There were no women or children in attendance. Just the fighters. These Indians looked ready. They were not chatting or laughing. Just walking quietly with guns and bows and lances in their hands. Régis Loisel had been right. These were bad Indians.

To this message our two captains only nodded and Lewis stood up and stepped away from his camp chair.

"Captain," he said hurriedly to Clark, "let us go meet these bad people. Perhaps we can persuade them toward the good."

So still was the air in that moment that I clearly heard his words offshore in the pirogue. I saw Clark make an odd little bow, and saw his ready grin flash in the sunlight. But the only sound which came from him was the metallic jingling of his sword chain as he hitched up the weapon and loosened it in its scabbard while following his senior toward the beach at land's joining of the sandbar. So quiet was the entire waterfront in that final pause that the lapping of the wavelets against the keelboat's side could be distinctly heard, while the harsh cries of the river birds wheeling over the stream a mile and a half distant pierced the ear as though uttered within a dozen paces.

It was then that three Sioux chieftains stepped from the dark cedar of the forest into the sunlight of the shore and came onward, not as if meeting our captains but as if stalking them. It was a sight to chill the flesh. Sun or no sun, I shook like a wet dog to raw wind.

"Watch it, Will!" I heard Captain Lewis say, the warning cutting off sharply, sibilantly.

Clark merely nodded, his right hand dropping to the horse pistol at his belt. The oiled gunsteel bite of the cocking piece engaging the trigger sear was the sole audible content of his reply. It was enough. Ten feet away the Sioux halted, stood stock-still, cruel faces expressionless. Lewis, playing to Clark's lead, let them wait. After what seemed an hour and was more in the order of three bird cries, he raised his hands in the prairie sign of "coming in peace."

Now it was the Sioux permitting the white captains to languish. In their own dark time, the central chief raised his hands in a return of the peace sign. His companions, however, made no move.

Lewis at this point sent for Cruzatte, who came forward and tried to speak with the central chief. He had no success. But the more desperate-looking of the two flanking chiefs had an obvious knowledge of French, and through this means was able to make Cruzatte understand who he and his fellows were.

The central chief, this fellow said, was known as Untongasabaw, Black Buffalo. The other man was Tartongawaka, Medicine Buffalo. His own name was Tortohongar.

Having spoken this last name with evident stress, he stood waiting as if to see his white confronters fall back in terror. Neither did, however, and Lewis inquired through Cruzatte, "Ask him how his name translates."

When the Sioux was given this question, his bronzed face paled.

"Tortohongar!" he repeated angrily. "Le Partisan!"

Lewis and Clark exchanged quick glances at this. So did the whole company. But Clark only nodded and said to Cruzatte, "Tell him we will talk to him anyway," and then stood there hard-eyed as any of the Sioux across from him while Cruzatte gave the rough answer back to the Partisan.

The famed chief flinched visibly.

"What does the Red Head Chief mean?" he demanded of Cruzatte, partly in bastard French, partly by signs.

The uneasy interpreter did his best to convey the temper of Clark's language but the task was beyond his command of the sign talk and the Partisan's comprehnsion of finer French. It was plain to me, watching from the white pirogue, that the infamous Teton had caught some of the challenge in Clark's statement and was returning it. Clark understood this, too. He took a long, deliberate stride toward the three chiefs, halting before Black Buffalo. Cruzatte, after a gulping look around at Lewis, followed him unhappily.

"Tell Black Buffalo," ordered Clark, "that Loisel has spoken well of him down the river. Say that we understand from Loisel, who does not lie, that Black Buffalo is a good man. Also say that we have been told by Loisel that the Partisan is a very bad man. Tell him we want to talk soft but that if this Partisan wants to talk hard with me, I am ready to let him try it."

Cruzatte gulped again, nodded helplessly, passed the red-headed captain's ultimatum along. Black Buffalo turned to Medicine Buffalo and spoke rapidly in Sioux. Both then spoke to the Partisan who first scowled murderously, then grinned vacuously.

"*Beaucoup, beaucoup,*" he said, waving at Clark as if the entire thing had been good Sioux fun. Then, in hand-signs to Cruzatte, "Come on, Frenchman, let's go to the soldier lodge and talk soft."

Not waiting for agreement, he pushed past Clark and Lewis, leading the way toward the awning. As if this were a signal, his move brought forth from the black shade of the forest a torrent of hidden Sioux women and children. These were accompanied by the usual complement of yapping village curs, a stray packmule or three, and one piebald old mare suckling a new foal. The entire cavalcade swarmed toward the sandbar, the scene going from incipient tragedy to gala holiday in less than a minute. "From murder to mardi gras," was the glib way George Shannon described it, but I was not so pleased as he and some of the others of my comrades.

The entire approach of the savages was suspect in my view. Perhaps it was the blood of my Pawnee mother warning me against these first of the true horse Indians. Again, it may have been because the Tetons were the tribe which had sold my father into slavery with the Shoshone. Or possibly the warnings of Régis Loisel about the ugly devil Tortohongar were playing in excess upon my French nerves. Whatever the reason, I warped the white pirogue nearer the bank of the sandbar. I had no concrete idea of what I intended doing in case of trouble, but by this time it was instinctive for me to stay close to Captain Clark and great black York when a situation deteriorated.

The chiefs now commanded their people to stay on the main riverbank, it not being considered fit that squaws and children sit in council. Half the warriors stayed with the tribe, the remaining half followed the three principal chiefs and our captains to the fly tent out on the fingerlike bar. Here Lewis resumed his camp chair, the undeniable hallmark of white mastery, while Clark sat cross-legged on the ground facing the chiefs. The latter were seated on white buffalo robes, their men in tribal rank behind them. The council now commenced.

Cruzatte moved up to stand midway of the two groups and attempted the beginning speech. At once I knew that he was in difficulty. He could not make the Sioux come around to French, which tongue they certainly understood, nor could he piece out the disparity with his limited command of handsign language.

Instantly Captain Clark was on his feet. His scanning glance fell upon the white pirogue and me.

"Ahoy, Frank!" he called. "Come ashore and see if you can palaver with these Tetongues."

Vastly frightened, I did as he bid. When I had splashed through the shallows of the bar and stood with him confronting the tall Sioux chiefs, the latter were already coming to their feet. Behind them their warriors were starting to move. It was an ominous moment. They could not have comprehended Clark's English order to me but they were clearly alarmed all the same. Lewis, ever steady, remained in his chair. York drifted up and came to a looming stand at Clark's elbow.

"Try to tell them," the latter now instructed me calmly, "that the big soldier chief wants to make a speech."

He meant Lewis, and I conveyed this fact by handsign to Black Buffalo. He signaled that he understood and that his side would wait and listen to the son of their great new father. Lewis then rose and presented the peace talk from President Jefferson designed to be given to every important tribe on the way up the river. Within the first minutes, however, I had fallen hopelessly behind him and the chiefs were making unpleasant signs to their warriors, the latter scowling and muttering and shaking their heads menacingly. Clark moved to Lewis's side.

"Better let me hand out the medals right off, Captain," he suggested. "They're getting set to go ugly on us."

"All right," answered Lewis, "go ahead. I believe you are right and that they mean to make trouble."

"Captain," said Clark, his eyes never leaving the muttering Sioux, "it's my opinion they mean a mite more than trouble. I'd say they aimed to settle us here and now. Look yonder on the bank while I talk with this bunch. Don't let them see you're any bit worried, now."

He began to talk with the three chiefs, gesturing importantly to draw their attention. While they watched him, Lewis stole his look shoreward. Cruzatte and I, with the others beneath the awning, did likewise.

It was a sobering view. Up behind the women and children of the original band stood a silently added audience of at least 100 newcomers. These late arrivals were all adult warriors and were painted enough differently from our prior guests to let us know who they were—the Sioux from the second Village of sixty lodges upstream I could feel my scalp pull tight. We were now faced with the total strength of the Teton Sioux, where we had carefully planned to council with them one band at a time on separate—and well-separated—days.

I am morally convinced that I was not the only one to feel the sudden eerie cold of that bright awning's shade. Sunleathered Peter Cruzatte was pale as a settlement storekeeper. Even ebony York seemed lighter by several hues. Clark and Lewis alone stood outwardly unchanged.

It was a proud moment, if fearful, for our captains. During it Clark said quietly, "The medals, Captain," and Lewis merely took the bright trinkets from the box by his

104

chair and answered matter-of-factly. "Be brief with them, Will; we've much else to do this afternoon."

18

I steered the white pirogue prayerfully into the main stream. Behind, on a sandbar, the council stood suspended in uneasy truce while my trim craft probed out toward the waiting keelboat. Aboard we carried strange cargo—Captain William Clark and five Teton Sioux. The latter were Black Buffalo, Medicine Buffalo, the Partisan and two noted fighting men, Second Bear and Considerable Man, all names contained on the list of good and bad men furnished us in La Charrette by Régis Loisel, and the last three marked very bad indeed. Our objective was as uncertain as our cargo, worse luck.

When the council had continued to go sour after the crisis of the medal-giving, the beribboned Jefferson baubles having failed utterly to impress the Tetons, Clark had conceived this sudden inspiration to take the big headmen, the two good and the three very bad, out to the big barge on a formal tour of inspection. The idea was to intimidate the chiefs with the armament of our principal vessel, very much a white man's bluff of course, but as Clark had said to me in embarking just now, "Hold steady lad. You never win without putting down your money."

I brought the pirogue alongside the keelboat now, and Clark and the Sioux scrambled over her low gunwale. The captain quickly showed his guests the swivel cannon, bow and stern; ordered the stern gun fired into the far bank to impress them with the weapon's "terrible long medicine," and then demonstrated how the lids of the deck cargo lockers could be cleverly raised to form a "war shield," from behind which a very few well-armed, resolute white riflemen might annihilate any number of reckless, ill-advised red savages.

The Sioux said nothing. If they were in any degree intimidated, it would not have been wise for any sane white man to gamble on the guess. They simply revealed no emotion whatever, either of appreciation or belligerence.

However, when Captain Clark, never at a loss with redmen, produced a bottle of trade whiskey, their attitudes underwent an instant, beatific change. One would have thought they had smelled water after ten days in the desert. The sight of that whiskey illuminated the ugly faces of those red devils. In especial was this true of the celestial halo bathing the grinning vulture's beak and lupine fangs of the Partisan. He ought to have been canonized on the spot—I mean by the swivel gun.

The Sioux went from insolent boorishness to shameless fawning at the pop of the cork. Captain Clark cautiously issued them but a quarter-cup each, seeking unobtrusively to retire the bottle at that mark. The Partisan, however, was ahead of him. Downing his dram, he threw the tin cup overboard and seized the bottle from Clark in such a rude way as nearly to upset the stout captain. I saw Clark's eyes take fire. He turned scarlet to the roots of his red mane, but he held himself in soldierly check.

"Tell that Indian," he ordered me, tight-lipped, "that if he touches me again, I shall break his right arm out of its shoulder socket. Tell him also, Frank, that I shall do it in front of all his people, so that the break will include his man pride."

I hesitated. This was a dire threat. A grand chief humbled before his people was thenceforth a ruined man. This much I knew absolutely from the teachings of my Uncle François.

"*Patron,*" I said "we must take care. Let me speak to him in another, less devastating way."

Clark's blood was up. He shook his head vehemently. "Say it as you were told, Rivet," he said. "Exactly."

Turning unhappily, I obeyed.

The Indians listened a moment, dark faces hardening. Then, Partisan tipped up the bottle and gurgled at it noisily. The warrior Considerable Man made a grab for it and succeeded in getting it away. He put it smackingly to his own lips and the other warrior, Second Bear, in turn took it greedily away from him. There ensured a violent, brief tussle before the bottle was gulped empty of its contents, then the three rascals fell to taking turns sucking and licking the neck of the dry container like brute, dumb animals. When, finally, the Partisan gave a coarse laugh and threw the bottle from him into the river, he had consumed perhaps—as his lion's share—the better part of a pint of raw whiskey in something less than five minutes.

In his pagan belly the fire was burning. With a dog's filth curse in mongrel French, he lurched deliberately into Captain Clark. I thought then that the finish was upon us. But I had forgotten my *patron*'s dark guardian angel.

York came over the side of the keelboat like a huge and shining black seal. He had followed the white pirogue out from shore, swimming to stay with his master. Hiding under the overhang of the big boat's hull, he had no doubt

107

planned to swim back, undiscovered, to the council site when I returned Clark and the chiefs in the pirogue.

But now he seized the Partisan as a serpent would seize a rat and would most certainly have killed the Sioux had not Captain Clark roared for him to desist. The giant Negro slowly lowered the Teton chief to the deck—he had raised him completely overhead to dash out his brains athwart the forecastle—and his master was able, through my swift assistance with sign language and forced smiles, to convince the five Sioux that York's performance had been part of their planned entertainment aboard ship.

The curiosity of the Indians in seeing the black man at close hand served to tide us over this chanceful moment. York was surely the first Negro of any description to be seen on the Upper Missouri, and the savages were unquestionably in awe of his enormous size and wild looks. Under cover of this respect, combined with the face-saving of Captain Clark's desperately invented lie, we were able to herd them back into the pirogue and return without further incident to the sandbar council site.

Here Lewis met us and, sensing the strain of our circumstance, quickly presented to Black Buffalo a laced red uniform coat of the kind worn by officers in the United States Corps of Artillerists, together with a cocked hat and a red, white and blue turkey feather. To Medicine Buffalo and the two noted warriors he gave peace papers. The Partisan got nothing, as was his surly half-drunken due.

During this second ceremony the Indians ashore came forward in a mass, and we stood on the bar virtually surrounded by Sioux. When the captains then announced that the meeting was done for the day and would be resumed upriver tomorrow, not an Indian moved. We knew then, instantly, that the entire thing had been planned by them in this way. They meant only to get all that we were going to give them, then bluff us out of more—indeed, out of all.

Clark took charge here without discussion. He told Lewis to engage Black Buffalo in the most fervent English harangue he might manage. Meanwhile he, Clark, would take the white pirogue to the keelboat, load her with riflemen and return. But the damnable Partisan was at the pirogue before we could board her. Laughing wickedly, he wrapped both arms about her mast, while two of his Sioux comrades blocked our way on the bar, and three more stood in the shallow, their hands laid to the mooring cable. At once Clark called, "Captain Lewis, come over here, sir!" Then, as Lewis moved to obey, he turned to me. "Talk to Black Buffalo," he ordered. "Tell him to call these devils away from our boat. If he will not make them leave it, I shall."

I had never seen him this disturbed in a thousand miles of the Missouri. At last his red hair and Scotch-Irish ancestry had the better of him. I knew that unless Black Buffalo might persuade the Partisan and his scowling warriors to abandon the pirogue forthwith, there was going to be a violence on that beach which could see us all scalped.

But Black Buffalo could no longer restrain his people. There was, instead, a frightening growl from the entire tribe and they drew in upon us so tightly at the pirogue's mooring that we were cut off from Captain Lewis, who was entombed now somewhere in the body of the mob-beast with York, who had been commanded by Clark to stay with the other captain "until death." But Clark, as ever, struck boldly.

Ignoring the Sioux holding the cable, he went straight into the pirogue, confronting the Partisan. The astonished warriors, staring after him, permitted me to scuttle past them and into the boat behind Clark. The latter, seeing me, merely nodded.

"All right Frank," he said, "you tell this throat-slitting pig precisely what I say: *If he does* not get *his damned filthy paws off that mast, I shall cut them off of it, and off of him."*

With the cold anger of the words, he slid his dress sword from its scabbard and made a lightning pass with it in a whipping slice aimed at the Partisan's beaded headband. The arc of the blade flashed in the sun. In the silence of the following hush, the Partisan's war feather, together with his proudly roached topknot hair which carried it, fluttered through the air and down upon the planking of the pirogue's bottom.

I thought, then, that the Partisan's vicious eyes would bug entirely from their places in his skull.

"Tell him," said Captain Clark evenly, "that this is only to show him that I mean what I say."

I rushed into a torrent of French and handsign pleadings with the dumbstruck Teton chief. I knew what that eagle feather and roached scalplock meant among his people, and I knew that the manner in which Clark had smote both sacred items from him had been a mortal insult. No possible question existed of Clark's understanding this too. Yet neither moved during my hoarse entreaty.

I shall never know if the Partisan heard my pleas, or if he did not. Certainly he never replied to them. He just slowly, slowly let his hands slide away from the mast of the white pirogue, his pit viper's stare never leaving Captain Clark's hard-set face.

Behind me on the sandbar I heard a mass indrawing of many breaths. I turned my glance to see that the Sioux by the dozens and scores were silently fitting arrows to bowstrings. In the same ominous pause I saw brave Shannon, with Drewyer, Colter, the two Fields brothers and half a dozen more of our most trusted men shoulder their arms. Then, in the same stillness which heard the loud knocking of arrows, the wonderful, chilling steel clink-clank of cocking rifle hammers was added.

In this breath-held vacuum of pending tragedy the Partisan struck. He came at Captain Clark with a skinning knife, a ten-inch blade keen as surgeon's steel. Clark, disdaining any advantage, threw aside his sword, accepting combat with bare hands. In the first rush the Sioux missed his stride, the knife narrowly slashing past Clark's ear. Instantly the white captain was under the extended arm. Seizing the redman's wrist, he drove the bony cap of his shoulder into the pit of the Partisan's arm-hollow, lifted him free of the deck, and threw him over his own bowed back down upon the planks with a boat-jarring crash. Before the Indian might recover, Clark leaped upon him, pulled him to his feet and doubled the knife arm up behind the savage's shoulder blade. They stood, thus, in full view of the Indian mob ashore. The drama held the watching Sioux from swarming over Captain Lewis and the white rifle squad. In such a quick and sudden stillness, the sound of the Partisan's arm being dislocated from its shoulder socket by the brutal force now twistingly applied to it by

Captain Clark was heard as plainly as the snapping of a branch in a silent forest.

The chief made a sound in his chest like the wounded animal he was. The sound was picked up and echoed by his fellows on the sandbar. It was a wordless, groaning "unnnaaghhh" which was the more eloquent for its tongueless nature. Captain Clark stepped away from the crippled Partisan. He picked up the Sioux chief's knife and threw it overboard. It splashed and sank in the clear shallows. The white captain turned and left the pirogue. Our riflemen ashore parted and let him through. The Indian pack also spread away, making an aisle. Lewis, still shepherded by York, came out of the press and stood with Clark. The only sound which came after that was the rasping muted twang of bowstrings being unbent, the soft rattling thumps of arrows being dropped back into quivers of elk and buffalo hockskin. All faces, dark red and pale white, turned to the pirogue.

The Partisan came away from the boat, head high. His useless arm, unquestionably in an agony of raw pain, hung and flopped at his side in the manner of a scarecrow's. He did not look either at his countrymen or at his enemies, but stared only straight ahead, face gray with shock. He went through the parted ranks of our riflemen, and those of his own motionless tribesmen. Only when he had crossed the long stretch of the river's bank and disappeared into the shroud of thick cedar timber, from whence but an hour gone he had emerged haughty and cold and cruel, did his fellow Sioux turn to follow him. And then they did it in the somber grieving fashion of a cortège departing the scene of some great dishonorable funeral.

Captain Clark kept his word. He had wrenched the arm of the Partisan from its socket and, with it, had broken the pride and the power and spirit of the Partisan. He had humbled and reduced in the full view of his tribal kinsmen the most feared of the upper river Sioux pirate chieftains. And he had done it in less than six full breaths and without a weapon.

It was no wonder that as they followed their menfolk from that fated sandbar the Teton women covered their heads with their blankets. The power of their people on the Missouri was finished. It had been broken with the Partisan's shoulder.

Next dawn, very early, in a consummate show of pure courage, Captain Clark, accompanied only by York, with myself as interpreter, went to the main Sioux camp, unarmed and unannounced, and with his great skill in such things replaced the Partisan's subluxated arm into its socket.

The Teton's relief from the enormous suffering of the dislocation was of course quick and complete. His seeming gratefulness was of the same quality but Clark, his rash act of mercy once done, viewed this sudden turn of Sioux heart with gravest reservations. We retreated immediately from the village and under cover of that same midnight stealthily resumed our march upriver.

But the Sioux were not easily done with us, as we with them, and in our very first camp above, they showed up in force and fawning humility, bearing with them 400 pounds of buffalo meat as a peace offering to our mighty captains.

The meat was 90 per cent bad due to the unseasonable hot spell obtaining just then, but Clark, his puckish sense of justice never deserting him, insisted we accept it and in return ordered an issue made to the Sioux of three barrels of overwhelmingly spoiled corned pork. Since we had for the past week been seeking some place in the river where we might dump this ptomainic cargo without killing too many innocent fish or down-river friendly Indians, the trade seemed right and fair to us all. However, Clark's generosity failed in its purpose, since not one Teton showed any least ill effect from this greenish sow meat and, indeed, they all plagued us incessantly for more of it.

These unwanted "peace meetings" continued day by day up the river, the Tetons refusing to abandon us. Our little company was for no minute deceived by this faithful attendance on shore. These were still deadly grinning red wolves trailing fleeing white sheep and waiting only the moment of weakness or unwariness which would provide them the proper circumstance for the kill. The strain for us grew intolerable. Captain Clark did not sleep for five days and nights and when, with the afternoon of September 30th we at last dropped our Indian river pilot—a Teton chief and brother of Black Buffalo, whom the latter had secretly supplied us to see us safely guided to the next nation above—the red-haired officer was at the brink of physical collapse.

His hand shook so badly he could not hold the quill and I essayed to take it from him and to write the closing entry of that memorable day for him. However, pale and sick as he was for want of rest, he rallied to take the pen back and to chide me with his infallibly bright grin for my "pusillanimous lack of faith in his staying powers."

Then, with me steadying the journal and holding it to the

light for him, he scrawled out the words which saw us finally free of the "murdering Tetongues."

. . . We proceeded on under a verry Stiff Breeze from the S.E. the Stern of the boat got fast on a log and the boat turned & was verry near filling up before we got her righted, the waves being verry high, The Chief on board was so fritened at the Motion of the boat which in its rocking Caused Several loosed articles to fall on the Deck from the lockers, he ran and hid himself, and we landed, he got his gun and informed us that he wished to return, that all things were now cleare for us to go on, we would not see any more Tetons &c. we repeated to him what had been Said before, and advised him to keep his men away, gave him a blanket a Knife & some Tobbacco, Smokd. a pipe & he Set out. we also Set Sale and Came to at a Sand Bar, & Camped, a verry cold evening, all on guard . . .

19

The days turned brittle cold now. Crying strings of wild brant and the great gray geese of Canada flew southward overhead. The gold and crimson, violet, umber and ochre of fall departed the hills. Brown and sear the prairies waited for the "white grass of winter." At dark the wind came prowling with the bit of ice in its bared teeth. By dawn the hoar frost silvered the lowlands of the river, making a lacery of the naked willow, limning the frozen feet of the low, close-crowding hills. It was an urgent, a warning time, and we responded to it.

But the river fought us each foot of the way. Her shallowing channels diverged into blind lagoons, her constantly silting current blocked ways by daylight which with previous dark had been open and clear. The winds, following us for so many weeks past, now came about into our faces. More and more the pole replaced the sail, the towrope, the oar. The barge would go aground a dozen times in any day's journey, the pirogues twice that in piloting the way. No man could bear more than thirty minutes in such freezing water and the wonder was that any of us survived those final fourteen days.

Even so—and indeed because the very loneliness and cold of those northern latitudes combined so bone chillingly with the Gargantuan labors of the river to keep us huddled to the blaze of each camp's fire—we had the chance and inclination to bring forward our various private journals of those last miles below the Mandans. Here is a specimen from my own:

Mond. Oct. 15, 1804
Camp news these past ten days is spare. One promotion, one demotion. Good fellow R. Frazer of Warfington's squad has been enlisted with the permanent company to replace Gass, who has been made Sgt., this on Oct. 8th. Yesterday, the 14th, J. Newman of the permanent party was court-martialed for insubordination, only the 2nd case in all these months and miles. Newman was sentenced to 75 lashes, which he got at once. He was likewise denied all status and ordered returned to St. Louis and discharged with dishonor from the U.S. Army. Frazer's joy at being chosen to go on beyond the

116

Mandan was touching. Because of some pride it may one day give his kin, I am going to copy the notice of his appt. from the Orderly book verbatim:

"Robert Frazer being regularly inlisted and haveing become one of the *Corps of Vollenteers for North-western Discovery,* he is therefore to be viewed and respected accordingly; and will be annexed to Sgt. Gass's mess.
Wm. Clark Cpt. &c.
Meriwether Lewis
Capt. 1st U.S.
Regt. Infy."

From the peculiar spelling, as well as the order in which the names of the officers appear, it is left to the imagination which of our captains made the foregoing entry in the company orderly book.

Musing here over the guttering flames tonight [I continued in my diary], it is difficult to forget the Arikaras, in whose land we now are. They are strange Indians. They even refuse our whiskey and told Lewis they were "surprised their white father would seek to make a present to them of a liquid which would make them fools." Aside from the ardent natures of their women, they are the most upright of savages. I think also, here in this cold, and lonely camp, of the Teton Sioux. And although my feet are virtually in the fire and my body cocooned in a fine Arikara buffalo robe, I shiver again at the memory.

We have picked up a Frenchman named Pierre Tabeau, said to be the agent of Régis Loisel for the Mandan and Sioux. As he speaks both of these tongues, I am momentarily relieved as interpreter. *Plût à Dieu* that M. Tabeau stays the winter. It is something to discuss Indian fine points with nothing but two hands and a bit of French to fill in the blank pauses.

The wind blows so fiercely tonight that the water from the river is driven like fine rain into our entire campsite. The dampness adds greatly to the misery of the mercury, which stands at minus 7° of the freezing mark.

We are camped on starb. shore below ten lodges of Arikaras, or "Rees." Chattering here upon the icy ground I imagine those snug lodges of earth and log with their friendly, bright-eyed dwellers, waiting so near and yet so damnably far from the chill fire and Frank Rivet. . . .

By next noonhalt we had cleared the Ree country, a not entire disappointment to me. As we rested, a Frenchman named Joseph Gravelines walked into our camp. He proved, as Tabeau before him, an employee of Loisel. Captain Lewis was delighted to hire Gravelines as an interpreter and from him we learned considerable of the Mandans, whose mysterious land we now approached.

After eating we set out again, all hands heartened by the talk with Gravelines. The wind, too cooperated. Out came the sails and away we went up the Missouri. The French boatmen chanted St. Louis ditties. The American soldiers responded with lusty ballads. Everyone lolled about the decks repairing gear, napping, or swapping lies in support of their manhood either as lovers, thieves or fighters. Given another hour of the fair wind and no fouling, and even Captain Lewis was seen to smile and say something pleasant.

At 2 P.M. we encountered a memorable blockade on the river—an antelope "harvest."

By a system of set fires on the outer prairie some wandering Sioux had compressed enormous numbers of the "goats" into a milling herd which they now, with wild shouts and waving blankets, were forcing to take the water at a shallow crossing. In the waist-deep channel the Indians were able to move about easily, but the antelopes were made to swim and were therefore rendered helpless. As we drew up, the naked warriors were wading unhurriedly among the poor brutes, skulling them with clubs or even mere large rocks. I counted fifty-eight dead antelope bobbing in the bloody shallows in the moments we pushed on through the carnage under full sail, and the Sioux cheerfully called to us that the hunt had been on "only a few pipe puffs."

It left me badly shaken to see these gentle things dead and dying and waiting to die, yet I heard Captain Lewis remark enthusiastically that it was but one of those rhythms of raw nature which if viewed objectively, must come to have a certain powerful beauty of its own. Well, perhaps. For me, I don't know. I still remember only the blood and the floating bits of bone and hair, together with the mildly sad and puzzled bleating of the babies looking for their mothers who could not answer them.

The following day, the seventeenth of October, was a bad one, the wind was hard against us from the outset. We

119

made but six miles by dark. Mr. Gravelines said that we were presently opposite the storied Black Mountain Range, the "Court Nou," as Captain Clark recorded it in his bravely original French. The Sioux name is He Sapa, the Black Hills. Captain Clark came to my bedding spot as I was nodding off that night and admonished me to cheer up, since he had a surprise for me tomorrow. I thanked him but slept badly, no least bit cheered by the prospect.

However, the weather warming and fine with dawn, and the wind came again happily astern, we hoisted canvas to glide away upriver, all spirits soaring. Directly following the start, at Mile Three of the day's log, we came to the mouth of an exceedingly fast stream entering from the west. Captain Clark waved over from the keelboat, pointing it out to me and bellowing, *"Luh Bullet! Luh Bullet!"*

Never dreaming this was his promised surprise, I waved back and fell to examining "The Bullet" indifferently.

Suddenly my eyes narrowed. The banks and cliffs of the racing tributary were literally paved with strangely embedded, perfectly round stones resembling nothing so much as a rocky kind of artillery shot—limestone cannon-balls, if you will—and it was when this comparison dawned for me that I understood Clark's atrocious French.

His *"Luh Bullet"* was my *"Le Boulet,"* the sinister and historic Cannonball River!

Here, of all places we might reach, was where my own personal adventure up the Grand Missouri began. This was the precise spot where the boat of my father Achille had upset and the merciless current swept him away into cruel Shoshone bondage. Here then would I reswear my vengeance against his red keepers. Let the fiendish Snakes beware. I was coming!

It was a splendid oath, little doubt, and salty, if only for the tears of righteous outrage which it brought to my brave eyes. But the damned Missouri obtruded on my high resolve and struck it low. From the Cannonball onward, the wind dropped dead, the water fell shallow, the men sullen. The salt of noble weeping was replaced by the inglorious stinging of blistered hands. *Aïe Dieu,* what toil! And what ingratitude from the Fates.

With this date, Saturday, October 20, 1804, we were forty miles north of the Cannonball River. With us now was a Ree chief claiming to have had a vision to go with us and "talk great new father peace" with the Mandans. The captains suffered him to stay. Also today Peter Cruzatte shot the first "grizzled" bear. These animals are well known to us by hearsay as the most extremely fierce of all bears. This one was a monster. He left behind a track of his paw into which three of my moccasin prints could be placed. Drewyer said Cruzatte was a fool and lucky to be alive. When wounded, these great bears nearly always charge. This one fled, crying like a dog.

During the night it rained, the drops freezing in solid, beadlike globules on the ground. Sunday's resulting cold was intense. It bit the tubes of the upper lungs. It stuck together the spittle of the lips. The wind, high again at dawn, suddenly fell off at our start, and it began to snow. It was our first fall, and a grim reminder how late we were in our race against the great freeze-over. Clark pushed us wickedly, Sabbath or no. Yet we made but seven miles.

Camp was early, enforced by physical exhaustion.

At Mile Four of the day's log we had seen the moldering traces of a second deserted Mandan town. The previous day, at late twilight, we had seen the first of these shadowy "ghost villages" of the past. There were three of them, the Ree said, marking the outer marches of the Mandan Nation. "Dead lodges," he called them, and accurately enough, we all thought, considering the ethereal silence which enshrouded their gaping doors and weed-grown sills. The third town, he said, waited on the north bank only two miles above where we presently sat huddled to the fitful warmth of Clark's mess fire, in that snowbound camp.

"Very soon now," he told the captain, deep-voiced and leaning intently forward, "the Mandan People come."

The events of the next four days magnified our tensions of anticipation. Now we *knew* that we were extremely near to our first great goal. It became suddenly a time for taking final stock, making final reassessments, for marshaling all men and *matériel* of the expedition for the critical entrance into the Land of the Mandan.

Men react to such strictures in unexpected ways, and very strange things happened in that tensing camp of the night of October 24th. Things such as Big Bat Deschamps coming up to me—to me, Frank Rivet—and blustering embarrassedly, "Here now, little rooster, little water rat, let us shake hands and say no more of any pirogue races to the Mandan villages." And such things as Captain Lewis calling me over to his mess and telling me, before his men, "Well, boy, you've done right well. I was wrong about you. You're a Rivet." And things, lastly, such as Captain Clark, under pretense of taking me to check over the white pirogue's anchoring, telling me that Gravelines had informed him and Captain Lewis that but for me the company would never have gotten past the Teton Sioux.

"Seems the devils spotted you, Frank," he said. "You must resemble old Achille to an eyelash. There's no other way to account for it, Gravelines says. They told him and Tabeau, both, that they let us go through because we had the 'son of the drowned man' with us. They must figure they owe you something for what they done to your father, eh? Anyways, Frank, we're even. I likely saved your bacon for you back at La Charrette, and you sure as sin kept mine from getting overfried back at the Sioux sandbar. One minus one, boy, it ciphers out zero."

"No, *Patron*," I said, head bowed. "you are much too generous. I am certain of your guardianship of me, whereas you only guess at what small good I have been to you."

"Pshaw!" He grinned. "Forget it. We're square."

We talked a little more, quietly; then he said good night and wheeled about to depart.

"*Capitaine!*" I called after him. "A moment, please. Do you think my father is alive?"

He turned back to me, frowning. "I don't know" he answered. "I've asked Gravelines about it and he claims the Tetongues won't say right out. They keep insisting he's '*tela nun wela*.' Gravelines says in Sioux that comes out 'dead yet alive.' So how would we translate it?"

"It's impossible," I said. "But do you then have any idea, *Patron*, why the Sioux should have such a strong feeling for my father that it protects his son thirteen years after? And protects even the friends of that son?"

"I said I didn't understand it, Frank."

"If you will not say he is alive, then, *Patron,* will you say that my father is dead?"

Clark set his blunt, red-bristled jaw.

"Frank," he said carefully, "let's leave it this way: a legend doesn't feed for thirteen years on nothing but Indian wind. Something solid is keeping that story about your father being a captive of the Snakes going the rounds of the lodgefires up in the country."

"But you don't think it's a good something, do you, *Patron?*

He peered at me closely through the gloom. Finally, reaching his decision, he nodded resolutely.

"No, sir, Frank," he said, "I don't."

I dropped my head again. He went away quickly, with his long driving strides, up the beach toward the beckoning cheery glow of the campfires. I was left there in the white pirogue with my Pawnee fears and settlement-bred lonelinesses, forty-eight hours and twenty-two miles below the villages of the Mandan.

The morning of the twenty-fifth was crackling cold. The wind was like an assassin's knife, it made little noise but went in deep. Being from the southeast, however, it permitted us to hoist the big sheet on the barge as well as the two small puffers on the pirogues, and so we were able to set sail up the Grand Missouri in a final style becoming to The Corps of Volunteers for Northwestern Discovery.

From Mile Three of this day, the banks of the river became dotted with smaller, more recently abandoned towns of Arikara and Mandan construction. It was in this mixed region, Captain Lewis told us, that the Rees lived with the Mandans when the former had been driven north by the persecutions of the Teton Sioux. Some of these town sites were fixed by the senior captain to be no more than five years empty.

Now suddenly, in the darkening afternoon, the bank eastward of river began to bloom with small parties of Indians of a tribe we had not seen. As we puzzled over them, our Ree chief began to show great agitation and to dance about on the deck and cry out in his bastard French, "*Mendannés! Mendannés!*" while pointing at the strangers, and we knew who those Indians were.

Ashore, the Mandans gathered in ever greater numbers following our boats upstream with repeated pleas for us to halt and take them aboard the "wondrous camp which fled on the water under the big white flag." This reference to the keelboat could not, of course, be accommodated, and the host on shore did not seem to care for this prohibition. Their numbers increased to a swarm, both afoot and on horseback now. We began to wonder belatedly about the true quality of their reported "general friendliness." Clark studied them through Lewis's glass for quite a while, with day's last light, and finally shook his head.

"All I know is that they're Indians, Captain," he said. "We'd best hold to the left bank and pick a good high campsite."

Lewis did not debate the suggestion. He hove to at once on the near shore, directly opposite to the main horde of shouting, gesturing Mandans. The night passed crawlingly.

The following morning, October 26, 1804, we solemnly

stood to the colors while Captain Lewis read aloud to us a brief commendation, but most moving, of our steadfast services to duty and to country in reaching this first, far landmark in our historic journey. We then embarked.

As the final day, its chronicle belonged in all justice to the permanent company. No quondam member could think to deny this canon. Indeed, my great honor lay in the opportunity to report that chronicle for whomsoever might come upon it in my own journal through the misting years ahead.

Captain Clark being disabled with a rheumatic seizure of the neck which took him with immense pain and suffering, the entry for the last day was written by Meriwether Lewis. Here is the way in which history will remember our arrival at latitude 47° 21' 47" and Mile Sixteen hundred from the mouth of the Missouri River, in the great adventure to unlock the 400-year secret of the Northwest Passage:

Friday 26th. We set out early with a southwest wind, and after putting the Ricara chief on shore to join the Mandans who are in great numbers along it, we proceeded to the camp of the grand chief four miles distant. Here we met a Mr. M'Cracken one of the North West or Hudson's Bay company, who arrived with another person about nine days ago to trade for horses or buffalo robes.

Two of the chiefs came on board with some of their household furniture, such as earthen pots and a little corn; and went with us; the rest of the Indians following on shore.

At one mile beyond the camp we passed a small creek, and at three more a bluff of coal of an inferior quality on the south. After making eleven miles . . . we camped for the night on the south side, about half a mile below the first village of the Mandans . . . The wind blew very cold in the evening from the southwest.

Two of our party are affected with rheumatic complaints.

Book IV
Charbonneau's Squaw

20

As with most events of extreme anticipation, our actual arrival among the Mandan fell short of what our imaginations had pictured. The historic Mandan Indians themselves were the first disappointment. Taller a little, and less gross in feature than the Otos, they were not so tall nor so strong-looking as the Teton Sioux, and not nearly so good-looking as the Rees. They did have intelligent and lively dispositions which were fundamentally friendly. And their women, if less comely than those of the Arikara, were no less amorous. The men were much easier to talk with than any Indians we had met, and one felt immediately that these were civilized Indians and, indeed, civilized men.

Due to the unlooked-for degree of this amicability, our captains were able, almost at once, to devote themselves to the pressing matter of constructing our winter quarters. Clark, of course, with his positive genius for workaday engineering was given the assignment of locating and putting up the military compound. He moved in his accustomed manner—quickly. On November 2nd, less than one week from our arrival, he chose a site three miles down the Missouri from the first village and upon the north bank. Work of clearing the land began that same day, and the very next day he had the French boatmen begin construction of the pirogue with which they would shepherd the big barge back down the Missouri. It was upon this second day, also, that he hired a man who was to loom large in our fates. This was Toussaint Charbonneau. He was taken into the company as an interpreter for the Minnetaree Indians. These were the Gros Ventres, or so-called "Big-Bellies." Since they had a reputation for harsh dealing with the whites and because their language was extremely difficult for white tongues to master, the addition of Charbonneau was considered an important achievement. For myself, I did not care for Toussaint Charbonneau, and I did not trust him. When I made bold to say something of this to Captain Clark, he laughed and said, "Look out, boy, you're behaving like a Pawnee," and urged me thereafter to attend to my work and leave the worrying to him and Captain Lewis. I accepted the order, but not in my heart.

In the first days that the log fortress was going up, Lewis held talks with the Mandan. He made friends with Black Cat, the grand chief, and was able to arrange for supplies of shelled corn, Indian meal, moccasins and other items of which our men were in some need, or at least desire. With Black Cat he arranged, as well, a formal peace with the ambassador Arikara chief from downriver, guaranteeing a state of friendly relations with the Ree and Mandan peoples, and securing the fealty of both to the United States and the great father in Washington. He gave out a vast quantity of Jefferson medals and peace papers and considered his time most well employed. I am certain that Clark did not agree, but the red-haired captain made his usual comment when it came to being critical of his co-commander. He said nothing at all.

There were five principal villages built about the mouth of the Knife River. Some were on the south, some on the north bank. Two of these main towns were pure Mandan, the other three were bastard Mandan-Minnetaree and Mandan-Anahaway Indians. Insofar as they may need to be entered here, the main chiefs of these combined peoples were Black Cat, Big White, Little Fox, Big Thief, Black Moccasin, White Buffalo, Red Shield and that ominous Minnetaree figure whom we had not yet seen or heard word from, Le Borgne, the One-Eyed.

But we had no leisure to build fears while building our fortress. Clark saw to that. We were permitted time off only for eating, sleeping, writing in our journals, washing our clothes and, upon rare occasions, for company hails and farewells.

These latter times were such events as the departure of Joseph Gravelines with the Arikara ambassador back downriver to pick up the Ree chiefs for the visit to President Jefferson, and the arrival in our camp on November 10 of a Pawnee chief who asked for the son of Achille Rivet and the Pawnee woman, Antelope. One may well envision the excitement which sprang up within me when, upon being asked by Clark what it was that he wished of me, the Indian replied that he was Chief Lame Horse, the father of

Antelope and the Grandfather of her half-white son.

Since I spoke the handsign language fluently by this time, Clark granted me the unusual privilege of meeting with Lame Horse in private. We were given the entire remainder of the day in which to discuss my mother and whatever else I might gain from my red grandfather of information on the Indians beyond the villages of the Mandan. I had no doubt that Grandfather Lame Horse would provide me with all I asked, and that I would in consequence be able to render my captains a considerable service of enlightenment upon the trials which waited them when winter passed.

I made my first mistake immediately, of course.

"Well, Grandfather," I signed to him, airily and with visible vanity in my mastery of the hand movements, "what do you think of your half-white grandson that you have come so far to see?"

The old man, it developed, did not favor the handsigns. He had some command of English, and even a little French. He did not mean to be talked to as though he were some ignorant savage come to trade ermine or otter for glass beads or grains of sugar.

"Boy shut mouth," he said, voice cracked as a bullfrog's. "Talk when told."

"What's that?" I asked, startled into a return to the English. "You don't want to talk to me?"

"Me talk," he said. "You shut mouth."

That seemed clear enough, and so I fell still and let him look it me. At the same time, I had a glance at him. He was short and had a big head. His body composed, it seemed, two-thirds of his entire height, his legs being very short

130

and so bowed as to defy description. Terms such as bulldog and bantam rooster spring to mind, but they pale in use. My grandfather was so bow-legged and so pigeon-toed that in the literal sense he could scarcely walk. His progress when walking was a hybrid of lame goose and drunken sailor. He waddled and rolled and pitched all in the same incredible motion, as he began to pace to and fro before the mess fire while studying me from beneath his hawk-nosed scowl. One could not say of his features that they were ugly. His face held too much of the sun and wind of many years. There was a gleam of dark pride in the old eyes which would not be denied. And he held himself erect as a war lance, even though he must have had eighty winters, or more, upon him. No, Grandfather Lame Horse was not common or ordinary.

What, by contrast, his fierce examination was showing him of his half-French grandson was presently revealed.

"Goddam," he said very plainly, and shaking his head in disapproval, "too skinny, too small in face, bad mouth. Not look like mother. Good nose. Big like father. Strong chin, eyes no good. Gray eyes bad. Mean and sneaky nature, always. White man's eyes. Skin too weak. Not dark. Thin skin, wound easy. Teeth all right. Jaw no good. Too narrow. No chew buffalo hock leather. No make bow-string, no make moccasin string, no make gutstring for repair saddle, bridle, rifle scabbard. No good chew anything. Grandson not much. Trip to see him long like hell. Goddam. Me go now."

It could be said that Lame Horse had made the same assessment out loud which young Pierre Dorion had kept to himself. He had come many miles across a cold country

131

in the belly of a hard winter to see this son of his only and dead daughter Antelope, and he had found not the Indian scion he had envisioned in his Pawnee pride, but a damned ribby and wretched half-breed boy looking much more French than Indian.

Stunned as I was by his sudden announcement, and his attendant gesture of rising to his full height and calling over his shoulder for his two companions to bring him his pony, I yet managed to find tongue to plead with him to stay, to desist, that we had not yet spoken of my mother, that I would talk at length of her, that I had missed her all these years as only a Pawnee boy can miss his mother when caught and held in the white man's lodges, and that it was only right and just that he, my Indian grandfather, should do this service to the memory of his sleeping daughter, who was my mother.

To this, he had a sledge blow for answer.

"Boy right," he stopped long enough to say. "Me remember duty to mother. That's why go now. Fast. Before maybe she see me talk with white son. Too bad. Good-bye, white boy."

That, then, was the end of it. He got up on his pony and rode off on the lope, friends following in haste. I ran as far as the river in pursuit, waving and calling for my grandfather to wait. I may as well have been hallooing the wind. Perhaps, better so. The wind sometimes turns around the whistles back. My grandfather did not. Neither did his friends. The last I saw of them, they were wading the Missouri at the shallow crossing of the first Mandan village.

That was a bad day for me. But those red gods of my mother's people were watching over me. They did not ride

132

away with my grandfather. The very next day, November 11th, they brought me another Indian gift far greater than Lame Horse.

21

How may one tell of Sacajawea, or Birdwoman, as the Shoshones translated her name? She was no more than a girl when we first saw her, sixteen summers Charbonneau said, and she was swollen big with the seventh month of her pregnancy. Yet when she came up the bank of the river to stand before Clark and myself at the construction site, and to murmur in her low voice, "I am Sacajawea, my chiefs, the younger wife of Charbonneau." I loved her. When she raised her eyes and looked at me, my heart stopped beating. For other women, from that moment, it never beat again. I loved Sacajawea beyond time, beyond place, beyond reason. It was that way in the beginning, that way in the end; it was the *all,* the final thing.

Even Clark, that rock, that granite carving of a man felt this power. And I saw him tremble to it, even as I trembled to it, and I knew, instantly, an envy, a jealousy, a challenge, which never was resolved.

As for Sacajawea, I thought that even in that brief encounter her luminous gaze lingered for a greater time upon the weather-beaten homeliness of the red-haired captain than upon my own narrow-faced métis features. But before I might make myself sicker yet from this mean suspicion, Clark, with his rough genius for treating with these simple wilderness folk, nodded to me and said, "Make her welcome, Frank. See what it is that has brought her downriver. Ask about the other squaw, too. I was told by Char-bonneau to expect his women, but you'll grant he didn't prepare us for anything like this."

Since Sacajawea had spoken in French, and since her older companion had said no word at all in any tongue, the onus of obeying my captain's order was inescapably mine.

Very awkwardly, I'm afraid, I conveyed to the young squaw the questions of the Red Haired Chief.

She replied that she had not originally intended to come to the Mandan towns with her husband, nor had her com-panion, the older squaw and other wife of the French trapper. But Charbonneau had sent for her, Sacajawea, when it was learned that the American captains sought an interpreter for the Shoshone language. It was thought by Charbonneau, she concluded, that while he earned his money interpreting for the Minnetaree, she might also be earning an equal amount supplying the same service for the Americans in connection with the Shoshone, the Snake Indians, when the expedition should go on, in the spring, to the distant Big Rock Mountains.

When Clark had me ask her why it was that she believed she might serve in this capacity—what qualifications she had for it—she replied quietly that she herself was a Shoshone Indian, captured five winters gone as a small girl of eleven years and little knowledge. But she had a good memory, she said, and had not forgotten the tongue of her people, and she was certain that she could help us when we should come to the land of the Snakes.

Considering her tender age when captured, Clark told me he thought it extremely unlikely that she could prove of any real or considerable value as a go-between with the

Shoshone, but that I was not to hurt her by revealing this fact. Rather, I was to inform her we were made glad in our hearts to see her and the other squaw, and that they might both camp with us to be near their husband. This I did, and Sacajawea, with a sad, soft smile that nearly tore my heart from my breast, thanked us both with a grace of word and gesture which left us, boy and man, blushing like country swains. In this case the woman was a mere girl, and a red Indian; the swains were the one a half-breed boy of nearly twenty, the other a middle-aging American soldier. There was, too, another factor which I am certain Clark considered as automatically as did I. This would be the husband; Toussaint Charbonneau, frontier legend, living fable, a man and name to reckon with. But a man who already grew old; who was gray and grizzled and somewhere upon the immediate approaches to fifty years of age. There was a further element—the unborn child—perhaps more patently a taboo than either Charbonneau's marital rights, or the disparate ages of Frank Rivet and William Clark. But I knew, as I stared at my captain there upon the bank of the Missouri, and while we both silently watched Sacajawea and the older squaw go down to their canoe and begin its unloading, that it was not I alone who was smitten at first sight with the strangely beautiful and compelling Shoshone girl.

22

Captain Clark built the compound in the form of a triangle, the apex toward the river. He drove us to the task like slaves, the increasing cold being his galley whip. In exactly nine days from the arrival of Sacajawea the last of what the red-haired captain called "our works" was completed. These works consisted of two rows of huts, making the legs of the triangle, which had an elegance more suited to stabling livestock than human beings. They were constructed of incredibly heavy ash and cottonwood logs, spongy, wet, fibrous and miserable to trim or shape. The dimensions of each of these "Mandan mansions" were fourteen feet square by seven feet high. Floors were rammed earth, ceilings raw plank. Across the open base of the triangle ran from a height of seven feet on the inside walls to a lofty eighteen feet on the outer walls, Clark's "works" in very real effect constituted a superior fortress which, upon the twentieth of November, 1804, was named by our captains in formal dress and ceremony Fort Mandan. As a final touch, and as only he might have conceived of it, Clark put up outside the gate a roadside sign containing our latitude of 47° 21' 47" and then, beneath this official business, added a crudely drawn arrow pointing southward down the rutted river trail and announcing laconically: ST. LOUIS, 1600 MILES.

For such acts did his men love him, and for such acts did they separate him from his co-captain and their real commander. It was perhaps not a fair judgment, but a most human one. If the record survives, let it note that nothing so endears the officer to the man as the ability to share a smile. Nor does iron discipline depend upon a steel face. No soldier of our company would have died the slower for Captain Clark than for the other captain. That soldier might leap the more quickly to answer Captain Lewis, but he would not jump harder or farther. A nice distinction, surely, but accurate.

With the fort finished and ourselves moved into it—none too soon, for upon November 13th we had seen the first block ice floating in the river—we were given some time to catch up our unofficial duties of which I personally had a most urgent one, and long delayed.

I had not seen nor heard of Sacajawea since that first day at the river. Clark told me that Charbonneau had purchased from some visiting Assiniboin Indians a tipi of the portable Sioux design and with this lodge and his two women set off "somewhere into the woods." Indeed, the captain added, Charbonneau himself, now many days overdue to report for duty, was being sought by Captain Lewis. Should I see him, I was to report at once. As for Sacajawea and the other squaw, no search had been ordered, nor was any contemplated. This dryly included fact, of course, merely doubled the ardor with which I now took the latter mission upon myself, uncommanded.

Yet for six straight days I combed those Mandan timberlands without result. My method was to pose as company meat hunter. My luck ran good and I was thus able to stay in the field with permission. Actually, after the first day, I did not go alone, but persuaded Clark to let me take York with me since I needed transportation for my game. It was on the seventh day that the big Negro dropped the towline on the Indian hauling toboggan and turned to me with his first grin since being assigned by his master as my pack animal.

"Mister Frank," he observed, sniffing the cold, flaky air of a swiftly thickening snowfall, "she's agoing to snow."

"Mister York," I replied acidly, "she's done already

137

snowed. Were you thinking of something else, perhaps?"

"Well, yes, sir, could be. How about you?"

"Damn you," I said, "it's none of your affair what I'm thinking of."

"No sir," he agreed amiably. "Not less'n you say so."

He fell silent, sniffing the snow again, shaking his head.

"She's agoing to be way too deep for what you're hunting, Mister Frank, less'n you find her pretty fast," he announced unexpectedly.

I could have shot him happily, but instead controlled my supposedly civilized superiority.

"York," I demanded finally, "do you mean to tell me that you've been hauling that miserable damned sled through these miserable damned woods for all of these miserable damned days knowing what I was looking for and yet you didn't say a miserable damned word the entire time?"

The grin spread, his head bobbing. "Oh, my, much worse than that, Mister Frank," he said. "I not only done knowed what you was looking for, I knowed all the time percisely whar it were."

"York, you don't mean it!"

"No, sir, not iffen you says so, I don't."

"No, wait, damn it, that's not what I meant and you know it."

"Yes, sir, I sure does."

I forced myself to think calmly.

"York, old friend," I said, "forget the hard words. Can you take me to her? Is there time before dark?"

"Course there's time. She's only ten minutes from the fort."

I wanted to bend my ride barrel over his skull. Rather, I

smiled forgivingly.

"Dear friend," I requested, "may I, just for the sake of old times down the river and by virtue of the dark-blood bond we share, ask you one simple question before we set out?"

"Why, surely, Mister Frank. You kin ask me anything you wants. And that's forever so."

"Well then," I nodded gritting my teeth "if you knew all the time that I was looking for Charbonneau's young squaw, why in the name of God didn't you tell me where she was?"

York looked at me, eyewhites walled in total innocence of my ire.

"Why, Mister Frank," he said in his gentle lion's rumble, "that's a powerful easy question. How am I agoing to tell you, when you don't ask me . . ."

23

Charbonneau's squaws showed pleasure at seeing us. They had been several days without the services of their lord and master and evidently they—the older one, at least—missed those services. This second squaw, a lean and hungry-looking she-weasel with a face as angular as Sacajawea's was oval, demonstrated a degree of cordiality not to be outdone by our memories of the Ree women. Spying York, as she came out of the cowskin lodge in answer to our hail, her dark features glowed. She called back into the lodge for Sacajawea to come out and see the métis boy, thus nominating herself as the object of the huge slave's visit. And when that rascal had obligingly patted her on the backside and suggested she come away with him on a sleigh ride through the trees, she lost no time in leaping on the toboggan and yelping at him to *"Marchons! Marchons!"* after the manner with which the northern Indians urge on their sled dogs.

Then I heard behind me the soft laugh of Sacajawea. I turned quickly back to face the Shoshone girl.

God's name but she was lovely! I could not speak, could not move, could not even think.

"Come in," she said in decent French, standing aside for me. "A friend of my husband's is welcome here."

Straightening, I looked at her.

"But I am not a friend of your husbands," I said. "I don't like your husband and I don't trust him."

She returned my look. Lowering her eyes, she again gestured for me to enter.

"My husband is a good man," she said. "Yet you are honest and say what is in your heart. So I will be the same. I like you. You don't look at an Indian with bad thoughts. I trust you. Come in."

I hesitated, charmed by the Indian thinking but alerted by it too. "If it is not proper to visit when the husband is away," I said, "please tell me."

"It is all right," she said. "Is not Wahiki here?"

"Wahiki?" I asked. "That's a Sioux name, isn't it?"

"Yes. Hunkpapa Sioux. It means The Bone. You see, Charbonneau bought her from the Sioux."

"A good name for her, Sioux or not," I replied, smiling.

Then, when she saw my blush of awkwardness, she at once waved her slim hand.

"Excuse it that I do not smile with you," she said, "but

it is that my people are more strict with their women than are some others."

As swiftly as I had blushed, I frowned.

"So I have noticed," I said bluntly, jerking my head toward York and the other squaw.

Sacajawea's patient voice only grew more gentle.

"You are forgiven, white boy," she said. "You could not understand that I meant Wahiki was not alone Sioux by name; she carried the blood, as well. She is no Shoshone sister of mine, as Charbonneau tells it. She is pure Hunkpapa."

"Oh," I said lamely, "I'm sorry, Sacajawea."

"It is already forgotten," she shrugged, face lighting to the sad, sweet smile. "Come in, Frank."

Once more I halted, heart hammering crazily

"How did you know my name?" I stammered.

"From asking about it, and about you," she admitted.

"From Captain Clark?" I demanded, half angrily.

"No, from Charbonneau, of course."

"What? Your husband? And he was not jealous? He showed no resentment of your interest in another man?"

"In another man, perhaps. He said you were but a foolish boy. He said when you came to see me it would be permitted that I let you in."

"Do you mean that Charbonneau knew I would come?"

"But of course. Charbonneau is very wise."

"Perhaps, but he's very old, too. I would think he would be suspicious of young men."

"Sometimes he is."

"But not this time, eh? Not with just a foolish boy?"

She laughed suddenly It was a soft delicious sound.

141

"Would you be worried when it is plain to all that I am soon to bear a child?" she asked. "I told you Charbonneau was a wise man. He doesn't waste time thinking about useless things. Come in, Frank, it's too cold standing here in this wind."

We spoke many things. Sacajawea was not shy, but appealingly soft of speech and manner. And she was gracefully feminine beyond any woman I had seen. Even bulky with child she was a creature of desire and exquisite femaleness. As she told me now of her past and present life, I watched her, utterly entranced.

She was, as I said, a slender girl. Her head was not elongated, as so many of the Indians, but rather small and round, Caucasian in shape. So, too, were her features Caucasian. Small ears lay flat to her head. The short straight nose was neither flatly Mongol like the river Indians, nor high-bridged as with the horse Indians. Her mouth, a little wide in the manner of Indian mouths, still had a form and softness not at all Indian. The teeth, of course, were perfect; I had not seen a healthy adult of her high plains race who did not have perfect teeth. But her eyes remained the most startling thing about her, even more so than the rare dark auburn color of her hair. They were not black or even dark or light brown in the normal Indian range of iris pigments. They were gray. They were as gray as my own eyes, although far, far darker, with that certain hint of green-blue seen in deep clear water, or in a rain-washed prairie sky of a cloudless sunset; and the lashes which framed them were thick as broomstem grasses. Her skin was a tigerish color, so light in tone that each blush was to be seen in Sacajawea's face as vividly as the face of the fairest French or American girl. Yet with all this strange beauty, she was always the purest of pure Indians.

One may say that being French and very young I add qualities to the Shoshone girl which no Indian maiden ever knew. The charge is fair but not true. Sacajawea was not only an uncommonly pretty young girl, she was a regal woman by any standard of any race. No man who ever knew her, was quite the same again.

Nor was it beauty alone which summed her gifts. Grace was hers, and good manners. Intelligence she had, and a lively humor with quick though gentle tongue. Dignity covered her every move. She could look like a queen while gutting an elk or jerking the boudins from the hot stinking belly of a dead bull buffalo. She was Sacajawea. She had no crown but her auburn brown hair, no gemmed circlet save the brightness of her smile, no scepter but the crude stone maul which crushed Charbonneau's cornmeal or drove the stakes of his hide tipi. But Sacajawea was a ruler of men's hearts by God's will. I knew this with the first word she spoke to me upon the banks of the Missouri, and I knew it now, as I sat in the lodge of Charbonneau and listened, heart afire, to her softly haunting voice.

She came to the end, moving her hands like fluttering birds, dark gray eyes shining in the half-light of the lodge.

"And so," she murmured, "there is my story. It is not, as I warned you, a simple tale. We are all the same, red and white. Our stories are much trouble and little joy, but we all see a better sunrise coming on the next day. It is as it should be. And now, Frank, what is your story?"

I answered her as briefly as courtesy would permit,

giving the plain facts of my history from the Pawnee camp to the college of the Jesuits. When I had concluded, she nodded soberly.

"Then it is true that you are métis, as Charbonneau told me," she said. "We are half-brother and half-sister, you and I. That's good. I like that."

"I'm not so certain that do," I replied. "It is not exactly as a sister that I view you."

I was bold with it and she understood my meaning.

"We must talk of other things," she said, gray eyes holding mine. "There is the matter of your father."

"Yes," I agreed, deserving the rebuke. "I was swept away with the tale of your Shoshone childhood, your capture by the Minnetaree, the manner in which Charbonneau was able to purchase you for a broken rifle and five old horses. The very next thing I intended was to inquire after Achille Rivet."

"I know," she said. "You're a good boy."

"I am bordering nineteen years old!" I said indignantly "Among your people a man is grown at seventeen, ready for his first warhorse and journey into battle when he is eighteen. And I am one-half horse Indian. I think I'm ready for my pony and my first fight. Yes, and for my first love, too."

She shrugged. I could see the curving gleam of her bare shoulders beneath the loosened fur cape.

"Frank," she said, "what makes a man different from a boy? Or a girl from a woman? Is it the years alone? I don't believe it. Thinking only of the hardships I have known, I am sixty winters old. Considering only those few happy times of my life, I am my actual age, sixteen summers

144

young. So what am I really? A woman or a girl?"

"You are a woman *and* girl," I said. "The most beautiful of both that I have ever seen."

She blushed deeply. "Beauty is like age," she said. "It depends upon who is describing it. I am certain that Toussaint Charbonneau sees me one way, and Frank Rivet sees me another way, and Captain Clark sees me yet a third way. That, too, is life."

I threw all caution to the snow-thick winds at the mention of the red-headed captain. "Sacajawea," I shouted jealously, "I love you! I don't care what Charbonneau or Clark see in you. I love you and shall wait for you and follow you until death moves between us. God help me!"

She might have laughed at the unguarded outburst, charitably passing by the excited speech as no more than ill-advised ardor. But it was more than that, and she sensed that it was.

"Frank," she said, "there is something you must be told. I do not return to you this feeling. I understand it; I know what it is. Its fire leaped up in my own breast that moment when I looked up the riverbank toward you and the red-haired captain. But it was not you, Frank, for whom the fire leaped."

She stopped, head lowered, not looking at me. My throat grew tight. I had been right from the first moment of my jealousy! That look which I fancied to see upon her lovely face when her eyes met Clark's had not been fancied by me but real; as real as the buffet of the wind beyond Charbonneau's lodge, and the sting of the woodsmoke within that lodge. If my life belonged to the Shoshone girl, her life belonged to the man who above all other men had treated

Frank Rivet as a human being. Her life belonged in the end to the same man as did mine. We were both bonded to Captain William Clark! No, it was worse than simply bonded. We were both bonded to him by love, and by hopeless love; for Sacajawea could no more be his mate in reality than could I be his son.

Still, we had come too far, Sacajawea and I, to turn back now. If she did not love me as a lover, if she could not answer to my own devotion, to my own passion, then we would go on as she felt it, as half-brother and half-sister of the Indian side. There could be no question, for me ever, of abandoning the slender Shoshone. I now told her so, and she accepted the situation.

"All right, Brother." She smiled. "For now it is the better way. We have a common desire, Frank, but it is not love. We both came to this place seeking the Shoshone Indians, you to find your lost father, I to rejoin my people with whom I shall then stay while Charbonneau travels on to the Big Blue Water with the American captains."

I nodded, her sober words having returned me to a sense of time and place.

"Yes, you are right," I said. "We both have the Shoshone to find before anything else. Indeed, as to that, what a blessing the good God has sent me in Sacajawea."

She looked at me quietly for a moment. Then, once more, the sad, swift smile brightened her dusky face.

"More blessing than you yet imagine, Brother Frank," she said. "For we not only look for the Shoshone together, but we look for the same bank of that people. It is my own tribe, Frank, which holds your father. I have sat as close to him as I do to you, across this smoking fire."

146

24

I was stunned, of course. It was a typically Indian revelation. She had known of my mission all this while, yet had chosen her own time and way in which to arrive at this bit of news for which I had labored like a galley rogue sixteen hundred miles up the Grand Missouri. The odds were, too, that not another human soul, no Charbonneau, not Wahiki, not anyone but Frank Rivet had been told this peculiar secret. That, as well, was the Indian way, and the way which made them such devils to deal with, innocent and friendly, or wicked and dire.

"*Good God!*" I breathed at last. "Why haven't you told me this before?"

Now the graceful shrug was back, the gleaming copper nakedness again showing briefly beneath the soft fur.

"You gave me no time," she explained.

"Well, there is scarcely time remaining," I said, "but please hurry. York and I must leave, or the captains will be out looking for us."

She tried to tell me what she could of my father but it proved maddeningly little. Achille Rivet had been brought into her village only a short time prior to her own capture by the Minnetaree. She had meant to ask her brother, who was the young second chief of the band, why the white prisoner was called "the dead man" and why, indeed, the Shoshone had purchased him from the Teton Sioux. But the Minnetarees had struck the Snake lodges before she remembered to put the question and so this was all she actually knew of Achille Rivet, who was called the dead

147

man. She was sorry. Did I forgive her?

Why, I could not say, but the mention of her brother being an important chief among the Shoshone caught my ear. An intuitive impulse told me to inquire about this young chief, and about the name of the band from whence he and Sacajawea came. But I had no more than posed the questions for my companion, and she no more than commenced to reply to them—first pledging me to hard secrecy, since even Charbonneau did not know she was the young sister of this powerful young chief—when there was a sudden rattle at the entrance flaps and the older squaw, Wahiki, parted the closed skins and dropped down on a pile of wolf pelts beyond the fire.

At this point York interrupted, protruding his head through the unfastened flaps and waving to me in some urgency.

"Come on along, Mister Frank," he said, "we'd best light a shuck out'n here. She's most dark and set to snow like hell. Ain't you done palavering yet?"

"No," I said irritably. "Come in and close the flaps. There are a couple of important things I must find out from Sacajawea; her folks have turned out to be the ones that are holding my father."

He obeyed me, black face beaming happily.

"Why, say, ain't that a passing grand piece of news, Mister Frank? This here little old Snake squaw's kin being the ones to have your daddy?"

I agreed that it was indeed good news and turned once more to query Sacajawea about her band and brother.

But again bad luck dogged the day. Before she might even open her mouth to begin her reply, the entry flaps

148

parted again and this time it was Captain Clark's shaggy red head, dusted white with snowflakes, which intruded abruptly.

"You lads had better be heading for home," he advised, eyes snapping. "Charbonneau is not five minutes behind me; I saw him saying good-bye to Captain Lewis as I set out from the fort just now. Eh, hello there, is that you, Charbonneau?"

Of course, it was not Charbonneau, and Clark was only terrorizing us, but how could we know? With him we went trotting through the early night, entirely grateful for the falling snow. Yet even as we went and even as I ought to have been burning with embarrassment over being caught with a young married girl in her lodge in her trusting husband's absence, I was not. I was aflame with another feeling altogether.

What was Captain Clark *really* doing at the hidden lodge of Sacajawea at darkfall of that cold and snowy night? Heart of Jesus, how I envied him then the love of Charbonneau's squaw!

25

That night when we had returned to the fort and when I had learned that Charbonneau had indeed reappeared, Clark sent for me. I suspected at once that he had serious matters in mind, and he did.

"Frank," he said. "I won't mince words with you. It's time we had it out in the open about the Shoshone girl. It's this simple; she's Charbonneau's wife. Do you understand what I mean?"

149

"I haven't touched her!" I said defiantly. "There's nothing to understand."

"Oh yes there is," he said quietly. "You're gone on her, lad, and it can't do either of you anything but harm."

He paused and I eyed him sullenly.

"Never mind the hard looks." He nodded. "I know what's eating you and it's not dismal as you think. I have no time or temper for that girl, Frank. You hear me?"

I heard him perfectly. I heard that he was jealous of me and trying to bluff me away from seeing her again.

"*Oui, Patron,*" I replied, still scowling. "I hear you all too well."

He took me by the shoulder. The grip made me gasp.

"Damn you, boy," he said, "don't you turn ugly on me."

He stood looking at me a long, angry moment, then eased his grip. He heaved a sigh, shoulders sagging.

"It's no fault of yours, blast it," he said. "She's enough to uncenter any man alive."

I nodded, saying nothing.

"Frank." he went on, "when we set out this spring, Sacajawea will stay here. I mean to tell Charbonneau that's definite; he's been after me to take her along. But with the baby delivered and her shape back, Lord knows what hard grief she would be to us all. Fact is, I'll see Captain Lewis about it yet tonight. Meanwhile, Frank, you and me will view it as two men who know where we're going to what we're doing. I take you to be a man, you see, and I expect you to behave as one. What do you say?"

Well, in truth what might I say? That I hated him? That he was a base liar? That I figured he was trying to throw me off the scent, while he ran it hot and heavy? I knew

150

better than that.

The fact the Shoshone girl had a deep feeling for this stout red-headed captain did not enter him into the same guilty column. Captain William Clark thought first of his men and his mission, and no Indian girl would change that.

"I say I'm sorry, *Patron,*" I admitted, head hung. "It's a bad thing to feel as I do about that girl. It makes me unequal to your trust in me."

"You'll get past that stage of it," he told me. "Work will do wonders meanwhile. And that I can give you."

He was as good as his word. He put such labor upon me that the wonder was I lived, much less thought of love. He kept me by his side, sleeping and waking. Our days together were sixteen and eighteen hours long. I even forgot the days altogether. They slid into weeks, and the weeks into months, and still he drove me.

When there came a day too bitter of weather for work, he would take me hunting. Often, on these trips, we would be away from the fort overnight, or even several nights, sleeping as we could in the open where darkness found us. One night the temperature on Captain Lewis's gauge was twenty-one degrees below zero when we dug our sleeping holes in the snow, and when we burrowed out the next morning the mercury stood at thirty-eight degrees below. It was on the next hunt, December 17th, that the cold fell forty-five degrees below zero, seventy-four degrees below the freezeline. We barely got back alive to the fort and would have died had such weather caught us farther off than we were. As it was, fifteen Indians froze to death in open camps that terrible night, and Captain Clark was treating frostbite victims the whole of the following day.

151

He saved many a blackened limb for the Mandans, too, and his reputation climbed mightily among them.

When the cursed northern winter gripped the land in this deathhold of subfrost, when neither timber nor hunting parties might be abroad, Clark still had work to spare. These times I would be put to sorting coal for the blacksmiths, and carrying it to the smithing forges, stoking their tempering fires, manning their bellows, whatever hot and dirty work needed doing.

These smiths were engaged in making war axes for the Mandans, who would trade nearly anything for one of the cheap iron weapons. Indeed, even for a 4x4-inch scrap of sheet metal, they would give eight gallons of corn. For an axe they would offer a complete storage hole of unshelled ears. Of course, when such whole grain arrived, it needed to be shelled off the cob and quite naturally Frank Rivet was given this privilege, too.

In the very heart of this terrible cold we were amazed to have an English visitor from Assiniboine River, a Mr. Hugh Heney, who had traveled nine days by dogsled with two Indian companions through this hell of glare ice and killing frost. He proved an extremely lively fellow and Captain Lewis entertained him much. With my half-breed's suspicious nature I doubted the validity of any such Canadian North West or Hudson's Bay company employee, and it was a fact that when Mr. Hugh Heney departed back into the snowy north, it was not three days when Charbonneau again disappeared, this time seemingly for good. The Mandan chief Black Cat advised Captain Lewis that Charbonneau had a history of friendliness with the British, but Lewis would have none of such "unfounded camp gossip."

For myself, the news that the squawman was gone again only reminded me of his wife. I longed forthwith to go and see Sacajawea once more. Clark had the antidote for that.

He put me with the carpentering crew finishing the interiors of the fort rooms. The last of this labor was done December 24th, Christmas Eve. Clark told the Mandans who visited us incessantly, that the next day was a holy day for white men and that the Indians must not come to the fort. He then shut the gates, issued two gills of whiskey per man and ordered a company dance. All hands fell to singing carols and trading their entire winter's pay or dearest possession for the next man's issue of liquor. I was able to deal off my own two cups of the poison to good friend George Shannon for a beautiful Kentucky rifle which thence forward was my constant comrade of the trail. Christmas day we all rested.

Next dawn the slave labor resumed, Clark this time detailing me to a forage unit sent to help the Mandans cut green cottonwood boughs for feeding their horses through the period of intense cold. It was remarkable how these little Indian ponies would stay fat on the tough, fibrous sticks of wood, but they did so. Considering that their adoring owners kept them in their lodges with them the winter through, these Mandan mounts were among the most interesting things about that gentle and cultured people. It was no wonder the Sioux coveted such animals and no wonder the British traders would come nine days by dogsled from Assiniboine River or three weeks by snowshoe from Turtle Mountain, to dicker for these pampered yet indestructible small brutes which could "run like

153

foxes and fight like wolves."

Still, by the time I had frostbitten my finger and cut my hands four times with the harvesting knife to feed the shaggy devils their damnable twigs, I would not have traded one gallon of shelled corn for a Mandan lodgeful of them.

But things were only commencing to tighten. When we had "hayed in" enough "boughs" to keep the little brutes temporarily from starving, I thought to sneak away from the fort to see for myself if Charbonneau were truly away from home. Clark of course, caught me at the gate. He had his squad of eight armed men behind him in marching order, and I knew trouble was somewhere not far from Fort Mandan.

"*Bon jour, Patron,*" I greeted him warily, "what is it that threatens?"

"Oh, nothing much, Frank!' He waved. "We hear there's some Sioux about and we're heading down to the south cache to pick up a load of meat in case it's true."

I noted then that the men were dragging the meat sled.

"Where is your black packhorse, *Patron?*" I asked, not seeing York. "Has he finally run off with the Indians?"

"No, but you're warm. He was in more trouble with some Mandan's wife last night. Captain Lewis has him under key for the day. Fall in."

"Fall in, *Patron?* Me?"

"You. With York locked up, you're the only scout I've got left. Shannon and the others are all out looking for Charbonneau. Step lively now All right, men, follow me."

I set off by his side, not unflattered even though circumvented. I nodded with some show of esprit, even.

"You may count on *my* lively step, *Patron,*" I said.

"I'll bet I can," he promised with a side look. "Especially if these Sioux turn out to be the Teton, eh?"

I dropped the grin and said no more. Somehow, Captain Clark always arranged to have the last worthwhile word.

26

To hold our meat supplies we had built stout pens of logs, strong enough to keep out bears and other prowling beasts. These were like hog pens roofed over and with trapdoors of solid planking which Clark kept under padlock and key. We had six of these meathouses scattered up and down the river and, since the one we were to visit was the principal one of them all, Clark had asked for some Mandan horses to help haul back our heavy sled. These animals and their three owners met us outside the fort a short ways, the whole party going cautiously down the north bank to the cache. I worked out ahead, with one of the Mandans. His name was Shahaka. It meant The Big White, and he was the first chief of the lower village. He was reputed to be a scout of note. I guess he had been told the same lie about me, for the truth was that both of us talked a great deal in French and smoked a respectable amount of tobacco and neither of us so much as suspected an enemy to be within smokedrift. In fact, we walked squarely into the waiting circle of Teton Sioux war party at the cache, still talking and puffing at our pipes.

"Greetings," signed the Sioux leader, a knife-cut murderer with a smile like a hunting lynx. "You are welcome to our camp." His evil grin widened and he swept a long arm about the clearing which contained the meat cache.

"We've been waiting for you a long time. You took long enough to get down here. Come on, hurry up. Open the trap. We want this meat." By this time he spied Clark and the rest of the company, closer across the ice of the frozen river. "Aha!" He brightened. "Isn't that kind of them? They even thought to bring a sled and some ponies to draw it, so that we would not have to pack the meat on our own horses. Only a Mandan could be so kind."

Shahaka and I exchanged glances, weighing our chances of making a break for it while the Sioux were momentarily distracted by the view of Clark and the meat sled. Evidently the Mandan's mind worked like my own, for when I bolted, he bolted, and we both raced shamelessly as any other two cowards toward the captain and his soldiers.

Although the Sioux fired after us, we took no wounds. However, our flight drew Clark into great trouble. He saw us coming and dashed at once to meet us, which was precisely what the damned Tetons wanted. They had laid up a number of their fellows in ambush of the river crossing, and Clark and our riflemen, running in off the ice, came squarely into this ambush. Of course, Clark fought his way out with truly admirable effect, getting his squad free of the surround with no serious casualties, but all too late, regardless. Before he might prevent it, the Mandan pony owners had given over their mounts to the Sioux and the latter had shot the lock off the meat pen. It was then but the work of five minutes for the Tetons to load the sled with our primest buffalo ribs and sides of elk, leap on the sled and drive it off into the woods yelling and laughing and firing their trade muskets in happy abandon. We were helpless to pursue them with our small band; there had been no less than three dozen of the devils, all well mounted on picked winter ponies.

Hence it was over and done with in ten minutes' time, and all we had to show for our valiant stand-off of the hated Teton was the fact that not a man had been wounded except for Shahaka, who got his injury diving under a down log to hide until the firing fell off.

"Well, boys," said Clark, examining the near-empty meat pen, "there's scarce enough to bother backpacking to the fort. I reckon we'd best just build us up a bonfire and hold a roast elk and hump-rib feed here and now. It's too infernal cold and mean with this wind for us to start back without rest and hot food."

The others agreed, as they always did with "Captain Will."

We began at once to lay the fire and get out the cuts of meat we wanted to roast. We had only begun to spit the frozen meat on green cottonwood boughs when one of the Mandans grunted something in his native tongue, and held up a dark red hand.

"Listen," he said in French.

We all listened. There is something about the sound of the order given in the wilderness among desperate men which commands attention.

And as we listened, so we heard.

The sound was wailing, long-drawn and menacing. It was a sound which has put up the hackles of fear in mankind since the first fire in the first cave. We all recognized it, yet knew, instinctively, that something was strangely different about it—something chillingly odd and

157

wrong. We all looked at the Mandan. Clark, it was, who moved over the Indian's side and said quietly, "Wolves?"

The Mandan shook his head. He was gray with fear.

"Not just wolves," he said. "That is the death-howl sound. They have the madness in them. *Le furieux.*"

"My God," said Clark softly. "Hydrophobia?"

It was Shahaka. who put words to it. *"Oui, Patron,"* he said, *"la hydrophobie.* And coming this way. They have smelled the meat. What must we do?"

Clark shook his head and scowled. We can't run for it. That's the one thing we can't do. They will attack anything that moves."

"That is true," said Shahaka. "Shall we climb into the trees?"

"In this cold? I think not. If they stay around the pen more than an hour or so, we would freeze up in the trees waiting for them to go. No, well have to fight them on the ground—somehow,

"One bite, one scratch," began Shahaka, but Clark cut him off.

"I know that. Be quiet. Think, don't whine."

He ran his eyes around the meat-pen clearing. Even for him the situation was a close thing. I could see the beads of moisture pop and run and freeze solid on his tanned cheeks. The hoarse, unnatural howling of the wolf pack broke suddenly, unexpectedly nearer.

"Captain," I said in English, so as not to alarm the Mandan, "if we are going to make a stand, let us fort up.

"Eh?" he said, almost distractedly. "How's that, boy?"

"The meat pen," I said. "It will hold us all. Let's get into it before those mad devils do."

158

He whirled on me, blue eyes alight.

"By the Lord!" he shouted. "That's it. Grab those Indians before they bolt. Inside, everybody!"

But the idea, if valid, was already too late.

Two of the Mandans, terrified by the burst of nearby howling, suddenly broke and darted for the river. Our men started after them, but Clark bellowed at them to come back, to let the Indians go. This they did, a third nearby howling of the pack bringing them about, white-faced. With the third Mandan, Shahaka, we all ran for the meat pen. Clark stood aside until the last of us were safely into it. Then, just as the rabid pack surged from the dark timber, he scrambled in and slammed shut the overhead trapdoor. The movement was so close to fatal lateness that the reaching jaws of one of the brutes cut six inches of rawhide fringe from the wrist of his hunting coat.

"Did he get you, Captain," I muttered huskily, afraid myself to look at the big-boned wrist.

But Captain Clark was not thinking of himself or his life. He was peering between the unchinked logs of the meat pen, out over the glare of the frozen river.

"Don't worry about me," he said. "Pray for those poor devils out there."

All eyes moved to the six black dots far out on the ice. Two were human dots, we knew. But the four behind the two were animal dots. Wolf dots. We watched, horrified, our own desperate situation for the moment forgotten. We saw the wolves come up to the fleeing Mandans, heard the twin reports of the two muskets, saw two wolves drop to the shots. We then saw the remaining two close on the redmen. There was a flash of knife and of clubbed musket

159

and foam-flecked yellow canine teeth in the pale light of the January sun. The remaining two wolves were killed and left limp upon the river ice. The two Mandans continued toward the dark trees on the far side of the river. But there was a difference now. Now, as they ran, they limped.

"God," said one of the men softly. "So much for praying."

It was in that instant that Shahaka, alone among us not held aghast at the fate of his fellows, cried out to Clark in sudden, strident warning; *"Patron!* Behind you—!"

We all wheeled from the riverward wall of the meat pen, then, and all too late.

We saw the wolf, and saw that it had somehow found an aperture in the pen through which it had forced its body. We stood paralyzed as it singled out Captain Clark and launched itself through the air at his face.

It was then that Shahaka hurled himself between them; and then that we heard the great jaws of the wolf go home in the Mandan's upper chest.

27

All I remembered was the smoke and the roar of my Kentucky rifle. I did not remember shouldering or aiming the long weapon. The heavy bullet of 200 grains struck the attacking wolf behind the left ear, shattering its spine and the base of its inflamed brain.

It died instantly and before it might make one more tearing slash at brave Shahaka's body. As it fell away from the Indian, Shahaka staggered and I leaped to support him.

"Don't touch him!" shouted Clark. I drew back, Sha-

160

haka sinking to the dirt floor. "Move away!" Clark ordered, and I pulled back. He had his horse pistol jerked from its belt scabbard and for a moment I thought he meant to kill Shahaka, either to protect us from the Indian's infection or to spare the poor fellow his own misery of pain and terror. But I was still far from knowing my captain.

The pistol belched its cloud of sooted flame toward the far side of the pen. Then I saw the second wolf halfway through the opening which had been discovered by its mate. Clark's ball took the brute in the face and it died as suddenly as had the first. Its deep-furred body, looking enormous at such near range, remained wedged in the entrance way, which now appeared to be the fault of one log having been chewed away by some marauding bear or wolverine. The dead wolf's carcass blocked this dangerous flaw for the moment and Clark said calmly, "Well, Frank, that was a nice shot you made. Risky but good. Come over here with your powder horn."

I moved to his side.

"Your own shot was not bad either, *Patron*," I told him, still breathing hard. "What about Shahaka, sir?"

"Shahaka is next," he said, unsheathing his knife.

It went quickly and very quietly from there. Only the sibilant breathing of the watching men, and the tooth-set pain noise of the injured Mandan broke the stillness.

Clark opened the fang wounds with his blade, making a crude cross-cut at each mark the wolf had put in Shahaka's skin. When he had the wounds thus incised and bleeding freely, he took snow which had sifted through the open chinks of the log pen and washed the wounds repeatedly,

161

flushing away the blood, scrubbing clean the edges of all the lacerations. He would allow none of us to touch the wound, or to help with the work in any way except to bring him snow He also ordered that none of us touch or go near the old snow from the wound-washing, which he discarded in a neat pile in one corner of the pen. When he had cleansed the fang marks as best he could, he washed his own hands and forearms in fresh snow, and turned to me.

"Now the powder horn, Frank," he said. I gave it to him, unstoppered, and he poured a trail of the black powder into all the wounds, mounding it high at each site. "Flint!" he barked over his shoulder to me and I struck it for him and got the pinch of moss fanned into life and handed it to him. He held its burning small torch, looking down at the dark-eyed Mandan.

"Shahaka," he said, "you must lie still while this medicine works. To help you I am going to have a man set on each of your arms and legs. Do you understand?"

The Mandan shook his head, and I repeated the directions for him in French. The he smiled. "I will need no men on my body. The wolf has bitten me but I am not afraid. I know you, Red Head Chief. Your medicine is strong."

We held him down, nonetheless. Clark lit the gunpowder with the moss *fusée*. It flared and ran. We could hear and smell the cooked flesh. Shahaka writhed beneath us like a red snake, then in a moment lay quiet. We got to our feet.

"From here," said Clark, "he'll need a bigger doctor."

28

On our way back up the river we kept watch for any return of the wolf pack. The rabid brutes had departed after we had shot half a dozen of their mates and the survivors had devoured the wounded brothers still alive. Ten minutes after the close of this bloody meal we were silently crossing the river on the ice, each man praying fervently that no "wolf dots" would appear behind us. They did not, and now we were nearing the fort with still no sign of discovery by the ravening pack.

Just south of the fort we came up with the two Indians who had fled and been attacked and bitten by the wolves. They had stopped to build a fire and examine their hurts. Clark tried to help them, to do for them what he had for Shahaka, but the circumstances were different. Here he had no absolute authority, and the redmen did not have to submit as Shahaka had in the meat pen. Nor would they.

When Shahaka, showed them his chest by way of convincing example of the Red Head Chief's medicine, his two fellows took exception to the fact that he, in their words, looked "like a piece of bullfat which has fallen in the fire," and refused absolutely to allow Clark to come near them. They had, they claimed, big medicine of their own for bites of the mad animal, and this they would trust before any "cooking medicine" of the Red Head Chief.

Shahaka, when queried by Clark as to this mystery cure for hydrophobia, was assured that the Mandan did possess such a medicine, which was made from the pulverized roots of a certain plant. Upon an agreement that Shahaka would procure some of this marvelous compound for Clark, our captain reluctantly permitted the two bitten Indians to stay by their trail fire, untreated. After we had gone on a ways, I asked him privately if he thought such a miracle—a medicinal cure for the bite and resultant disease which had held humanity in dread for centuries—did, indeed, or could possibly, indeed, exist here among the Mandan, and he only shook his head grimly.

"Frank," he said, "roots or no roots, I wouldn't trade places with those poor devils for all of the Louisiana and the Columbia and Canada together, with a guaranteed map of the Northwest Passage thrown in. Inside thirty days they'll start the first signs. Then you won't even be able to say, 'God help them,' because not God, nor nobody, can help them then."

"How about Shahaka?' I asked.

"Shahaka's got a good chance. We got him fast and scrubbed him deep and burnt him severe. He'll live, I'd say."

We talked no more then, for uptrail we saw a familiar figure approaching on a sharp dogtrot. It was Charbonneau, shown up again and carrying urgent news for our blunt-jawed company "physician."

"Can you come, *Capitaine?*" He panted. "It is Sacajawea. Her time has come, but the baby will not move out."

I could see Clark's ruddy color lighten.

"How long has she labored?" he said.

"Since this morning."

"My God, man it's four o'clock in the afternoon!"

"*Oui, Patron;* that's why I have come for you."

164

"Why not sooner?" demanded Clark, hard-eyed.

"I have been away, *Patron*. Only this noon did I come back. You know I have been trying to find out something about the British for you."

Again Clark eyed him.

"Yes," he said icily. "Either that, or something about us for the British, eh?"

"*Patron!*"

"Shut up," said Clark, "and lead the way."

Clark got the baby that night. He did it with the potion of crushed rattlesnake buttons which was Indian medicine, pure and simple. Sacajawea, fourteen hours in hard labor, the baby coming breech-to and her first child, had been near death from exhaustion. Clark gave the powdered rattles only in final desperation. He had no idea they might work. And who but God can say? The fact remains that twelve minutes after their administration the young wife of Toussaint Charbonneau was cleanly delivered of a healthy male child. We all thanked *le bon Dieu,* except the weary and triumphant Clark. The latter came to me outside the snow-whipped tipi of Charbonneau, where, with York, I waited hunched beneath my winter furs, and said, "It's a boy. I've named him Pompey for Roman reasons." When, in response to this news, I breathed thanks to our deity, he grimaced and added, "If you want to thank any god, thank that of the Indians. It was that red recipe of those rattler buttons that delivered her. They do what the Indians told us. You never saw such smooth and strong contractions of big muscle in your life."

That was William Clark: engineer, doctor, soldier, frontiersman, midwife, chemist, mechanic, boatman, cartographer, Indian fighter, Indian lover, explorer, plainsman, river pilot, simple believer and captain of American Presidents. What Clark could not do, was not worth doing. Somehow, though, his comment struck me as callous. "Why didn't you name him Frank, or Bill or Meriwether?" I complained. "You know, something to remember at least one of us. What has Pompey got to do with it?"

Clark didn't seem to hear.

He struck one knotted fist against the other, eyes blazing with pride.

"Pomp," he repeated, as though to himself. "My boy, Pomp. By God, but I'm glad."

Well, I was happy as well, I suppose. Yet, from the moment when her child became an actuality, the Shoshone girl, as I saw her, was indeed Charbonneau's, but Clark's by right of saving. Their claims to him, also gave the two men claims to Sacajawea, which I might not share. The thought would not leave me. It stayed with me all of the following month of February, into the first week of March and the breaking up of the river ice; then, toward mid-March and the threshold of that springtime which would see us embarked again up the Missouri into the unknown territories of the Assiniboin, the Sioux, the Absaroka and the Snake. In the whole time I did not go near Sacajawea, or the cowhide lodge of Toussaint Charbonneau. I worked with my captains and my comrades, trying to forget the girl, in preparing for the continuance of the adventure. The effort was heroic but absurd. There was no hour of it in which the memory of the haunting dark gray eyes did not follow me.

There were diversions, true. For example, that notable

eighth of March, upon which we received word that the great Le Borgne had come down to the Black Cat's village and wanted to see the American captains. Both captains, York, myself, Charbonneau, and six picked men of our company composed the party which went up to the lodge of the Mandan to meet with the famed "One-Eyed" chief of the savage Minnetaree. We were seated by rank, which gave me the very good position of being to the left of Clark, while York crouched, as ever, to his right.

The council was to begin, as always, with the pipe-smoking by all white and Indian hands of the great aromatic tobacco of the Americans. But the instant that Le Borgne stalked into the lodge and saw York, the visiting chief literally dropped his pipe and his reaching tobacco-hand, to stare in disbelief. This condition was compounded when, under the prodding of the Minnetaree's stare, the giant slave uncoiled his near seven feet of black bone and muscle to "stand for examination," as his master succinctly put it.

Le Borgne was totally bemused.

He walked around and around York. He measured him with his spread arms for width, and with his rifle barrel for height. He felt of the kinky wool which capped his bullet head, then tried rubbing off his black color by spitting on his own finger and scrubbing vigorously with them on the slave's hide. When York's pigment failed to come off, Le Borgne pronounced the towering slave a bona fide wonder and offered Captain Clark twelve prime ponies and two virgin daughters for him. Clark did not accept the deal and, after another hour of smoking up our tobacco, the Minnetaree leader got up from the fire and without another

167

word of thanks or farewell stalked out of Black Cat's lodge.

Immediately after his exit there was a commotion outside the lodge and a very frightened Indian woman ran inside from the village street and prostrated herself before Lewis, who was still seated with Black Cat.

This woman, Black Cat nervously informed Lewis, was one of the wives of Le Borgne. She had deserted the head chief in favor of a man who had been her lover before she wed the One-Eyed. Now the man had abandoned her and she had been hiding from Le Borgne's embarrassed anger in her father's lodge. Thinking to gain some intercession from the American captains, apparently, she had come to Black Cat's lodge in this reckless manner.

Almost before this could be told Lewis, Le Borgne himself had come back into the lodge to stand looking calmly at his faithless mate. Seeming to dismiss her, he sat down again and smoked an entire pipe with Lewis and Black Cat, passing the time in discussion of Indian morals in such matter. He explained that to steal a wife was a transgression which might ordinarily be settled by a gift of a good horse to the insulted husband by the repentant thief. Another moderate settlement might be achieved where the errant wife admitted her sin and claimed sorrow for it. Indeed, said the Minnetaree chief, he had so forgiven another wife not long ago. She was quite young and had eloped with a youth of her own years. Feeling herself wrong, she had returned voluntarily to Le Borgne. He had then sent for the guilty young man who naturally feared the worst. However, Le Borgne had only asked him and the young wife if they still loved one another, and when they honestly and bravely admitted that they did, he had told them to go with his blessings and be happy, and he added that he had even given them a fat young mare to carry their belongings. At the same time, he wanted the white captains to understand that a situation like this present one with the older wife was another kettle of boiled dog altogether. When a man and a woman made a voluntary elopement and then the man spurned the woman, the husband's honor was placed in an impossible shadow. Some discipline must be visited upon the woman in these cases, Le Borgne now stated, and he hoped the Americans would excuse him while he carried out this necessary punishment.

Thinking he meant merely to whip the woman, shameful treatment but not serious, Clark and Lewis nodded their agreement. Le Borgne, taking the piteously weeping wife by the hair, led her to the doorway of the lodge and there killed her with a single blow of his tomahawk, letting the body fall across the entrance. Stepping over it, he said to Black Cat, and as calmly as he had talked with Lewis and Clark, "She was a Mandan, Pocopsahe. If any of her relatives wish to look for me, I will be in my lodge." Amazingly, Black Cat only replied, "No one will come from my people; the woman was wrong."

There they left it and there Clark told Lewis we would be wisest to leave it. All of us returned to the fort not very hungry for the noon meal.

Other "diversions," and some as fearsome, followed the killing of Le Borgne's wife.

On the following day, March 9th, one of the Indians who had been bitten by the wolves complained of stiffness in the neck and an inability to swallow water. Recognizing the dread signs, the brave Mandan went into the timber beyond the village and shot himself through the head. His fellows burned the body and buried the ashes deep in the forest.

Clark explained to me that the delay in symptoms developing was probably due to the fact the fellow had been bitten in the legs, the poison thus taking longer to travel "to the brain." He said that evidently the other Mandan had not taken the disease. But he was wrong.

Three days later, March 12th, the second of the bitten Indians felt the stiffness and the morbid fear of taking water. Moreover, he showed in the deep, odd croaking of his voice that terrible "sign" which marks the disease in its furious stage. Taking the warning, his fellow Mandans bore the poor fellow on a willow matting to the nearest of our empty meat pens, and there they imprisoned him in the freezing cold, no cover but the stout boards of the trapdoor, no bed but the mothy wool of an old Buffalo robe. He began to cry out like a wolf in eight hours. By nightfall he was foaming at the mouth and biting the wooden pales of his cage. He died in unspeakable torture during the black-cold belly of the following night. The Mandan heaped dried faggots on the pen and burned it to the ground. They then carried all its ashes to the river and let them be "made clean again" by the Mini Sosi, the mud-painted waters of their Mother Missouri.

Shahaka, the chief Clark had treated, remained well and of good spirit. "Fool's luck," Clark called it, but the awed Mandans knew better. From that day no least wish of the Red Head Chief went untended among them.

In three days, March 15th, Charbonneau disappeared

again. Two days later Shahaka, moved apparently by a gratitude, came to report that he had seen him meet four British agents in the forest. More, he had risked his life to creep in close and hear what was being said. And what was being said was that Charbonneau should desert the Americans after leading them astray when they went on, and that he should work among the Mandan, meanwhile, to incite them to revolt against the Americans even before the expedition might again move on.

Faced with this information upon his return, Charbonneau unexpectedly confessed and Captain Lewis, even more unexpectedly, forgave him and rehired him as our Minnetaree guide and interpreter.

To my astonishment, Captain Clark agreed.

"Don't fret, Frank," he replied grinning, when I had made known my outrage at this leniency, "A thief took in the act most often makes the holiest saint of all. From here, old Toussaint will be so feared we're trailing him, he'll likely behave pure and mild as sweet milk. Besides, I'm going to take along a little antidote to make certain he don't clabber up on us again."

When I pressed him for the answer to this "insurance," he ginned again, and shrugged in his simple way.

"It's Shahaka," he said. "I'm asking Captain Lewis to sign him on as our guide to the Snake country. Shahaka claims he's been there, all the way to the Big Rock Mountains, and Charbonneau ain't. The captain won't be too keen, but he'll give in. He's a mite doubtful of Indians, you'll recall."

"Yes," I nodded, "and half-Indians, too!' Clark passed the remark by and we said no more.

171

29

The days were now spent increasingly in the work of preparation to travel on. The men wove boat cords and towropes of wound grass and braided elkhide. Others toiled at building the six new small canoes which, with our two old pirogues, would compose the fleet for our renewed assault on the Upper Missouri. The big keelboat, with Warfington's squad of soldiers and French *engagés* of Baptiste Deschamps, would go down to St. Louis when we departed upstream, bearing all the various trophies of the expedition to this point back to President Jefferson. In all this accelerated labor, personal affairs languished; we were eager to be off and sailing once more for the Columbia country with the advent of spring.

It was March 20th, I think, when I first heard of Sacajawea's illness. Knowing Clark had been visiting her the past day or so, I confronted him immediately. I assumed his calls had been in his capacity of company physician, and so demanded to know the worst. Unhappily, he was prepared to give it to me.

"I will tell you something, Frank," he answered bluntly. "If we cannot determine what ails that girl, she's going to die. I halfways think, for that matter, that she wants to."

"To die?" I cried. "But why, in God's name?"

"I can only guess; I think it's something to do with her getting left behind when we go. Listen, boy, she seems to have a particular attachment for you, maybe you could get her to tell us what's wrong."

"I would try it, *Patron,*" I agreed, frowning. "But if she

172

won't talk to you, who we know she—"

"Bother that nonsense!" he snapped. "Damn it, Frank, we're faced with keeping a fine young girl from dying!"

"Yes, sir," I submitted, coloring. "I'll try, Captain."

"Good boy!" he said, thumping my shoulder bruisingly. "Now be off with you and make her talk. We haven't much time and neither has she."

I left him and went down to the lodge of Charbonneau and called out to know if Frank Rivet might enter.

At once the wondrous voice, grown distressfully weak, answered that "Brother Frank" was always welcome in that tipi, as in the heart of she who lived within it.

I nearly wept. But, controlling myself, I entered. I would have thought myself prepared for anything, but I was not. Sacajawea, that child of beauty and desire, lay haggard and hollow-eyed. She looked old and ugly. There was, too, in the close confines of that cowhide lodge, the unmistakable air of morbid disease and of death not far off.

"What is this, Sister?" I asked, forcing myself to smile. "Do you pine away here because the captains will leave you behind? Because now you will not see your brother who is the young chief. What was his name, now—"

She looked away from me. I saw the shine of the tears.

"Cameahwait," she answered softly. "His name is Cameahwait."

"Oh, yes, Cameahwait," I said, though I had never heard the name before. "And you did say he was the second chief?" I talked only to distract her, to get her mind at ease, but she replied with quick, low-voiced pride.

"He is now the first chief," she said. "Since I have been ill, Wahiki has heard secretly from the Assiniboin that the

173

old chief is dead—Kooskiah is dead—and that Cameah-wait has been named Grand Chief of the Shoshone in his place. But you must say nothing, Brother Frank. I have pledged Wahiki, also. I would not want Cameahwait to hear of my shame, to know his little sister has been left behind by the white captains."

I sank to her side, taking her thin hand in mine.

"Sacajawea," I pleaded, "is there no way that I may help you? Take a message to Cameahwait, anything?"

She shook her head, and I saw the new tears roll.

"If I cannot go with the Red Head Chief and with you, Brother Frank, I would rather die."

"But you have the baby, now. Surely, you will live for his sake. You must do it, you must live. Please!"

"I will live," she murmured, "when you have come back and told me that Captain Clark will take me with him."

It was hopeless, but I nodded as if it were not.

"And if I promise to go see him this moment, will you begin to smile and to fight for your life?"

"I will," she signed," when you return with his word."

I could force no more from her. True Indian, having stated her position, she would not alter it, nor repeat it, nor defend it. I stood up at last to go. In my heart I realized I would not have the courage to return with Clark's denial. When I moved to the entrance flaps, pausing for the final backward glance, I knew that I would not see her again.

"Good-bye Sacajawea," I whispered.

Outside, the cold of the March wind and the wet snow was no colder than the fear which clutched my heart.

At the fort, and only to be true to her commissioning of

me as her *coureur d'amour,* I sought out Captain Clark. Spying York on post outside the door of Captain Lewis's quarters, I asked after his master and was told a conference of great urgency went forward within at this instant.

"Concerning what?" I said quickly.

"The big ice start to break," said York. "The whole damn river she begin to flow pretty quick."

I could hear the river ice grinding. If not yet truly open, the Missouri had commenced to loosen—the sign we had all been awaiting.

"Who all is inside?" I demanded.

"Cap'n Lewis, Cap'n Clark, old Charbonneau, Big Bat Deschamps, all sergeants. They even got Shahaka in there. Hell, everybody. Big meeting, Mister Frank."

"Any notion what it's about, other than the ice?"

"Sure, Cap'n Clark says they ain't yet figger no way to make sure they get horses for the portage over the Big Rock Mountains. That's the main thing they're cracking about. How abouten them packhorses?"

"Damn!" I said. "I thought it was a granted fact we would get the horses from the Shoshone—that they had all the horses there were, or are, out there in that country."

"Sure, sure, but that ain't the problem, Cap'n Clark say. It ain't just finding them Injuns, it's separating them from them horses. We cain't move less'n we figgers some way to talk them Injuns inter helping us."

I knew that. Men could not move our heavy goods over the high passes. For that, only horses would do. Scowlingly, I started past him.

"Well," I said, "I've no help for that. All I can add to their gloom is my own bit of bad news. Sacajawea's dying."

"Oh, no," said York, dark face clouding. "Is she sure enough agoing to die, Mister Frank? Pore little thing."

"She will die," I said grimly, "unless I can get Captain Lewis to let her go along with us."

York shook his head. "It ain't only him," he said. "Cap'n Clark don't want her going along neither!"

"I realize that, God knows," I muttered bitterly.

"Too bad," said York, "that Sacajawea ain't the Injun the captains is looking for. You know, the one to go along and talk them Snakes out'n their horses. But we's got to get us some big chief what draws abouten eight feet of water with them Shoshone for that job. Ain't agoing to do us no damn good dragging out some pore little old sick squaw gal what they ain't seen for five years and who wasn't nobody in particular amongst them nohow. Ain't that so, Mister Frank?"

Of a sudden the great light broke.

Intelligence flooded the dark corners of my French-Pawnee brain.

"My God, York" I yelled, "if you weren't so ugly, I would kiss you! Here, hell, I'll kiss you anyway." I did so, too, and then shouted, "God bless you, black genie. Stand aside!"

Within the surprised council room, I was received with all the respect and accommodation of an idiot. Captain Lewis ordered me thrown out and it was only Clark's intercession which spared me long enough to speak.

"*Patron*," I gasped to the latter, "may I please ask of Shahaka and Charbonneau one single Indian question?"

"Go ahead," said Clark. "Be brief, Frank. We're in serious business here."

"And I, Captain!" I cried. "Listen to this."

176

I wheeled upon the Mandan and the French squawman.

"*Mes amis,*" I ordered, "tell me at once, and without second thoughts, who is the Grand Chief of all the Shoshones?"

Shahaka and Charbonneau stared at me with near-equal degrees of compassion. It was the Mandan, because he like dme, who answered for both.

"It was until very recently the old chief, Kooskiah," he said. "But he has just died this past moon, the Assiniboin say. The new Grand Chief is a very young man. His name is Cameahwait. We do not know him."

"Aha!" I shouted. "You do not know him and neither does Charbonneau, or any man, red or white, in this room or in the Mandan villages. Am I correct? Do you deny it?"

"Are you preparing to tell us, Rivet," interrupted Lewis sharply, "that you *do* know this new Shoshone Grand Chief?"

"No, sir," I returned boldly. "But I am prepared to tell you, if you will grant me the opportunity, that I know his sister."

Lewis's face froze. "His *sister?*" he said icily. "This better be no joke, Rivet. Your age won't save you again."

"I'm not here to save myself, Captain," I answered him defiantly. "I'm here to save you; I've brought you your Shoshone horses, sir."

Clark, who had been watching intently now moved in.

"Out with it, Frank," he said severely. "You've beat around the bush quite long enough. Speak up."

"Yes, sir, and thank God for the chance to do so," I said, facing Lewis rashly. "It's Charbonneau's squaw, *Patron,* young Sacajawea; she's the one that's Cameahwait's sister."

The silence in that room was thunderous. No man there, American, French, or Mandan, but understood instantly the historic significance of the discovery.

With the long-lost "little sister" of the Shoshone Grand Chief guiding our party into the land of her fierce and war-like people, the expedition's crucial problem of portage from the headwaters of the Missouri, to those of the mighty Columbia River in the far side of the Big Rock Mountains, was as good as solved. Thanks to Sacajawea we would get those good Shoshone horses, and get them in friendship and gratitude for our returning the child so brutally stolen by the cruel Minnetarees, blood enemies of the Snake people. She was a better pawn than any big chief; a bigger bargain than ten Charbonneaus. She was, in effect, our passport into the land of the Shoshone.

Clark simply took my hand, rugged face bright with pride. "Frank," he said, "by damn, boy, you're *my* Pawnee!"

BOOK V
AWAY TO THE
BIG ROCK MOUNTAINS

30

I was not permitted to bear the news to Sacajawea, this being considered the province of Charbonneau. But Clark was subsequently able to tell me he had never witnessed so startling a change as that which took place in the Shoshone girl when informed she had been accepted back into the company. She began to gain and in only four days was out of her couch doing light work about the lodge.

"She wants to live now as bad as she wanted to die before," Clark told me. "It didn't hurt any, either, when I told her it was you got her the chance to go along."

I blushed and thanked him, but still got no opportunity to see Sacajawea for myself. However, this was no fault of Clark's. The crowded business of our departure simply would not make room for such errands.

It was March 25th, I have said, when the river began to break up in the main channel. It was in the aching cold blackness of the morning of March 30th, about 2 A.M., when the fort was brought awake by a tremendous vibrating of the ground and, then, a shattering, monstrous explosion. Half our numbers ran out into the compound, pantless. The other half stayed in its blankets and hoped they had not heard what they had heard. Outside, it was coal-seam dark, but Charbonneau called out from his bivouac by the gate that it was no earthquake, no end of the world, but only the "bore ice" going out of the great West Bend above the villages of the Mandan.

"*Sacristi,*" he shouted excitedly, "that's the old big jam herself! By God, that will break her old boudins loose. Now you will see, *mes amis*. Now the Grand Missouri will show you how to open a channel. God's name! By daylight that damn river she will be up one foot of water!"

Next morning with first dawn Captain Clark was down at the main bank checking his rise-and-fall gauge. York and I, accompanying him by order, shivered in the chill

179

frost and cursed the damned Frenchman for a filthy liar. But when the captain came back up the bank a moment later, he was waving the gauge stick jubilantly and shouting, "Eleven inches, by thunder, eleven inches!" So Charbonneau was a scoundrel by only one inch.

And the river continued to rise. Nine inches that day; five inches that night. With daybreak of the thirty-first we had over two feet of new channel draft in twenty-four hours.

The normally sedate Lewis joined rough Clark in uncloaked expressions of joy at this release of the bore jam. It meant we should have "traveling water" ten days ahead of season's expectancy. When, on that same thirty-first, just at twilight, we heard a high, thinly crying string of Canada geese working northward overhead every man in the company felt his hackles rise in concert with Captain Clark's flow gauge.

Next day, April 1st, nature put the seal on her certainty of the early start by sending the first rainfall since October 15, 1804. Now the upstream snow-melt would be on in earnest. The Missouri would grow swiftly deeper with each passing hour. Winter was finally departed. The great gray goose had come again. The rare sweet smells of the new spring were flooding down the turgid mother stream. The cargoes, both for our own elated Columbia party and the dejected St. Louis returnees, were stowed and battened. The Mandan and Minnetaree farewells were said. Detailed last-moment rechecking of all items and itineraries was completed.

By sunset of Saturday, April 6, 1805, we were ready.

This would be our last sleep at Fort Mandan. There remained only the matter of releasing and reading aloud at

180

company assembly the carefully selected names of the crew to go north, a formality only, which would be performed after Sunday services on the morrow.

Before God, what wondrous dreams there were that night!

31

With the mishaps which always plague a departure, our pirogues were not ready to leave Fort Mandan until late Sunday afternoon. Postponed, also, was the reading of the company roll. It was four o'clock, the big keelboat destined for St. Louis loaded and manned, when Captain Lewis had the sergeants assemble the full complement at the fort landing.

Sergeant Patrick Gass, who had taken poor Floyd's place, read the orders for the upriver party in a loud clear voice: "Sergeants: Gass, Ordway, Pryor; Privates: Bratton, Colter, Collins, Cruzatte, Frazier, R. Fields, J. Fields, Gibson, Goodrich, Hall, Howard, LePage, Labiche, M'Neal, Potts, Shields, Shannon, Thompson, Werner, Willard, Windsor, Whitehouse, Wiser; Black servant, York; Interpreters: Drewyer, Charbonneau; also, the wife of Charbonneau, and young child; Mandan Indian guide, Shahaka . . ."

I waited through a moment of crushing stillness, but no more names were spoken. Gass was furling the scroll. The men were forming up to go aboard the six canoes and two pirogues that composed the new fleet. Black Cat and all his tribesmen, down to see us off, began crowding in upon the beach. I stood alone, stunned.

Presently York came up to me, dark eyes shining with

compassion. He started to speak but got only so far as, "Mister Frank, this old heart beat mighty sad for you"—when Captain Clark followed him and dismissed him.

"Frank," the latter then said, "I done all that I could for you. Captain Lewis simply refused me. He said there never was any question of you going beyond the Mandan, His position is that your return to La Charrette and your aunt and uncle is incumbent upon him as commander. As co-commander, I put your case as best I could, but you can see it wasn't good enough, lad. I'm sorry," he concluded, "there's nought more I can do."

"But why? Why, for God's love?" I cried, "If I was to go back, why keep me in this hell all winter? Why did I not get sent back last autumn with Old Dorion? It was assumed I would go all the way with you, *Patron*. Everyone believed it."

"Yes." he said, "including me, Frank."

I began to shout. My spirit cried out that a forceful stand would yet win me my rightful place among the north-sailing company. But if I thought to overwhelm Clark, I had reckoned without the other captain. Meriwether Lewis came up on the trot from the beach and readied boats. As always, he spoke evenly and carefully, neither condemning nor praising nor palliating, but merely stating the case and its disposal.

"Rivet," he said, "we have given your position every consideration. We can find no place for you in this expedition. You have served us well, particularly in the matter of the Teton Sioux, and I will provide you with a citation to this effect. However, other brave and good men, too, are being sent back. Our reasons are plain. From this point, each man must be selected for a special service capability. I give you in example Charbonneau, Drewyer, Shannon, Shahaka. As for your father, lad, we shall do all in our power to locate him, and you must know that Captain Clark and myself can certainly attend the case of Achille Rivet better than you personally might hope to."

He paused, since I would not look up at him nor give any sign of understanding.

"He has a very hard head, Captain," I heard Clark say quietly, and I could envision Lewis's brief nod.

"Rivet," demanded the latter now, "have you nothing to say?"

I raised my head only so far as to stare at his chest.

"Yes, sir," I responded, "you may keep your citation; I don't want it."

"Lad," said Clark, touching my arm, "that was an unkind thing to say."

"Let him be, Captain," said Lewis. "It's a hard blow."

Clark moved half a step forward. "He could still go, Captain," he suggested. "Let him mess with Charbonneau and Shahaka. I've spoken to Charbonneau about it. The old man says, 'oui-da,' yes, indeed. As for Shahaka, you know he's fond of the boy."

"And so," said Lewis curtly, "is Charbonneau's squaw. You know we talked that all out last night and agreed on it. Do we now propose to debate it again?"

"No, sir," said Clark, "we surely don't."

"Good. Now then, Rivet, we want your word that you will go in good faith with Warfington and the Frenchmen back down the river. You know, boy, that you've a poor record for doing what you're told when it comes to boat rides."

183

I merely shook my head obstinately. This captain had been against me from first meeting in La Charrette. I could thank him for nothing—and curse him for plenty.

"Well, boy?"

At last I looked up.

"No, sir," I said angrily, "I will not give you my word."

"Think about it, Rivet. But be quick."

"I've thought, Captain. If you want me to stay behind, you had better shoot me."

"You're saying you'll try to follow us?"

"Not try, Captain—I *will* follow you."

"Corporal Warfington!"

He said it instantly, as if he had planned it this way all along. As well, it seemed that Warfington and his soldiers were upon us almost before Lewis called them.

"Corporal," said Lewis, "put Rivet in arrest. Confine him in leg irons and remand him to the custody of Deschamps on the keelboat. You will not release him until you are three days down the river. Consider him and treat him as a military prisoner meanwhile. Is that clear?"

"Yes, sir," saluted the corporal. "Come along, Frank."

Sunset, and the sad, insane cry of the loon echoed from the still-watered slough to river's west. Chained like a dog to the mast of the big keelboat, I hunched beneath the naked spar and shivered to the bird's eerie call. Off east, the prairie was already darkened by a misting spring ground fog. Westward, the sky was clear above the ragged silhouette of the timber on that bank. Downdeck, the French boatmen lolled about the cabin and tiller. The high water and unobstructed current carried the barge along with small-craft lightness and speed. Updeck, I could see Deschamps seated with Warfington. Their backs were to me, feet braced on the towrope coils in the prow. Off the starboard bow, a hired pirogue with Warfington's soldiers and a local French steersman led the keelboat like a pilot bird. To the larboard, heading the pirogue, was a canoe carrying two friendly Arikara Indians.

"*Oui, mon corporal,*" I heard Big Bat's deep voice say in reply to a question from Warfington, "you are right, of course. I do not intend to run all night. Only so far as this bend that we come to even now. Lay to, Jules! Warp in carefully there. Watch the deadheads."

The helmsman answered smartly, bringing the big boat in to a fine beach. The pirogue and Indian canoe followed quickly. Big Bat roused himself and strolled down toward the mast as the others made to disembark.

"Well, little François," he greeted me loudly "what are you thinking now? Don't tell me. You think that you can escape in some way? What a goose!"

He glanced swiftly updeck to see where the men were, especially Warfington.

"Listen," he said, lowering his voice, give me your word you will try nothing, and I will unchain you after it gets good and dark. You know, François, I must be discreet. The corporal has his orders, naturally."

"Yes, he has," I answered "but I won't lie to you, Bat. You unchain me and I shall flee at first chance. I will die rather than go down river."

"I know, I know," he rumbled. "I would too in your place. They were wrong, the captains were wrong. They had no real reason to send you home."

185

I shook my head.

"I'm not so sure of that," I said. "True, I don't like Captain Lewis and true he despises me, but I believe he is honest, that he does what he thinks is right."

"Well, God's blood! Is that some great triumph to be honest? Christ was honest and look what it gained him. Now, Judas Iscariot was a damned scoundrel, but he made money at it. Where's the choice? You want to be honest and dead, or a filthy bastard with your pockets full of silver?"

"Bat," I admitted, "you are a deep thinker, but never mind that. I need a small favor just now. Give me a moment, unchained, so that I may attend to nature before you go ashore."

He at once unlocked my fetters and led me to the boat's gunwale. "Well, all right," he said. "But come on, hurry up with it, then back to the mast!"

He turned away carelessly for a moment as he gave the order and in that same instant I crouched and sprang to go over the side, leg irons and all. We were in shallow water and I felt I could make it to the bank and into the willows before he might stop me. But the movement of crouching to spring, alerted him and betrayed my hope. He whirled, quick as a panther, and struck me down with a swiping blow of his left forearm. It was a backhand blow, striking my nose and breaking it certainly. I lay helpless on the deck, head spinning.

Big Bat dragged me back to the mast and rechained me to it. He then sloshed a bucket of river water over my head and stared at me disappointedly.

"Muskrat," he said, "you grieve me. I trusted you and

186

you showed treachery. Is this the reward of that honesty we spoke of but a moment gone? Eh? Well, what is it you say, little traitor?"

I shrugged and spat blood toward his boot toes.

"Damn the luck," I said.

"Just that? Nothing else, François?" His voice was grating with resentment. "Well, now, see the pay I get for being kind to you. All the way up this cursed river I looked out for your life. There you were fouling my boat and strutting and puffing out your little métis chest in front of the others, scratching dirt in the face of Baptiste Deschamps. And Baptiste? Hell's name, little water rat, Baptiste was taking care of you every oar sweep of the way. And why? Very simply because your father, Achille, taught me all that I know of the Mother Missouri, and I loved him better than my own father, whom I never knew. Hah! You didn't know that I was a natural child, did you? But I am, yes. And the devil with it. But your father, ah, there was a man! How do you think I felt about not getting to go on with the expedition and help look for him? Eh, monster? And you? How about you? You try to jump over the side and swim for the willows when I show a moment's charity. To make Big Bat a fool once more. Well, no, boy, that's the end of it. You stay on that mast now until we get down to the Rees and maybe even to the Teton Sioux. I will make you understand indebtedness, little water moccasin."

He stormed ashore, following the last of the others. There was already a bonfire and soon there was singing and dancing on the beach. I could smell the coffee before long and then the roast buffalo and the tobacco smoke later on. It made me weak, and very, very sad. There was nothing that I did right.

Finally, one of the soldiers came out to the boat and brought me a bone with a shag or two of meat on it. Also a tin cup of spring water. I thanked him and asked if he were to be my night guard. He said, no, that he believed Deschamps himself was going to "sleep" watch over me. My heart sank at this. The soldier was not too bright a fellow and I felt there would be some reasonable chance to get his gun away from him were he to prove my keeper. But Big Bat slept with the delicate ear of the kit fox, and the quick wits of a wolverine. I drank my cold water and chewed my cold bone and felt all hope drain out of me with the increasing chill of the bottom mists now swirling about the keelboat. It seemed an eternity before Big Bat came aboard and sent the drowsing soldier off to his blankets on the beach.

I tried a little talk with the *patron* but found him not in the mood. When I lonesomely pressed him to know if anyone had given him a farewell or good-speed word of any kind for me, he shrugged and growled that none had. He had not seen Charbonneau or Sacajawea, and York had been busied on some last-moment cargo-shifting for Clark. Shannon had come to see me, of course, and Drewyer and two others of the men. But I supposed, being honest with myself, that it was Sacajawea whom I had expected to come more than any of them. The others were soldiers for the main part and saw things as soldiers. What had befallen me might well have befallen any of them. It was purely a matter of duty's line. But the Shoshone girl? What could be her excuse? Why had she not come to see me? To speak me some word of good will or regret? Or, if nothing more, of gratitude?

For these sorrowful queries I could find no answers. Neither would Big Bat help me look for any. When I made the final attempt to enlist him in conversation, he grunted sleepily and replied, "Look, muskrat, lie down in your dog chains and shut your mouth. I grow weary of your yappings. Moreover, don't be thinking of ways in which you might reach me and get at the key to your padlock. Do you think I am a fool? The key is left on shore with Corporal Warfington. He comes aboard with it in the morning, no sooner.

Meanwhile, I want to sleep and I want you to sleep. So be a good boy and sleep, eh?"

That was the finish of it. I couldn't get another syllable from him and his next answer was a deck-rattling snore. I believe that in that moment, with the leg-iron key out of reach ashore and Big Bat snoring so lustily, that had I gun or blade I would have turned them upon myself, not him. *Aïe Dieu,* what fortune.

Alas, I was no more than I had been in La Charrette that rainy May twelve months past, with no human friend in all the world save one, and he had deserted me along with Sacajawea. Where are you, Captain Clark, I thought, so near and yet so fearsomely far away from me? Do you nod over your fire tonight up there on that other lonely bank above the Mandan towns? Do you think of me as I think of you? Can you hear my lonely heart crying out? Can you feel me calling to you over all these muddy-watered miles between us?

No, you can't. You don't care. You don't hear. You don't feel. For if you did, you would have found some way to

189

send me a message to let me know you cared for Frank Rivet, and that you had not forgotten him in his darkest hour of hopeless need.

An impassioned flood of entreaties of the mind perhaps; but, even so, it was no less startling, no less wild, than its immediate flesh-and-bone materialization.

Beyond Baptiste Deschamps, snaking over the gunwale of the keelboat from the river side, slid a thick black arm. It was followed by a glistening coal-black face and gleaming ivory-toothed grin which lit up the darkness of that fogbound deck of despair as no earthly candle ever could.

I was wrong once more. Clark's message had arrived.

32

York came dripping over the gunwale. He stole across the deck and came to a halt over the slumbering Deschamps. I could see that he carried some weapon in his hand. Frantically I waved my arms to attract his attention. When he looked my way, I motioned him to come over to me. With clear reluctance, he quit his prey, glided to my side.

"Must we harm him?" I whispered. "He has been good to me. Can't you do something else?"

York scowled, thought hard, nodded in halfway agreement.

"Mebbe so," he muttered. "Lemme think."

He squatted down, great jaw buried in one hand. Suddenly he raised his head, his marvelous grin spreading. His other hand at the same moment dived into the pouch which he wore belted about his naked middle.

"Hoo hoo," he said, "I knowed there was something else what I brang along just in case. I surely am pleased that you done reminded me of it, Mister Frank."

"You black scoundrel," I said, "I could strangle you. You're crazy. But you can't help it. What have you brought me? An African good luck charm? A Jefferson medal from Captain Clark?"

The sarcasm, of course, was wasted on him. "Well, now," he said, grinning more broadly, still, "it's from Cap'n Clark, all right, but it sure ain't no African voodoo. This here is plain good old American voodoo. What you think of this, half-breed boy?"

The hand came out of the pouch now, huge black fingers holding up for my closer inspection the brass key to the leg irons which bound me to the mast of the Lewis and Clark keelboat.

"My God," I gasped, "where did you get it? Have you been ashore and killed Corporal Warfington?"

York didn't answer. He was watching Big Bat Deschamps, who stirred slightly in his sleep. Relaxing, the big Negro placed the key on the deck within my reach, his hands silently unfastening the pouch at his waist. I now recognized it as the birdshot pouch of Captain William Clark. As well, I realized it was the weapon with which York had previously meant to assault Big Bat. And not alone previously, but presently, I tried again to gesture him away from the sleeping *patron* but this time he would not heed me. I heard the sodden "tonk" with which the shot pouch met the skull of Baptiste Deschamps, then the small groan with which Big Bat slumped into that other sleep

191

which has no snores.

York returned, dragging the burly *patron* behind him.

"Get them irons off'n your leg, Mister Frank," he commanded. "We got to get shut of here. This ain't no healthy spot for us Pawnees."

I understood his grinning instruction. Removing the irons, I relocked them on Bat, one about his ankle, the other through the eye bolt in the mast.

"He's anchored," I said to York. "Let's decamp."

My companion shook his head, no longer grinning.

"Got to anker his mouth, too, Mister Frank," he muttered.

I watched, astonished, as he gagged Deschamps with the latter's wide belt, trussing him within half a minute so tightly he could not have uttered a mouse's squeak. He then tied his hands behind him with equal speed and skill.

"Where did you learn that?" I challenged him, as he turned to me. "Not following Captain Clark, I'll guarantee."

He wagged his curly head, answering very softly. "I learned that a long time ago in a far-off place," he said. "That's the way them Arab slave hunters cotched us niggers across the water. They hit us on the head and tied us up and throwed us in the bush and left us lay. Sometimes we was there a week. When they came back the pore nigger was a long time dead from no water. Bad times, long, long away, Mister Frank."

"Yes," I said. "I'm very sad to hear it, York."

He came closer to me and put his enormous hand to my arm.

"Don't be sad, Mister Frank," he said. "York's damn

192

glad them Arabs cotch him. Elsewise, however would this nigger have come to know you, and to serve Cap'n Clark?"

We said no more.

I followed him obediently over the side. The water was freezing cold. Now and again we had to push off small blocks and cakes of dirty honeycomb yellow ice still tumbling in the high current. How we made it to the far bank I will never understand. Suffice it that I was nearly dead from the cold when our feet touched bottom and York carried me up out of the water onto a sandspit three-quarters of a mile downstream of the keelboat camp.

Over on this side the mists were thinning. Peering ahead into the alder thicket beyond where we had landed, I thought I saw a fire, and I was right.

"Come along, boy," said York, not able to hide the outright happiness in his voice, "you've got more friends yet to find."

"What?" I cried. "More friends? Me? Here in this wilderness? *Vous avez fait des merveilles!*"

York, who had gained much French the past year, spread his hands deprecatingly.

"Not me, Mister Frank," he said. "I ain't worked no wonders. It's just that us pore dark-blood bastards has got to hang together."

Perforce, and shiveringly, I followed him through the alder tangle toward the cheery beacon of the firelight. When we had come through the screening limbs and stood at the edge of the hidden campsite, I halted, dumbstruck.

Beyond the fire three Indians had risen to greet us. One was faithful Shahaka, the "big scout" of the lower Mandan village. One was homely, bony-faced Wahiki, the Hunkpapa second wife of Toussaint Charbonneau. The other was a slim, haunting-eyed Shoshone squaw, also known to me, and to my lonely heart.

"*Bon soir,*" Brother Frank," said Sacajawea. "Welcome to our tipi."

33

They had brought me a set of Mandan buckskins, the gift of Shahaka. Wahiki furnished a handsome pair of Hunkpapa moccasins. As I changed into the clothing, roast elk tongue was being taken from its spit and the steaming coffeepot removed from the heating stones. While I ate ravenously, the various stories of all concerned with the rescue were told me.

The original idea had been Sacajawea's, her impulse being the simple Indian one of repaying in literal kind any debt; I having been the one to see that she returned to the land of her people, she must be the one to see that I went there also.

She had subsequently sought out the aid of Wahiki, who had felt to be of help because I had been the one to bring black York to see her at Charbonneau's lodge. The next step had been the enlistment of Shahaka and his canoe, the only free craft in the expedition flotilla. This rakish Mandan scow, a hybrid of birch bark and buffalo hide, had been a risky method of transporting four people down the flooding Missouri to ferry back a fifth person, myself, but all had wanted to go, and in the Indian philosophy the want was master to the act. Shahaka had fallen in with the spirit of the conspiracy, he said, because he liked to talk French with me and because we had been great scouts together in the fight with the mad wolves, an event destined to take front rank in Mandan folklore if Shahaka had anything to say about it.

The third arrangement had entailed getting the spare leg-iron key away from Captain Clark. Here, Sacajawea had called in York, who had happily agreed not only to filch the key from his captain, but also to furnish his own great muscles to the adventure. All had gone smoothly from there, and now the sole remaining problem was that of sneaking back upriver and into the sleeping camp of Clark and Lewis without discovery. As York put it: "Happen Cap'n Clark cotch enny of us out'n our blankets come daybreak, we is all disastered."

The Indians concurring this judgment, we kicked out the embers of the fire and made for the beached canoe.

The return voyage missed tragedy half a hundred times. The overloaded craft rode with her sides a bare four inches above water. One cake of ice, one bobbing snag, even a clump of floating bank sod, would have put us under in the racing black cold thunder of wild tides about us. But through some miracle of navigation we made safe landing one-quarter mile below the sleeping camp of the expedition at something like fifteen minutes of four o'clock in the morning of Monday, April 8, 1805.

It was already paling in the east when our craft grounded and we got out of her. There was here, however, a sudden change of spirit on the part of Shahaka. The Mandan chief in repassing his village had grown overwhelmingly homesick. He now informed us that he was going back with

195

Wahiki, and asked Sacajawea to explain his decision to the Red Head Captain and to tell him that Shahaka was sorry to thus leave the party but he could not help the way his heart hurt for his old village when he saw her once more in the night.

Nothing I could say would dissuade him, either. Within five minutes of putting us ashore, he and the bony-faced Hunkpapa squaw had poled the leaky canoe back out into the current and been swept away toward Fort Mandan. York fled as swiftly in the opposite direction to reach Clark's bivouac and replace the stolen key and birdshot pouch ere the red-haired captain might awaken to apprehend him in the act, and I was left alone in the predawn grayness with Sacajawea. For a moment neither of us spoke. We stood awkwardly and looked at one another. Then it was the Shoshone girl who broke the mounting hush.

"Brother Frank," she murmured, "more remains to my debt than this, and I will pay it. You must stay out of sight for one week. You will need to follow us by land during this time. You cannot have a gun, for a shot would not alone warn the captains to look behind them, but it would bring the Indians looking, also. Remember, within this week we enter the Assiniboin country, and they are very bad Indians. They are white-haters always, brother, and they will not provide you time in which to explain to them that your mother was a Pawnee. Do you understand this?"

I nodded mutely, unable to think of what to say.

"Now," she continued, "because you must hide as you travel by day, lest the Assiniboin see you, and you scarce dare light a fire to warm by at night, lest the American captains or their meat hunters see it glow behind them, I have brought you some few things of need."

"*Mais oui,*" I said, "for this. I thank you; but you must not risk further penalty to yourself by serving me in this manner. I forbid it, Sister."

She shrugged, the sad smile lighting her face briefly. "Don't argue, Brother Frank," she said. "That's woman's work."

She then produced from the nearby brush the articles she had brought for me. These contained a sleeping robe of finest winter calfskin, a knife, axe, flint, steel, a food packet of elk jerky and, lastly, a black-and-white eagle feather and an otter-fur warrior's head circlet.

Sacajawea took up these latter ornaments quickly. The light was coming definitely in the east, now, each minute increasing the danger of discovery and, almost certainly in that case, of forced return for both Sacajawea and me to the Mandan villages.

Her swift fingers busied themselves with Indian skill on the lank black locks of my shoulder-length hair. In moments she had dressed that hair into a near-perfect warrior's horsetail braid hanging between my shoulder blades. As quickly, she slashed the eagle feather slantingly through the braid, twisting it into place so that it would fall away and "droop" in that certain Indian way so difficult for the white man to imitate. She then placed the otter-fur headband as it should be worn, and stepped back.

"Now," she said, "from a hilltop far away, you are a 'Big Belly.' That is the Minnetaree feather and headband. If the Assiniboin see you not too closely, they may leave you alone. They are more friendly with the Minnetaree than with the Mandan, which is to say they are more afraid of them."

I took her hands in mine. "Sister," I said, "this Pawnee gives you his heart once again. Will you keep it this time?"

She turned the luminous gray eyes upward, searching my face. Finally, she nodded, taking her hands away.

"For a little while," she said softly, and turned and went quickly toward the screening timber beyond the beach.

That Monday, as I followed on shore, the expedition made fourteen miles on the river. Tuesday, it was twenty-three and a half miles; Wednesday, eighteen and a half miles. Wednesday night's camp was on a willow point of the south bank, just above a looping bend in the river. This was the camp which Lewis named "Little Basin" in the journal.

Next day, Thursday, Clark had the boats going early, and made nineteen miles. The country remained open and difficult for me to find hiding as I traveled. I had to hang far back to avoid detection, this increasing my Indian worries. In the afternoon, late, I saw a band of red horsemen on the south side of the river. They watched Clark and Lewis and our boats, then rode slowly after them for some miles. I recognized them as Assiniboins from the Sioux style of roaching their forehair, or "scalplock," but did not feel inclined to signal them that a Minnetaree "brother" waited opposite them. Still later that afternoon I did have an Indian visitor on my side of the stream, however. It was almost sunset and I was resting in some burned-over scrub in the bottoms waiting for darkness to cover my sneak past the white camp when, suddenly, I heard the brush crackle. Whirling, I waited with drawn knife.

Presently the enemy put his head out of a nearby clump

of tall weeds.

"Ooowwrrr-ruff," he said, and stood there watching me to see if he should run for his life, or advance and be recognized.

"All right," I called softly to him, "give the countersign."

"Aaarr-ruff-arr?" he asked hesitantly.

"That's close enough," I replied. "Welcome to my tipi."

He came out of the brush, skulking cautiously, ready to elude any motion I might make suggestive of the boiling pot, a fate from which he was clearly a starving fugitive. Seeing that he was actually watching my hand with the knife in it, I laughed and put the weapon away. He straightened and wagged his tail the least bit.

"Come on, *mon ami*," I called to him. "Come over and have a sniff of me. I'm no Minnetaree dog-eater. This costume was loaned to me by an Indian friend. Here, look, I'm as white as you are."

I lifted off the otter-fur headband and pulled out the eagle feather.

"See?" I said. "Just as I told you—we're both white."

Well, as a matter of fact, we were both about half white, but equal any way that the color was viewed. My dark French and Pawnee hide was quite as filthy and coated with mud and dust as his own. Also, we were nearly of the same gauntness and desperate state of nerves. But my words seemed to have calmed the newcomer, and he genuinely responded to the removal of the fur browband and the black-and-white feather. It was plain to me that here was a dog which felt very much about Indians as did I. Which was very much against them, indeed.

"Arrowrrr," he said, his mind decided in my favor, and trotted over to me, tail inscribing a happy arc, jaws split in a melting smile of canine delight at finding a safe human friend at last.

I gave him a tentative pat on the head, as Indian dogs are notoriously given to the free and fast bite for any hand extended to them. But he meant what he said and from that moment of our miserable introduction in the burned-over Missouri River bottomlands, the white and ugly-spotted refugee from the Assiniboin boiling pots and Frank Rivet, the La Charrette stowaway, became comrades of inseparable faith.

We sealed the compact an hour later by sharing my supper half a mile upstream of the camp. We did not talk a great deal, since my command of Assiniboin and his of French were somewhat slight. But we managed what half-breed ingenuity we had, and with that unspoken affinity which is the universal loyalty of unwanted fugitives the world over, to make our feelings understood. I called him Omar, which name he seemed to accept.

Friday, to my immense relief, Clark and Lewis went only six miles to the mouth of the Little Missouri River. Here they camped and spent the day in making celestial observations and overhauling canoe bottoms scarred by the shallowing channel of the big river. Omar and I rested. We both had sore feet. The ground over which we had come was bare, rocky, sandy, tough. The grass, even, was tough. It cut like wire. The streams flowing into the Missouri were all rotten with salts and not fit to drink. There was little timber save right on the river. We made many detours in seeking cover for our advance. Oftentimes we traveled more miles than the boats, never did we travel less, and always we were in danger of discovery. That night I went hungry. Omar shared the fast.

Next dawn Clark again had the boats on the water before the sun came. And he sailed them twenty-two and a half miles having a following south wind on his quarter all the daylight hours. The country, again, was hell. But it was tougher and furnished better hiding. We passed through an abandoned Assiniboin village of forty-three temporary lodges. Some of the fire spots were still warm. Omar growled and behaved as though he were seeing red ghosts in every track in the village dust. His hatred for his recent Indian masters seemed surprisingly grand. He made a fine travelmate and steady friend, but I would not have wanted him for an enemy. He had the most enormous tushes I had ever seen on a domestic dog, two and one-half inches long by my guess, and he was quick to show them upon the least excuse. Indeed, this remarkably big and ugly splay-footed, piebald, evil half-wolf of an Assiniboin mongrel was the epitome of the savage hunting companion of primitive man, and it heartened me accordingly to have him by my side.

As the afternoon wore on we witnessed a strangely fearful sight—vast numbers of the carcasses of dead elk and buffalo putrefying along the shores of the Missouri. These beasts, in the literal thousands, had apparently been swept under the ice during the spring and held there entombed until the main bore at Great Bend broke free. They had then been spat out here on these lonely banks to lie in their silent wind-rows. The stench of them and the green-blue hordes of blowflies swarming their ripe putrescence made me quite ill, and even Omar looked a bit pale.

By that evening the river had become more than a mile wide and was running deep and hard. Now, with that devil's luck which had been dogging me the whole of the way on my desperate attempt to stay up with the company and still keep out of sight, Clark chose this night to make his camp on the opposite, north bank. I was too weary and, moreover, angry to attempt the swim over the widened flood by dark. Therefore I lay down for my fitful sleep where I stood on the south bank, vowing to let tomorrow attend its own troubles. Faithful Omar, as was his practice, took the first watch lying with me ear-pricked and alert to any sound of the night. His low growls awoke me after what I thought was but a little while, and I drowsily answered, "All right, all right give me a moment to get my eyes open, will you?" Yet when I did get myself thoroughly aroused, I saw that it was already graying in the east. I saw something else, as well: on a point above the Lewis and Clark camp, on the same north side of the stream, were gathered no less than sixty Indians. By their weapons and the way they sat naked on their painted ponies I understood them to be on the business of war in general. And by their poised attitude above the still-sleeping white camp I could easily guess their specific plan of attack.

The situation admitted of no malingering on my part. It was now for me to decide between self-preservation and duty to comrades who had deserted their duty to me.

The decision was soon made. I was starving. My footgear was gone. My feet were in shreds. I had broken my axe chopping iron-hard driftwood. This was the eighth day from the Mandan villages. We had come, I was certain, well over 100 miles from the lodges of Black Cat and Le Borgne. Baptiste Deschamps, by this time, must be 300 miles down the Missouri with the big barge. How could I be returned, and to what?

It was settled, then. If the captains would send me back from the maw of this lonely, fierce and enemy-ridden territory, they would send me back from the bowels of hell itself.

Voilà tout, I would do it.

Calling Omar after me, I went into the river. The crossing was dangerous. Three times I thought I was gone, but each time I struck a slick of quiet water or a sandbar undersurface which I might float or touch bottom in rest. Omar made nothing of the swim. He was, if part wolf, also part otter. He paddled around at the rest spots, waiting for me with all the confidence and lack of care of a hen mallard circling tired chicks in still slough water. By the time I hauled myself, gray-faced and panting, out upon the north bank I was beginning to wonder if I had not taken up with a *loup-garou,* an unnatural dog of the other world.

Regaining my wind, I struck out up the bank toward the camp. If the Assiniboin were to attack, they would do it in this same gray of the borning day. I quickened my pace to a laboring dogtrot. At the bivouac, I made out Clark's position by recognizing the black bulk of York sprawled near him. Guards were out but they were down at the river watching over the boats. I did not bother with them but went directly to the captain.

"*Patron,*" I whispered, shaking him by the shoulder. "Wake up! It's me, Frank."

"Eh? Who? What—?"

He came up on an elbow, the big horse pistol whipped

out from beneath the blanket and pointed at me. Seeing me, he broke into a totally rewarding grin and said, "Well, God bless you, boy, I am that glad to see you I could cry!" Then swiftly to business. "What the devil did you say?"

"Assiniboins, *Patron!*" I replied. "Half a hundred or more of them. Dire-looking bunch. Mounted and moving this way. They're painted for war, Captain!"

"You certain, Frank?"

"Absolutely."

"Ordway!" he bawled to his sergeant. "Roll out your men. Indians on the prowl."

While the camp aroused, I followed Clark over to Captain Lewis's bedding place. Here, to my joyful surprise, I saw none other than Shahaka coming up on the run with Toussaint Charbonneau. The Mandan's homesickness had proved but passing, and he had rejoined the company that past midnight, only hours ahead of my own return. We were eventually to pay the same price for our absences—with and without leave—of being left out of the journal from Fort Mandan forward. But for the moment we knew only real delight at the reunion. As for Captain Lewis, in the moment we rushed up to him he was just toeing into his moccasins and reaching for his long rifle.

When he spied me it was an uneasy sighting. But before he could say a word Clark had said it for him and had left him no way to go but along with us.

"It's our boy, Frank Rivet, Captain." he announced flatly, "come back to finish out the river with us."

Lewis looked at him long and hard. Clark stood to the challenge, jaw clamped, eyes defiant. At last, to my amazement if not to Clark's, Meriwether Lewis suddenly elevated both hands as though Clark had the big horse pistol stuck in his midriff. I could not say that he smiled but I will swear that he wanted to.

"All right, Will." He bowed. "I surrender. Welcome back, Rivet, but what is this that you've brought with you?"

I glanced behind me to see Omar skulking and baring his fangs silently.

"That's Omar Khayyám, sir," I said. "He's an Indian pointer, sir. Very rare breed. Never misses on the flush."

Lewis tightened his sword belt, picked up his rifle.

"Omar Khayyám, eh?" he said, eyeing me.

"Yes, sir, after the old tentmaker of the same name, sir. I found him wandering in the wilderness and have been sharing my loaf of bread and jug of wine with him."

Lewis nodded.

"That's 'singing,' not 'wandering' in the wilderness, Rivet," he corrected. "Indian pointer, you say? How does he do on Assiniboins of an early April morning?"

"Splendid, sir," I answered. "They're his best bird."

Lewis glanced at the rifle company forming up under Ordway and Pryor and falling to behind Clark and Shahaka and beady-eyed old Toussaint Charbonneau.

"Very well, boy," he said, "let's go and see if he can put us up a fat brace for breakfast."

34

In that Sunday camp of April 14, 1805, we stood 1,721 miles from the confluence of the Missouri with the Mississippi River. The only name for the site was that given it

205

by Shahaka, who called it Two Lean Antelope from the fact that the total game the hunters brought in there was a brace of ribby female "goats."

It might, however, have been given a more noble title by the imaginative Mandan except for the fact that, when we surprised them, the Assiniboins would not fight.

Our rifle squad caught the Indians coming off the bluff trail. They let them start walking their ponies quietly across the meadow and then suddenly presented themselves from among the trees, Captain Lewis, cold as comb ice, in their van. Shahaka stood with him. It was a very big silence.

Then the Mandan chief informed the leader of the Assiniboins that he might save as many lives as the Americans had rifles pointed at his warriors. If he were inclined to believe this and to see things in a reasonable light, there would be no shooting. If he were not friendly and wanted a fight, all he needed to do was to move one hoof of one pony in the direction of the Quiet Chief—Lewis—and his deadly sharpshooters.

The Assiniboin thought it over. They certainly knew who we were and who the Quiet Chief was. In our winter with the Mandans many small bands of Assiniboins had come to see the famous American soldiers and to meet their sturdy captains. This chief had been among those visitors. He remembered the riflemen and he remembered Meriwether Lewis.

The Indians did not like Lewis as they did Clark, and Lewis could not handle them nearly so well in most cases. But in battle pose, in outrightly hostile confrontation such as this present stillness, the Quiet Chief was, if possible, even more effective than the Red Head Chief. The difference with the Indians was the contraposition of fear and affection. Clark liked them, Lewis did not; the red brother understood the distinction keenly.

Little Calf the Younger now decided that the silence had lasted long enough. It came to him that his sixty to our six was not the certain massacre he had envisioned. The element of surprise, always the attacking Indians' greatest weapon, had been lost. His stomach for slaughter on a mutual basis failed him. He nodded to Shahaka, then turned and shouted at his warriors.

"Hopo!" he yelled. *"Hookahey!"*

These were Sioux exhortations amounting to "Come on, let's go someplace else immediately!" and the warriors did not linger to examine the suggestion. Within thirty seconds there was only a lingering drift of pony dust to mark the area from which the murdering band had departed. We did not make light of our easy victory, as might be supposed, but returned at once to camp, struck it swiftly, and ourselves wisely obeyed the injunction to *"Hookahey!"*

It was still barely sunrise when the last of our hastily loaded canoes pushed off from the beach at Two Lean Antelope.

To designate this camp so important to Shahaka and me, and to demark in so doing another of Captain Meriwether Lewis's unsung generous sides, consider the entry in the company journal made by Lewis in which he covers entirely his concept of the importance of our return to the command, together with the importance of my timely warning of the Assiniboin war party and the narrowly averted massacre which its fierce members undoubtedly planned.

Sunday 14. We set off early with pleasant and fair weather: a dog joined us, which we suppose had strayed from the Assiniboin camp . . .

Well, at least he did not show complete ingratitude. At least he remembered Omar.

35

From the camp of Two Lean Antelope, the adventure assumed new urgencies for us all. Would we find the Snake Indians? If we found them—when we found them—would we find Cameahwait with them? Would he still be the grand chief? And, if so, would he consent to sell us the number and quality of packhorses, which we must have to portage the Great Divide; to get over that vast spine of the Big Rock mountains which separated the headwaters of the Missouri and the Columbia?

The miles toiled under were as painful as those below the Mandan. They took the same fierce toll of strength and spirit; interminable hours in snow-cold water cording the rapids and the bars; endless hours rowing against the current when following wind failed; countless and cursing hours of poling the ever-shallowing, ever-swiftening Missouri into the teeth of obstinate winds which never seemed to fail. These all took the measure of our wills, as they had on the lower river. Yet to them, up here, was added that ineffable loneliness of endless grasslands unbroken by bush or tree, against which Captain Clark had warned me at Cedar

Island. This was the "big stillness which hurts the ears," thus described for us the past winter by Shahaka in his interviews with Captain Lewis. It was my mother's country, and the country of Sacajawea's mother. Entering it, we entered the approaches to the land of Cameahwait's people.

Here the feeling was that the engulfing plains were an ocean of liquid grass rather than a scape of solid earth. The illusion caused literal sickness. Many times we were grateful for towrope, setting pole or thick-shanked oar, their greater pains of backache, blister and rock-cut feet offsetting the nausea of *le mal de prairie.*

Despite the abundance of game, the men became depressed and melancholy. On Friday, April 26th, we reached the mouth of the fabled Yellowstone River, the Rochejaune of the Canadian trappers. Resting, we went on, passing Martha River, Porcupine River, Two Thousand Mile Creek—named for the distance of our journey to its mouth—Big Dry River and Poplar River, to come, on Wednesday, the eighth of May, one month and one day from the villages of the Mandan, to this opaque, strange-watered Milk River.

From this place, the Missouri grew wide, shallow and clear. The captains commenced at once to despair of having draft enough to carry us to the Big Rock Mountains. The country began to alter again, as well. The earth became pale-colored and sterile. The chokeberry and fleshleaf thorn set in, replacing the hyssop and honeysuckle. There was no recognizable timber.

On the fourteenth we passed Gibson and Sticklodge Creeks. On the seventeenth we charted Rattlesnake Creek. We had as yet seen no sign of Indian life. Abandoned lodges, even, were scarce. We saw one dead Indian, a squaw laid out on a Sioux platform, her belongings beneath the scaffold, her pet dog killed and left at the foot of the structure to go with her into the Land of the Shadows. Now and again, at some crossing place of the buffalo, we would see the barefoot pony tracks of some vanished-ahead-of-us red horsemen, and that was all. It was weird and disturbing and, Captain Clark privately confided to me, dangerous.

On May 20th, of a hawk-lonely midday, we reached yet another landmark in safety, this the large river called the Musselshell. It emptied into the Missouri from the south side, 2,270 miles from St. Louis, in latitude 47° 0' 24" north. Its water was greenish yellow and there was a sparse rash of timber along the dry hilltops flanking its arid confluence. The trees broke the lonesomeness a little.

Shortly before this camp a handsome small river joined the Musselshell and Clark entered it on his charts as Birdwoman's River, this being the Shoshone translation of Sacajawea's name. I thought it poor enough reward for this brave girl without whom we stood no chance, or precious small, of conquering the Big Rock traverse. But Clark said to me, "Poor it may be, Frank, but permanent. Long after you and me are six foot under, her river will still be flowing on this map of mine. And besides," he added, with his puckish grin, "we ain't yet over that divide, boy, with or without Sacajawea." Since there was no standing against such logic, let alone against the sunshine of that grin, I submitted.

On the twenty-ninth we came to a jewel-green stream which Captain Clark named Judith's River for what reason he would not at first confide, but then told me it was for his sweetheart back in Virginia. This was Julia "Miss Judy" Hancock, the dear and true lady whom he hoped to wed if God and our good luck should bring him once more to the Old Dominion State.

I thanked him for the little secret and told him that I was very glad to hear about his lady. Which I certainly was. It gave me considerable relief in the directions of his intentions toward Sacajawea. Or it did, at any rate, until I glumly remembered that, not ten days gone, he had named another scarcely less lovely stream for another and scarcely less lovely young lady. And so I was returned to my jealousy and stalked off from Clark and would not eat my breakfast, but sat on the rocks down by the river, glaring at the Argalia goats, or big-horned animals, at play upon the far, southside cliffs of "Miss Judy's" thrice-damned tributary namesake.

We suffered on, successfully passed up the difficult Ash Rapids, and came to and went by Slaughter River. On June 2nd, late, we came to a grinding halt at the juncture of the Missouri with another quite large and rolling river which neither of our captains knew, or were prepared to see in that place, and which at once posed the most grievous of decisions for them both, and for the expedition.

The situation did not lessen in its ominous shade but took on added, even more compelling, hue from Lewis's carefully restrained language in the journal. Wrote the senior commander and "quiet chief":

Monday, June 3: . . . It now became an interesting question which of these two streams is what the Minnetarees

211

call the Anmateahza or Missouri which they described as approaching very near to the Columbia . . .

Lewis, for all his soldier's trained behavior, was a mercuric man. He was far more emotional than Clark. His shifts of temper ranged from elation to depression almost daily. His spirits rose, fell, ran in shoal water, grounded, backed off, shot the rapids or sank as suddenly and startlingly as the gyrations of a loose canoe. But he always bobbed safely back up from his deep plunges and if his moods sometimes puzzled Clark, they never defeated him.

And Lewis knew this. When the night was dark enough, he was wont, as few men of the command knew, to seek the council of William Clark. The midnight previous to that vital entry of June 3rd was dark enough. At that time he came looking for my captain and, if I were uninvited witness to the meeting, I was nonetheless as privy to it as the stillness of the sleeping camp and the summer stars might conspire to permit.

As we traveled it had become the custom of Clark and Lewis to headquarter in a sort of command tent which was a large cowskin Indian tipi, transported, set up, taken down, maintained in repair and, in general, fully housekept by Sacajawea. She herself stayed with Charbonneau in a small dog-tent pitched to the rear of the big lodge. Also bivouacked near by was George Drewyer, Lewis's emergency interpreter and favorite of the camp.

The concourse of this "family" often grew a bit strident for Clark, who was the most natural man I ever knew and who could and did prefer the bare ground to the billowy bed of boughs or gathered grasses. Particularly on a balmy prairie night would he seek the outer air and on many of these latter occasions he sought me out and bedded by me on "guard edge" of the encampment. Owing to my half-breed's nose for the noises of the night, together with Omar's similar talent for "winding Injun," I had become somewhat of a camp watchdog. Since I also had aspirations of one day becoming Clark's "Drewyer," the captain's visits were doubly welcome and heartening. It was already a point of great pride with me that I had begun to hear myself referred to by the soldiers of the corps as "Clark's Pawnee." So it was that Clark and I, on this occasion had smoked, small-talked, grown weary, spread our robes and said good night about eleven-thirty.

Sometime afterward, and when I ordinarily would have been asleep, I heard someone coming. It was York guiding Captain Lewis. I held still, pretending slumber.

"Will?" I heard Lewis call softly, and at once my captain was sitting bolt upright and answering, "Yes, Captain, over here by the flat rock."

Lewis came up, York properly hanging back to squat, out of hearing, on the sandy beach.

"Is this young Rivet with you?" asked Lewis, pointing to my blanketed form.

"It's him," said Clark. "But no matter, Captain; he's dead to the world. What was it you wanted?"

Captain Lewis, in reply, only tightened his words. "You know what it is, Will. It's these two streams. If, after ascending one of them to the Rocky Mountains, possibly even beyond, we should learn that we are wrong and are not following that river of these two which does lead to the Columbia, or heads nearest it, and so be obliged to return and take the other, then we should not alone have lost the traveling season, two months of which have already elapsed, but would likely find the men so disheartened as to induce them to abandon the enterprise. As bad, perhaps worse, they might not quit, but continue without spirit, yielding us a cold obedience in place of that warm, wondrous support hitherto provided us. Will, if we guess wrong on those two rivers, we can face a revolt and attendant failure of everything."

Clark bobbed his head sympathetically.

"It could be, Captain," he agreed, "but I doubt it very greatly. It appears to me but a matter of examining our ground mighty damned careful before we trust our full weight on it. Don't you think?"

Lewis shook his head.

"The trouble is that I don't think," he said. "I seem unable to think. The gamble intimidates my mind."

"Pshaw, that ain't so, Captain." Clark spread his long arms deprecatingly. "Let's just start by sending two canoes, with say three men each, up both rivers tomorrow morning. At the same time, we can send out land parties to scout the high country between and to spot the lay of the two drainages from the best elevation they can find before dark. Depending on what they bring back for us, we can commence to worrying about it then. That's to say tomorrow night, Captain, rather than this one. We agreed?"

I knew that he was smiling and, from Lewis's grateful reply, imagined that the sober captain might be also.

"Will," he said, arising, "you always make it sound so beautifully simple."

Clark's answering chuckle was not flippant, but warm and kind. "Shucks, that's easy, Captain," he said. "All it takes is the right kind of a mind."

I could see Lewis's head move in thought. "That's so," he said, "it surely does; and thank God that you have got it, Will."

"You mean the simple mind, Captain?"

Again the smile was in Clark's comment, but this time I could see Lewis's deliberate headshake denying any jest.

"No, Will," he replied, "I mean the right kind of a mind."

There was a brief spell of silence then, and I could feel the bond of strength and faith flowing between these two remarkable men. It was Lewis who broke it first.

"Well, thank you once more, Will," he said. "I'll see to the canoes first thing in the morning."

"Yes, sir," responded Clark. "I'll get Ordway and Pryor to detail the land parties. Good night, Captain."

Lewis, who had started to turn away, stopped. He looked back at his fellow soldier for a long moment, then nodded softly. *"Good night, Captain,"* he said and walked off straight and square-shouldered up the rise to the buffalo-hide tipi.

36

Next day the men dispatched to examine the two rivers returned without information of a kind to permit the captains to take any decision. Clark and Lewis then understood they would have to do the job themselves, and at greater length. It was determined Clark would take the

South Fork, Lewis the North. Nearing 11 P.M. Clark alerted Sergeant Gass, R. and J. Fields, Shannon and York to stand by to go with him. Departure time was set at earliest light. Hearing of the orders, I sought out Clark and importuned him in regard to enlisting me and my Assiniboin dog Omar, as Indian guards for his group. When that plea failed, I reminded him of my skill in shooting the fierce grizzled bears, asking if he did not think it good insurance to name me and my Kentucky rifle to his company on that ground alone. To this, he laughed and gave in. He did not expect, he said to meet either more Indians or bears than he might handle, but there was, he admitted, something fetching about a boy and his dog all the same. At this, Omar growled wickedly and showed his fangs, and Clark nodded to me and said, "Well, anyway, there's something to be said for a boy. Uh, remind yourself not to let that brute in the canoe tomorrow, Frank. No, bother the canoe. We'll walk. I'm sick of the river . . ."

We walked. We walked for forty-eight hours and until I thought my feet would fall off. And the weather! Heart of Jesus, it *snowed* that second night of June the 4th. And cold? It was so damnably cold that we could see the breaths of the buffalo standing across the river from our camp three-quarters of a mile off!

That night I slept under the same robe with York, who gave off heat like a hibernating bear. It was comfortable enough until along about 3 A.M. he began to suffer some wild African dreams, and I fled his bed cursing all blacks. For the remainder of the night I hunched to the watchfire with Omar, burning my belly and freezing my buttocks in the time-honored dilemma of the plainsman.

I do not know how long it was before I slept, but when I awakened to Omar's warning growl, the light was growing faintly in the east. Some other things were likewise growing in the east. Three of them. And they were coming as silently down upon our sleeping camp as any Assyrian wolves upon the peaceful fold. But they were not Assyrians and they were not wolves. They were grizzled North American bears, looking big as buffalo to me and the ghostly gray of the dawn behind them, and making no more noise than that dawn. They were thirty feet away when I opened my eyes, twenty feet away when I reached for my rifle.

"*Patron!*" I yelled. "*Dépêchez-vous! Gare! Gare—!*"

It was Omar, really, who saved our lives. The fearless Assiniboin cur leaped at the leading bear and took a hard grip on his flank. This caused the bear to rear and turn in order to swipe at the dog. His action, together with his tremendous roar of amazement that such a mite of an animal would dare assault the king beast of the Upper Missouri, disturbed the other two bears, both of which veered off to pass around their leader, and around our waking men. In this moment, I managed to get the Kentucky piece shouldered and let off. Its ball took the first bear in the breast, bringing him down to all fours with the most agonizing cry of pain. He saw me, sensed that I had been the one to hurt him, and came for me on a lumbering gallop. Omar fell away from his flank and was trod underfoot by the huge brute. I rolled to my right and in under a shelf of river rock which, praise God, was occupied by York. The bear, in his blundering charge then, fell upon this rock rather than upon me.

York, who carried no arm save an espontoon—a stout staff with hooked or barbed steel head—now gave a roar nearly equal to that of the bear. And with the roar, he drove the steel of the espontoon into the bear's rear quarter. In the next instant, the big Negro had rolled out from under the rock and came to his feet, still grasping the handle of the espontoon embedded in the bear's rear. He then amazingly—and using the haft of the espontoon as his whip handle—"cracked" the bear away from the campsite and down upon the sandy beach below. The time thus granted was crucial. Clark drove a bullet into the bear's chest, the other men following suit. The heavy balls could be heard whacking into his flesh, and in at least three places he was spurting blood in fountain quantities from bullet exit holes.

The poor brute gazed about, distracted.

His companions had disappeared back into the timber, his body was on fire with pain, his small brain sick and confused. Turning, he lunged into the river and swam for a tiny island near by. Our company, now reloaded, fired six more rounds into him as he swam. Yet he made the island and lived half an hour, roaring and coughing and groaning in almost human despair and agony.

His measurements exceeded those of the big bear Captain Lewis had shot below Two Thousand Mile Creek, and which had taped eight feet seven inches nose to tail. This bear, to be called "Omar's Bear," was nine feet six inches long, six feet eleven inches around the breast, four feet five inches around the neck, two feet three inches around the middle of the foreleg, the talons of the foot being thick as knife hafts and five and three-quarters inches in length, and the total weight as estimated by Captain Clark and

George Shannon was said to be in excess of 800 pounds.

That he had meant to harm us, no man of our camp doubted. Also, that Omar's growl and my following French cry to "Look out!" had voided that intent, went uncontested. The incident, even if but one more in the long series of attacks made upon us by these damnably vicious "grizzlies" of the upper river, served to sober us all and led, I think, to Captain Clark's conviction that we had come far enough up this fork. Shortly thereafter he gave the order to return and with sunset of the sixth we were back in the Main Forks Camp. There two bits of dismal news awaited us. Sacajawea had become violently ill again and was believed dying. Lewis was still missing, and no word of him had come in by scout or runner from up the North Fork.

The men were very quiet. While Clark hurried to do what he and his medicines might for the Shoshone girl, I crouched outside her dog-tent shelter with the husband Charbonneau and the black servant York. Others of the company waited with us in the dark. I could distinguish the voices of Shannon, Gass, Reuben Fields, and several others. If not in the same way that Clark and I loved her, then in their own and various respectful ways these hardy adventurers had come to favor the Indian girl who was the first one of her red race that they had felt to be a woman, as a woman, and not as an ignorant savage.

We all talked of Captain Lewis and his missing men, and of the dark possibility of failure at this far time in our strike toward the Columbia, and of what Captain Clark would do should his beloved and previously infallible "superior" prove truly to be lost.

There were no answers; not even any guesses. The talk

fell off. We all sat watching the dog-tent, waiting for Clark to come out.

37

It was nearing 1 A.M. The other men had drifted off and sought their blankets. Even York had gone to bed. Only Shahaka and I waited outside the dog-tent with Charbonneau—and Charbonneau was asleep on his haunches.

When Clark at last came out, he did not disturb the French squawman, but signaled for Shahaka and me to follow him off a ways. This we did. He halted in front of the big lodge.

"Well," he said, "I don't know if we can help her or not. She's got something low in the belly. I give her opium and bark poultices over the groins, but this only relieves her pains briefly. It seems much the same thing that killed poor Floyd. I fear something will burst in her, as it did in him."

"Is there nothing at all we may try?" I asked desperately.

"Yes," he answered carefully, "there is something. She spoke of getting her to the Pool of the Morning Glory. She said Shahaka would know the place—"

"Aye," said the Mandan chief, "Shahaka knows this pool. It is a spring, the biggest one that any Indian knows of. It comes out of the ground up there above the Great Falls close to Medicine River. It flows upward from the ground with such force that its center stands higher than the prairie and it looks like a great blue flower, like a morning glory, growing there."

"And its waters are curative?" asked Clark.

"They are sacred, *Patron*."

"And blue," I said, somewhat cynically.

"Yes, blue," nodded Shahaka. "So blue that they stain the Missouri for half a mile below where they fall into it."

"Well," said Clark, "that's pretty blue, but it doesn't help us. We're a long ways from there and we'll never get that girl up to there to that pool in time. It's impossible."

"The water would help her, all right," decided Shahaka, ignoring him. "The Indians drink it as a flush of the entire body. It purifies the bowel, takes the poisons out of the gut."

"That's what we need, true enough," agreed Clark. "But we are just too damned far from it, worse luck."

I looked at him through the darkness, an idea beginning to glimmer in my mind.

"How far would you say we are from it, *Patron?*" I asked quietly.

"Forty miles," replied Clark hopelessly with a sigh. "Maybe fifty."

"Well, *Patron,*" I said, "we French have a saying for such distances. Surely you have heard it—the one concerning *Mahométan et la montagne?* If we cannot get Sacajawea to the water, *Patron,* we must get the water to Sacajawea."

He stared at me. Even in the morning blackness I could see his eyes widen.

"By God, you've struck it, Frank!" he said.

"He has spoken a true thing, *Patron,*" agreed Shahaka. "And I can help in this matter. I can guide the way to the blue water. We can go in my canoe. If the wind will blow up from my country, south and west, we can be back here with that water in three days.

Even as he said it and even as my pessimistic Pawnee side

221

said there was no breath of wind, and had been none for two days running, and none for a week from the southwest, a light breeze played across our faces from down the river.

"A freak," I said, half aloud. "A gust induced by the heat of the day rising in the night's coolness."

Captain Clark said nothing but wetted his forefinger and held it up into the air.

Shahaka watched him, as did I.

The breeze steadied and did not die. It came on soft and strong and from down the river toward the country of Shahaka, the Mandan, and my heart beat faster than a bird's.

"What's the direction, Captain?" I said, steadying myself.

"*Southwest!*" he said softly, triumphantly.

Then, smacking one knotted fist against the other, in that odd habit of his, he added tersely, "Get the canoe, Frank, and rig the sail. By God, there's a chance . . . there's just a crazy, half-breed chance!"

Shahaka and I made tremendous sail the remainder of that night. I think by dawn we must have come thirty miles. And the wind held. All we needed to do was steer the canoe, now and again voiding her away from some snaggle of rock with the paddles. By noon we had come another twenty miles and Shahaka, pointing to a small island which he seemed to recognize and which lay dead ahead, suggested we beach there "and listen."

When we had grounded our absurd craft and were standing on the little rocky spit, the sloshing of the paddles and the slap of the wind against our sail for the moment quieted, it came to me with a racing thrill where we were. The sound of the Grand Missouri roaring was like no sound imaginable. It filled not alone the ear, but the mind, the heart, the imagination and the very soul—it filled the eye. Looking now where Shahaka directed me, I saw off to the south a monster cloud of what I took to be steam rising from the prairie, and then I knew. The Great Falls of the Mother Missouri! We were there! We were just below that scene which probably no white man had ever seen! I trembled almost as with dread.

"Marchons!" I shouted to Shahaka. "Come on! Come on!"

How can these poor words tell of the scene which waited us around that sweeping south bend of the river? Between the 250-foot-high ramparts of ochred earth, the "smoking water" vaporized by the cascades rose in a veritable cloud. As we stared, this cloud was swept away repeatedly by the wind. Each time it drove the spume away, the snarling river would replace it. And through all this interchange of misted waters the dropping sun slanted to make rainbows which overwhelmed the senses. I counted hundreds of these in the first moments of rounding the far downstream bend.

It took us, even with sail, another five hours on the river to come up to the actual foot of the first falls. Thus it was very late sunset when we were at last within near sight of the awesome spectacle.

Again I knew the nameless, eerie dread. The river, where it went over, was 300 yards wide. On the leftbank side 100 yards of water fell vertically for no less than eighty feet over a solid rock precipice. The other 200 yards of water on the right bank lost the same eighty feet of elevation in a raceway of rock-toothed cataracts running upstream 400 yards. It was this devil's downplunge which boiled up most of the steam while the sheer precipice furnished the greater part of the now-deafening cannonade of water. Below the precipice and the raceway the flanking walls of yellow rock channeled the entire Missouri into a mad foaming bore of white water no wider than seventy-five yards. It absolutely made the heart stop to see and hear it. But Shahaka, shouting in my ear, assured me that this was not the Great Falls, at all, but only the first small breaking of the water which now continued for ten miles upstream to Medicine River and the Morning Glory Pool of the blue water. I was too overcome to answer him anything.

In the deepening gloom of the twilight, we steered our leaking craft for the near shore, upon which the pool lies, and where we must land since the river cannot be crossed at any place within the falls. Hiding the canoe in brush and high grass, we took the buffalogut water bottles and set out over the steepening plain. By midnight, with fair luck and hard driving pace afoot, we had found the fabled pool of "medicine water" and filled our bottles.

I could feel the power of the place. The vast fount arose only some few paces from the bank of the river. In the dark its bubbling water seemed indigo or cobalt blue in color. But even at night and only by starlight one could see their dark stain streaking the clear-bottomed flood of the main river. The river, too, at this point below its confluence with the Medicine River—which Shahaka told me was called Sun River by the Shoshone who regarded it as a holy place—was a spectacle in itself. It was at least 1,500 yards wide, and smooth as melted green glass, where it pooled itself for the great plunge downward into the ten miles of its falls. Yet we had no time for such scenery. My companion wanted to be away from the noise and power of that place, and so did I. We dog-trotted much of the way back downstream. Even with the heavy bottles of the blue water, four of them carried two-and-two by the Mandan and myself, we made excellent trail time. It still lacked an hour of full light when we came again to our cached vessel.

Loading the precious water, with ourselves and our nervous wolfdog into the rickety craft, we pushed her out from the rocky sandbar. The downfalls swirl of the current caught her immediately, and spun her away. We did not talk, saving our breath for fighting the river. We had come far and we had the blue water. But we were still half a hundred miles from the Two Forks Camp and the question was now one of the rotten skins, spongy cottonwood ribs and molded rawhide bindings of Shahaka's canoe. Would the foul craft stay afloat another full day? By his apprehensive stirrings and whimperings amidship, Omar clearly did not think so. As for myself, I knew very well what I believed, and it was negative. But Shahaka, looking at my worried Pawnee scowl in the first rosy tint of the coming sun, waved a dark hand and read my mind as clearly as if he had a private porthole in my forehead.

"*Oui,* Brother Frank," he said in French, "I think so that she will do it. Maybe . . ."

38

Shahaka was right. At somewhere after 10 P.M. that night and within plain sight and wading-water distance of the beach at Two Forks Camp, the canoe foundered and went under. Omar, Shahaka and I, with the waterskins, sloshed ashore. We found Clark in conference with Lewis, who had come in that same night at 5 P.M. Clark at once took the water from us and went with it over to the dog-tent of Charbonneau. The squawman was gone but Saca-jawea faintly replied to Clark's low call. "Wait here," the captain instructed Shahaka and me. "I will call you if I want more water."

I do not know what was in that blue water. Many things, I suspect, at least after its night and day in the fetid, stinking bags of buffalo boudins. But whatever its medicinal prop-erties, the fact remained that in one hour Clark was back outside saying the Shoshone girl had rallied in a most incomprehensible manner from drinking about two quarts of the Morning Glory water. She had better color, fuller pulses, steadier respiration. She would live now, Clark thought, though his opinion had been the opposite for the past seventy-two hours. I did not go into the tiny lodge but went to its door and called in to Sacajawea that it was Brother Frank and that I had prayed for her to be eased of her pain. She answered with the usual poesy of the Indian that she could see my head against the stars and that she knew it was her brother there, and her heart was made glad by my voice. There was a pause during which neither of us spoke, then I asked her if she were free from fear now. She replied that she was, and that I had made her so. "I know, Brother Frank, that it was you who brought the blue water. My poor body and my tired spirit thank you."

"It is nothing, Little Sister," I said in French. "Your voice growing stronger is payment tenfold for the water. I will always do for you that which I am able to do. You must know this. Rest quietly now. Sleep and get well again."

I heard her long grateful sigh of assent. *"Bonne nuit, mon frère,"* she murmured through the darkness. "I still keep your heart which you gave to me."

Early next morning Clark and Lewis consulted with the crew members, and with one another, seeking to arrive at the answer of which river was the Missouri. Lewis had come back from his exploration of the North Fork convinced that Clark's estimate had been correct and that the South Fork was the true Missouri. But the remainder of the company stoutly held with Peter Cruzatte, the premier riverman, that the silted color and slower current of the North Fork made it the true river. The South Fork, they pointed out, ran too clear, too swiftly and too far due south. For a time it seemed that there might be some genuine reluctance of the crew to go by the southern fork. It was when this feeling showed itself that Clark called Shahaka and myself as witness. "I have been withholding information," he grinned, "in the interests of examining the question without prejudice. But we now know the South Fork is the main Missouri and it is time we heard the testimony of the experts." As the assemblage gave him a community frown, he waved at Shahaka and myself.

"Rivet here and the Mandan have just got back from a scout up 'my' fork," he continued. "They went to the falls and all the way to the Medicine River."

Lewis at once challenged us, and I told him it was true. He was far from pleased. It had been his own plan to push ahead of Clark with a few men and so be first to see this famed landmark. Now, patently, he did not relish being beaten to it by a naked Mandan and a half-breed Pawnee. I saw at once that any gain I might have made in his favor was now irretrievably lost. Nonetheless, I stood firm. *"Mon Capitaine,"* I told him, "we need not argue the matter; we have brought back proof."

"Proof!" he asked raspingly. "What proof?"

"You have heard of the blue water, *Capitaine?* The Morning Glory Pool of the Mandan legend?"

"You mean the supposed artesian fountain below the Medicine River?"

"The same, *Capitaine;* the one whose waters stain those of the Missouri blue for one-half mile where the river is a full mile wide."

"Well, what of it?"

"I have some of that blue water. We went to get it to treat Charbonneau's squaw. Ask the *Patron.*"

He swung back to Clark, who soon enough convinced him that the thing was as we had said it was. Some of the men went so far as to pour a little of the water from one of the buffalo-gut bags into the South Fork to see if it would stain the water. Of course it would not, but Captain Lewis was well above the need of any such childish demonstrations. He did not like the way in which Clark had handled the whole thing but typically he said nothing. Like the good commander that he was, he recognized the important meaning of our mission and so gave his orders. They were simple enough.

"We shall proceed by the South Fork," he announced, "as soon as we have completed the *cache* to be made here at Marias River"—the name he had given the North Fork.

'We will unload and hide the red pirogue, burying most of her burden in the Indian manner, distributing the rest of her cargo, and her crew, among the canoes. This work will be completed by sundown tomorrow. Sunrise, eleventh June, I shall leave with four men overland. Captain Clark will follow with the boats by the river as rapidly as he may be able. And, men, may I remind you that your loyalty and good will are our chief comfort in all these difficult matters. Captain Clark and I could not have made one-half this journey without your remarkable devotion. Now, let us all go, each to his task, and with every speed. The season grows late; our Louisiana gamble may yet be lost if we do not bend every hour of time and ounce of our strength to the winning. God bless you all, and let's get to work!"

The men cheered him. And when the echoes were done they fell to the work of beaching the big pirogue and burying her precious goods for our return use with a joyous spirit which saw the entire job completed and the Marias River Camp cleaned up for our next dawn's departure with the sun still three hours high on June 10th. The emotions of the men sharpened yet more.

Only the Great Falls portage lay between us and the long-sought Land of the Shoshone. Our difficulties were done; it was all plain sailing from here.

BOOK VI
LAND OF THE SHOSHONE

39

On June 16th we reached the foot of the Great Falls rapids. Camp was established on a large creek which fell in on the south side and which, because it would be our base for the overland passage around the falls, Captain Clark named Portage Creek. Work was at once begun upon the wheeled trucks for transporting our canoes by land. While the canoe-carriage builders were busy, Clark struck off upstream to survey and stake the portage road. The balance of us toiled to draw up into the creek the five canoes and the cargo from the white pirogue, which would be cached here as the red had been at Marias River.

On the eighteenth Clark was back and all was ready. The canoe wagons, with wheels made of sawed rounds of cottonwood log and axles fashioned from the mast of the abandoned pirogue, were in position. However, the wind came whooping up with such sudden violence that Clark ordered a lay-over and sent our crews to hunt and dry meat. Meanwhile, he himself once more "ran up" to the head of the falls and established our base camp at the upper end of the portage at Whitebear Islands, two miles above Medicine River, this making the whole distance of the portage to be seventeen and three-quarter miles, a hellish course considering our means of getting over it. But

Captain Clark was not a man to consider. He left that part of the work to Meriwether Lewis.

As for the latter, he was now ahead somewhere with Charbonneau and Sacajawea, scouting and hunting. Now, on the eve of our departure up the portage, came a note from him to Clark: "I reached camp," the missive said, "to find the Indian woman extremely ill again, and much reduced by her indisposition. This gives me much concern as well for the poor object herself, with the young child in her arms, as from the consideration of her being our only dependence for a friendly negotiation with the Snake Indians upon whom, of course, we depend utterly for horses to assist us in our portage from the Missouri to the Columbia country."

There was more, but more was not needed. If there had been any mystery previously about the nature of Lewis's mercy, it was now clear. He did not dare lose "the poor object." She was his key to the lock of the Big Rock Mountains, and, without her well, why labor it? He had admitted the matter.

At last, on the twenty-second we began the portage. Its tortures would not be believed. The wagon tongues broke repeatedly. The feet of the men, with the rock and cactus, were pulped masses within half the distance to Whitebear Islands. We made eight miles that day and fell to the ground without blankets or food when Clark released us from the wagons. Several men retched and vomited from exhaustion. Two had to be bled for collapse.

Clark went forward next day to resurvey the route, and managed to cut off more than 900 yards by changing his stakes.

We spent the day sewing double soles on our moccasins, for in addition to the prickly pear we now had a new condition of pain. The rain had led to the ground's being cut into knife edges by the hoofs of a tremendous herd of buffalo— 10,000 animals Captain Clark believed—which passed in our van while the earth was still wet. The sun then poured down, drying the cut dirt into rocklike hardness. This footing, a purgatory to pass unburdened, became, when tottering beneath a 100-pound backpack or straining to haul the half-ton canoe wagons, a torture indescribable.

Next day we resumed the mournful journey. Its true hell cannot be told. Suffice it that two small mosaics of its destructive pattern be taken from the journal. Wrote Meriwether Lewis, after five days of this creeping march:

. . . Finding it impossible to reach the end of the portage with their present load, in consequence of the state of the road after the rain, he [Clark] sent back nearly all his party to bring on the articles which had been left yesterday. Having [himself] determined to go up to the Whitebear Islands . . . he left one man to guard the baggage [myself, Frank Rivet!] and went on to the falls accompanied by his servant York, Chaboneau [sic] and his wife with her young child.

On his arrival there he observed a very dark cloud rising in the west which threatened rain, and looked about for some shelter, but could find no place where they would be secure from being blown into the river if the wind should prove as violent as it sometimes does in the plains.

At length about a quarter of a mile above the falls he

found a deep ravine where there were some shelving rocks, under which he took refuge. They were on the upper side of the ravine, perfectly safe from the rain. . . . The shower was at first moderate, it then increased to a heavy rain, the effects of which they did not feel: soon after a torrent of rain and hail descended; the rain seemed to fall in a solid mass, and instantly collecting in the ravine came rolling down in a dreaded current, carrying the mud and rocks, and every thing that opposed it.

Captain Clark fortunately saw it a moment before it reached them, and spinning up with his gun and shot-pouch in his left hand, with his right clambered up the steep bluff, pushing on the Indian woman with her child in her arms; her husband too had seized her hand, and was pulling her up the hill, but he was so terrified at the danger, that but for the captain Clark, himself and his wife and child would have been lost. So instantaneous was the rise of the water, that before captain Clark had reached his gun and began to ascend the bank, the water was up to his waist, and he could scarce get up faster than it rose till it reached the height of fifteen feet with a furious current, which had they waited a moment longer would have swept them into the river just above the great falls, down which they must inevitably have been precipitated . . .

A bit later, and in a separated situation of the cyclonic weather which seemed to distinguish this Dante's portage of ours, Lewis commented:

. . . He [Clark] now . . . returned to the camp at Willowrun. Here he found that the party sent that morning for the baggage, had all returned to camp in great confusion [from a sudden ice storm] leaving their loads on the plain. On account of the heat they generally go naked and with no covering on their heads. The hail was so large and driven so furiously against them by the high wind, that it knocked several of them down: one of them particularly was thrown on the ground three times, and most of them bleeding freely and complained of being much bruised. Willowrun had risen six feet since the storm, and as the plains were so wet that they could not proceed, they passed the night at their camp . . .

There was another entry, far shorter and more singular, made five days later when we were engaged in packing the last of our goods from Portage Creek to Whitebear Islands. Wrote Lewis on July 4, 1805:

. . . We had intended to dispatch a canoe with part of our men to the United States early this spring; but not having yet seen the Snake Indians, or knowing whether to calculate on their friendship or enmity, we have decided not to weaken our party which is already scarcely sufficient to repel any hostility.

On July 14th we finished the portage and set sail for fabled Three Forks of the Missouri River, our beaten spirits restored. But the increasing wild beauty of the land, now turning truly mountainous, proved only a portent in reverse of our prospects.

Five days later we came to that ominous great canyon-portal of the Missouri, concerning which Captain Lewis was moved to create the following title and description:

". . . The river appears to have worn a passage just the width of its channel of 150 yds. It is deep from side to side nor is there in the last 3 Miles of this distance a spot except of a few yards in extent on which a man could rest the soal of his foot . . . From the singular appearance of this place I called it the Gates of the Rocky Mountains . . .

The entry was not alone singular in appearance within the imagination of Captain Lewis. At this far way station of the journey, 2,600 miles from the Missouri's juncture with the Mississippi the expedition stood within the shadow of final failure. Both of the captains understood the foreboding nature of the threat. From the Gates of the Mountains onward, every effort to locate the missing Indians was redoubled. But we saw no Shoshone. Clark, probing far ahead, saw no Shoshone. Lewis took over with stout Shannon, brave Gass and crafty Drewyer. They saw no Shoshone.

The days fled in silence. The river shallowed, grew fat, limpid, lazy, crooked. She became choked with islands, girt by granite narrows. Her waters turned clear as green bottle glass. She lured us on through a vista of continuously more bizarre scapes of level meadow, upflung spire, conifered forest and sunbright creeks. And towering over all, dazzling the eye, awing the mind, firing the imagination, loomed the eternal snows of the Big Rock Mountains.

Yet constantly above this vaulting grandeur crouched the eternal loneliness which had haunted our venture from the time of my return to the company at Two Lean Ante-lope camp. The men grew quiet, apprehensive, unreason-ably taut of nerve. The only cheering news was Saca-jawea's improvement in health and her subsequent delighted recognition of certain landmarks along the river as definitely those of her Shoshone homelands.

On the twenty-seventh day of July we came to the mother source of the Missouri River at the legendary place called Three Forks. What we found of the Shoshone there was precisely what we had found of him since entering his empty and silent land of shining mountains. We found nothing; not an old lodge, a dead horse, a starving dog, a discarded moccasin.

That night, hunched over what must have been his most uncertain campfire since leaving Fort Mandan, Captain Lewis confided his unspoken fears to the journal:

. . . We are now very anxious to see the Snake Indians. After advancing for several hundred miles into this wild and mountainous country, we may soon expect that the game will abandon us. With no information of the route we may be unable to find a passage across the moun-tains when we reach the head of the river, at least such a one as will lead us to the Columbia, and even were we so fortunate as to find a branch of that river, the timber which we have hitherto seen in these mountains does not promise us any fit to make canoes, so that our chief dependence remains on meeting some tribe from whom we may procure horses.

For myself, and my own neglected memoirs of our far

236

journey from the villages of the Mandan, I had even grimmer visions. That night, huddled forlorn and alone by the dying embers of Clark's mess fire, I wrote:

Three Forks, the French call this mountain-locked and lonesome place, and for reasons which I cannot isolate, its wild beauty and deep stillness build up within my breast a prescience of restless fears which seems in some strange way related to the name and its meanings. I am left with the dark premonitory image in my mind of three roads which will soon no longer travel together. Will they have names? And will those names be Clark, Frank, and Sacajawea? The wandering breezes of the night are warm, the winking embers of the fire, bright and friendly. Yet I shiver and draw my blanket about my shoulders. The métis blood is strong. It is pagan and feral and it can feel things no white blood can feel. *Something* is waiting for me here.

40

Even now, I cannot say why, from this seeming paradise of calm beauty at Three Forks of the Missouri, I commenced to suffer that oppressive air of personal foreboding which was, so soon, to engulf me in the concrete realities of my separate fate. Perhaps it was Sacajawea herself who served the warning note.

It was in the long prairie twilight of the twenty eighth of July that I came upon her strolling alone on the sanded beach of the forks. When I hailed her, she smiled and said in her sad sweet way, "You startled me, Brother Frank; but

237

now I am very glad to see that it is you."

I bobbed my head happily.

"And I am glad to see that it is you, Sacajawea," I answered, "*without* your husband and your little baby."

To my considerable relief, she laughed at that. "Poor Brother Frank," she said, "if it is not Charbonneau, then it is little Pompey and if not he, then Captain Clark. You and I, we have no time for us, eh, *frère François?*"

I frowned a bit, thinking of Clark.

"What about the *capitaine?*" I asked. "Does he still make your heart beat like a bird's?"

She shook her head.

"No, not like that any more. I was wrong. He stirs me, it is true. But then, he stirs you as well, and also the others. He is that sort of man. But I think of him now as you might think of your father, Achille Rivet. It is more than one feels for just any father. A sort of spirit quality is added. Do you understand?"

"I think so. But Clark is not old enough to be your father." I could not let that pass unchallenged, the shards of my somewhat broken jealousy still lying underfoot. "Do you know that he has but thirty-four summers?"

"Yes, he told me his true age. He told me, too, that I must not think of him in an untrue way. He said his heart belonged to another woman and that I was only a child to him. He thought much of me, he said, but I was to think of him as I thought of Cameahwait. I might come to him for anything except the love of a man for a woman. He said I was to remember that."

"Was that all he said?"

"No, he said also that I was to make you under stand that

238

there was no man-and-woman love between him and Sacajawea."

"Why did you not tell me this before?"

"Well, it seemed awkward. I didn't think you would understand."

"You were probably right," I admitted ruefully. "But as we Americans say, 'better late than never.' I'm pleased to hear how it is now, Sacajawea. You see, I knew about Clark's promised woman back in the United States. I'm glad he told you, and that you and I are now the same way about our *capitaine;* and you know that we are his foster children?"

"Yes, that's the way it is, Frank." She left the "brother" off, and I did not think accidentally. My own heart began to bound unreasonably.

"Sacajawea," I said, reaching for her hands, "do you remember a moment like this in the dawn light of that camp at Two Lean Antelope? We stood as we stand now, alone, on the sands of the river, with our eyes talking?"

She gave me her hands, lovely eyes downswept.

"I remember," she murmured. The touch of her nearly took my voice. The feel of her slender fingers gripping mine well nigh unstrung me. I forced my words thickly.

"I gave you my heart to keep for me," I muttered. "Do you still have it?"

"Yes, I have it."

Our hands tightened.

"And what," I said, "will you do with it now?"

Her answer was to tighten her grasp so that it hurt my hands. I thought I would smother for want of breathing.

"Sacajawea," I said, "you must reply to me. What will

239

you do with my heart?"

"I don't want your heart!" she said with sudden fierceness. "I never asked you for it! You forced it upon me!"

"And, now?" I demanded. "Now—?"

"Now, I don't know, Frank. I can't answer you."

"Sacajawea—!"

The great gray eyes swept upward then, meeting mine. I went crazy, seizing her in the grip of a madman. And, for an instant, she yielded. Her lips met my own in a kiss that burned into me a lifetime of love memories.

But the fire was torn away from me in the same moment that it blazed up. Sacajawea cried out savagely and low-voiced, and wrenched herself from me to leap back.

"Sacajawea," I pleaded desperately "it was a mistake; I apologize. My feelings wronged me. They tricked me. Please forgive it. It was such a thing as will happen. A summer night's madness. A half-breed's hot blood. What can I say?"

The grey eyes found mine through the deepening twilight.

"Say no more, Brother Frank," she told me. "It was no mistake. We felt what we felt. The mistake would be to deny it."

"My God, Sacajawea! Don't talk like that."

"There is no other way to talk, Frank. We won't lie to one another. That's a worse way to talk"

"I don't know how to take you," I told her, finally. "I think one minute you understand me, then you turn Indian on me and I don't know what you mean. What do you mean, Sacajawea? I mean about us, now?"

She dropped her eyes. The spell seemed faded.

"I am Charbonneau's squaw," she said.

"You mean his wife," I corrected gallantly.

"No," she denied, savagely harsh and quick, "I mean his squaw. He is my husband but I am only his squaw."

"But I thought you were married?"

"As an Indian only."

"Sapristi! There were no vows? You exchanged nothing?"

"He exchanged nothing; I gave my girlhood." She raised her head. "Frank," she murmured, "would you like me to tell you how it was?"

I nodded wordlessly, and she reached me her hand. "Take it," she directed, "and walk with me. The night is our friend. She hides us in softness. See now, the light is gone at last, only the stars guide us."

"There will be a moon soon enough," I reminded her nervously.

"We have an hour, Frank; we may never have another."

She gestured with the hand. I stared at its slender grace, knew that I did wrong, fought the temptation and lost.

"You are right, Shoshone girl," I said, taking her hand in mine. "Let us follow the stars."

We rested on the soft curl of the warm buffalo grass, where it grew down to water's edge, and where all about us grew tall cottonwood and dense willow to screen the place with nature's clean decency. The moon was only now tipping the rim of the prairie with its warning soft orange glow. All about us hung the enchantments of the summer night.

"Among my people," Sacajawea was saying, "the man

241

is the only master of his women. He is permitted to barter his wives or his daughters as he will. The Shoshone father often sells his young daughters to men two times and more their own ages. But the girls live with their parents until the time of their womanhood. Since I have been these last five years captive, you will understand that I have not yet been delivered to my future husband in our band. But I had been sold to him by my father, you may be sure, and by our laws I am still his wife, even though Charbonneau may feel otherwise by virtue of the price he paid the Minnetarees for me in his turn."

She paused, reaching for my hand. Our fingers met. "Do you know how Charbonneau acquired me, Frank? You think that he saw me as I am today, a woman grown, and desired me and asked me to share his lodge? Ah, no. He purchased me for five winter-thin ponies and a rusted gun when I was but eleven summers. He kept me as his daughter. Then, when I was still scarcely fourteen years old, he took me into his lodge and told Wahiki to go away and sit down by the creek for a little while, until he might call out for her to return."

Sacajawea trailed of her low words and I felt her hand tighten on mine with the memory. I put my arm about her shoulder, cradling her face on my breast. Her dark hair, fluffed and sweet in the prairie breeze, lay upon me warm and light.

"I know," I said. "I know . . ." and did not really know anything, but only felt.

"This very camp here at Three Forks," she continued, "is where my people were staying when the scouts came gallopingin saying that the Big Bellies were coming right behind them. Well, those Minnetaree devils fell upon us even though we fled three miles up the river. That's the northwest fork, over there. Do you see the one I mean?"

"Yes, yes," I said. "Please go on, Sacajawea."

"The Big Bellies killed four of our men and four of our women and all of our young boys they could catch. They took all of the girls they caught and carried them off, including myself and my friend Lost Girl. But Lost Girl escaped on the march back to the land of the Minnetaree, and it was I who was sold for slave to Charbonneau, and I alone."

I waited for her to go on, but she seemed to have told me all she intended to of her life. As well, she appeared to have done all she meant to do for that time, or forever.

Before I might move to halt her, she withdrew herself from my arms. The next moment she was standing over me, poised to flee.

"Be still!" she warned, laying a slim dark finger to my lips. "We have stayed too long, Brother Frank; *good-bye, Pawnee boy!*"

I did not care for the way in which she so urgently whispered that last good-bye. I was warned, too, by swiftness of the kiss she leaned so lightly to place within the hollow of my neck. But she had fled and faded into the shadows of the night before I might think to restrain her, or even to reply in kind to her strangely hurried adieu.

I stood alone in the rising light of the moon. No, not quite alone, either. My heart and I stood together there; I knew in that moment, as surely as I knew the moonlight, the starshine, or the soft purling tongue of the river, that Sacajawea had answered my question: she had given my heart back to me.

This was the moment that the cold crept into me. This was the time, I am certain, when that nameless dread of approaching, separate ends put forth in me its first and evil rootling of despair.

41

The remaining time at Three Forks was intolerable. The beauty of the place evaporated. Due to its marshy nature and the humid air from the slow channels merging, the gnats and mosquitoes became monstrous. The camp was ringed with stacked biers which were kept burning all night, since sleep could be had in no other manner. Game, as the Mandan and Minnetaree had told us, had already begun to become scarce. The buffalo were gone. Elk were increasingly rare. Deer, a new red species with long tail, became the staple meat of our diet. Because I was now hunting full time with George Shannon, for Captain Clark's mess, and our daily minimum of meat to feed the total company of thirty-two person was four deer, or one deer and an elk, or one fat buffalo, it may be imagined what toils we hunters endured when camp meat grew thin and wary. To stalk and secure a quarter ton of meat each twenty-four hours had been child's play before. Up here it was giant's toil.

Even so, Captain Lewis still would not permit the use of our Mandan supply of parched Indian meal, and Captain Clark fell victim to a mysterious malady which refused to respond to laudanum, Rush's pills, Glauber salts, hot sweats and blooding. At this time Sacajawea returned to following Charbonneau about like a dog and give me no further decent opportunity to speak with her.

It was accordingly with a feeling far stronger than relief that I heard we were to break camp on the morrow, and that Captain Clark was much improved and wished to see me.

When I came up to him, he was propped in his blankets, fully dressed, studying the company journal. When he saw me waiting there, he smiled and waved me to sit down.

"Well, *Patron*," I said, "it's good to see that you are better."

"Less worse, Frank" he correctly wryly. "I've still got the weaks in my nether limbs, but the fever's down and I can stand."

I grimaced unconsciously. "So long as you can stand, we shall go on, is that it, *mon capitaine?*"

"You hitting at the captain, Frank? You think he drives me where I don't want to go?"

"No, sir. But I think he pushes you a little, now and again."

He studied me a moment.

"You look fair miserable, boy," he said at last and quietly. "What might be your trouble?"

"Nothing," I said.

"Nothing," he repeated, "spelled with a capital 'S,' as in Sacajawea?"

"Yes, sir," I blurted. "I guess you could say that."

"Ah," he said softly, "it was a lovely night. Don't tell me any more, boy. I can guess the rest." He shook his head, lowering his voice. "Frank," he said, "you had best walk mighty cautious. The Shoshone have strong rules for the game you and that little squaw have been playing."

I started to protest, to deny any such game, but he would

245

not be interrupted.

"You shut up," he ordered, "and listen. I don't care to hear your denials. You're my chore, boy, and I aim to handle you the way I see fit. You've been mooning around that Shoshone girl ever since she set foot at Fort Mandan. You've give yourself—and you've give the girl—ideas about her that just ain't so. Let me read you something, Frank. I want you to see this girl as some others of us see her. Listen to this."

He took up the journal upon which he had been working.

"This is Captain Lewis's entry for a day or so back. He is writing of Sacajawea and the way she was captured at this site by the Minnetaree. There's no use going over it all, but attend what he puts down here in summation: 'The Minnetarees,' he writes, 'pursued and attacked them, killed four men, as many women, and a number of boys; and made prisoners of all the females, of whom Sacajawea, our Indian woman, was one: *she does not, however, show any distress at these recollections, nor any joy at the prospect of being restored to her country; for she seems to possess the folly or the philosophy of not suffering her feelings to extend beyond the anxiety of having plenty to eat and a few trinkets to wear. . . .*' "

His words faded, and he put the journal down again. "Frank," he asked patiently, "does that sound to you like the girl who told us she would rather die than not go on with us to the land of her people? Does it sound like the brave, tough, faithful servant of our company, who has come all this long way without complaint? Does this match the picture you and I have drawn of this Indian girl?

Well Frank—?"

I shook my head, the admixture of anger and sadness rising in me simultaneously.

"No, *Patron*," I said, low-voiced, "you know that it does not. Why do you even ask me?"

"I ask you, Frank, for a damned good and serious reason," he answered. "Captain Lewis is a highly educated man and a skilled professional soldier. He is also a Virginia gentleman, the best friend of my life, and he would no sooner tell a conscious untruth than he would strike a woman or a defenseless child—and remember that Sacajawea is both of these things, Frank. Remember it hard, boy, and think on it hard."

I tried to do as he bid, but could make no sense of the order. Again I had to surrender to my heart rather than my head.

"I'm unable to do as you ask, *Patron*," I told him.

Clark nodded silently, put his hand on my shoulder. "You have got to see the point, Frank," he told me gently. "Captain Lewis doesn't make Sacajawea any thing but what she is, or what he thinks she is: a simple savage employed at government expense to gain us audience with the Shoshone Indians. That's why I read you the passage, boy. We're coming near to the end now. What's happened with you and Sacajawea the past couple of days is just her way of letting you know this fact. Your Shoshone sweetheart has said good-bye to you. It's over, don't you understand?"

I shook my head in desperate denial.

"But why, *Patron?* That's what I can't understand. Why?"

"Why?" he repeated after me, the big hand again finding

my shoulder. "Can't you guess why, Frank? Her people are near. She senses that. In one day, two days, a week possibly, we will find the Shoshones. When we do, it's done between you and her and she knows it is."

"How is that?" I said, feeling a presentiment of great fear. "What is done, *Patron?*"

"You are, Frank." said Captain William Clark. "Sacajawea is going on with us over the mountains. You ain't."

42

For a moment Clark's information was more than my mind could cope with. Then its cold truth froze my marrow.

"*Patron!*" I gasped. "You cannot mean it! I, not going on with you to the Columbia?"

"That's it, Frank, you're staying with the Shoshone."

"But, *Patron*—"

"But nothing, boy," he interrupted. "Me and Captain Lewis talked long about you. When we saw we wasn't going to get over the mountains and back this season, the way we planned, we both figured you'd be safer wintering with the Indians than going on with us. Besides, boy, you're forgetting something that Captain Lewis ain't; I mean your father. He's the whole reason the captain's let you come this far. Now you know that, and you know where your duty lays. It's here, somewhere, with Achille Rivet. Admit it Frank, you've let Sacajawea make you look shallow and small through forgetting your father. That ain't Captain Lewis's fault, nor mine. It's yours."

We both fell silent.

There was no way out for me naturally. I could not real-istically expect Lewis to add my father to the already taxed concerns of the Corps. Neither could I expect to simply find my father and then say to him, *au revoir,* continuing merrily over the mountains with the Americans. My entire motivation, from La Charrette to the villages of the Mandan, and from Milk River to Three Forks, had been to seek out and to find—*and to restore to freedom*—my cap-tive father. First Clark, at some risk, had supported this motive. Then Lewis, himself, had given in to it when con-fronted by the dedication to its purpose which I had shown in following the party all of the way from Fort Mandan to Two Lean Antelope. Now I could not ask either captain to understand that which I myself had not truly understood until this very moment when reminded of it by Captain Clark's honorable admission of the company decision to leave me with the Shoshone.

But I knew the truth: from La Charrette to Fort Mandan I had followed the American commanders in their gallant adventure to beat the British to the northwest ramparts of an unknown empire; and from Fort Mandan to these present forks of the Missouri, I had followed those same comman-ders and that same rash Louisiana gamble *and* an Indian waif known as Sacajawea. Never, saving perhaps for the first inspired moment in the woodbox of my aunt Célie when for the first time I heard that my father might still live, had I honestly been driven by the given excuse of looking for Achille Rivet. This truth came very hard to me now.

It came even harder for me when I tried to state it for Captain Clark. I struggled, I stumbled, I bumbled and began again. It was no good and I knew it was no good. At last I tossed my arms wide.

"*Voilà!*" I exclaimed, "I don't know how to say it, *Patron,* but I mean to go with you over the mountains. *Le bon Dieu* will have to look after my father, as he has done so far. I won't stay with him, or with the Snakes. I stay with you, or I die. That's final."

He nodded, without smiling.

"Dying is always pretty final, Frank," he said, "but this time you'll do as you're told. If you want to die about it, that's up to you. I can only tell you what Captain Lewis has decided and what I've agreed to. You'll stay with the Shoshone, boy, and *that's* final."

43

How strange, how small, how untoward our individual endings. For fifteen months I had traveled over two thousand miles of wilderness with death and disablement as my daily companions. No hour had been free of its small danger, no day or week lacking in its great one. Cold and hunger and pain had been mine. Heat and exhaustion and fear had shadowed me, awake and resting. Half-breed and métis and mongrel I had been called, and worse. Yet all of this had been accepted happily and with fond hope. I would be an American, I would be a white man, I would be as my companions, if only I bore what they bore, endured what they endured, did not cry out nor complain when they did not. What a poor fool, I! And what a vain protester in the end.

We went on up the northwest fork, named the Jefferson by Clark and Lewis in honor of their President. It was not in one day, or two, or seven, as predicted by Clark, that we found the Snake Indians, but thirteen days. On August 11th, Meriwether Lewis, working out ahead with Drewyer and John Shields, saw the first Shoshone. The man took fright at their approach and fled, but our men kept upon his track. This led them, on Monday the 12th, to an Indian trail of very ancient markings back in the mountains. This trail led west, and upward. It took them to a high ridge, which it traversed by a narrow gap. To their immense excitement they found, upon threading cautiously through this pass, that the falling waters of a clear streamlet on its other side flowed not their own way but *westward!* They had crossed the Divide! They stood on the headwaters of the Columbia!

The following day having taken the Indian trail down the far slope, they encountered the first of the Shoshone and were able to communicate through Drewyer and the sign language that they sought the Snake Grand Chief, Cameahwait.

It was three days thence, August 17th, when the remainder of us, following tediously up the Jefferson with the canoes by portage and tow and pole, heard a far hail and looking ahead, saw several Indians mounted on elegant horses standing on a granite headland watching us.

At the sight of them Sacajawea, who with Clark, Charbonneau, York and myself was walking ashore in the fore of the canoes, gave a wild cry like none any of us had heard. She began at once to dance about like a demented thing, and to suck noisily upon the fingers of her right hand. At this, Charbonneau turned to Clark, showing some spirit of his own.

"That's the sign of recognition," he shouted. "Look! See, she sucks the fingers, then shakes them at the Indians.

251

They're her people, *Patron*. We're looking at the Shoshone!"

It does not seem fair that my own words express this greatest hour in the expedition's fate. All that the Americans had gambled upon, all that Sacajawea meant to them and to their government now marched with Captain William Clark toward the nearby band of Cameahwait. With that band waited the horses of the Snake Indians. Or, if they did not, then disaster waited for the Corps and its bold commanders around that last bend of the river. The answer hung upon the turn of history's card within that coming hour. I was there with Clark and black York and red Shahaka to see it. If in my breast some emotion lingered of anger against my fate, of deep feeling that but for Frank Rivet and his discovery that Sacajawea was the sister of the Shoshone Grand Chief, this entire company might well have finally starved for horses; if, in fact, some shreds of this unsung contribution still cut at my insides with its keen blade of remorse and half-breed's fierce resentment, then it may be forgiven of me, and understood, that I yield to Captain Meriwether Lewis for the telling of how that card of history was turned in the council at the high bend of the Jefferson.

Let the Quiet Chief tell it. It was he who found the Shoshone.

. . . While the boats were performing the circuit, Clark went towards the forks with the Indians, who, as they went along, sang aloud with the greatest appearance of delight. They soon drew near to the camp, and just as they approached it a woman made her way through the crowd toward Sacajawea, and recognizing each other, they embraced with the most tender affection.

The meeting of these two young women had in it something peculiarly touching, not only in the ardent manner in which their feelings were expressed, but from the real interest of their situation. They had been companions in childhood, in the war with the Minnetarees they had both been taken prisoners in the same battle, they had shared and softened the rigors of their captivity, till one of them had escaped from the Minnetarees, with scarce a hope of ever seeing her friends relieved from the hands of her enemies.

While Sacajawea was renewing among the women the friendship of former days, captain Clark went on, and was received by Captain Lewis and the chief, who after the first embrace and salutations were over, conducted him to a sort of circular tent or shade of willows. Here he was seated on a white robe; and the chief immediately tied in his hair six small shells resembling pearls, an ornament highly valued by these people, who procured them in the course of trade with the seacoast. The moccasins of the whole party were then taken off, and after much ceremony the smoking began.

After this the conference was to be opened, and glad of the opportunity of being able to converse more intelligibly, Sacajawea was sent for; she came into the tent, sat down, and was to interpret, when in the person of Cameahwait she recognized her brother; she instantly jumped up, and ran and embraced him, throwing over him her blanket and weeping profusely: the chief himself was moved, though not in the same degree. After some conversations between them she resumed her seat, and attempted to interpret for us, but her new situation seemed to overpower her, and she was frequently interrupted by her tears.

After the council was finished, the unfortunate woman learnt that all her family were dead except two brothers, one of whom was absent, and a son of her eldest sister, a small boy, who was immediately adopted by her.

The canoes arriving soon after, we formed a camp in a meadow on the left side, a little below the forks; took out our baggage, and by means of our sails and willow poles formed a canopy for our Indian visitors. About four o'clock the chiefs and warrriors were collected.

We explained to them the purposes of our visit and the necessity of requesting them to furnish us with horses to transport our baggage across the mountains, and a guide to show us the route, they to be amply remunerated for the horses, services, etc.

The speech made a favorable impression: the chief in reply declared their willingness to render us every service. He concluded by saying that there were not horses here sufficient to transport our goods; but that he would return to the village and bring all his own horses and encourage his people to come over with theirs. The conference being thus ended to our satisfaction, we then distributed our presents which much pleased them. . . .

So it was that the expedition was assured of its horses by Cameahwait and the main band of the Shoshone. Some details of minor nature remained, as inevitable in any barter with Indians. But the word of Sacajawea's brother

254

had been given and the mountains would be crossed with baggage animals furnished by the Snake Indians of the Big Rock Mountains. The Shoshone words, *"Ah hi e!"* had been spoken with the American captains, meaning, "I am much pleased, I am much rejoiced," and the Snakes would honor those words. Hearing Sacajawea so assure Clark and Lewis upon leaving the council with her brother, I could not help but wonder if one of them, Clark at least, might not see fit at this moment to come over and give me a personal *"Ah hi e!"* for my part in providing those precious Snake horses. But he did not do so. In fact, he and Lewis at once went into a conference of their own, and most intent about it, too. The upshot of this was that the expedition must be made to move on quickly. It was decided that Clark should depart with an advance force in the morning. He would take tools for canoe building and when he got far enough down the Columbia, or its first, best tributary, to where there was navigable water and fit trees, would commence construction of new dugouts. There he would also send back word to Lewis, who would meanwhile be bringing all the baggage forward from the cache at Shoshone Cove, on the headwaters of the Jefferson, to the main camp of the Cameahwait band. This camp lay west of Lemhi Pass, on the Columbia side, and it was here that the captains planned to begin the great portage through the remainder of the Big Rock mountains to that point where Clark would have found his canoe water on the Columbia or its best tributary.

As well, Clark was to take with him on the first part of his journey Charbonneau and Sacajawea, dropping off the latter in the Shoshone camp so that she might lend her personal effort to the collection and selection of the best possible pack animals. With her, as far as the Shoshone camp, would go two other members of the expedition. One would be Shahaka, the Mandan ambassador. The other would be François Rivet. And, ah yes, excuse it; there would be also a third member departing the main company at Cameahwait's village. His name? Omar Khayyám, of course. His tribe? Assiniboin. His profession, his rank of service to the company? Watchdog and enemy smeller.

44

It required eleven days and nine horses to move the baggage of the expedition over the Divide via Lemhi Pass to the village of the Cameahwait band on the headwaters of the Columbia. No respite was taken here. Captain Clark, probing down the forks of the Salmon River, returned to say that water transportation by this route was impossible. The Salmon, called The River of No Return by the Shoshone, was nothing but one solid white froth of deafening cataracts. Moreover, its sheer rock walls offered no track even for passage on foot, and no horse could possibly pass down it to the main Columbia. This intelligence created the gravest of situations for our captains.

The season was now far gone. Cameahwait said that within the next week snow storms would commence. The salmon had already disappeared from the Lemhi River, upon which the band had its fish weirs. They were nearly gone from the Salmon River itself. The game was leaving the high country to go below. In weeks, even within days now, life could not be supported in the mountains. The

Shoshone would leave as soon as their white guests did, for if the Indians did not go quickly back over Lemhi Pass to the hunting country on the Missouri side at Three Forks, where traditionally the Shoshone people wintered, they would die in the mountains. A precisely similar fate awaited the white men if they did not now go at once down to the land of the Chopunnish, the pierced-nose people, where food might be found again and where canoe water began once more on the Columbia River.

Clark and Lewis did not linger to debate this advice. The situation was reduced to what the Mandan Indians had warned us it was all the previous winter. Despite Jefferson's dreams, there was no easy, short, one- or two-day passage by land from the headwaters of the Missouri to those of the Columbia. There was only a choice of hard, long passages. And as to ways of making even those passages, there was no choice but the packhorse, bred and trained to survive those barren heights where there was no major game in any season, and where the only sustenance was that carried along by the traversing party.

This confrontation with the cruel facts seemed to strike Lewis heavily. Clark had ceased to believe in the short passage some time ago, but Lewis had persisted even to Milk River and beyond in believing that the distance to the Pacific was far less than it actually was, and that the expedition might yet hope to reach its shores and return in the season of 1805. Now all that was far behind. The question was one of simply getting out of the mountains and down to the Columbia lowlands in what was left of the season for that year.

In trading with the Shoshone the past week, Captain

257

Lewis had procured another twenty horses, giving the expedition a total of twenty-nine mounts. These were young and strong animals and had been selected by the senior captain with an eye to two main qualities, those of bearing burdens and of serving to grace the company stewpot, of which the latter was to prove vital.

During that same week I had made my inquiries after my father. In this business, Clark being absent on the Salmon River scout, Captain Lewis did me just and kind service. By his offices with Cameahwait, using Sacajawea as intermediary, it was learned that Achille Rivet, known as "the dead man," did indeed reside with the Shoshone. As the legend of the lower river held, he was originally sold as slave, but subsequently treated as tribe member. Presently, he enjoyed full respect of the band and, also, fair health and happiness of spirit. Insofar as Cameahwait might tell us, all seemed well with my long-missing parent. However, and unfortunately for any last outside chance that I might persuade the captains to permit Achille and me to accompany them to the Columbia, my father had only "just now" departed to visit a neighboring band of Shoshone over on the Stinking Water. When further interrogation revealed that Cameahwait's "Stinking Water" was Captain Lewis's "Philanthropy River," passed on the Missouri side by the expedition on August 8th, three weeks gone, my heart admitted final defeat.

My fate was sealed. Since Cameahwait's band would pass the Stinking Water going toward their winter camp at Three Forks of the Missouri, it was decided that I should ride with the Indians, collect Achille Rivet from the sibling band, and continue with Cameahwait's people until spring brought the expedition back over the mountains, homeward bound. It was even arranged by Lewis with the chief—smoked over and hands shaken upon it—that the Shoshone should wait with me and my father at the forks for the rendezvous in early June, a full month later than the Shoshone usually lingered in those Missouri lowlands. Considering the very real reasons of fear in which these people of Cameahwait's held the Minnetaree and Sioux buffalo-hunting bands, this concession was a major one, and was, moreover, an act of entire faith and friendship toward me on the part of Lewis. Yet my mood at the time did not permit of any such charity in judging the "Quiet Chief's" decision to abandon me. So it was with no relinquishment of my inner hurt that, upon the morning of August 30, 1805— a gorgeous, sunbright, warm and summery mountain day—I sat with black heart upon a slope outside the camp of Cameahwait's Shoshone, watching and waving after the departing figures of my comrades.

There had been no formal good-byes. What might one say of farewell to such men as brave Drewyer, keen-eyed George Shannon, roguish, childlike York and red-haired, homely Captain William Clark?

If I opened my mouth, my heart would have cried out from it. Had I faced them, my tears would have washed out their respect for me. No, I was doing all that God had given me the courage to do, simply by crouching back upon the mountainside to wave my *bon voyage!* from its sunlit safety. Hence my surprise was doubly great to hear Clark's familiar quiet voice sounding at my shoulder there above Cameahwait's lodges. I whirled about in reply to its calm greeting.

"Patron!" I gasped. "You, here? What has happened?"

"Nothing yet," he said, grinning, as he got down from his fine spotted horse. "You didn't think I'd leave without shaking hands with my Pawnee, did you?"

He came up to me, big hand held out. I took it and we shook somewhat awkwardly. I was weeping. I had to hold my head to one side. If he saw the tears, he made no sign that he did. After a moment, our hands parted.

"Well, *Patron,*" I murmured, "many thanks. You know that my heart rides with you. It was a fine thing for you to come up here and take my hand."

"Frank," he nodded, ignoring my sentiments, "I'll say only this by way of good-byes: Captain Lewis has promised that we shall pick you up on the return trip. To his vow I'll add my own personal word. I'll be here, boy, come what may." He paused, studying me. "You know, lad, that time is bound to get mighty long and lonesome for you before we see one another in the spring. So when it does, you just think of Captain and his promise, you hear?"

"*Patron,*" I said, "I can't speak. You can see me crying. Do you want those damned Shoshones down there to think that I'm a woman? Go on now. Leave me alone."

He laughed and clapped me on the shoulder. "By God, Frank," he said, "you'll do to pole the river with! Come along here, I've brought you some things." He turned back to his mount, and I followed him. "All right," he said, unhooking an old Mandan cornbag from his saddlehorn, "here's what we've got."

His freckled and hairy fist dived into the bag and came up with a beautiful double-cavity Kentucky bullet mold, which I recognized at once as the very treasured property of my fellow scholar, George Shannon.

260

"Shannon says you stole the blasted rifle from him, you may as well have the mold that fits her like a sweetheart's kiss. He says good cess to you, and God favor your tribe."

The hand dived into the bag again. "Drewyer just sends the knife," he said, handing me the shimmering Sheffield blade worth its weight in platinum this 2,500 miles from St. Louis. "You know Drewyer. He's French. It must have hurt him something fierce to turn loose of it."

I nodded dumbly, and he reached into the bag again.

This time it returned with a weird trophy likewise well known to me. It was a carving of elephant's ivory, an exquisite African charm pendant from a solid gold slave necklace of Arabic link.

"Thank you, *Patron,*" I said gulping. "Next to his life, that's the most important thing in the world to York. It's all he owns. I wonder that he would part with it."

"I don't," said Clark. "You were his only friend, Frank. That's why you got the trinket. I reckon you'd best keep it, boy; I doubt you'll garner another one in this lifetime."

"Yes sir," I said, and pocketed the exotic bauble.

"Hold on," he said, "there's more—"

He then gave me a Jefferson medal of the first class, the one reserved for grand chiefs, complete with its red ribbon and clasp. He didn't put it about my neck, but only nodded. "Just put it in your warbag and let it set. The day'll come when you'll look back and get a little eyeshine out of it. It's from Captain Lewis, boy; and you know he ain't give one of those to any man in this company. He meant it to do you proud. See that it does."

Again I gulped and bobbed my head.

"Now, Frank," he said, "There's only you and me left. I

261

got something I'd like you to have, too. I've noted you casting green eyes at it ever since the Teton Sioux."

Before I might guess his intent, he had unbelted his famed horse pistol and draped it, scabbard and all, over my shoulder. "It shoots two inches high at fifty paces, dead-blank at twenty-five," he said. "Keep your powder dry and your flint handy, boy"

He turned and swung up on his Shoshone mount and I had to run to catch at his stirrup. He wheeled the horse away from me with a flourish and a wide bright grin, however, and cried out, "Stand back, there! *Allons donc—!*" Then he spurred the nervous brute down the mountainside in a dashing shower of rock and loose talus. I gazed after him, throat tight, eyes brimming.

Later, I thought of a thousand farewells to say. All brave, all noble, all quick of wit. That day no words came.

45

I had never seen an entire Indian camp on the move, much less been a part of such a migration. Hence, the trip with the Shoshone back over Lemhi Pass and the Continental Divide to the Missouri River side of the Big Rock Mountains was an event of some genuine excitement. When a rollicking nomad band of 400 people, together with 700 horses, 100 and more weanling foals and old packmules, and the several score of mongrel dogs which are as certain as flies to follow Indian camps, begin to move and to make noise at the same time the result is startling. Men shout, women scream, children wail or bawl or shriek with laughter. Stallions challenge shrilly, mares squeal and bite, colts whicker and kick, mules bray, dogs howl or snarl in endless fights, and the nerves of even the half-white stranger suffer the exercises of hell.

But, ah, the compensations! Due to my status as Clark's protégé, I was permitted to ride at column's head with Cameahwait and Shahaka. I was mounted in accordance with the privilege of one of the young chief's superb buffalo horses. This animal was one of the prized "appaloosies" descended—or stolen!—from the herds of the Chopunnish, the Pierced-Nose or Nez Perce Indians of the Columbia country. His color was a bright blood bay, the entire rump wildly splattered with white blotchings, the face blazed, all four feet stockinged, the braided mane and "buffalo-bobbed" tail a shining blue-black. His name developed to be something which neither Shahaka nor I could translate from that reasonably adequate amount of the Shoshone tongue imparted to us by Charbonneau's squaw during the winter at Fort Mandan. It was something betwixt Sun Dancer, Red Runner, Sun Lance and Bright Arrow, Shahaka guessed. With typical Indian generosity he further suggested I take my choice of these options, since the way that I spoke Shoshone made the selection academic at best. Accepting his council for what it was worth—nothing—I gave the appaloosa a handsome Indian name in English.

Red Lance he was, from that day forward, and as noble a comrade as Omar Kyayyám, or any other.

So it was with understandable Pawnee pride that I rode that first day with Cameahwait and the Mandan, Shahaka, at the head of the long Shoshone column winding upward to the granite gap of Lemhi Pass. And as I rode, I began to

263

listen to the Mandan emissary and the young Shoshone Grand Chief commence their exploratory talks on the idea of the great Indian peace proposed by Lewis and Clark. Thus, by the time we reached the top of the Divide and paused there to rest the horses, I had fallen into the rhythm of the guttural language and graceful handsigns passing between the two chiefs and was able to gather what Captain Clark would have called the "drift" of Cameahwait's legendary speech at Lemhi Pass on that thirtieth day of August, 1805.

"My Mandan brother," the young chief began, "this Shoshone uncovers his ears to your words of peace. If, as the white chiefs say, the Mandan are able to keep the peace with the Teton Sioux and the Pahkees (Minnetarees), then the hearts of my people will be big for Shahaka and his people; but if you must fight the Sioux and we both must fight the Pahkees, let us then do it now. The white soldier chiefs have shown us how straight they shoot with their remarkable guns. They have told us they will be our friends and fight with us against our enemies. They say you Mandans will do the same. They even say that they have the promise of the Pahkees to keep the new peace. Maybe this is so; I would like to believe it. What do you say, brother?"

Shahaka then replied that he believed the peace would be kept by the Minnetarees and that the Minnetarees truly would kill no more Shoshones. He expressed his conviction that the people of the dreaded Le Borgne respected and feared the long guns of the Red Head Chief and the Quiet Chief, and would behave as promised, and leave the Shoshone in peace.

To this, Cameahwait nodded soberly. He straightened,

gazing eastward down the trail to Three Forks and the Missouri winter camp, fierce eyes alight.

"It is done then," he said softly. "The Shoshones will keep the peace in the Big Rock Mountains. The Mandans will do the same on the Big Muddy River. We vow it together, you and I. The Shoshone will be safe to visit you, you will be safe to visit the Shoshone. And the white men will be safe to visit any place in the Indian country. It is good. It is as it should be. Let us touch the hands upon it." The two Indians touched their finger tips briefly—a contract never to be broken—and that was the whole of it.

What a simple and delightful people! What a pity, too, that the white man could not decide his truces so bloodlessly! But then, this pagan truce would not endure either. It would end, no doubt, as any white-inspired Indian treaty, in despair and little else.

I wondered, though, even as the glum thought struck me, if in this case, such would truly be the end. And, looking at the beautifully muscled Cameahwait and the tough, good-humored Mandan, I suddenly—and with a lifting sweep of my own Indian spirit—decided that it would not. This time it *could be* different.

Suppose, I told myself, that the Mandan and Shoshone *did* keep the peace they promised to make in the name of Jefferson's captains? Would not then all the land from St. Louis to Fort Mandan to the Big Rock Mountains be opened to the Americans? Surely it would, for the ravages of the warlike Indian tribes had been the only real obstacle to travel and settlement in that vast Louisiana, and Jefferson had correctly understood this. Now, should the captains but secure the last link—the agreement of the Nez Perce to keep the peace—would not this entire great northwest country become, in fact, the exclusive province and property of the United States? It would, it surely would, I knew. And when I realized this truth, there upon the silent mountain, I realized, too, that enormous gift of vision which had been shared by the President and his sturdy captains.

Granted only success with the Nez Perce, Clark and Lewis had secured all of the Louisiana to American use and had won their boat race with the British while still 600 miles from the mouth of the mighty Columbia and the shores of the Sunset Sea!

What a remarkable pair! What strangely driven and devoted men were these! What soldiers, what explorers, what engineers! What geographers, cartographers, botanists, biologists, hunters, scouts, envoys, physicians, stargazers, midwives, menders, traders, statesmen, chemists, cannoneers! Ah, *quels capitaines!*

Reining the red appaloosa around to face back whence we had come, and whence I had parted with the expedition, I sat very tall upon his back and raised my right hand in stiff, proud salute to the West and my vanished comrades of the Corps of Volunteers.

"What are you doing, Brother Frank?" called Shahaka impatiently. "Don't make us wait for you. Come on now, it's a very long way down to Three Forks and the buffalo country. Forget your friends. They have gone to the Columbia and you are returning back the other way. That's life."

I wheeled the appaloosa about once more, eastward this time, and rode on with Cameahwait and Shahaka down the Missouri side of the Great Divide.

46

The actual miles back down the eastern slope to the head waters of the Missouri and the Stinking Waters confluence were not many; as nearly as I judge, some sixty-five or seventy by the Indian Road, generally following the banks of the Jefferson River. But Cameahwait was in no hurry after that first day and first long ride, which took us down from the 8,000-foot highlands of Lemhi Pass to the lower canyon of the Jefferson at 6,000 feet.

Here we camped in a slight widening of the chasm which the Shoshone euphemistically described as Valley of Sunshine. I failed to concur. Even at 6,000 feet and August not yet gone, the mountain air had the bite of a scalpknife in it. If I might guess, the temperature was freezing at sunset. In the morning I did not have to guess; there was three-quarters of an inch of ice rimming the back pools along the river.

As the sun rose, I scanned the Divide above to see if the "big snow" had come during the night. It had. The towering pass and the range on either flank of it was solid, glistening white. Black clouds whipped and strung above the peaks told of high winds and still more snow to come. I shivered and sought out Cameahwait. His only comment was, "Eat your break fast and don't worry."

Now, on that second day, I again rode Red Lance at the head of the procession. We made good time since the lower way was naturally more open. Our camp that night was at the mouth of a fine valley called The Beaverhead by the Shoshone. With the third sunset we had descended another 1,000 feet and were at the confluence of the Stinking Water. With dawn of the fourth day, we were off up that fine stream, riding only hours away from journey's end of the 2,500-mile hegira from La Charrette to the land of the Shoshone.

Before the sun stood straight over our heads, I would see my father, Achille Rivet.

The scene was one of intense drama: the Indians felt it as exquisitely as I. Even the dogs seemed to fall silent. For the time it took Shoots Straight, the chief of the sibling village to find my father and to bring him to the riverbank gathering of both Shoshone bands, I do not think a cur whined or a colt whickered. There was one sound in the expectant hush, however, and that was Cameahwait's rich voice. It spoke in lowered tones, for my ear only. And its tones warned me in the last second of our waiting that something was not right. My eyes stabbed at him, watching for quick handsigns.

"I think you should know," he was saying, "that I sent your father here when I heard the white men were coming with you, his half-Indian son. I did not think even a half-Indian would want white men to see his father thus."

"To see my father 'thus'?" I signed to him. "In God's name, what do you mean?"

He did not comprehend my questions, but Shahaka, standing with us, spoke to him and he nodded and said to me, "Wait, you will see: I thought only to make you ready for something which is not good."

My heart froze. It was a kindness, I realized. But an Indian kindness. God knew what it hid, or threatened.

I was not long held in this torture. There was a stir on the far side of the Indian crowd and its ranks parted to reveal Shoots Straight coming toward us with a tall gray-bearded white man held by the arm and guided as a small child, or a man whose sight was gone.

"God's name!" I blurted in French. "He's blind!"

Shahaka, who plainly knew more than I had been told of this moment, only shook his head and replied to me in the same tongue and with singular emphasis.

"Not in the eyes, Brother Frank."

Shoots Straight and the tall white man stopped in front of us. I stared at Achille Rivet. Shahaka was right. He had no fault of vision. It was not his eyes which were empty, it was his mind.

The Indians waited, as they would, compassionately still. How is it that one knows when a fellow creature has lost his tenuous grip upon the world? What is there about the demented that we can see at a glance the brain has departed? Achille Rivet had that look. My father was fine of feature, handsome, straight-limbed, almost noble in bearing, the most exciting figure of a lost frontiersman; and he was mindless as a toddling child.

In the silence there upon the bank of the Stinking Water, Cameahwait said softly to me, "You will see how it is, Pawnee boy. Some damage to the brain from his long time beneath the flood waters. He is as the Teton Sioux told us, *tela nun wela,* dead yet alive. Do you understand now why it was that I did not want the other white men to see him in this altered way?"

I struggled to make reply, to state my thanks, but could not. The words simply refused to form.

"Come along, friend," said Shahaka, touching my arm. "There is no more to be done here. We have seen. Now it is for us to decide. Your father seems well, moderately content, even, in a sad way, happy. We shall just have to talk about what to do."

I permitted him to lead me off to one side, the Shoshone politely turning their eyes away from us, "giving us their backs," as they put it. This was their sign of respect for a stranger's sorrow, and it impressed me, reaching my heart.

"Shahaka, friend," I murmured, "you are two times my age, and a chief of your people. I know you to be wise and brave, also to possess a kind spirit. What would you do?"

He shrugged, palms spread outward.

"What an Indians always does, Brother Frank: talk."

"But with whom? Who can answer what I must ask!"

"Well," he said, "I would begin with those who know your father the best; Shoots Straight and his band."

"Yes," I nodded, "perhaps that would be good."

"And Cameahwait," said Shahaka. "He's a smart Indian. I would follow his words pretty carefully, I think. Besides, it is he with whom you and I must spend the winter. It is only common courtesy to include him, don't you think?"

"I do, yes" I admitted. "Will you speak with him and see if will arrange a talk with Shoots Straight and his elders?"

The Mandan chief smiled, his weathered, dark grin repressed but well pleased, in the Indian manner.

"I have already done so," he said. "Come, young friend, they are waiting now at the lodge of Shoots Straight."

Well, one must live with the red man to know even one-tenth of his good qualities. The Indian is like an ice-

270

berg; only one-fifth of his true self shows above the surface. The rest of him lies deep and silent and he does not expose it for any white man, fearing injury, betrayal or death for his trust. In this case, Shahaka, simple and pagan savage, had acted in a sensitive and right way that would have defied most educated men to equal, much less to surpass. Nor did the chief of the Stinking Water band prove any less equal in fact and compassion.

Shoots Straight explained that I was young, with my life before me. I had no need to burden myself with the care of a person who was happy where he was, and who was welcome in that place, also. "If you take this poor creature whose mind no longer thinks as our own, and you bring him to your people, in the settlements, he will not be happy any longer, and neither will you," he told me. "But if you leave him with us, he will be safe, and he will stay as you have seen him today. You know that the Indian looks upon such ones as touched by the Great Spirit. We are bound to care for these heedless ones, and to respect them. It is a pleasure for us, because we believe in this way. Shahaka tells me that your people do not. This is not to speak ill of your people. In ways they are kinder than the Indian is, Shahaka says. For one thing, they are more gentle with their old ones who are infirm. But we are all different, and your people are cruel to these strange creatures which the gods have put their hands upon. So I say to you, Pawnee boy: leave your father with us."

There was a pause then, while Shahaka brought me into full understanding of all that had been said. When I had it in my mind, I touched the fingers to the brow in the direction of the chief, and made the sign for him to continue.

271

"We live to the south of this place," he said, "many days travel. On the Wind River, down in the Wyoming country. It is not so deep with snow there and we find more elk and easier living. By the time that we return to the buffalo country next summer in the July and August moons, the American captains will have passed back through here and you will be with them. No white man, while we live, need know that your father is as he is. You can let it be known that he *did* die on the great Missouri River where the Teton Sioux found him. You can say that and you will not lie, my son. The man that you saw here on this day is not the father that sired you. He is not the father you came to find. He is not the father that your Pawnee mother, Antelope took vow to follow and make moccasins for, and to bear men children by. That father is dead. Go, young white and Pawnee brother. Bury your dead and depart in peace. That is what we say; what do you say?"

In truth, what could I say? When the proposal was made known to me by Shahaka in all its details, I rose and went to Shoots Straight, saluting him as a son salutes the father in this dark race. With the handsigns I replied to him that my heart would remember him forever, that his words were good, and that they were true. I told him that I believed he was a fine man and that if I ever might, I would repay him and his tribe, unto the third generation.

At this, he smiled warmly, coming to his feet in turn. "Be a good boy," was all he said, "brave and gentle like your father."

That was the brief, strange nature of the way in which I came to find my father, and to leave him, on the banks of that far, foreign river in the Big Rock Mountains called by its Snake Indian dwellers the Stinking Water. Of course, I went to visit Achille Rivet later in the day. It was my thought that some sight or sound of me could release his imprisoned memories.

The meeting led, however, only to another discovery which served but to make more certain my resolve to have him travel southward with the Wyoming band: during the entire hour I spent with him attempting to arouse a spark from the old days, he uttered no intelligible sound.

It was then that Lost Girl, who had learned a smattering of French while captive of the Minnetaree, and who had come with me to help me try to reach the mind of Achille Rivet, told me that in all his time with the Shoshone my father had spoken no word of any tongue. He had made no human sound at all, really, except the sounds of the body, such as to cough, to sneeze, to raise stomach gas and clear the throat of obstruction. He even laughed without noise. But oh, wait—yes, he did make another sound. He whistled. He whistled beautifully. He whistled sweetly and poignantly and melodiously and cheerfully as the prairie lark. Yet this truly was all. Past that he was mute as the mountains.

When I learned this, I took the tall white man's hand in my own. I pressed it and spoke the Shoshone word for farewell. He smiled as though he understood and pressed my hand with good will, nodding vigorously. Then, next moment, he dropped my hand, as quickly, and wandered off in the noisy, laughing train of a group of Shoshone children passing by just then bound for the river to bathe. As he went, I heard the high, sweet trill of his lark's whistling song, and saw the youngsters wave back to him and

273

beckon him happily to come along with them. Lost Girl informed me then that he loved the little children and acted as guard for the smaller ones of the band. He would permit no harm to come to them, had rescued many from drowning, from falling into fires, from walking or running over high places, and the like. The children, in repayment, gave him an especial love which, even as I stood watching its visible evidence, warmed the breast and spirit.

Here, I thought, this man belonged. Here he was wanted. Here he was important to these nomad, carefree people and to their gay, bright-eyed children. So be it. I was very glad I had come to see my father and to speak to him and to shake his hand. Now I knew that what I did was the right thing to do. Now I could go away with a quiet heart. I spoke quickly to Lost Girl and we went away from there, leaving my father with his Shoshone children.

I never saw him again, nor heard of how he fared. But, when the dew lies fresh and the sun bright upon the buffalo grass, I can still hear the cheery lark song of his parting whistle, falling from afar and happily.

Book VII
Fort Mandan and Farewell

47

Next morning the lodges were struck and loaded aboard the travois ponies before the sun was into the valley. All was cheerfulness. No feigned sorrow or false sadness for these red wanderers. Next summer they would meet again. How joyous would be that time! But presently, with a great tootling of eaglebone flutes, a waving of tasseled lances and a showing off of painted horses, the combined peoples moved off down the Stinking Water. At the joining of that stream with the Jefferson, one band went south, the other band went north. Within minutes the dear friends and relatives had lost sight of one another and the mountain stillness had resettled as completely as though there were no Indian nearer than one thousand miles to that remote confluence.

It was the time-bound way of my mother's people I soon learned. Where the red man passed he left the land as he had found it. No stones were rolled aside, no great trees felled, no course of any stream altered. No scars whatever were put into the ground, or upon its cover, which survival did not demand, or worship direct. No fields were plowed, no fences built, no foundations dug or laid. This was their mother, this wild earth. She bore them, she suckled them, she sheltered them and in the end she hid them. One did not cut the face of his mother. He did not waste her blood, nor shear of her hair. Neither did he scrape away tier skin, nor disturb her poor bones. He was her child and she cared for him as he cared for her, jealously, and it was not in his comprehension that he should cause her pain.

The weather having moderated, our band traveled at no great pace. We hunted, swam or fished in the river, made numerous halts for horse racing and games of stick-and-ball. At these times I was joined more and more by Sacajawea's funny little friend Lost Girl. We went well together and I did nothing to discourage her tagging after me. I knew it for a habit of Indian women, so we had no trouble and, by the time the band reached three Forks of the Missouri River on September 5th, we were good comrades.

Now, at the forks, the Shoshone quickly turned to making their winter camp. In the Minnetaree raid of the past year here, the band had lost all its lodges save Cameahwait's own big sixteen-pole council lodge. In the interim, they had made do with brush and pole shelters, and with willow-framed tipis covered with blankets, horsehides, trade goods or whatever "skins', would suffice. It became imperative, therefore, to replace the traditional buffalo-hide lodges which had been lost. This led to an immediate search for the herds. I was privileged to go on this scout, which set out the morning after our arrival at the forks. No women went along. Shahaka and I were employed as outriders for this crucial Shoshone hunting band due to the Mandan's long tongue. He had, in a word sold us both to the Snake Indians as the greatest scouts of the high plains.

But again, incredible luck was ours. Within the hour, we rode over a long swell of prairie and saw in our van, shooting close, a beautiful herd of young bachelor bulls. They were about 100 in number, rolling fat, unhunted and quiet as pasture cattle. Slipping back over the crest of the rise, we walked our horses up the river for a mile, then let them run full out for the Shoshone hunters following in our wake. We came up to them, guided them back to the rise, and found our herd had grazed even closer to our covert.

Cameahwait then separated his hunters, half of the sixty total number going far out around the herd and getting into position on its downstream side. Then, at a signal from the

Grand Chief—a barking wolf's cry—both downriver and upriver hunters attacked simultaneously, and even though the Shoshone were armed exclusively with short lances and old smoothbore Hudson's Bay muskets, such was the close stalking of the buffalo that the harvest among them was extremely great. Of the 100-odd animals, eighty-eight were down on the ground when the last balls had been exploded and last lance hurled home. In the history of the Big Rock Mountain Snake people, no hunter had exceeded this one in skill and fortune. The honors were unhesitatingly given to Shahaka and myself, and these honors were scarcely the less important for the fact that within the next unbroken skein of forty-seven days, not one other head of buffalo was seen at Three Forks, or within five scout camps of that place.

The squaws preferred cows for their lodgeskins but since they had been living in brush huts through a hard winter and long summer, our bullhides were welcome indeed. The weather god also cooperated. For the following two weeks fair skies and warm sun prevailed. The hides cured and the meat dried on the jerky racks. By the end of September the new lodges were dotting the sheltered meadow cove at the forks, the dried buffalo beef was baled and stored, the Shoshone were gorged on fresh cuts of all the delicacies—boudins, livers, hearts, tongues, tenderloins, backfat strips and humpribs—the pemmican was pounded and sacked in its gut bags, firewood was hauled and stacked, the horses were turned out on the rich grass of the river thickets, where they might browse the cottonwood twigs and dig for the sun-cured prairie hay the winter through, and the people of Cameahwait were ready for the blizzard giant to begin his five-month rule of snow and ice.

The first great storm blew down upon us. October 3rd. For eight days and nights it raged, seating us in our snug lodges. It was as midnight at noontime. The wind howled like a prowling wolf. The temperatures plummeted to zero, to ten, to twenty, to forty below zero. We did not see the blue sky until late in the morning of October 11th. Then it was for only an hour or two. Following this, the snow commenced again, although with less wind and less Arctic cold. We were able to be outside again and to move between the lodges and to see our friends. The Shoshone told me that in the memory of the oldest living member of the band there had been no single storm such as this one wherein the daylight had vanished and the wind been so terrible that no movement outside the lodges might be risked. It was evident to them all, they said, that but for the big buffalo kill the entire tribe might have perished there at Three Forks in the awesome, icy wind.

The natural result of this conviction was the elevation of Shahaka and myself to tribal first rank. Cameahwait called a council of all the old men during which he recounted the above indebtedness and then said he was honoring the occasion by giving me his Shoshone war name of Tooette-cone, which meant Black Rifle. Cameahwait also gave to me the peerless buffalo horse, Red Lance. Overcome by this gesture, the aging father of Lost Girl stepped forward and presented me not only with his daughter but with a fine new lodge of eight skins to go with her. Here was a chanceful moment, for I might not refuse this gift and accept Cameahwait's. Hence, I made the receiving speech as gracefully as possible, content that I could persuade

278

Lost Girl to allow me to joy the sanctity of my new home with no more company than Shahaka and Omar. This confidence, too, was. misplaced. The Mandan was voted a lodge of his own. Then he, the empty-headed jackass, thinking to spare me the embarrassment of having the old father sitting around in *my* lodge the while Lost Girl and I made the acquaintance moves, selflessly offered to share *his* lodge with the toothless old chief. I could more happily have knifed him, but for the sake of the spirit as well as the outright letter of the Shoshone law in such matters, I bowed to his charity.

This, I remember clearly, was on the morning of October 14th. At sundown of the twenty-ninth, having been afoot in the mountains for twenty days and nights, with only one blanket, his bow and arrows, fire tinder and a packet of dried fish, the aged Shoshone guide Toby appeared at Three Forks. He was the Shoshone guide supplied by Cameahwait to take Clark and Lewis on through the mountains and down the Columbia River as far as the camp of Twisted Hair, the Nez Perce main chief. The old man was the only Shoshone of the band who had been all the way to Nez Perce country, and so was the only guide Cameahwait could supply our captains. Nonetheless, due to Toby's extreme age, Cameahwait had worried lest the ancient warrior would not be able to remember the trail to Twisted Hair's people, and so be able to safely bring the American captains and their men to the Nez Perce camp. Now the dramatic, unexpected appearance of old Toby at the Three Forks camp on the Missouri side of the Big Rock Mountains posed a sudden fear that a bad fate had overtaken the expedition, and that he had deserted it, and returned to his Shoshone homeland.

Toby, however, told a different story. He had, he claimed, made such good time on the return trip from the camp of Twisted Hair, only because he had used the secret Indian route going by way of Traveler's Rest and down the Missouri slope by the Blackfoot River; a route, which, had our captains known of it when coming up the Missouri, could have saved the expedition untold weeks of agony. This "Nez Perce road to the buffalo country," as Toby called it, had, he insisted, permitted him to come down from the Divide in *seven* days, as against the incredible *fifty-two* days the expedition had taken to reach the same point via Jefferson River and Lemhi Pass.

As for Clark and Lewis and The Corps of Volunteers, he concluded, all were safe in the camp of Twisted Hair, which Toby had found for them as charged to do by Cameahwait, and were being restored with good food and kind treatment after nearly starving and freezing to death on the terrible Lemhi trail to the land of the Pierced Noses.

His own story was not much. He had stayed with the American chiefs only long enough to be certain the Nez Perce meant to treat them well. Then he had turned back homeward, leaving quietly in the middle of the night, and refusing to accept one penny of the pay promised and due him for his services. He had simply made himself a set of rabbitskin snowshoes and with no food but that one little bag of dried salmon, had come back through those freezing mountains, utterly alone.

The tale was well nigh unbelievable, of course. Yet, strangely, the truth seemed to shine like a beacon light from the dark eyes of the old man who told it. In the end,

I cast suspicion and doubt from my mind. Be grateful for what you have heard from this old Indian, I told myself. Accept his story and take strength from it. Let it keep you warm until the springtime comes again and all last questions are resolved.

I shook hands with the old man and thanked him with lifting heart. I believed now that my comrades were indeed safely on their ways to the Sunset Sea. I believed too, that the captains would surely triumph over the remaining journey down the Columbia River and return. I was certain that, come fair June and the new young grass, there would come also down that ancient Nez Perce buffalo road from Traveler's Rest to the Missouri and our Shoshone winter camp at Three Forks, Captain William Clark, beloved black York and crusty old Toussaint Charbonneau.

And, ah, yes. With old Toussaint, God willing, would come my shy and sweet-mouthed young squaw, Sacajawea!

48

For the remainder of the winter at Three Forks I was comfortable and contented in my new lodge. Lost Girl lived with me. She was a bright thing and companionable Short, thick-set, bow-legged, large in face, foot and hand, she was the female opposite of her slender friend, Sacajawea. There was never between us the love a man and woman normally might know in circumstances such as ours. She accepted this fact. It was enough for her that she might serve "Brother Frank," and if she yearned to be treated as a woman, she did not reveal the want to me.

Thus we dwelled, with savage Omar, in our warm lodge with some happiness and not a few good times. We knew, also, some sadness and some hunger and as cold the red man always knows. An old mother might fall and thus shatter a hip on the ice, dying inevitably of the pneumonia induced by lying helpless and inactive. A toddler would play too near the tipi fire, tumble in and be burned severely. An older child might break through a rotten crust of comb ice on the river. A hunter would come afoul a crippled bull elk and be gutted or sliced half his length in working carelessly with the downed brute. These things happened. The Indians understood that they would. They nursed and buried their unfortunate, shaved their heads in mourning, wore ashes on the face. But always they went on with their lives, brightly, cheerfully, expecting better things the next day, not bemoaning their fortunes when they did not get them.

There were diversions. Lost Girl found somewhere a ragged and forlorn camp bitch and induced Omar to look upon her with fondness. The resulting litter of spotted wolfings shared our lodge with us, and with their unlovely parents through the turning of the year and until they were of pot age. Then Lost Girl, enlisting the gullible Shahaka, spirited the entire brood out of camp one black and howling night to avoid the certain ending of all Indian dogs in the cooking kettles. I did not learn until two moons later that the little squaw had found a nursing wolf bitch denned up in the riverbank above the forks. She had then waited until the she-wolf was away hunting, added Omar's offspring to the wild brood and stayed to be sure the foster dam took the strays to suck. She did, evidently, for later on we saw a pack of half-grown wolves coursing an old cow elk near the campsite, and five of the pack were as piebald with white patches as any settlement mongrel. So impressed were the Shoshone that they named the site Spotted Wolf Camp, and it was so known in their folklore from that time.

Then there was the exciting interlude when some of our hunters found a frozen, starving and far-lost band of French trappers, nearly dead, who had been caught upon these high reaches of the Missouri by their greed to take the last beaver they might before the snows. The bad blizzard of early October had surprised them, forcing them to make a winter camp and attempt to survive until the ice went out of the Missouri, and they might escape down to Fort Mandan. These men proved to be those same ones our captains had met in the week I was trailing behind on the way to Two Lean Antelope Camp, and of whom Captain Lewis speaks in the journal. But they had a surprise with them which would have startled my captains as greatly as it did me, and which, of course, was never included in the journal.

When I saw this bulky, square and loud-voiced bull of a man, who was the sole one of the sickened Frenchmen still on his feet and able to walk unaided, my heart leaped joyfully.

"Impossible!" I cried, actual tears of gladness streaming down my cheeks. "No! God's name, it cannot be you—"

But it was he, and with his riverhorse's bellow he replied to my greeting as feelingly as I had given it.

"Hell yes!" shouted Big Bat Deschamps, enfolding me in a brown bear's hug. "Skinny chicken! Water rat! But of course it is I. Here, let me look you over—"

It developed that he had taken a strange course upon

recovering his senses from York's skulling blow on the keelboat. "It was this way," he told me, while drinking willowbark tea in my lodge and letting Lost Girl minister to his less hardy mates. "You see, François, the blow on the head restored me my few brains. I saw that I had been wrong not to go beaver-trapping with these French fools when they first invited me to go. So I just bade adieu to Corporal Warfington and set out to catch up with these friends of mine who are over there dribbling their tea down their chins. Pah! They're all females and the sons of sheep. I have done little but wipe their noses for them ever since coming up with them at the Yellowstone. But come, little rooster, what of you? What of your brave *patrons?*"

I told him our history to that day and he shared my feeling that Clark and Lewis would prove equal to challenge of the Columbia, and that I should surely see them in May or June as they had promised. When he said that "I" would see them, rather than that "we" should do so, I thought it odd. Querying him on it, I received a sobering answer.

"François," he said, "over there in our buried cache of beaver, we have a fortune. I would never linger in this Indian nation one day that I did not need to. When *Capitaine* Clark comes up this river from Gates of the Mountains to keep his word with you, Baptiste Deschamps will already be long started down the river for Fort Mandan. We will be rich, my *confrères* and I, and we do not mean to risk this wealth by waiting for the summer sun and the buffalo grass."

"And you will go when the ice goes?" I asked sadly.

284

"Yes," he said. "By mid-April at the latest. You should come along, François. The *patron* would understand. He would advise it, I think. Why take chances?"

"I don't know," I admitted, "it's a great temptation . . ."

By the end of March, Deschamps and his men, restored by the care and kindness of the Shoshone, were constructing the rafts to carry their peltries down the stream. Soon after, they dug open their caches, and in the second week of the Soft Moon of Showers, the Shoshone April, the beaver peltries were baled, tied, loaded and lashed to the rafts. Big Bat and his Frenchmen were ready to sail. The waters were high and swift, the wind fair, the weather warm and clear. It was more, I thought, than an overpoweringly lonely half-breed youth might endure, that coming farewell on the spring-freshened banks of the mother river. I fought with all manly resolve to be equal to it, and to my rendezvous with Captain Clark. But even my Indian friends deserted me.

In the very last moment, Shahaka gave a great shout, advising one and all to pay attention. He had changed his mind, he said, and would, after all, accompany his French friends to Fort Mandan. That is, he would, he added, if there were room for one more than himself aboard the straining rafts. At this, Big Bat laughed and said there was always room for one more aboard a French *radeau,* as there was in an Indian lodge, but that he hoped the "one more" was not too big. Shahaka assured him that this was not the case and, to my amazement, produced a suddenly demure and smirking Lost Girl from the crowd of her Shoshone relatives thronging the debarkation beach.

I had thought my lodgemate and Shoshone housekeeper to be particularly merry the past few weeks, but had given it no consideration. I had even missed her a handful of nights and had understood her to be at Shahaka's lodge caring for her father. Hence, when the Mandan chief now came over to me, somewhat sheepishly, I was not altogether unprepared. "Brother Frank," he said to me, "I had thought to speak to you when this first happened. But the woman assured me there had been nothing of husband and wife between you, and so I believed her. You know that I would never violate the laws of the husband." I at once reached out and touched Shahaka on the left shoulder with my right hand, the sign that all was understood. "Mandan friend," I announced loudly, "you make my heart glad. Of course this woman was no wife to me, but only a true comrade, a sister. Take her to your lodge and to the Mandan people. Tell them that she is the cousin of Cameahwait and that this great Shoshone chief sends you with this fine Shoshone woman as a respect gift. Let her be Cameahwait's second blessing to the cause of peace between the tribes, as his sister Sacajawea was the first blessing. Go now, and good hunting."

Well, this oration proved an excellent, if expedient, move. Everyone was made happy by it. Even Big Bat had to admit that it was quite a speech.

"Skinny chicken," he bellowed, "you are no longer so skinny! I am going back down this damned mother river of ours and I shall report to Uncle François in La Charrette that he need no longer lament his broken ankle. I will assure him that there is once again a real Rivet upon the Missouri. You agree, François?" Perforce, I agreed. One did not argue with Big Bat.

At my concession, he laughed shatteringly, and yelled for Shahaka and Lost Girl to be aboard. Then he slashed the mooring ropes and himself leaped from shore to the dangerously overloaded deck of the first raft. The next moment the roaring spring tide had caught the clumsy craft. With its smaller mate bearing the other three Frenchmen, it swirled out into the channel, went lunging off down the river.

As far as I could see Big Bat, I could hear his brawny voice carrying above the cannonading of the swollen waters. *Quel hippopotame!* I thought. And, no sooner had I thought it, than I realized its truth. When Baptiste Deschamps swept out of my sight and out of my life around that far bend of the raging Missouri, I had waved good-bye to the last great king of the riverhorses.

I realized something else, too. I may have waved good-bye in the same moment to my last chance to escape.

With Big Bat, Shahaka and Lost Girl gone down the river, never to return, I might spend the remainder of my natural days among the Shoshone Indians waiting for a white captain who would never come.

49

Until Meriwether Lewis and William Clark had come to this distant land, no known white man had penetrated it. Now, with the Fort Mandan Frenchmen departed and with my brave comrades of President Jefferson's expedition still somewhere upon the far side of the Big Rock Mountains, dead perhaps at the bottom of the mighty Columbia or perished from disease, starvation or Indian treachery along the unknown trail, it could come to pass that no other white men would venture this way in my time.

I was now and truly alone. The realization brought a second uneasy fact to bear. From this moment I would be an Indian: when those rafts of the Frenchmen swept out of view, the half of me which was white departed with them.

The identical thought, strangely, seemed to invade the minds of Cameahwait's people. After turning away from the beach that morning, they ceased calling me "Panani" (Pawnee), or "taba-bone" (white man), and referred to me exclusively by their Shoshone title, Black Rifle. I was treated by them in all other ways as an Indian. Abandoning my own lodge, I lived with Cameahwait, hunted when he hunted, hungered when he hungered, slept when he slept, smoked when he smoked and, within the moon, was in every respect save that of taking a squaw, as pure a Shoshone as the youthful chief himself.

In the anxious weeks of waiting to learn if my comrades would return, I came to know those kindly, courageous people as few, if any, white men had until that time. It seemed to me, thus, only an act of justice to leave some picture of them behind so that they might be recalled as they were, rather than as they might become with the benefits of civilization.

The Snakes, as they were universally called, were not a numerous people, numbering but a few hundred souls divided into seven small bands. They lived from May to September in the Big Rock Mountains on the Columbia side, subsisting mainly, and miserably, on berries, boiled salmon, grubs, grasshoppers and the roots of the camas lily. In the fall they recrossed the Divide to hunt buffalo on the Missouri side, and to winter there, usually at Three Forks. In early spring they again resorted to the mountains to man the salmon traps until first snow flew

Notwithstanding this Spartan life amid the rocks and cold of the lofty Divide, they were a gay and cheerful folk encloaked with that special dignity reserved for the hard-pressed tribes of earth. They were particularly bright and trusting with strangers and always honest, a very raw quality in Indians. Like most real men they gambled and smoked excessively, but they neither begged nor importuned nor fawned upon the white man as other Indians invariably did.

Theirs was a male society. A man purchased or disposed of his women to suit his convenience or his purse. Male children were seldom corrected, never punished. As soon as they walked and talked, they were considered their own masters. To control was to corrupt, the Shoshones felt. The girls were less favored, although both sexes were unspeakably spoiled.

The virtue of the squaws was for hire. Most husbands would lend their wives for any token. However, if the freedom were taken without his granting it, blood would surely flow. Moreover, the errant woman would be as severely censured by her red sisters as would be any white settlement spouse. Even so these people treated their women with far more respect than any other tribe and they never pushed them shamelessly upon the white man as did the Sioux and Arikara. As to drudgery, the Snake women were as badly mated as any. They did *all* of the work. The men knew only one thing, to kill the enemy and to shoot that game which must be shot for the camp pot.

The Shoshone had the finest horses of any Indians, obtaining their seedstock from the Spaniards in Santa Fe, whence they journeyed to trade once or twice in each decade. From these same Spaniards they also obtained the large mules which the other tribes so envied and for one specimen of which they would quickly offer three prime horses, five good horses, two squaws, a fine rifle, or a virgin daughter.

The Snakes did battle only on horseback and would run from almost any enemy force if caught afoot. As a result of their dependence upon their mounts, they were the most amazing horsemen of the plains. They had also one unique weapon which, combined with their matchless riding, made them feared even by the Sioux and Minnetaree with their superior guns. This was the *poggamoggon*. It consisted of a wooden handle two feet long bound in rawhide. To one end of this, by a leather thong, was tied a heavy round stone in a buckskin balled pouch. At the other end a wrist thong prevented the rider losing his whiplike bludgeon while at the breakneck gallop. The havoc which was wrought by this whirling rock in close quarters was awesome.

The horse was ridden with only a hair-filled saddle pad held in place by a braided horsehair surcingle. The bridle was one thin rawhide thong looped about the lower jaw. The Shoshone used also the Spanish looped rope or catching line, by which they easily captured any running horse and used it as well in war to draw the enemy off his mount and drag him to death over the ground. No other Indian I had seen used this rope in such ways, although Cameahwait said that his father acquired the art from a captive Pierced Nose man, and not a Spaniard.

The Shoshone were an unlovely people to look upon. Grossly short, they had broad flat feet, coarse knees and slack long arms. The hair was worn to the shoulder. At that time, however, most of the men had the hair shortened in sign of mourning for friends and kinfolk killed in the Minnetaree raids of recent years. Cameahwait himself had cut his hair to a roach-maned length all over his head because of these losses. He looked odd but vastly fierce. Unlike the others, he was as tall nearly as I, with no heaviness.

For dress the women wore togas of antelope, mountain sheep, or muledeer skins trimmed with fox, beaver or wolf, girdled at waist and reaching but to mid-thigh. Beneath, they might or might not wear antelope leggins. Only the children fancied beads pendant from the neck. The adults preferred their bangles hanging from the lobes of both ears. The claws of the grizzled bear were of course the premier decoration, with elk's teeth and salmon backbones being in the second place of favor. The men wore eagle feather and otter fur headbands, the women nothing on the head in any season, while the children went naked, toe to head, from April to first snow.

Generally, then, these were the homeliest, the happiest, the poorest, best humored, most intelligent, hardy and trustworthy of all horse Indians encountered by the expedition in my time with it. To live one's life among them would not be by any means the cruelest of fates and I vowed anew that were I forced to it, I would accept the fact and permanently become one of their number with good heart. But oh, how I pleaded in private with my Savior that this possibility should not come to pass! And how I prayed aloud and yearningly on a second dark-skinned subject so near and yet so far from Three Forks.

Ah! Sacajawea! The time grows long, the hope surpassing faint. I die for you each day a little.

Through May I expected no sight of Clark and whatever of the company might appear with him. Even as the forepart of June passed I calmed myself with thoughts of the delays encountered on the Missouri, and reasoned the Columbia would be scarcely less difficult. It was when the fourth week dragged by that I began to know an empty cold in the pit of the belly. I tried to ease the fear with hard work. The buffalo had returned that spring and I fired the "black rifle" dawn to dusk in effort to help Cameahwait and the band get in enough meat to enrich their long poor season in the high country. June proved sunny. The buffalo jerky dried swiftly. Soon, thousands of pounds were prepared. The Shoshone then were ready to set out from Three Forks, their winter camp, and return over Lemhi Pass to the salmon fisheries and their mountain summer home. Only their vow to the American captains to have me at Three Forks in June held them now.

And in truth it was a great bravery they showed in staying with me, for with the buffalo had come their inevitable red shadows, the Mirnnetarees, the dreaded Pahkees of previous dark history here at Three Forks. By midmonth two Minnetaree scout parties had been seen far off, and the Shoshone nerves mounted. When, on June 30th, a third party of at least three dozen Pahkee braves was seen but one easy day's ride to the east of our camp at the forks, Cameahwait called me to him. Even as I responded to his summons, the squaws were striking the

292

lodges, the young men running in the pony herd.

"Toettecone," he told me gravely, "a time has come for this Shoshone to say good-bye to his brother. I wish you would come with us. We all wish that you would come with us over the mountain to the salmon fishing. What do you say to that?"

"I don't know what to say," I answered honestly.

"Well," he said, "you can see that I can no longer hold my people here. Already we have stayed too long. The Pahkees are all about us."

I nodded glumly. "Yes, I know. It's a bad thing. Do you think my captains will come this way again, Cameah-wait?"

He shook his head. "No, I don't think so. The Sunshine Moon is gone. This is its last day. Something has happened to your captains."

"This is possibly true," I admitted. "And you will not wait with me any longer to make sure of it, my brother?"

"You can see the lodges coming down, Tooettecone. I have no choice. I have kept you here as long as I promised your captain. My part is done."

"Again true." I sighed. "But my honor makes me stay and wait for them. They would think me a woman if they came and found me not here but fled back into the mountains with you."

Cameahwait struck his chest in sudden anger. I thought for a bad moment he would put his *poggamoggon* to me.

"I do not *flee* into the mountains," he answered, scowling. "I go into them. The salmon are running high in the streams over there on the other side. Don't you say that I run away!"

293

"Of course I don't say that," I apologized. "What do you take me for, a *taba-bone?*"

"No," he said. "You're no white man; you're of your Pawnee mother's people. Here, take my hand on it, brother. Grip my fingers and remember this winter we have spent together. Remember, too, that I gave you my war name and my second-best horse. Those are proud things. Honor them. *Ah hi e!*"

"*Ah hi e!*" I replied, and took his hand in mine. We exchanged grips silently, briefly.

Then he stood up and walked past me out of his lodge and I never had another word with him. Indeed, I was nearly brained by the lodgepoles being struck above me by his impatient squaws and within the hour the Shoshone winter camp at Three Forks, hereafter to be known in their legends as the Spotted Wolf Camp, had been leveled to the ground.

In another thirty minutes the final pots, pans, old ladies and young babies had been loaded aboard the pack animals and the travois ponies stood burdened with the poles and rolled skins of the lodges. There were no shoutings, no children's howls or laughter, no tootling of the eaglebone flutes or willow whistles. This was a silent, hurried departure and even the dogs were instinctively quiet. The only noises were from the horses and mules and even these were muted, since the young men drove the herd so pressingly its members were granted little time to whicker or bray their complaints. By noon, less than three hours from the return of our Shoshone scouts, I sat alone at the Three Forks of the Missouri River, my only comrades Omar Khyyàm, Red Lance, the lonesome whisper of the wind prowling that deserted fork timber, and my haunting fear that Cameah-wait was right—that Captain William Clark was not coming, and that I had accepted the best of all possible chances to get a Minnetaree musket ball through my guts by voting to wait for the Red Head Chief at Three Forks.

50

The first week in July passed. Omar, Red Lance and I moved ceaselessly from one fork to the other. We never bedded on the same ground two nights. We never made fire. We never discharged the rifle.

The impulse to leave Three Forks became well nigh irresistible. It would have been so easy to sneak up one of the several small tributaries of the main forks and to hide there in relative safety from the prowling bands of Minnetaree buffalo hunters. But I realized that should Clark come and find Frank Rivet not waiting, he would travel on.

Another three days inched by, seeming a month. I seriously consulted the idea of building a canoe to slip down the Missouri with Omar, abandoning Red Lance. But the noise needed to fashion either a dugout or a raft were too risky. Besides, I had given my axe to Cameahwait's wife and had only Drewyer's knife to carpenter with. As well, I hated to leave the noble horse.

But for fierce Omar, I would have weakened and starved in those latter days of my July skulking, since the little supply of Shoshone jerky which I could carry with me was soon exhausted. Omar, however, could give lessons to any lynx in pest hunting. He worked day and night to fill both our shrinking bellies with wood rat, rabbit and ground squirrel. Desperation mounted nonetheless. By the eleventh day of this diet I was reduced to devouring those dog-caught varmint things, intestinal content and all. On the twelfth day, except for an ermine skin and head which I seized to force away from Omar, I went hungry altogether. On the thirteenth day I determined to shoot a deer or elk if it cost me my long Shoshone braids.

Directly, I made my stalk of a fat young cow elk and put her down with one ball through her neck vertebrae. Half an hour later, as I built my fire congratulating myself on my good fortune in not alarming the Minnetaree to my presence, I thought I heard the familiar strike of pony hoofs on flinty river gravel. The following instant I knew that I heard Omars one and unmistakable "Indian growl."

I had Red Lance grazing near by under bridle, and I went aboard him without bothering to investigate the identity of my callers. Once under gallop, a quick glance back showed me they were the Minnetarees. I yelled on both Red Lance and Omar and we went away from that place, the Pahkee lead splashing rock and sand and broken twigs all about us. Undiscouraged by their indifferent marksmanship, the Indians left half their number to finish butchering out my elk, sent the remaining dozen braves on in my track at a purposeful, relentless lope.

The sun now was no more than four hours high. This left little chance to run until darkness might hide my friends and me. The only maneuver I could think of was to turn up the Jefferson and let Red Lance show his mountain breeding by outdistancing the prairie-bred mounts in the steep rocky going. Away we shot, then, up the latter stream for forty-five minutes the strategy worked well enough to keep the Pahkees out of rifle range behind us. Then, in negotiating a sharp, sandy bend in the ascending bank, Red Lance twisted his foreleg. I at once felt him begin to go rough beneath me and knew that my next decision was the simple choice of a place to die.

Immediately ahead lay a rock barricade. Seeing it, I slid off Red Lance and gave him a whack on the rump. But he would not leave me, and instead limped after me as I ran for the rocks. Omar, of course never left my side. It was in this moment of animal loyalty that the Minnetarees burst around the bend below and came whooping toward our fortress. Crouching low, I drew a fine bead on their chief and shot him through the throat at seventy paces. He went floppingly off his pony, jamming the next two mounts behind him and knocking them down into the bank rubble with their masters. Three down. Nine still coming. There was no time to reload. I pulled Drewyer's Sheffield blade, making ready to take one more of the red devils as they swarmed in on me. It was in this posture that I heard the sweetest sound to a lone white man in the wilderness world.

It was the booming, distinctive bellow of Tennessee and Kentucky long rifles, accompanied by the magnificent obscenity of English-American curse words of encouragement, that roared home upriver and behind my bouldered fort.

Overhead I heard the whistling passage of the rifle balls. In the next instant the Pahkee horses commenced to rear and fall. Four went down and the charge upon my breastworks degenerated. Pausing only to pick up their wounded fellows, the Indians retreated in total rout down the river. I turned, then, to identify my rescuers and was granted the thrill of my lifetime to see the brawny figure of Clark standing in the bow of the leading canoe. Behind him, in the remaining four craft; were Shannon, Shields, Windsor, Gibson, Bratton and some seven or eight others of my old friends. Almost at the same time, I recognized the canoes for those we had buried at Shoshone Cove at the headwaters of the Jefferson, and I knew then what had happened: Clark had returned from the Columbia by way of the Lemhi Trail rather than by the Nez Perce buffalo road. Had he taken all those tortured extra miles just to pick me up at Three Forks? I could not say. But when he stepped ashore and we embraced, I wept openly.

The men, old comrades all, made no awkwardness over my display of emotion. In fact, Shannon and Shields, hardiest of the lot, shared a tear or two with me in their gladness to find me alive and well. We must have looked like crazy men, hopping around and embracing and shaking hands upon that lonely mountain shore.

I was quickly delighted to discover that with the crew had come withered Old Toby, the Shoshone guide. He had found them digging up the cache at the Cove and insisted on coming back with them to make certain Clark did not forget to stop for me at Three Forks. After the aged warrior and I had exchanged hugs and respect signs, I asked him if he would come over in the rocks and look at my dead Pahkee chief. "Tell me," I said, "if you have ever seen him before. I would like to remember him, should he prove a worthy kill. He had my name on his bullets." A moment later when the old Shoshone had bent over the staring-red face of the Minnetaree whose throat I had blown out, he gave a loud cry and straightened up.

"*Ah hi e!*" he said. "This the Pahkee dog called Ten Sleeps. He is the one who stole Sacajewea and Lost Girl and killed our young men for whom we still have our hair cut. You have done a great thing for the Shoshone people, Tooettecone. Wait until I tell this to she who follows us close behind on the river!"

At this, I whirled upon Captain Clark.

"*Patron!*" I cried. "Sacajawea is with you and you didn't tell me!"

"By Tophet!" he exclaimed grinning. "I knew there was something I forgot. Well, anyways, there's your answer coming yonder round the bend."

He flung out his arm, upstream. There, just rounding into view, was the sixth of our cached canoes. In its stern, steering, crouched giant black York. Amidship, balancing cargo, wielding no paddle, performing no least labor as would be his squawman's prerogative lounged Toussaint Charbonneau. In his lap, chubby arms trailed at play over the canoe's side into the green water, little Pomp, the baby born to Sacajawea at Fort Mandan, laughed and chortled happily. And at the bow station, paddle fishing in the sun to fend the racing craft free of rock and snag through the cataract, Sacajawea herself bent and toiled proudly as a reed in high wind.

My heart thundered. Clark had come and he had come as I had asked God to send him—with York and Charbonneau and Charbonneau's slim squaw at his side. No man could have been happier, and not die from it, than was I in that timeless moment on Jefferson River.

51

Clark soon enough ordered the men back into the canoes. He had to meet with Ordway at the mouth of the Madison, he said, since the latter was overland with fifty head of prime Snake and Nez ponies from the cache at Shoshone Cove. Because the distance was not too great, he suggested that we share the walk back to the forks with my lamed mount.

In that time apart from the others, he told me the full tale of the expedition's harrowing "ride" down the Columbia and the following hard winter at Fort Clatsop near the issuance of that great river into the Pacific Ocean. The construction and occupancy of that post, he assured me, would establish for the United States its territorial title to the northern reaches of that great wilderness empire, toward the settlement of which we had all embarked in the beginning.

The captains had won that boat race to the mouth of the Columbia, Clark said, and the British would from this time forward have to confine their excitation of the Indians to their own Canadian provinces. As for Captain Lewis, he was heading via the Nez Perce short cut for Great Falls portage with the remainder of the company. He would there raise the cache and restore the white pirogue, proceeding down the Missouri to its confluence with the Yellowstone, where we would meet him. For our part, we were to strike overland with the horse herd which Ordway was bringing, coming out, if possible, near the headwaters of the Yellowstone, then exploring down its valley to the rendezvous. Ordway, leaving this present day from Three Forks, would take the canoes on to Lewis at Whitebear Islands and Great Falls. After the expedition was reunited at the mouth of the Yellowstone, it would descend with all speed to Fort Mandan. Within scant weeks thereafter the whole of the American people would know what William Clark was that moment confiding to Frank Rivet on the banks of the Jefferson River in the faraway Big Rock Mountains.

I then told him of my time with the Shoshones; of the strange odyssey of Big Bat and the Frenchmen, the departure of Shahaka for his Mandan homeland, the return of Cameahwait to the Lemhi country when June had passed with no word of the company.

When I had finished, Clark looked at me questioningly. "Well, Frank, " he said, "is that all? Ain't you forgetting the main part? What about your father, boy?"

It was instantly in my mind to try some lie on him. Then, as quickly, I knew better. But for Clark, I would never even have seen my father, never known his fate. I bowed my head and answered him quietly with all the truth.

"I'm powerful glad you told me," he said. "I already had the story from Toby He gave it to me on pledge it would stay with me. But I wanted it from you, straight, Frank. Now I think we'll just keep it between the two of us the same way old Toby handed it on to me. Eh, lad?"

"Yes, sir " I answered. "That's the way I decided."

"A good way, too, Frank," he agreed quickly "I may want to tell Captain Lewis some day, but that will wait. As for Toby he's going back over to the Lemhi as soon as we skeedaddle. The story of Achille Rivet can go with him. I doubt any white man will hear it again in our time. Or leastways be able to follow it out. What do you say, boy?

301

That strike you as right and fitting?"

I nodded, throat tightening. "Yes, sir, *Patron,*" I said, "it does."

He caught the difficulty of my words—alert, bright eyes at once probing my face.

"Anything else?" he demanded, head cocked.

"Nothing of importance, *Patron,*" I answered, coloring awkwardly. "Only that the Lord has been good to let me be your Pawnee."

He looked at me a moment, then nodded in that dry-voiced way he had when cornered by his own emotion. "Well, Frank," he said, "coming to that, now, maybe He ain't been entirely too bad letting me be your captain, neither . . ."

We set out eastward from the forks of the Missouri at 5 P.M. Ordway had already departed for Great Falls with the canoes. All spirits were high. I had seen no opportunity as yet to speak with Sacajawea but I believed this matter would adjust itself at quite an early convenience. Her brief greeting at the bend of the Jefferson, given in Shoshone and with the lowered, sidelong look which only she could effect, had left me no other conclusion. When, with that remembered throaty murmur she had said, "Greetings, Brother Frank, these eyes are made glad to gaze upon you once again," my heart had taken crazy wing and was, in fact, still sailing high above the dusty column of our plodding horse herd.

We did not go far. Clark had only wanted to remove his camp from the forks over to the Gallatin, and for the same reason of wandering Indians which had kept my thirteen days alone in that place so sleepless. At Mile Four from the forks, in a lovely stream-bank meadow well opened and situated for defense of our precious Snake and Nez Perce herd, he called the halt for the night.

I prepared at once to chaperone Sacajawea off into the nearest river-bend bower, but had only begun to imagine ways and means toward this end when Shannon spoiled everything by appearing with two fat spikehorn bucks slung over his packhorse. Nothing would then do, naturally, but that a deer roast ensue. And of course who might better gut and butcher the main dish than Sacajawea? I accepted this fortune, telling myself that all was not lost. Charbonneau, being old and much worn, would surely seek his blankets early and alone. It should then be merely a matter of enlisting York to nursemaid little Pomp while his slim mother and I strolled in the hush of evening. But when had such luck been mine?

As soon as the deer was done with, I was given the twilight watch of the pony herd with York as my companion guard. This honor fell to me because the Indians loved to run off horses either early or late in the day, and Clark considered me his best man on this most difficult of guard shifts. York made the two hours more tedious yet, because he wanted to relive the adventures we had shared last year, and to renew the comradeship we had then formed. I wished that I might help him in this direction, but I found myself unable. Something had changed. In the year apart we had lost contact. We were two different men now. No, I was different. York was the same.

He made me see this truth when, after a desultory hour of trying to engage my interest and emotions, he shook his curly head sadly and said to me something most strange indeed.

"Good-bye Mister Frank," he said, "you's growed up on me while I been over the mountain."

"Good-bye? Grown up?" I echoed. "What the devil do you mean? Of course I'm grown up; I'm very nearly twenty years old. But what's this talk of goodbye? I'm not leaving that I know of."

He nodded, still sad-faced, still soft of word. "That's so," he said, "you don't know it but it's already happened to you. You ain't my white boy no more. Now you're Mister Frank for sure. It ain't never agoing to be the same again."

"York," I said carefully, "what isn't ever going to be the same?"

"Me and you, Mister Frank. I'm still here but you done gone away That's how come me to say good-bye to you just now. You understand that?"

I thought, then, that I could see what he was trying to tell me. It was that I had departed his world in the year we had been apart. He was still of my world because he was a slave to it and could never escape its white-man boundaries. But I had escaped his simple earth of childlike pleasure and carefree adventure by the elementary process of becoming a man. York was right. His half-breed white boy had gone away. All that remained, for him, was his Mister Frank.

Putting my arm about his huge shoulders, I did my best to allay his sorrow at the parting. But words would not do the work. What language speaks for the injured trust of a child whose only friend has left him alone and frightened

304

in the night?

We started early next morning, crossing the river and proceeding on a southwest course to the forks of the Gallatin River, a distance of twelve miles. Crossing the south fork, we found the Indian buffalo road which Sacajawea had said would take us over the Divide to the Yellowstone drainage. After three miles on this road we came to a lovely meadow on the middle fork, past which we could all plainly see the high notch in the mountains through which the Indian trail passed to the Valley of the Yellowstone. Here we camped for the night.

Next day we went up and through the pass, Buffalo Gap on Clark's maps, and on down to the Yellowstone, a total distance of but eighteen miles. Captain Clark regarded this as a signal bit of information, but the only memory I retained of the Buffalo Gap passage was that it marked another day of failure to get Sacajawea aside. I did not get near her at next dark, nor, indeed, the next after that. The reason was a conspiracy of nature. That fourth day from the Three Forks drainage and the first along the Yellowstone, we saw a country of wondrous wild beauty, with much game, but there was no timber of canoe size in it; not as far as the eye might strain was there standing a solitary tree trunk large enough for dugout manufacture.

No little concerned, Clark gave the order to press on downriver. Regathering the straggling horses, we drove them eastward. Before long we were into a terrain of low barren hills, extremely dry and rocky. Almost immediately the horses commenced to go lame. Their unshod feet were unused to any such unrelieved and flinty going as that

305

which distinguished this part of the Yellowstone.

These rare Shoshone and Nez Perce horses were of great potential value to the expedition. The whole reason for their presence was that they represented enormous trading worth among the Mandan, Sioux and Minnetaree Indians, and, through this fact, our captains hoped to conclude a really binding truce among the three tribes on their return to Fort Mandan. They counted upon the near-certain assumption that with such elegant horses to offer in token, or bribery, to the Partisan and Le Borgne, these two key chieftains would greedily control their dangerous tribesmen until the government of the United States might impose upon them some more permanent, trustworthy authority.

Again, it was Sacajawea who, as she had a hundred times since leaving Fort Mandan, provided the ready intellect to overcome a hazard of the journey which might otherwise have imperiled its entire outcome. The solution of the "sore hoof" problem was so simple that at first men laughed aloud at it; all, that is, save Clark. The red-headed captain was the shrewdest natural engineer and frontier mechanic of his time. He at once understood and approved of the remedy.

"Horse moccasins?" He grinned at the Indian girl. "Why not?"

And so they were made. Buffalo were stalked and shot and the heavy leather of their calloused and thickened hock-skins taken and made into hoof moccasins following a Shoshone design likewise furnished by our priceless Bird-woman. Only the rear hoofs of each animal were shod, for Sacajawea said these bore the main weight in climbing and descending such hilly country as we were in. She was, of course, right. The "Injun shoes" worked to perfection, only one animal lost to lameness. We thus came into camp that fifth night, July 17, 1806, with forty-nine heads of sound horses, and incredible 98 percent survival from Shoshone Cove on the headwaters of the Jefferson.

Relief proved short-lived. The following morning at 11 A.M. smoke was seen from the mountains, south-southwest. Sacajawea said it was Absaroka, or Crow, smoke, and that now we would surely lose all the horses, since the Crows were the acknowledged master horse thieves of all the Indian tribes. Clark only nodded and doubled the herd guard.

We camped that sunset of July 18th, having made only eighteen miles. The night was passed safely but in the morning of the nineteenth more smoke was seen behind the ridges away from the river. And this smoke was north of the stream, where the other had been south, letting us know we had the Crows—if they were the Crows—on both flanks. In consequence, Captain Clark ordered the advance halted while he took York and myself on down the river to scout the way ahead. Vastly uneasy, I settled into a mood of Pawnee gloom from which I did not emerge until late afternoon when, from downstream, arose such an ominous sound of eerie whining and whirring that York and I at once crowded in on Clark most anxiously.

"What is it, *Patron?*" I asked. "I never heard this noise before. It is some new kind of storm? Some strange cyclones or hurricane of the high country?"

Clark shook his head, as puzzled as I. It was black York who answered the query, eye whites showing in fear. "It's the Bible plague out'n Egypt, Cap'n," he said to Clark. "The one the Jews run into and that destroyed all that their sheep they eat, and all that their ox chewed on, and all that

307

their ass he gnawed on. I done heard it before, Cap'n. When I was a little boy in the Sudan. No other noise like that one in all the world, Cap'n. It's them. It's the Egypt plague."

By now the keen and wailing had swelled to piercing volume. At the same time the sky began to darken. In a moment the vanguards of the host were singing and chirring and falling whistlingly among us. The shrill sounds of their vibrating wings and grating mandibles put a nameless dread deep into each of us.

"My God," said Clark quietly, "they're grasshoppers. York was talking about the plague of locusts in the Bible. Come on, hurry it up. Into that stand of dead willow yonder. No forage in there to attract them."

We got into the dead timber and tied our terrified mounts hard and short. We ourselves sat on the ground, backs braced together, and fought the things away from our mouths and noses so that we might simply breathe and live. In ten minutes the advance had passed up the river, leaving the ground, and each stalk of weed, brush, or, least-leaved tree, coated black with crawling, stinking, popping and squirting "hoppers."

"All right," said Clark, still quiet. "Untie the horses and mount up."

We obeyed without question. Our horses, after getting accustomed to the cracking pulp of the voracious horde underfoot, went along at a steady lope toward our upstream camp. But no matter their good gait, it was not swift enough. By the time we reached Pryor and the herd, the Valley of the Yellowstone, from riverbank to mountain wall, lay bare of leaf and grass to feed our dearly bought horses.

Faced with this disaster, Clark moved boldly. All hands

were detailed to drive the herd forward to a point downriver where we had discovered some acceptably large trees standing near water. Two of the largest of these were subsequently felled for canoes, and the hollowing crews worked on them until dark forced the halt. The plan was that canoes, because made of smaller than ideal trees, would be lashed together into a twin-hulled craft, thus bearing our entire baggage and the main number of our party down the fast-running Yellowstone to the rendezvous with Lewis at its confluence with the Missouri. A small and select force of riflemen scouts would meanwhile proceed by forced march through the hills away from the river. This march would take the precious horse herd overland all the way to Fort Mandan, moving only at night when Indian attack would be more frustrated in forming or in finding the places of ambush so dear to the red heart.

The company was undivided in this new emergency and for good reason. While we had been building the canoes, Sacajawea had found a war moccasin and discarded horsehair halter, the design and workmanship of which let her know unquestionably that our shadowers were the Crows. Thus, Clark's plan of traveling with the horses only at night and short-cutting through the hills would cut the odds against an "Absaroka steal" to the vanishing point. Spirits revived as they always did under the Red Head Chief's cool leadership and warm camaraderie. Were one a gambling man that night of the twentieth of July, 1806, he might have gotten any odds he named against the Crow Indians depriving us of one head of our fine Nez Perce horses.

As a matter of record, he could have collected on his wager, too. For the Crows did not steal one horse.

When the dawn shift of guards was sent out to the herd in the mist-gray morning of July 21st, its startled members discovered twenty-four of the prized animals to be missing. No sound had been heard in the night. No sight of Indians had been caught in day's first light. Not a mare had nickered or whistled in alarm. Even Omar had slept like a puppy, no least whimper or suspicion wrinkling his ugly snout. Yet one-half our horses were gone and even in full sun's glare of ten o'clock in the morning we had still found no hoof-mark, no moccasin print, no lost or mislaid personal article of clothing to assure us what Indian agency, if any, had spirited our stock away into the apparently empty air.

It was a tribute to Sacajawea that, when she shrugged her slim shoulders, pointed up the Yellowstone and announced the single word "Absaroka," not a man there but nodded his head and knew the Shoshone squaw was right and that the "greatest horse thieves on the high plains" were now the richer by two dozen head of invaluable Shoshone and Nez Perce spotted horses.

Yet what was Captain Clark's sole comment in lieu of reprimand or condemnation for this tragedy? Said he, behind his wry and sun-warm grin: "Don't lose heart, boys, cheer up; we've still got the best part of them left!" By which he meant that we still had twenty-five of the horses to the Indians' twenty-four.

52

Despite Clark's charity in forgiving the horse guards he spent two full days, the twenty-first and twenty-second, seeking to determine the direction of retreat taken by the

Indian thieves. Meanwhile, the men worked swiftly upon the canoes. By noon next day the craft were completed. Clark, immediately upon his return, ordered them launched. Both floated well and he then had them lashed side by side in the manner he had learned from the Nez Perce on the Columbia. The twin dugouts, twenty-eight feet long, eighteen inches deep, twenty-four inches wide, would handily float our slim baggage and all of the company save the handful the captain had chosen to accompany the horse herd in its night-driven flight to outrun the Crows and get to Fort Mandan without further loss. That "handful," I now learned, was to consist of Pryor, Shannon and Windsor, with myself as sort of supernumerary scout, this honor arrived at from the fact that in Red Lance, now recovered from his lameness, and Omar I had the best possible equipment for the task. My curses at this great luck did little to change it. As always, where William Clark had figured something out, there was no better answer. Hence, I saluted, forced a smile, resigned myself to my fate.

However, and before too long, this latter factor struck me as being altogether too foul to be accepted as, purely accidental. All the old jealousies returned. Clark was deliberately scheming to get me out of the way. He had even designed this midday departure so that I might not have even the small solace of that night's opportunity to make a last desperate try at getting Sacajawea aside. How despicable of him! How entirely unfair! How completely unlike him!

But I had still not learned my lesson about this remarkable man. From La Charrette to the land of the Shoshone

311

he had fooled me, and now, preparing to depart down the unknown Valley of the Yellowstone, he fooled me again. At the last moment, even as my horse-herding comrades and I were saddling our riding mounts, the red-haired captain came sidling over to us, pawky grin at work.

"Well, boys," he announced "we've all worked like fieldhands this morning and I reckon we could each of us use a few hours of lay-over time. I allowed we'd have us a rest this afternoon and a good feast tonight off of that last mess of buffalo ribs we got left. Then we can set sail first thing tomorrow, bright-eyed and full of fight. What do you think of that?"

Naturally we all said we thought it was a prime idea and that we could well use the time to mend our gear and go over our marching plans. Shannon and the other two soon moved off, but Clark remained watching me rub down Red Lance. Saying nothing, he loaded his pipe, lit it up, got it going. This done, he eyed me speculatively.

"Well, Frank," he said, "you appear pleased enough with the delay. Or ought we to call it a reprieve?"

I went right on rubbing the horse. "Yes, sir," I answered, "thank you very much, *Patron;* I'm pleased enough."

"Thought you would be," he nodded. Then, glancing about to make certain we were free of listeners. "Thought you might be interested in this, too—I'm making a scout up the river this afternoon to have my own look for some Crows Labiche and Shields think they saw. Figured I'd take old Charbonneau along with me." He peered up at the slant of the sun. "Looks to me as if he won't stand much chance getting back till late—well after dark I'd say."

I quit rubbing the horse. Straightening I faced him.

312

"Patron," I asked, "how long after dark?"

For answer he said nothing, but only stood watching me, the pipe's smoke curling around his cocked head in a halo of fragrant innocence. Finally he nodded in his wry, dry way, eyes beaming.

"Long enough," he said, grinning, and went stomping off toward the riverbank whistling as cheerily as if neither of us had truly good sense.

For a moment I waited motionlessly. Then I recovered. My imagination vaulted. My pulses raced. That night I would see Sacajawea! Ah, the mere thought, the simple consideration of it! Well, yes, simple would be the proper word.

With the whole of the long, lazy summer afternoon in which to pursue my purpose, I spent the time like a rich man. I deliberately squandered it, knowing that in the velvet dark to come each of its tantalizing hours would be repaid me a thousandfold. I was the drunkard with the full bottle hidden against his wild thirst. I knew I had to reach behind the certain rock, or into the chosen hollow stump, to retrieve the medicine for my delicious pain. And so I wantonly dawdled, watching Sacajawea move about the camp, play with her child, work, laugh with the other men, cast the occasional luminous and smoldering eye in my direction, and in all such ways, delicious and self-exciting, I permitted my senses to riot under this idiot's delusion of time being my total slave.

With sunset, I was ten feet tall. At late dusk, having seen Sacajawea glide away toward the bowered riverbank, and being myself in the act of turning to follow her, I heard the upstream clatter of unshod pony hoofs running hard over rough Yellowstone rock. The next instant Clark and Charbonneau had slid their lathered mounts into the circle of our fire's light.

The captain said old Toussaint had found the Crows. They were in large number, uncertain temper, and very near by. Indeed, they had almost caught Clark and the grizzled Frenchman. Only the superior fleetness and sure-footedness of the latter's Nez Perce horses had saved them. But now it was we who must show equal speed and sureness to save what remained of our precious herd from the emboldened red robbers. The herd was immediately gathered up and brought in from its meadow pasture. The last animal was roped securely to a hastily strung fireside picket line. The rest of the night was spent in emergency turns at guard by one-half the full company at a time. The awake half would divide its work between keeping the fires burning brightly and in patrolling the outer perimeters of the picket line. The other half tried for nervous catnaps, rifle and pistol to uneasy hand. The extreme measure was certified by the all-night calling of the Crow warriors in the timber both above and below our campsite. Their querulous fox yelps, loon cries, whippoorwill whistles and turtledove mournings went on until sunrise. But when the red ball of the sun came at last probing up the long Valley of the Yellowstone, we could once more thank the never-sleeping genius of our red-haired captain: We still had our horses and our hair. Breakfast was tense and burned, however, and Clark was not long in sending for me.

"Frank," he said, "I want you to remember that you're my Pawnee. I'm trusting the safety of these horses to your Indian side, do you hear? Pryor is in charge, but I'm looking to you to scout for him so careful that he don't lose

314

a head 'twixt here and meeting up with Captain Lewis."

I was still brooding over the hurried return which had aborted my meeting with Sacajawea, but in view of such straight talk and high trust from Captain William Clark. I could take no other action than to accept the commission.

"*Oui, Patron,*" I said, "I shall do my best. Perhaps it will be that the Absaroka will tire of the trail. Or they may decide they already have the better part of our herd."

He shook his head quickly. "No, Frank, you look sharp. Them devils will be after you. They want those prize appaloosie stud horses. Them and the big Shoshone black."

"All right, *Capitaine,*" I said. "Was there anything else?"

For the second time he shook his head.

"Nope," he said, "all you got to remember is the one thing; you're Clark's Pawnee. That'll get you there, I'm betting."

"Thank you, *Patron,*" I replied, nodding uneasily, and spurred Red Lance after the departing herd.

My last thought in looking back at the crossing below, and seeing the reloaded canoes sweeping out of sight down the racing Yellowstone, was not a thankful one, however.

It was in my mind that Clark's Pawnee was bound for the same oblivion as York's white boy.

The feeling rode with me away from the river. It rode with me still into the rocky silences of the Yellowstone's thin-timbered hills. And it rode with me yet when, three camps later, in the dead of night, the cursed Crows came down upon our lonely bivouac in final deadly stealth, to run off the remainder of our horse herd.

The loss of the priceless animals was my personal fault. We had been generally charged by Clark—and I had been specifically warned by him—*not to move the herd by day,* but at night only, when the Indians would be far less able to run it off. Yet once away from our captain, it had been I who had convinced brave Pryor that no Crows were following us and that Clark's ban might be safely ignored in favor of the more natural "drive by day, rest by night" order of trail herding. I used as a part of my excuse the wet weather we had encountered since leaving the Yellowstone. Now tragedy had fallen upon our vital mission. Yet my comrades would not permit me this sole blame. Rather, they advised I say nothing to Clark of the misfortune except that we had been the victims—all of us—of a fate, which might not have been averted by any reasonable vigilance. I knew far better and my guilt lay heavy as stone within me, Moreover, the ultimate cruelty of the Crows was still to be discovered. Its burden, now added to my betrayal of Clark's trust, set brutal seal to my guilt.

This time they left us not one horse, not even my brave and beautiful Red Lance. And the way that they did it—the only way in which they could have done it—was an old and vicious and brutally designed devil's trick. They came beneath the cloak of twilight, luring out our choicest guard, Omar, with offers of tainted meat, or perhaps, as we never knew, of an Absarokan camp bitch. And then, when they had him so decoyed, and far enough away, they slew him in the ancient, silent way, with steel through his guts and only the cold stars and tongueless rocks to bear him witness.

Thus it was that we found Omar Kyayyám with daylight.

He was pinned so fiercely to the hard, dry earth by the razored blade of the Crow lance which had killed him that only by crude butchery could we have freed his rigid body.

I forbade my friends to touch him. They helped me to cover him with a cairn of heavy stone, so that no skulking carrion eater should come at him, and we left him there with the shaft in his heart to show that he had died as he had lived.

A tout seigneur tout honneur. Let the epitaph suit the truth. Bravery and death are brothers.

53

We packed what we could of our supplies upon our backs and set out to strike the Yellowstone once more. Afoot as we were, we had to have a constant source of wild meat upon which to depend for survival. In the dry hills through which we had been force-marching the horses back from the river, hunting was practical only with mounts to give chase to the fleet antelope and wary deer. But when luck deserted a band of travelers in that alien land, it did not abandon them part way. Our last sleep from the river, we were attacked in the night by a band of buffalo wolves. The brutes bit Pryor through the hand and would have made it his throat, except that he awakened in time to throw up his arm and fend them off. His cry alerted Shannon, who was quick enough to shoot the devil, which had hold of Pryor's hand. Next moment Hall, Windsor and I fired, and the combined roars and flashes of the guns drove the pack away.

What had brought them so desperately into our midst was our backpacks containing our supplies of dried buffalo beef and backfat, and these supplies they had seized and devoured to the last scrap. Why they should openly attack us could be explained, then, by one of two grim choices: either they were starving or they were sickened with hydrophobia as had been the pack at Fort Mandan. If the latter, brave Pryor faced death alone. If the other, we all faced death together. The first thing, in either event, was to treat Pryor. Recalling the gunpowder therapy which Clark had saved Shahaka's life that previous time, I had my comrades bind the sergeant tightly, then administered the same harsh measures. When the flaming powder had sizzled out in the wounds, we bound the hand in strips from our leather shirts and forged on for the Yellowstone. That afternoon, late, we reached the stream and learned that it was indeed hunger, not hydrophobia, which goaded the wolves.

The country, to eye's reach, was barren of game, a grass fire having burned through it recently to destroy what game pasturage ordinarily grew there. This we were certain was an Indian-set fire, probably ignited by the Crows before they got all our horses and planned to starve our herd into uselessness to us. Cursingly we examined the blackened scape. Finally the incorrigible Shannon grinned his quick Irish grin and said, "Just think, boys, here we are in this paradise unencumbered of captains and with no need, even, to worry about the weight of a morsel of meat aboard our weary backs. We are free men in a free land. Isn't it marvelous?"

The others, required to grin back at him, did so acidly.

"Sure is," spat Windsor, getting the dust from his parched throat. "These tears you see in my eyes are just plain, pure gratitude."

"Why, hell," said Pryor, fighting the pain of his torn hand, "we ain't begun to count blessings. Just think, we might have been forced to go with Captain Clark and the others in them clumsy canoes, making no more than sixty, eighty miles a day through this lovely country, Why dear Jesus, I reckon we'd ought to get down on our knees in thanks this minute. Then, again, happen we had best wait till this burnt ground cools off somewhat."

It was my turn to be cheerful and I knew it, but I hesitated frowningly. Pryor's remark about the canoes tugged at my memory. "Suppose," I finally said, and with some care, "that we consider these canoes you just mentioned, but without the grins and caustic comment."

"Of course, lad," said Shannon at once, "and let's consider those canoes without our axes, too. Do you propose to whittle them out with our skinning knives?"

"Not for a minute, lad," I mimicked. "All we need it two good-sized bull buffalo."

Pryor frowned now, sensing something but not sure of it. "Is that a Pawnee joke, Frank?" he asked.

"Well," I said, "it comes from Pawnee country anyway, Sergeant. Do you recall old Dorion's story down on the Platte about the Pawnees making those round bullboats from buffalo skins, and how they went on swift, shallow water better than any canoe? Well if we could get two good bulls, we could use their skins to make a couple of those boats for ourselves and be out of this blasted desert in one day."

"Oh, wonderful! Wonderful!" exclaimed Shannon. "Now why didn't the rest of us think of that? But pardon me, maybe it's the smoke down yonder, but I'm blessed if

I see those two buffalo of yours tiptoeing around in those cinders. Which way ought I to look for them, Frank lad?"

More in despair than rational hope, I shrugged and gestured below.

"Why that way of course, George my boy."

They all followed my outflung arm, not thinking, any more than I, to see anything.

"My God," gasped Windsor, "where did *they* come from?"

The question was sound, and we all stared in disbelief. Where, indeed, had those two old bachelor bulls down there, soot-black with fire smoke and grass char, wandered from in precisely this nick of time to save our threatened lives?

God alone understood, perhaps, but we wasted no moment inquiring of him. Shannon and I made the stalk, since we were the best riflemen. Both of us made long, beautiful, one-shot kills, and necessarily so, for the burned-over river bottom offered only its rocks and cottonwood skeletons for cover, putting second shots in the realm of no meat. Within the hour, however, we had our bulls skinned, the hides stretched and fleshed. By sunset the willow frames were finished and with twilight we had the green hides pulled about them and sewed fast with backgut and hock tendon threads. Pausing only to butcher out the best cuts of the two carcasses and to swiftly broil some of the tongue and liver to fill our twenty-four-hour-empty bellies, we loaded ourselves into the ridiculous-looking craft and pushed off into the churning current.

The Indian bullboats were seven feet in diameter, with a slender willow hoop at top and one at bottom fastened together with sixteen willow ribs. They were thus a perfect bowl some eighteen inches deep, drawing not over six inches of water, fully loaded. We were all therefore certain that death by drowning awaited us at the first bad water, but the skin saucers shipped not one drop of water in the entire descent of the Yellowstone and we reached the Missouri in one delightful week. We found there a note on a pole left by Captain Clark for Captain Lewis, and so, happily—or as happily as we might, the loss of the horses considered—we turned our Indian "buffalo bowlers" down the parent stream and, on the eighth day of August, 1806, came up with the red-headed captain and our other comrades at their camp below White Earth River.

At this place, and in a line such as the raven might fly, we were less than one hundred miles from Fort Mandan! What a thrilling thought this would have been but for the nature of our reunion. As it was, Clark behaved with all his usual granite forbearance. He had known, he said, that we faced great odds to come through that Absaroka country with the horses. He did not consider it our fault that we had failed. The loss of the herd was a hard bit of fate, but would need to be borne as we had borne other blows as wicked or heart-wrenching. He would, he assured us, find some way in which to soften the matter with Captain Lewis, whom he expected down the Missouri each hour now. Meanwhile, we were to believe that the major accomplishment and his principal relief was our safety and survival.

"We can always buy more horses, boys," was the soft-voiced way he put it, "but where am I going to find more Shannons, Halls, and Windsors, and where, indeed, more sons of old Achille Rivet?"

It was when he said this, when he included me with particular fondness and separate naming that I knew I would have to confess to him my perfidy my comrades had loyally glossed over in their reporting of the calamity. When Pryor and the others had departed, I stayed on to keep this rendezvous with my honor and my devotion to William Clark.

"*Patron,*" I began, "there is more that you do not know; something that I did, and which my companions vowed not to reveal against me. But I cannot let this shadow rest on them, when it is I, alone, who have cast it."

Clark looked at me in his quizzical, kindly way. "Go on, boy," he said quietly. "We've never had no secrets. No time to start harboring bad news now."

I told him, then, how those horses had been lost. How it had rained all of the second day and how, because of that cloudy cover, I had decided to ignore his order to travel only at night and had gone on under that storm the full day. Hence, how, when the third night fell, both ourselves and the horses were too weary to go on, and how, of course, we had made that muddy camp where Omar had died for his duty and where we—where I in paramount guilt—had shirked ours.

When I was done with the shameful tale, I knew that at last I had transgressed the limits even of my captain's long sympathy and stout support of friendless métis boys.

He never uttered a word of criticism, nor gave me one glance of censure. Neither then, nor later, did he permit me a single evidence of ill will or resentment. But when we parted, with his big hand patting me as reassuringly as ever, I understood the wound I had struck him.

As surely and as irrevocably as I was no longer York's white boy, so inalterably was I no longer Clark's Pawnee.

54

The following two days we loafed on down the river holding back for Captain Lewis to catch up. With Fort Mandan nearing and with my failure to deliver the vital horse herd and my inability to come to some terms with Sacajawea—at least in my mind—a great uneasiness began pervading me. I tried to think ahead to La Charrette and Uncle François and Aunt Célie and what a hero I would be at home, but it was no good. I could not make my imagination proceed past Fort Mandan. For some vaguely sinister reason my thoughts refused to carry me past that point. I gave the attempt to force them to do so, solacing myself with hard work on the river and ashore.

We had gone on from our nooning of the third day only about two miles when I spied, cleverly hidden in the bank rushes, a canoe lying on the north side. Accordingly, we turned in to investigate. Imagine our first delight upon discovering that the canoeists were not enemy Indians but brash young Americans out on a bit of beaver plewing. The names of the two were Dickson and Hancock and they had put in the recent winter as enforced guests of the Teton Sioux, our old friends from the Cedar Island days. Escaping but a few weeks ago, they had come upriver past the Mandan villages and what they now had to tell us on that score changed our pleasure to rude shock.

There was a wide-scale Indian war threatening in the entire Northwest, centering in that area where we had done our most intensive missionary work. Despite all the peace promises extracted by Clark and Lewis on the upvoyage, the

Mandans and Minnetarees were now fighting the Arikaras; the Assiniboins were at war with the Mandans; the Teton Sioux, as usual, were killing members of all four tribes.

This was potentially disastrous news. It meant that the bargaining position of our captains with the various Missouri River tribes, already seriously reduced by our loss of the Nez Perce and Shoshone "trading horses," was now placed in final jeopardy. It meant, as well, that I myself must now face the fact of personal complicity in this cruel trick of history upon President Jefferson's brave captains.

All the principal chiefs of unimportant reputation, Le Borgne, Black Cat, Big Man, Chechawk, Shotawhorora, even the grim Partisan, had made Clark and Lewis tentative promises to sail back down the Missouri with them on the return voyage as guests of the white man's new American Government. A dozen of the lesser chiefs in all four of the primary tribes of Mandan, Minnetaree, Assiniboin, and Sioux had likewise expressed willingness, even interest, in sharing this "journey to meet the new father."

Now, all of this amity, this triumph in-the-round for our captains, was done with. Any Indian war going as hotly as Dickson and Hancock reported this one, could mean but one thing: the Red Head Chief and the Quiet Chief would be lucky to secure one rheumy-eyed old squaw to go with them down the Missouri to Washington.

What could I tell myself, viewing this dismal fact, except that even in the last mile I was a failure? Watching Clark bid farewell to the two American trappers, I wished only that I might have died with Omar, or been taken captive with Red Lance, rather than bring such lasting disgrace op the name of Rivet on this Grand Missouri where the men of my blood had roamed with pride since the days of the Vérendryes.

Dear Lord, what other sorrow could await me? One other, I told myself. A slim and slender sorrow, the deepest, most poignant and impossible sadness of them all—Sacajawea.

We drifted on, camping that night at Goatpen Creek. The name was used by Clark on his charts because of the brush trap built there by the Indians to catch antelope. But the place had for me more of the aroma of real goats. Nothing, I was determined, was going to rearouse my spirit. For me, the essence of adventure had vanished. I even shook off Clark's fatherly attempt to reinterest me in his journal entries. I took one brief glance at his remarks for Goatpen Creek Camp and was discouraged. After four thousand miles and two years, he was still worrying more about mosquitoes than the course of empire! Noting the fact aloud, I expected him to be angry at my surly insubordination, but he only laughed.

"Frank," he said "I know what's eating you, boy, and it ain't me or my notes. I wish it was. We could likely fix it then." He had suddenly, in the space of the few words, come from laughter to the hard center of my dilemma. It was another of those gifts of his, which so set him apart from ordinary men, yet did so in a quiet, inside way which left no anger but only stirred the heart to listen and agree. I nodded in abject silence in this instance, and he went on compassionately.

"Now, lad," he said, "I want you to do something for

me. What you got can't be cured excepting in one way. That's to understand it. I know what your disease is, boy, and so do you. But I maybe know a little something else about it that you don't. I've lived with it eleven months longer and a great deal closer than you have."

"You mean Sacajawea, *Patron?*" I said, then added, hopelessly, "What is it you wish me to do about her?"

"Come along with me," he said, "and take a good, long, last, hard look at her. I've invited the two of us over to Charbonneau's fire for supper."

"That's all? " I asked, frowning. "Just go there and eat and look?"

"You don't even need to eat," he answered, "just look."

I stared at him. Far, far back in my mind a glimmer of his meaning began to filter through.

"You mean," I said, "that you want me to *really* look at Sacajawea. Is that it, *Capitaine?*"

"That's it, Frank," he nodded. "But, suppose that after I have looked I still don't see?"

He studied me a moment in his turn. "Don't you French have a saying for that?" he asked.

"Do you mean that no man is so blind as that man who will not see, *Patron?*"

"Something like that, Frank. Will you go?"

I put down the journal notes and stood up.

"Surely, *Capitaine,*" I said, "Let us *both* go and see."

Clark was right. I was shown a Sacajawea that August night over the Goatpen Creek campfire of old Toussaint Charbonneau that I had never seen. Clark had wanted me to see an Indian woman, as she was, and that is what I did see; a squaw, a Shoshone slave, serving an aged French white man who had bought her for a few horses and worked her ever since as though afraid of having made a poor bargain and wanting to secure full return on the investment before it might die on him. Clark lifted the curtain of this bargain long enough for me to witness my true love in her full Shoshone pigments. I *saw* Sacajawea that night.

I saw her begin the evening by killing a fat, friendly puppy, with which I had seen both her and her button-eyed infant laughing and playing that same noonhalt. She seized the squealing mongrel by its hind legs and knocked out its brains against the nearest cottonwood sapling, and dropped it, still jerking, into the kettle of hot stones and steaming water where it would boil, ungutted and unskinned, for our supper.

I refused to look at Clark, but knew that he was regarding me calmly the whole time. When she came back to the fire and settled herself opposite me to stir the puppy in the pot, I could not take my eyes from her. The change in her within one year was startling. Her face, once so oval and lovely, seemed now, in this harsh firelight, plain merely. The nose had bridged higher, the mouth stretched wider, the cheekbones protruded more flatly and pronounced. The teeth, formerly perfect, were presently showing edge wear and yellow stain of nicotine from her use of the stone pipe. Even as I watched her now, Clark deliberately gave her a twist of his burley and she bit off a ragged mouthful it, before passing it dutifully to Charbonneau. Cheeking the stringy quid, she made a cud of it and commenced chewing it as contently as any buffalo cow. When it hit the side of the boiling pot and sizzled loudly, a portion splashed over the iron rim into our supper, she laughed gaily. Staring at her, I saw a dribble of the brown juice leaking down her chin, unminded.

The meal passed somehow. After it, she vied with Charbonneau in belching to show her pleasure with the puppy fricassee. I at last allowed myself to meet Clark's steady eyes. He merely nodded imperceptibly and arose from his cross-legged Indian position.

"It grows late," he said to old Toussaint. "The dog was very good, Charbono. *Beaucoup* dog, eh?"

"*Oui, Patron. A beaucoup près.* Will we travel early tomorrow?"

"Same as today. We'll drift along."

"Good. Rest well."

"Thanks," said Clark. "Come along, Frank."

I hesitated, looking at Sacajawea. She glanced up, feeling my eyes upon her.

"Oh," she murmured in French, the throaty voice and luminous gray eyes suddenly luring as ever, "good night, Brother Frank. Sleep well."

"Good night." I nodded stiffly, and turned and went away with Captain William Clark, mind and spirit benumbed.

When we were out of sight and hearing, the latter stopped and lit up his pipe. "Well, Frank," he said, "what did you see?"

"What you wanted me to see, *Patron,*" I answered, "an Indian squaw."

"You saw it good?"

"It's all changed, *Patron.* The girl that I saw at Fort Mandan is gone. She never came back over the Big Rock

328

Mountains. You left her somewhere on the Columbia."

"That girl," said Clark slowly, "never existed, Frank, saving in your own imagination. The squaw you saw tonight is the girl that is Cameahwait's sister, Charbonneau's squaw—Sacajawea, Birdwoman. She was never nothing more, nor less, than these things."

I nodded, mute to say more, and he gave me his quick shoulder-squeeze of reassurance, and went on to leave me there alone, that I might follow him in my own time when my feelings had regathered and steadied themselves.

I did not tarry long, only long enough to look back at the gleam of Charbonneau's dying fire, then ahead where the sturdy figure of Captain Clark could still be seen by dim starlight. I nodded then to myself, knowing that once more my captain had seen the right, where I had not.

"Sacajawea *was* Cameahwait's sister, and not mine. The third sorrow no longer lay in wait somewhere unknown. As York's white boy and Clark's Pawnee had faded in their separate nights, so Sacajawea's Brother Frank died silently beneath the winking, cold, high stars of Goatpen Creek.

55

Next day at noon, while halted to repair one of our skin boats which had torn its bottom we were all inspired by the sight of Captain Lewis's boats sweeping into view from upstream. Our joy was short of life, however. Captain Lewis had been shot in the thigh the day before by Peter Cruzatte in a hunting accident. He lay now, helpless to walk or even to sit erect, in the white pirogue. Clark went at once to tend him, working to cleanse and rebandage the injury. He returned to our boats with the news that Lewis had a dangerous wound, but that no major artery had been severed, and no bone struck. If infection did not set in, he would recover, but he would be helpless for weeks. Moreover, in view of his delicate condition, he must suffer no shocks or startlements whatever, and the piloting of the white pirogue thus became a matter of utmost importance. I was surprised and deeply affected to be asked then if I would take over the pirogue and act in my old capacity as her steersman.

"Yes, *Patron,* thank you," was all that I could say to Clark's request, but I felt much more than that.

Clark now determined, in view of the need to get Lewis downriver, to consolidate the company. The skin bullboats were ordered scuttled and sunk to the bottom of the stream, all hands were put into the larger canoes, Clark transferred with me to the white pirogue and we departed forthwith.

Next morning Clark was needed to run ahead in the lead canoe, and I was left alone with Captain Lewis aboard the pirogue, alone, that was, except for her normal boat crew and for the Charbonneaus, who had been assigned to ride in her for reason of whatever woman's attention the squaw might provide the restless patient. Lewis was in a very high fever now, his pain considerable and the fears for his life mounting. The date was August 13th, an uneasy omen indeed, for it was also a Friday. The wind, as though favoring our urgency, switched to our beam quarter and arose to blow spanking-stiff. Under sail and steering only, we raised the mouth of the Little Missouri by 8 A.M. Not pausing, we swept on. With sunset that evening, and with Captain Clark's signal to turn shoreward and encamp at the confluence of Miry Creek, we had made a run of eighty-six and one-half miles and stood but nineteen miles by water above Knife River and the villages of the Mandan.

But this was not the remarkable thing about the day. What made it memorable, and made me remember it, was what happened after Clark's signal to turn in off the river and before our prow grated on the sandy beach at creek mouth.

As I returned the red-headed captain's wave and shifted my tiller to obey its direction, I saw Sacajawea swaying up the pirogue's center planking toward my station. I thrilled as I always did to see her native grace and thought that, in the rosy flush of the sunset, she looked again as enchanting and lovely as of old. Yet I was able to watch her approach and to anticipate her greeting with a steadiness completely alien to my earlier excitements. I was even able to smile at her and to wave lightly, and to mean both gestures. I was relieved, too, to see that she reacted as easily.

"It is good to see your face happy again, Tooettecone," she said. "Do you feel happy?"

"No," I said, "but I have reached some understandings with myself. I have some peace now."

"I can see it, " she nodded. "I am the same, I think."

We looked at each other for a long moment, something of the past being exchanged guardedly. Then she dropped her glance in the old shy way.

"Captain Lewis would like to talk with you," she murmured. "He asked that you come now, before we reach the riverbank. He wants to see you alone."

I thanked her, glad of the excuse to depart. Forward, I found Lewis lying on his folded white buffalo robe, face gray with pain. "Yes, *Capitaine,*" I said. "The squaw said you wished to see me." He nodded, motioning me to sit beside him where we both might see one another without turning. After a moment he spoke, the words costing him a great deal in effort.

"Rivet," he said, "Captain Clark has told me about the horses and about your acceptance of the blame. I won't lie to you; those horses meant a very great deal to me. But I think it's only fair to tell you that American scouts aren't the only ones who lose horses—American captains do it also."

He paused, and I asked him carefully, "*American* scouts, *Capitaine?*"

"That's what I said, Rivet. Wasn't it Captain Clark who said us Americans have got to stick together?"

Clark had said it indeed. But it had been so long ago and at a time when this stricken captain was so hostile toward me that I was astounded at his memory of it. I nodded my head with difficulty.

"*Oui, Capitaine,* it was he."

"And now me, eh, Rivet?" He hesitated, gathering his thoughts. "The truth is, lad," he continued, "that I let a bunch of Atsina or Blackfeet jump me up on the Marias River and run me all the way back to the Missouri. It was only pure luck that we hit the river just as our canoes came down from the Great Falls portage. We were able to hail them, transport our baggage from horses to canoes and be off again before the Indians might come up to us. But I left seventeen head of mighty good horses standing there on the riverbank whickering us good-bye, and not a thing to do for it but wave back to them and let them go. How many was it you lost, Rivet, twenty-four?"

"Twenty-five, sir; they got my own horse, too."

"Well, you see, we're only eight head apart."

"Merci, capitaine," I muttered humbly, "but I failed my mission, and you did not. So I am still destitute finally."

He brought himself painfully up to one elbow. "Listen to me, boy," he said. "You say I didn't fail my mission? Well, you're wrong. I failed it, all right, and it brings our hopes lower than any loss of horses. The President, and I, and mostly I, were certain that some tributary of the Upper Missouri reached the Canadian fur country. I vowed it could only be the Marias. As far back as Traveler's Rest I planned my entire company's route to prove my point, and to find for Mr. Jefferson that water trail by which American commerce might carry the fur trade of the Saskatchewan country to American markets. It was a large part of our original commission in this undertaking, Rivet, and I now tell you that I found no such pathway. Moreover, there is no navigable American river, tributary to the Missouri, by which one may reach territory north of fifty degrees. You failed, lad? If you want to talk of failure, see this captain. Talk with him. Ask an expert. Inquire of Meriwether Lewis how to fail. He can tell you."

He fell back, perspiring, violently, and paper-white. After a frightening moment, he continued.

"This leg," he said, "I don't know what will become of it, or of me. I wanted you to know that your captains are not so blind, or dumb, or halt. You've done your part, Rivet; you've been a good soldier, a good citizen. Let yourself remember it."

I sat in silence, completely overcome. This was Captain Lewis, the Quiet Chief, the man I had disliked from La Charrette to Shoshone Cove, and who I thought had disliked me.

At last I stood up.

"I don't know what to say, *Capitaine*," I told him. "I don't have the words."

He nodded, the smile a thin gray line. "We're not great talkers, you and I, eh, Rivet? Not about ourselves, at least or between ourselves, that is"

Again the long pause, and I could not decide to go, or think of anything more to stay for. But there was more, something more, something he now told me in his perversely oblique way.

"Oh, Rivet," he added, looking away from me, "Captain Clark spoke to me when last we were at Fort Mandan about restoring your name on the permanent roll of the company. I have told him, just today, that I would now do so."

He lowered his head and his voice. "You see, lad, we've left you out of the journals all this time since leaving the Mandan, entirely by my own direction. It seemed to me that you had earned the deprivation. But now, it seems to me, as well, that you have earned relief from the penalty. Hence, my promise to Captain Clark that, when the expedition returns to St. Louis and the final record is set down, the name of F Rivet, of La Charrette, will appear in the permanent company."

I stammered, trying to say something of my gratitude. He was at once brusque, permitting me no moment of acknowledgement.

"Look, sharp, yonder!" he ordered me. "Get back to your post. I don't think that man at the tiller is taking the boat in at all properly. Jump to it, do you hear!"

"*Merci, mon Capitaine,*" I managed. "I hope God watches you well." His only answer was a tight-lipped groan of pain.

The next moment, the pirogue was running in under a low shelfbank and Cruzatte and Labiche were leaping ashore to tie her fast. When they had, I lashed the tiller and sat alone in the thickening twilight for a long time.

Surely Clark was not the only remarkable one of Jefferson's oak-and-iron captains. Perhaps he was not even the more remarkable of the two. I learned that on August the thirteenth, 1806; the day that Meriwether Lewis made me a permanent member of The Corps of Volunteers for Northwestern Discovery.

Our fears in regard to the Indians proved partly justified, partly enlarged beyond life. Our arrival at Knife River and Fort Mandan next day was greeted by the greatest demonstrations of joy and affection at our safe return. Even I, coming again to the villages of the Mandan, as I had first come to them, at the tiller of the white pirogue, felt something of this dark people's good heart. The enthusiasm rallied Captain Lewis, who improved enough to sit up and to take some active part in the ensuing talks. Clark, of course, was sanguine always. A man with a more incorruptible center of good will for his fellows never lived. As before in our winter's stay at Fort Mandan, the Indians simply swarmed about him, all wanting to touch him, or have him touch them, being thus given some of his strong medicine for themselves. York, also, was bathed in the reflection of this love for his master, and the giant slave roused up from his depression of the past weeks to become his old self once more, the ivory grin and apish antics which so delighted the redmen and women being restored to fullest activity. Even old Toussaint perked up and began to look ashore for Wahiki, his old and favorite wife, among the crowding ranks of Black Cat's main village. The surprise was Sacajawea. Looking to see what shades of happiness she might be demonstrating at this return, I observed an expression upon her face which I had not seen there in many months. It was the hauntingly sad and wistful look which I had noted when first she came ashore upon these very beaches at the outset of our winter among the Mandan. Stirred by it, I moved to her side in the press of the crowd greeting us as we disembarked. When she saw me at her elbow, I thought the look only deepened.

"What is it?" I said. "You're not happy, like the others. How is this? Are you thinking of the Shoshone?"

"No," she replied, "not the Shoshone."

"What then? Why should you be sad?"

"I don't know. Something seems to say to me that all is not right. You know that this is the place where I first saw you and the Red Head Chief. Coming back to it, I feel sad. It's like saying good-bye, Tooettecone."

She was talking like an Indian again, even to employing my Shoshone name. It made me uneasy, and I resented it.

"Nonsense," I said abruptly. "You're behaving like a squaw. Stop it."

She shook her head. "You cannot lie to me, Tooettecone," she told me. "Your face is sad, too. You feel this thing also."

"Stop it!" I snapped. "That's enough. I feel nothing."

She nodded and turned quickly away. To my amazement, I saw tears in her eyes. I started to push toward her, then halted. Belatedly, it came to me that she was right. I did feel sad. I felt that way for days. The anxiety about

336

coming again to Fort Mandan had settled in upon me far up the river. Why should I so resent the same nameless disposition in Sacajawea?

I was given no chance to answer my own demand. Clark and Lewis were not of a mind to tarry among the Mandan. Runners were sent to the Minnetaree upriver, and to the Arikara downstream. Smoke fires were built at the same time signaling the various local chiefs to come into the main village of Pocopsahe, the Black Cat. We of the company were meanwhile given work in refurbishing the pirogue and our canoes for the long voyage home. We even worked through the night by the light of Mandan cornstalk and cattail rush torches. As we did, the chiefs began to come in. There had been no similar gathering in all of our previous months among these people.

From the north came haughty Le Borgne, grand chief of all the Minnetaree, his one eye gleaming as fiercely as ever. Up from the south for the Arikara came Kagohweto and Pocasse, the main chiefs whom we had known passingly on the way up the river. From north of north came three chiefs of the greatest power. These were from Assniboine River, Turtle Mountain and the Saskachain. Their appearance and friendly mood gave our captains considerable new hope that the reports of Indian war were largely exaggerated, if indeed not false altogether.

The ensuing council, however, sobered their momentary optimism. The war was real enough, the chiefs hastily assured them, or at least the threat of it was real enough. In fact, the American captains had returned only in time to delay a final, full-scale clash. On this hardening note the talks commenced.

The first day was devoted to the visiting non-Mandan chiefs. It failed utterly. All of the important leaders, including Le Borgne in particular, expressed interest in reestablishing the peace wrought by Clark and Lewis during their Mandan winter, and before, on their way up the Missouri. But not a single chief would now agree to return with the expedition to visit the new father in Washington. The reason was the Teton Sioux. The latter were bloodily at war. No question whatever of that. For any Indian of the northern bands to attempt to pass through the Teton country by the river, or by any other route, would be the same as suicide. Moreover, the Assiniboin and Minnetaree did not think that the Arikara chief who had gone last with old Pierre Dorian to Washington had ever lived to reach the new father's big white house. If he had lived and was all right, why had he not returned this spring to the land of the Mandan with word of his journey? And if the Teton Sioux had not killed that Arikara chief and old man Dorion, where had they been all this time?

These were questions our captains could not answer, and next day the Mandans were asking the same questions in their council meeting.

For this meeting the complete hierarchy of the Mandan Nation turned out: Black Cat, Neighing Horse, Old Woman, Little Raven, Big Man, Coal, Red Shield, Wolf Medicine and Littlecherry all were there and all anxious to please and to help the white chiefs. They brought so much corn and gave it so freely with no word of trade in exchange that it would have filled our boats three times over. But of individuals prepared to travel on with us to Washington they produced not one more than had their wilder brothers of the

338

north, or their craftier ones of the south.

Accordingly, the captains were soon reduced to accepting this universal fear of the Teton Sioux. The Mandan council broke up in the same despair as that of the Assiniboin and Minnetaree.

For the third day and its council, not a single chief appeared, and Clark and Lewis devoted the entire afternoon to individual efforts to seek out the various name chieftains and try to alter their opposition, or induce even one of them to change his mind and go with us. But as the sun dropped swiftly, the last candidate, Little Raven, who had earlier in the day promised Clark he would go, suddenly switched about and said that he had to think of his women and children. Argument was worse than useless. He became hostile in his attitude and would not even accept the American flag which Lewis belatedly offered him. In this extremity the departure was at last ordered. The time was set for next morning. The feelings of the Corps plummeted. The mess fires were quiet.

But God was good to me now. In the very darkest hour of that hushed evening he sent a messenger to me with the power of repaying in some small way my debt to my captains and to my new country. The messenger was the main chief of the second Mandan village. He had been absent from the councils of the first days and, even more oddly, had not been available for individual persuasion this third day. His name translated into "The Big White," but I knew him far better by his Mandan name. It was Shahaka.

We greeted one another with genuine emotion, then he "shared" some of my tobacco, loaded his extra-large visiting pipe, lit it with an ember from the beach fire by which he had found me, and got, finally, to the point.

"Pawnee brother," he began, "for two days I have been out in the woods examining my heart. I have avoided the American captains as a coward like the others. I did not want to say no to them. Now I have reached a decision."

"Yes," I said, "what is that?"

"Do you remember," he said, "when Cameahwait and I touched the palms in peace on the mountain?"

"Yes, it was a fine moment."

"More than that, Brother Frank, it was a true moment. In it we vowed to keep the peace and to help the white man."

"Yes, that's so, Shahaka. I remember it."

"Well, then, here I am," he said, and that was all.

I stared at him.

"What do you mean, here you are?" I asked, at last.

"I am ready," he answered calmly. "In the morning I will go with you to see the new father in Washington."

There it was, as unadorned as that: the second biggest Mandan of them all, ready to face that unknown voyage down the great river, from which his friend the Arikara chief had never returned, and to do it because he and Cameahwait had put their hands together on it in the lonely council hall of Lemhi Pass, twelve moons gone and long forgotten.

"Strange," I muttered to myself, "of them all, you held the truest, Mandan friend."

"Eh? How is that?" he asked, reaching to take a little more of my tobacco while he thought the conversation had taken my mind from its open pouch. "The truest of them all, you say? In what way? And of which ones do you speak?"

"Never mind," I told him, rising happily and touching

him on the shoulder, "come along and tell the captains what you have just told me."

There were delays the next day, as there always must be. First it was John Colter deciding he wanted to stay up the river with Hancock and Dickson. Colter was a solitary kind of fellow, much addicted to long times in the field alone and often given up as lost by our captains. He was now inspired by an Indian tale, told him since our arrival, of a weirdly wonderful and frightening spirit land which lay at the source of the Yellowstone. This place was known as The Smoking Water. From what Lewis could gather it must be of extensive volcanic origin, containing both hot rivers and eruptive springs. It was considered taboo by the Indians.

Surprisingly Lewis granted Colter his leave, discharging him with honor and full pay. No other fellow of the company resented the privilege and in fact all gave Colter something of value—ammunition, knife, powder horn and the like—to further his comfort and safety in the wilderness. He left that midmorning, before our canoes had embarked downstream. If he met with fair fortune, or foul, or if he ever found his hell of hot smoking rock and fuming water, I know not, for he was never seen again by me.

Next it was Le Borgne, the One-Eyed, returning unexpectedly with his chiefs to see us off. Since this was a signal tribute, canny Clark, on the spur of the second, ordered the bow swivel of the white pirogue dismounted and given over as a gift of state to the all-powerful Minnetaree.

Le Borgne was suitably overcome by such munificence, never understanding, or needing to, that the little cannon was put out of order and rendered totally unserviceable;

the sheer idea of an Indian owning the white man's exclusive medicine was all-encompassing in its political implications. And Clark comprehended this fact on the instant.

"If the Grand Chief of all the Minnetarees will accept this gift of American power," he added hastily, and in the correct rolling tones of Indian oratory, "the White Father in Washington will entrust to that chief—to the great Le Borgne, the One-Eyed—the keeping of all the peace in all this land of the upper river. Receive this iron medicine cannon, now, my chief. Until we return to you again, may you remember that its magic power of the lightning and thunder will serve you as your authority to represent your new father over all other Indians from the Omahas to the Assiniboins."

The stroke proved inspirational, achieving in one overleaping vault of the imagination all the influence upon these restless savages that had been previously lost with the theft of the Shoshone and Nez Perce horse herd. Le Borgne was staggered by the weight of the charge and vowed upon his father's honor and the grave of his mother and the bravery of his own seed for seven generations to come, that he would keep the peace until his American friends might come again to this land of the Mandan at the five villages of Knife River. As with tough John Colter, I never knew what became of that small and shining cannon of brass and iron. But for the day and for the hour it served its appointed role in its country's destiny as few guns ever have.

Following the genius stroke of the useless swivel, however, the Indians would not yield their fear of the Sioux and no one of them, saving the brave Shahaka, would board our flotilla in response to the final stirring appeal now delivered to them by their trusted friend Clark.

Worse yet, this last-minute display of the "Teton fever" proved contagious. Old Charbonneau, until that moment pledged to go with little Pomp and Sacajawea aboard the canoes to Washington, now suddenly announced new plans. "You will understand it, *Patron*," he said, shrugging uncomfortably to Lewis. "With no Minnetaree now going with you, you will have no use for the interpreter of that tongue. I'll not go, all things considered. Not me, and not my squaw, and not my young son."

Lewis was angry with this shilly-shallying, since it was not the first instance of the old Frenchman's evanescent honor.

"What will you do?" he demanded sharply. "There's apt to be a war up here, you must realize. I trust you have no intent to go over to the British of the North West Company?"

"Nothing like that, *Patron*. You've been fair with me."

"You don't fear an uprising?"

"No, *Patron*. I'll go back up to the Minnetaree country for the winter. The Sioux doesn't bother Le Borgne."

"I see. There's no changing your mind, then?"

"I am decided, *Patron*. My services are done."

Lewis nodded in his old abrupt way. Time was flowing by with the river, and it would not waste like water.

"Very well, Charbonneau." He gave the name his own form, as did each American. "You have been serviceable to us, and your Snake wife particularly useful among the Shoshones. Indeed, she has borne with a truly admirable patience the fatigues of so long a route encumbered with the charge of an infant who is even now only nineteen months old. If you will see Captain Clark, he will pay you off."

That, so far as I ever heard, was Captain Meriwether Lewis's eulogy of Sacajawea.

Clark, naturally, warmed his own parting with that humanity which was so genuinely his. But even he failed inexplicably to see in the odyssey of Charbonneau's soft-spoken squaw what I had seen in it. Or, for that matter, what I yet saw in it. But he was Clark all the same.

As old Toussaint went up to him to claim his money, he took the grizzled Frenchman by the hand with real feeling. He did the same with Sacajawea, then picked up and embraced little Pomp. The latter, unlike a true Indian, wept profusely over the good-bye. Clark himself was visibly moved.

He explicitly urged the Charbonneaus to relent and to come along as originally planned. The expedition would take them to any point on the lower river they might wish.

"I understand," he said to old Toussaint, "that you are from the Illinois country. Why not go with us to that part of the United States, at least? I would feel vastly better to see your wife and child in such civilized surroundings."

"No *Patron*." the old man said, "there is no employment down there for a squawman. What could I do? How would I feed my family? No one remains alive there who would remember me, either. Who would care if I came back?"

These were questions without answers. Clark knew that. "I believe you are right, Toussaint." He sighed. "Yet you know that I have grown as fond as any father of our boy Pomp. Will you not let me take him down the river with us, so that he may grow up with me, in the United States? I will send him to the best school, Toussaint. He will be reared a white man, as you and I were. What do you say?"

Now it was that I saw tears in the eyes of the old Fenchman. He even made no pretense about wiping them with his grease-blackened buckskin sleeve.

"*Capitaine*," he answered, "I am touched. If the child were weaned, he would go. I know his mother would say the same. We both trust you and want you to have the boy. Can we send him to you in one more year? He will be ready to leave his mother then, and I will bring him to you myself. We would hold it an honor for you to rear him in such a manner as you thought proper. Do you say all right?" Clark agreed to this and all at last seemed completed.

Lewis quickly gave the order to embark, and I went aboard the pirogue to my station at her tiller As the canoes began to load and the human freight of the pirogue to follow suit, however, a low voice spoke to me and, glancing up, I saw Sacajawea standing on the bank above. At once I sensed that this was no ordinary visit, and the thrill which ran through me made me weak. The pirogue lay anchored bow and stern by shorelines. At my station we were somewhat removed from the excitement of the boarding. The bank was only inches higher than the gunwale of the white craft. I moved ot stand as near her as I might. We were perhaps a half dozen feet apart.

Only then did I see that she wept silently. I could not speak. Around our parting, the curtain of this stillness closed softly. For us, the crews, the captains, the Indians did not exist. There was only the swift fleeting of time, and the restless tide of the river. Even a word would have destroyed the enchantment. But we stood still as deer upon the hill at twilight, our senses tuned to a communion past any sound of tongues.

It was thus, at last, that I beheld Sacajawea.

She was never the dream of beauty which I had seen step ashore from Charbonneau's canoe at the beach below Fort Mandan. No more was she in actuality the brute female shown by the campfire at Goatpen Creek. It was not in her mind to love me, or Clark, or old Toussaint, or any white man, apart; it was in her heart to love us all, together. We were the strangers in her land. Unto us she was bidden by her inner light to show the way, to lead us through the wilderness, to guide us and go with us, as Ruth went. If she was less than a Shoshone saint, she was inestimably more than a Charbonneau's squaw. Dismissed in the journals by Lewis as "our Indian woman," and by Clark as "the squar," she was something beyond the imaginations of either captain to ensnare, or of any use to describe.

And what was her reward, other than Lewis's laconic admission that she had been "particularly useful among the Shoshones," and Clark's embellished statement that she had "accompanied us on our route to the Pacific Ocean in the capacity of interpretess"? It can be stated precisely; *nothing*.

For I had seen Charbonneau paid off by Clark not ten minutes before and the sum which the old Frenchman received from a grateful government for his and his wife's hard work, plus the cost of one horse and one lodge purchased for "Charbonneau and his squaw in the interests of the Public Service," was to the entire penny, five hundred dollars and thirty three and a third cents.

It would come to fifty cents per day for Sacajawea's part, had she been paid for half of it. But she was not. Her lord and master valued her on a par with the captains. Insofar as I saw him that day, old Toussaint gave not one dime to his tender, gray-eyed squaw.

All of this and much, much more, came into my mind as, with the sister of Cameahwait, I stood breath-held and staring through our private world of silence amid the Indian tumult and shouting which would so soon die at the departing of the white captains. Sacajawea knew, and I knew, that if I departed with those captains, it would be forever. No man of us in that homebound crew meant in his heart to come again to that far, fierce Mandan land. What was said good-byes here must endure. There would be no others.

For myself, I could not say this last adieu. For the dark Shoshone girl there was no tongue to tell it either. But we were Indians and there was a sign.

Sacajawea put out her hand toward me. I looked quickly up the decking of the white pirogue. Cruzatte and Labiche were at the mooring lines ready to cast off. Clark was just coming aboard, following Leid in the litter. Athwart the gunwale at my feet lay the long black rifle. At my belt was the hunting knife of Drewyer. In my heart was madness. I picked up the black rifle. The pirogue stirred only a little to my step, as I went ashore and fled with Sacajawea.

56

As I sit by the fire composing these last notes, I am alone. It is the half of the cold-wind moon, November. Outside the lodge which Charbonneau and I built in late

347

summer, the blizzard giant has begun his icy-footed stalking of our frail lives. But the old man and I built well. We are safe, and our families with us. Our lodge is of the Arikara-Mandan design, round, log-walled, low and earth-chinked to withstand the most vicious storm or deepest snow. We can live, if need be, for many days without hunting. Our supplies of buffalo beef, pemmican, Indian cornmeal, wild onions and the other roots our women know, and which they gathered with their elkhorn digging hoes while Toussaint and I brought in the prime fat bullmeat, are plentiful and properly cured. They will feed us well until the ice again goes out of the great river.

We lack no comfort meanwhile. The pounded earth floor of our spacious home is covered with the prime autumn robes of the curly cows taken in their richest sheen. The same fine cow robes rest in foot high piles where we sleep back from the fire. The thick furs of wolf, fox, lynx, sable and otter lie also scattered in careless abundance. They hang, as well, from the roof timbers in ordered rows, where they will wait for the spring thaw and transportation to the Americans at Fort Mandan, or to the British of the North West Company, at Turtle Mountain. Our center fireplace of flat river stones, dished inward and glazed with clay, channels its smoke directly upward through the escape hole at the roof's apex, while it spreads its heat radiantly outward to warm the entire building. The outer timbered entranceway, so cleverly designed by Charbonneau, baffles the most cunning or slashing assault of the arctic cold and gale winds which prow this harsh far northland so mercilessly and long. We are, too, a well-chosen family. There are no malcontents among us, and each one does his work gladly. As willingly we play, when it is time for that, and otherwise and in all ways we live our pagan lives in better shelter, spirit and safety than all but the most splendid of our white counterparts in their civilized haunts. It is thus that I am content here and that I am reasonably assured that my return to my mother's people, for all the rashness and métis irresponsibility of its sudden decision, was the rightful and most logical choice. Indeed, for the grandson of a Pawnee chief, the adopted tribesman of the Lemhi Shoshone and the avowed brother of Cameahwait, Lost Girl, Sacajawea and the Hunkpapa Sioux squaw Wahiki, it was the only choice.

Yet when I am alone for a little while, as now, and when I remember my captains and my brave companions in The Corps of Volunteers, the calling of the other blood comes from afar and poignantly. We were heroes then, and heroes together. We were more, we were Americans together. No less than Captain Lewis had told me that. He had said I was an American scout. Not a Pawnee, or a half-breed, or a squaw keeper. An American.

There is no gain in thinking back, I put it from my mind. Sacajawea and the bank of the river lay beckoning within my step. The dark hand which I loved waited there above me in the August sunlight. I knew the price of what I did, and I still reached out and took that hand.

When I left untended the tiller of the white pirogue, I left untenanted my place in the white world. That stern captain and that stout one would not forgive me this last transgression. The one might accept it in his gentleman's firm way, the other might even sympathize with it through that wondrous affinity for the young which was his. Yet neither of them could forgive it. Both were soldiers in the end. I had served them well, then deserted them. No soldier does that and is forgiven by any other soldier.

In the spring I will go away. The spirit which called me north from La Charrette, now calls me west from Fort Mandan. There is the Oregon country out there. I yearn to go across the Big Rock Mountains as my captains did. I want to see that mighty Columbia, to meet those fabled Nez Perce people, to reach and see the sunset ocean, and to visit again with sober Cameahwait, spry Toby and wandering Shoots Straight.

I hope my large family will come with me. We make a strange company but a happy one. There is lusty old Wahiki and Lost Girl, that homely imp who was supposed to wait for Shahaka but who decided she would rather winter with Sacajawea, her Shoshone girlhood friend. Then there is little Pomp and old Toussaint and young Birdwoman. Ah! What good times, if now and then uncivilized, we have.

But Charbonneau grows creaky in the knees. He says he does not care to chase the Crows who stole my horse, Red Lance. He vows he has no interest in climbing Lemhi Pass or seeing Traveler's Rest again. Nonetheless, he is a good old Frenchman.

There is a possibility, he feels, that I may have the same slender guide who took Clark and Lewis to the land of the Shoshone. Of course that will depend on Sacajawea herself in some small part. Mostly, however, it will resolve itself into a matter of how well we make out in our winter fur sales at Fort Mandan or Turtle Mountain. If we prosper and I am then of a mind to make an acceptable offer, he might consider the release of his younger wife. The older one, Wahiki, suits him somewhat better in any event, or so he avers. If I could promise to pay him something considerable in advance and on account, why then the proposed transfer of Sacajawea might well become even more tolerable to him.

Of course this is only winter talk. The prospect is at best intangible, but for the moment God has been kind and I am living where Sacajawea lives. What the new grass will bring, only the April rain can say. For myself, I am resigned to my chosen future and to this consignment of my memories to its care.

I close with some reasonable hopes that what I write may reach the captains. Among these words is the instruction that whatsoever of wages or rewards may be due me for my small part in the expedition, they be paid over in St. Louis to the account of my uncle, François Rivet, of La Charrette. With this inclusion the account is balanced, the debt discharged. When the springtime comes again and Charbonneau takes little Pomp to Fort Mandan for the agreed delivery of the child to Captain Clark in far off Virginia, the old Frenchman will bear with him for Clark, this trail-stained diary.

God rest you both, stout Clark and sober Lewis. You truly were and forever will be Jefferson's captains. Yet only one of you was my captain. Will you remember that, *Patron?* And with it will you remember me? When these hundred years have gone and then another hundred fled, as well, will some other distant youth such as I, hungry to prove his honor to his flag, read in that wondrous crude and misspelled journal which you kept so well and faithfully, the name of François Rivet? Will I be there, *Patron?*

Outside, the winds howl laughingly in reply to my poor question. I hear the voices of my family returning from the village of the Minnetarees, near which we have our low round lodge. I hurry to close these covers, consigning what lies between them to the judgment of my father's people with this last thought: Should any man see this testament and seek to know its truth, or the honor of its transcriber, let him search for my name upon the journals' muster of the permanent company of the Corps of Volunteers.

It is F. Rivet, of La Charrette. Do you see it there . . . ?

Center Point Publishing
600 Brooks Road ● PO Box 1
Thorndike ME 04986-0001 USA

(207) 568-3717

**US & Canada:
1 800 929-9108**